The Workplace

By

Billy Harding

The *2nd* Will Hardley Novel

This Novel is a work of Fiction.

It has certain Autobiographical events that were used as inspiration in its creation, it is not however an Autobiography.

For this particular Story, the characters are all fictionalized due to the Novelist's imagination.

Any resemblance to actual persons living or dead, or certain events is purely coincidental.

Other than that, there's demanding customers, agreements along with disagreements and staff members who are simply just trying to get to the end of their shift.

6

I dedicate this Tale to the following people:

Kelly – My real life *'Firecracker'*.

Your friendship we forged in the Fires/Pitfalls/Dramas of Work were and continue to be a great source of comfort and strength to me after all these Years we have known each other. Thank you.

Nicola – For basically being there for me from *Day One* (literally).

Your quiet resolve, your patience and laughs we had on the Job were completely ours to cherish. It's safe to say you were probably one of the most consistent and stable working relationships I ever had throughout those Years. Here's to those *Kitchen Days*.

Adem – For simply being one of *the* most Mature Teenagers I have ever met.

Professional yet hard-working with a Heart of Gold. Mate, you're the Legend and I am so proud to call you one of my Friends.

To any Person/Individual I worked with over the Years and we were able to have a laugh even when it was the most busiest of times on Shift. We were run down, fed up and had it up to *here* with the most pettiest requests from customers, it must have been worth it if we were still able to crack a joke to cope with the day. Cheers for that & the many Memories.

& finally:

To Michael Sadler who very sadly passed away during the Summer of 2020.

You were a joy to work with my dear Co-Worker. Your dry Yorkshire humour, your penchant for a quick cigarette, your imperious gaze when you had your specs on. I'll never forget you or your traits.

Thanks for being there on my Final Shift.

Rest In Peace.

Prologue

September 3rd, 2010.

Riverside Shoppers Complex.

Friday.

10:29 am.

He was breathing a bit too heavily for his own good.

Having just rolled up into the bus depot next to the shopping complex the nerves were now starting to kick in, which told him he was going to completely flop this interview he was heading for. '*I don't have a chance in hell, there, simple.*' he thought as he disembarked the bus looking upwards to see a lone plane flying high in the sky wishing with all his might that he could be working on that up there instead of down here on the solid ground. Shaking his head far too vigorously which got him the odd look from one or two people waiting for the bus to admit new passengers Will Hardley decided to head into Riverside Shoppers Complex through the Debenhams entrance and stopped his fleeting yet fanciful thoughts of working on an airplane to concentrate on the impending job opportunity that was awaiting him at 11:00. It had just gone 10:30 in the morning so he had made it there in good time from his bus journey all the way from Hornchurch. He had heard stories from some of his former college friends and co-workers at his part-time job that one of the two bus routes that went to Riverside weren't that reliable at all but so far it proven him wrong, and it had sped through the towns such as Upminster then the side roads in the back routes on its journey to the place, sure it had gone through other places like Ockendon which had a bit of a reputation in some of its parts for being rough but there had been nothing alarming as he had sat on it too nervous to think about anything but this job opportunity he had been presented with by one of his close girls mates from his Media Studies classes in his College days. Will was now freshly graduated as well as having been working in a part time waiting job at a Silver Service Restaurant over the course of the Summer, but he knew from certain loaded comments by his family that the part time job he currently had just wouldn't cut the mustard to make him last the distance in life so there had been suggestions that he needed to start looking for a job which offered more of a wage and more full time hours, naturally he had looked and found nothing that had grabbed his attention fully until he had been speaking to his girl mate Ashley Hays from College. She had recently nabbed herself a Customer Service Job working at the In-House Commercial Restaurant based in Riverside Shoppers Complex Stores and they needed more staff to fill their numbers. Will had three different waiting jobs under his belt from when he had begun working in the Hospitality Industry from seventeen, so Ashley had naturally text him straight away more or less ordering him to Riverside having put in a good word with the Management Team about his previous Employment History. Now here Will was on sunny September morning making his way to a job opportunity he for some reason felt like he didn't have a shot at getting at all, even with Ashley encouraging him to just go for it the night before when they had been texting back and forth about what the job entailed. Will was making his way out through Debenhams and into the main part of Riverside itself now, it was pretty quiet for a Friday considering it was the final weekend before most of the kids started going back to school to begin their new Academic Terms. *'I guess the kids are just lying in. Lucky buggers. Wish I was them right now rather than being here, why am I so nervous?'* Will was trying to shake the unpleasant thought swirling around in his mind like a thunderstorm of self-doubt that refused to let up. Each step he took he swore it let out a clap of thunder that was teasing him with words like *you're not good enough* or *they'll take one look at you and laugh hysterically*. Ashley had told him what to wear for the job, everything in black including his socks weirdly, talk about stripping down your identity to a blank canvass. He had floated the idea of wearing all black trainers, but his Mum had given him 'the look'. That look that spoke so much to him without his Mother having to speak or describe a word in what it actually meant. *'Don't even think about wearing any form of comfy trainers when it comes to a job interview young man'* he could hear her words pierce the thunderstorm like fork lightening, and he knew wearing shiny new black work shoes was the correct thing to do even if he had, had to dish out on £30 for them. *"I'll make a good impression on the new shoes if I don't even get a look in at least.'* Will was nodding his head in reassurance to himself as he continued walking through the complex to his destination. He passed other stores like JD Sports, Carphone Warehouse, Accessorize, HMV, River Island, Brother2Brother and smaller boutique clothing shops that sold what was clearly Designer Label only clothing and nothing on what would be considered the affordable scale of money every day people earned. He saw Primark on the way and of course it spanned all three levels of the complex. *'Figures they would take one of the biggest Units out of the entire place.'* Will thought even if he weren't a big fan of their clothes despite being the cheap but cheerful option of the High Street these days. Truthfully, he wasn't looking forward to being part of an In-House Riverside Department Store that included selling clothes as well as housing a Restaurant upstairs along with a separate Cafe' downstairs. He could just see himself being told to go help out on one of the tills on one of their Clothing Departments and staying there rest of the day like a soulless robot, but he hadn't even got the job yet, so he pushed that image well out of his mind despite the internal storm playing out still. *'Now Ashley told me to go up the escalators at WHSmith's then walk down past Starbucks and its right next door to another small independent Café.'* Will thought as he saw the waiting escalators right where Ashley said they would be and just the like rest of the Complex they were eerily devoid of many or any people at all going about their shopping experiences. Will felt like he was in the film 28 Days Later and he was ready for some flesh-eating zombie to spring out and devour him. Nothing happened of the sort as he went up the moving stairs and there was Starbucks which had the first signs of actual shoppers he had seen, *'of course they would be getting their coffee fix first.'* Will noted as he saw the queue just starting to edge out of the popular coffee house chain with expectant but patient faces of people of all different ages. "Talk about invasion of the *Americans*..." Will muttered as he slowly walked past the queue making his way down one of Riversides overly large extension corridors. They had added this one and were nearing completion of what was going to be known was the East Walk of Riverside which would have a lot more big named Restaurant-chains all claiming the available Unit Spaces right by the lake or river which had been how Riverside had gotten its name. The extension corridor was basically what connected the old building to the new part and there were of course more shops on the way including another designer wear shop called Choices which was right opposite the independent Cafe' called 'Spreads' Ashley had told him about and then just off kilter from Choices was his destination awaiting him. Simply titled as 'The Restaurant' it was obviously another extension of the In-House Department Store that Riverside had added on when the extension corridor had been constructed for the East Walk so of course the management in charge of the Riverside Store had capitalised on the readily available Unit Space and the obvious profit they could see in the Company Venture so here it was, a consumerism wet dream if Will ever saw one before. Will's potential job was on show before him, and he felt even more intimidated that he was now here standing outside of it. He saw how small the independent 'Spreads' was next to 'The Restaurant' but despite comparing its size all of the tables in 'The Restaurant' were full all barring one or two odd ones still available. *'Loyal customer base in there then.'* Will noted as he studied the dimensions of the place. It was large space but not exactly huge and you could tell it was an added extension of the established In-House Store already in place. Will saw it connected to the Kids Wear Department of the Store inside, but it had security scanners either side before you entered so 'The Restaurant' was a definite add-on, it still looked relatively new as well, probably less than a couple of years old. Will could tell this place had about a hundred covers to use in total so that meant it could get busy quickly and experience high turnover at the same time if customers didn't want to dawdle for long, one quick coffee order then on to the next person willing to part with their hard-earned cash. *'This could turn into a busy afternoon shift at any of the other places I have worked at if I snapped my figures or twitched my nose like Samantha off of Bewitched.'* Will amusingly thought which calmed him down a little. It had a long countertop with a glass service opening for coffees followed next to it by another biggish glass display case for a rather large amount of different cakes and scones to tempt customers to part with even more of their money, *'consumerism is quite literally screaming at me right now.'* Next door to the coffee machine station behind the counter was what must have been the kitchen area, three-quarters shielded from the public eye but an open entrance with no door, on the shop floor itself was a two-way door that permitted entrance to the back area, but he couldn't see in there, at least not yet anyway. Near the door was another small service hatch opening with heated lamps on one level for hot food to be dispensed from the mostly sealed off kitchen. Now that Will had arrived at his destination he was getting into the zone more and focusing on what he needed to do to sell himself, he had his CV at the ready in a plastic sleeve and he was taking a few measured breathes in and out to relax as best he could, the thunderstorm in his mind was now settling, it felt even like it had blown over like it was off in the distant trying to taunt him, but he paid it no mind. Now was the time to go get himself a new job if he could that it. Then a voice pierced his concentration snapping him back into realities grip of the here and now.

"Will..." the voice called out "...over here Mr!"

A girl wearing a black hat and all black uniform with the Riverside logo adorned to it was bouncing up and down on the spot from behind 'The Restaurant' counter at the coffee machine. It was Ashley his college friend and she was giddy at the mere sight of him. Ashley was just a little bit taller than Will at five foot nine; she had light brown hair with a few whispers of blonde dye still left in it, a pointy but cute nose which helped prop up a pair of small black spectacles and a small cheeky grin for good measure. She came round from the end of the counter through a swinging door designed to not let the customers in to her workspace, her adorable green eyes were alight as she came out to greet Will with a welcoming hug. "Eek, you made it! And your early too Will, that'll go down well with Derrick." she was excited for him as she released him from her hug looking at Will's slightly confused but adorable face.

"And Derrick would be?"

"Oh, silly me, sorry. He's the *Assistant Manager*."

"Not that main *Manager*?"

"Ah no, he's not here today but Derrick is the one I have been singing your praises to, so you've got nothing to worry about in that Department."

"Oh, so no pressure then..." Will gave his friend a wide eye look of alarm, but Ashley only laughed at his continued nervousness. "Will you have three part-time jobs worth of Waiting Experience to fall back on, you'll be fine!" Ashley gave him another reassuring hug which he happily accepted. "So, Ashley are you enjoying this job then?" Will asked her as he took another look around the place. There were about half a dozen covers with customers all sitting with different forms of coffee and the odd breakfast item. All was calm and quiet, but Will felt like come the lunchtime rush it would be crazy, he could practically feel the change in the air. "Well, I've only been here about six weeks myself, but the weekend shifts can be pretty brutal." she started explaining which got Will's attention.

"That busy huh?"

"Oh, like you wouldn't believe honestly..."

"Sounds like my first waiting job as a runner..."

"Wait a minute, not that chain of Italian restaurants, the ones that completely screwed you over then dumped you unceremoniously from the job once they were up and running after their first couple of months of being officially open?"

"Yep. That's the one..."

"Oh babe..." her Essex accent coming through thick and strong now "...this place doesn't have that mentality; they want people to *last* here."

"You've already got that impression after six weeks in the job Ashley?" Will asked genuinely curious but Ashley was beaming from ear to ear in confidence.

"Yep absolutely this job..."

"...Speaking of *this job* Ashley, don't you have coffee's to be making?" a new voice spoke out of nowhere, it was female. Both of the young friends turned at the sound of the new voice. It was an older woman in her mid-thirties, curvaceous but she carried it well, she was dressed all in black with a matching skull cap on top of her head and her chocolate brown hair meticulously placed up within it, not a strand was out of place, Will knew she was a pro just from seeing her the first time. Ashley jumped to attention at the arrival of this new person; she looked like someone not to be messed with in Will's initial assessment. "Oh Nat!" Ashley almost squawked

"Sorry yes I'll get right back to that, I thought Sallie was on coffee with me also though…?" Ashley looked back at the obvious empty station not seeing anyone else there; Nat though was also looking with Ashley then rolled her eyes clearly annoyed. "Ah yes your right, I bet you any money she is talking to one of the Chefs in the kitchen *again*..." Nat stopped as a high-pitched womanly laugh came from out of nowhere in the semi-sealed off kitchen area which seemed to confirm Nat's suspicions about the errant member of staff, "...that'll verify that then. Sorry about that Ashley, if you don't mind making that coffee order that's just come through I'll really appreciate it, I'll look after your friend and I'll deal with the wayward *Sallie*." Another very loud laugh came from the kitchen again which got a further shake of her head in more annoyance from Nat "...I'll deal with *her* in a bit. Thanks again Ashley" she finished as Ashley left Will with Nat who inspected him with her eyes, Will felt like he was being observed for any inconsistencies; however, Nat dropped the inspection and gave him a warm smile of greeting instead. "Sorry about all that..." she offered him her hand to shake which Will took and reciprocated firmly "...I'm Natalie Hardley, but everyone calls me Nat, welcome to 'The Restaurant'. It's Will isn't it?" But Natalie didn't get an immediate response as Will was now laughing as he continued to shake her hand for longer than necessary.

"You're kidding right? *Hardley* is your surname?"

"Yes? Wait? Don't tell me..."

"Yep" Will beamed "my surname is also *Hardley*."

Natalie was now laughing herself at the amusing encounter as they finally stopped shaking hands. They were both laughing together at their shared surnames despite not being biologically related to one another. "What a small world, *Will Hardley* and *Nat Hardley*. Who would have thought?" Nat chuckled some more as Will relaxed around her; she didn't seem as intimidating as before. In fact, Will had a gut feeling they would get along rather nicely if he were successful in this interview today.

"So how are you feeling today Will? Nervous or excited? Both I bet?"

"Well honestly right now, yes a bit of both really, not sure what to expect..."

"Ah don't worry it's not as involved as it seems, you brought your CV I see for Derrick?" She indicated the document in the sleeve which Will handed to her; she scanned the contents quick but efficiently seeming to approve its contents on the initial basis. "Looking good. Yep I like that, that'll do us nicely, I'm sure Derrick will approve..." another piercing laugh came from the kitchen and Nat looked off into the distance with a tightened face. "I tell you what Will..." Nat began "...take a seat at one of the tables near the two-way door, I know Derrick said your interview was at 11:00 but he is in a meeting with one of the managers for the Store at the moment that's rather *conveniently* run over its time slot." Nat was shaking her head at this "since we aren't employed by the Company fully these things happen I'm afraid, the joys of being Sub-Contracted these days. Make yourself comfy and I'll go work my magic about prying him from his meeting…" another loud laugh came from the kitchen that had a rather obvious dirty undertone to it made one of the customer's look up in annoyance which Will and Nat both took notice of. Nat tucked his CV in the wallet under her arm and smoothed down her black Riverside work shirt, "…and if you'll excuse me I'll just go deal with *that* in the kitchen…"

"The overly-happy Sallie I presume? The rather loud laugher out back there, it doesn't sound entirely work appropriate if you don't mind me saying so?" Will finished Nat's sentence for her and she looked at him surprised but also somewhat impressed. "Seems to me your catching on already *Mr Hardley*" Nat turned around and walked away double time to deal with whatever was going on in the kitchen with the unseen Sallie and one of the Chefs. Will was quite curious to know what exactly this employee was doing with the Chef that was getting a louder laugh each time a new one sprang from her mouth, a few naughty suggestive thoughts sprung in his mind, but he was a young impressionable red-blooded nineteen-year-old after all. Nat disappeared out back and Will heard her begin with an abrupt "right, what's going on..." only for the two-way revolving door to close and drown out anymore of her putdown speech. For now, Will just wanted to get his interview going with the still absent Derrick and be done with it, *'no point in delaying the inevitable.'* he was starting to get a little nervous again but a quick smile from Ashley at the coffee station calmed him. Checking his phone for the time it was almost 11:15 so this meeting Derrick was stuck in with the management was either serious or seriously tedious. When he finally graced Will with his presence five minutes later only twenty minutes over the allotted time he had agreed upon Will could tell immediately that it fully settled into the tedious factor. Derrick was a man who probably sat around the good six-foot region, with spiked hair that was gelled, a toothy smile that definitely needed a trip to the dentist and a suit with no blazer that needed a good press after it had been washed at least twice you could tell when it came to the management hierarchy in this place he was very much the middleman and he was fully aware in the knowledge of this also. Being an Assistant Manager obviously afforded him not only a lower wage but clearly very few Managerial powers that he could exert over the staff in 'The Restaurant', but he did it all with a smile in place which Will liked about him from the off so he introduced himself with as much confidence he could muster. "Will Hardley I presume, related to our Nat are you?" Derrick did a double take at Will's CV with a laddish-like attitude when he saw the name on the paper which made Will laugh nervously at what was becoming an inside joke. "Ha, I know it looks like it but me and Nat only met today just over twenty minutes ago much to our joint amusement." Will made sure he was perky; alert and his shoulders were raised at the ready to show eagerness which Derrick seemed to be impressed by. Scanning his CV, he had gotten off of Nat, Derrick looked at him a few times then proceeded to just look at Will some more like he was getting a read on him, then he intentionally looked at Will shoes tucked under the table.

"New shoes?" he asked Will.

"Err, yes actually..."

"I like it, wanting to make as big an impact in those first few moments..."

"Well, I thought it would look good..."

"No, you didn't, your Mum did though right?" Derrick looked Will dead in the eyes, but he did it cockily to not pile on the pressure, Will went a shade of pink at this question.

"Guilty as charged I'm afraid." Will laughed with his hands held up in surrender and Derrick chuckled with him, a good rapport had developed between them already. Derrick was nodding now along then took another quick look at the CV then back to Will.

"Three part-time jobs in the Hospitality Sector I see. Still in your current part-time job now?"

Yes, I'm actually on shift there tonight at 6:30 as it happens..."

"Ah I see, they have no idea you're doing this right now do they?"

"Nope. Not a clue in fact..."

"Good way to be if your ever looking for a new job. So, what time can you stay till today?" Derrick dropped the question out of nowhere for Will who was thrown completely off balance by it without warning. Blinking he re-focused trying to stay on Derrick's wavelength.

"I'm a... sorry you lost me there for a second..."

"Can you stay, say till 4 this afternoon? Then you can go do your shift at your other place?"

"Erm, well yeah I can stay till then I have nothing else planned for the day, it's just..."

"Just what?"

"Well, I thought it was an interview only?"

"It was..." Derrick began then he paused to entwine both of his hands and inspect Will some more, he had a habit of just staring which made Will feel rather naked. If this were the time he was with a hot guy about to get down to some dirty business Will would have pounced on the waiting sexual liaison with abandonment, this feeling however was something else altogether. He felt like today was about to get a whole lot more interesting in this job opportunity.

Derrick resumed "...yes it was an interview. I've seen your CV, I like it, your dressed in the appropriate clothing for the job which I'm sure Ashley told you to do so that means you follow instructions well, that also means I have already made some form of a decision..." Derrick unfolded his hands and seemed to be waiting for Will to ask the obvious.

"What's the decision?" Will asked Derrick.

"Will..." Derrick got up from the table "...can you stay for a trial today? Preferably till four pm if you don't mind? By two pm though however I will have a good idea of where we both stand with each other agreed?" Derrick held out his hand to shake Will's. Will got up and accepted it, it was another firm one. A sign of confidence in him. The thunderstorm of nerves that been swirling in Will's mind earlier were nowhere to be felt in his body and it made Will feel good, he felt like he had a real shot all of a sudden.

Released from their handshake Derrick got down to the matter at hand. "Right" he clapped his hands together in vigour "Nat, get out here Mrs!" he called out back; Nat came strolling from out the kitchen area to stand next to Ashley by the coffee station, the loud laughing from the still unseen Sallie had now been stopped by Nat's timely intervention.

"Yes boss?"

"Nat my love can you get Will here to put his coat up somewhere out back and anything he might want to store with it. Then can we get him introduced to the rest of the team on shift and show him where everything is based, we'll get him running some food orders and coffee's to customers and make sure he knows how to properly clean down a table. How does that sound my Supervisor?" Derrick finished with is arms folded without looking at her, he was back to inspecting Will again who was all of sudden rather getting used to it, it was like he was mentally approving him for the job already. Nat was nodding her head slowly and looking back from Will to Derrick carefully but seemed to be giving her own mental approval of Will as well. Ashley was looking at Will proudly.

"I think boss..." Nat began "that that is a rather good idea. Meet me out back Will; let's get you set up for the day" Nat made her way out back through the kitchen to meet him. Derrick smiled at Will and he only used his head to indicate him to follow her.

"Don't let me down now Will ok?"

"You got it..." Will stopped for a second then decided to just go for it "...*boss*."

Derrick laughed at this. Will then headed off to meet Nat through the revolving door. The rest of the day sort of passed in a blur. Will cleaned tables, he ran food orders out to customers under Nat's supervision with a smile in place, he took coffee orders on trays carefully made by Ashley to other customers making sure he asked about how their individual days were going and if they needed anything just to call for him, Ashley didn't stop smiling at him all day, he was even taken upstairs by Nat for a quick fifteen-minute teak break and to be shown where staff could get away from the stress of serving customers. Nat showed him the on-sight HR Department and Switchboard areas where customers rang through to make enquiries. It was all a lot of information dumping in one huge adrenaline filled hit. Then he came back and waited on more tables, he chatted with the two Chefs in the kitchen who were polite enough, he met the loud-laughing Sallie who was another curvaceous woman like Nat but a little bit bigger and she seemed to bark more orders at Ashley rather than actually helping her make coffee's Will noticed while she seemed to be looking at one of the Chef's in the kitchen a lot more than she should have been, Nat Will noticed didn't miss a beat of any of this. Before he knew it, it was gone three-thirty in the afternoon by the time Derrick came back to him who seemed to have gotten dragged in to yet another tediously timed management meeting that overran again. "Honestly Will..." he was openly frustrated "...they have meetings here just to say that have had a meeting! It makes no sense." He was looking over some paperwork in a corner table well away from the serving station now and he had asked Nat to cover Will on the floor while he spoke with him. He wasn't looking at Will much this time, but he was successfully multi-tasking in the same instant.

"So, Will, how did you find today?"

"Err well..." Will was trying to find the right words for the day that seemed to have literally flown by. He had seen a lot, spoke to a lot, served a lot and Ashley was right, it could get crazy busy here. Will had known the lunchtime might have been crazy but not as crazy as it was to actually work in it. Nat had been there to support him throughout and no customer had come across upset by a delayed meal or coffee though, so he knew he had handled it well.

"Well?" Derrick asked again.

"Well, I gotta say Derrick, it was tough, but it was fun actually. Nat was a real help and so was Ashley so I didn't feel like I was drowning out there like I first thought I might." Will seemed satisfied to leave it at that and Derrick was now back to looking at him nodding that he agreed with his assessment of the trial.

"Good thing you said that because I think you did bloody well."

Derrick floored Will with the compliment as he turned pink with embarrassment again "I have here Will a contract for you. It's a contract of employment, fancy signing it?" Derrick said casually. Will was now jaw dropped.

"You mean the jobs mine?"

"Hit the nail on the head there didn't you?"

"Oh my god Derrick, I don't know what to say!"

"How about, *yes give me a pen*?"

"Yes give me a pen! Thank you so much for this as well..."

"No problem at all kiddo. now before you sign on the dotted line there's a few things about the job I have to run by you. Firstly, you'll be on a basic 20-Hour Contract but you will never be working that as everyone here in their Contracts receive immediate overtime, so you'll essentially be a full-time worker here in the Restaurant under the official Employment of the *Orbit Group*. They basically have their own Contractual Agreement in place with the company who run the Riverside In-House Department Store to staff all nine Restaurants' the company have in the business up and down the Country, not that many we know but they always talk about expansion these days. Your hourly rate will

£6.75, and everyone works all weekends, but their days off will be on the staff rota during in the week, also since we are sub-contracted to the *Orbit Group* we do not receive In-House Staff Discount but we have to wear their uniform since we are representative of them. How does that all sound to you Will?" Derrick finished by sliding the single page contract over to him with a pen at the ready. Will looked at the contract briefly then back to Derrick this time inspecting him. Derrick sat there impassively waiting.

"Derrick, you have just changed this nineteen-year-olds life with his first full time job. I know *exactly* how this all sounds to me" Will finished by picking up the pen and signed his name to the contract, his first ever full-time employment in his life sealed at a pen stroke. Derrick smiled and reached out to shake Will's hand again who took it confidently.

What a day this had turned out to be indeed.

"Now that, that's all settled I thought you deserved a little something..." Derrick made a gesture with his hand over Will's shoulder and Will turned to see Ashley coming over with two drinks on a tray, she hadn't stopped smiling all day at Will her cheeks must be killing her. "Derrick thought me, and you could celebrate by having a hot chocolate together, to toast your new job!" Ashley placed the two hot drinks down on the table as

Derrick got up grinning as he went, and Ashley took the vacated seat. "I'll leave you both to it but Will I have your details now so I will get you on the staff rota to start in just over a week's time since you said resigning from your other part-time employment doesn't require that much notice. I'll text you your *official* start date and look forward to seeing you then." Derrick moved off to go talk to Nat on the shop floor as Will nodded eagerly. Ashley was now practically bouncing on her seat for him.

"Ah Will, you smashed it today!" Ashley took one of the hot chocolates she had made for them while Will took the other; he was on cloud nine right now.

"You really think so? I thought I was doing just ok really..." Will took a sip of the hot drink and the sugar fix felt good down his throat, Ashley was shaking her head in happy disagreement.

"Oh no not at all, even Sallie said you kept up a good pace during the lunch rush..."

"What Sallie who has hardly done any work today except tell you all day to make hot drink after hot drink while she ogles at one of the Chefs? Is she a Supervisor like Nat?" Will asked Ashley who almost snorted out her latest sip of hot chocolate. "Don't be daft Will she is the same level as you and me!" Ashley giggled with a hand over her mouth as Will's jaw dropped again in shock.

"You're kidding right?"

"Nope, sorry!"

"Christ, she has a bit of an attitude on her shoulders then I see..."

"Yep but I just let it go over my head; she's been told by Nat to cover me while we have our celebratory drinks before you leave today."

"Oh, so now she can't ogle anymore at the Chef with her tongue practically hanging out her mouth!"

"Will you cheeky Gay boy! Oh, you wouldn't know of course..." Ashley stopped talking as she intentionally busied herself by drinking some more of her hot chocolate, but Will wanted to know what else she was going to say.

"Know what Ashley?"

"Oh nothing..."

"Bullshit. Come on. Spill it!"

"Ok, ok..." Ashley began by putting down her hot drink then looking mischievously at Will, she had some real good juicy gossip to tell.

"...Well, she's doing you know what with..."

"With? Wait not..."

"Yep. She's shagging one of the Chefs and their both on shift today!"

"Obviously, it's the younger one? She's a cheeky cow."

"Oh yeah of course, no doubt. There's is one *other thing*..."

"There's more?" Will asked, he needed to know right there and then.

"Yep..." Ashley said, "...she's already married, and the Chef is too!"

Will's head snapped round at that the now busy Sallie who was making coffees with her back to them. Little did she know that she was the source of his and Ashley's rather animated conversation. Yes Will Hardley had earned his first ever full-time job and he had inherited all the gossip that went with it too.

It was going to be an interesting experience from here on out.

"So, Will I have one more thing I wanna know..."

"Oh?"

"Nothing bad of course. I just want to know; how long do you see yourself working here for?" Ashley asked as she finished what was left of her hot chocolate.

Will looked around the Restaurant deep in thought, he saw Nat chatting to customers, he saw cheating Sallie still making coffees while stealing glances into the kitchen at the young Chef she was having it off with, he saw other customers were wrapped up in their own situations as well, Will just smiled at all of it. He finished his own hot chocolate then placing it assuredly on the table and turned back to look at Ashley with a grateful smile.

"Truth be told Ashley; I honestly don't actually know currently. I guess we will have to embark on this new adventure together and simply see where the wind takes us. Who would have thought it though? You and me working in a job together after we left college behind only just a few short months ago, it really boggles' the mind".

"I'll tell you what though Ashley..."

Will looked around at the workplace in consideration.

"...it's gonna be a hell of an experience!"

One

Exactly Six Years Later.

Riverside Shoppers Complex.

Saturday.

11:25 am.

'Six. Fucking. Years! Happy Anniversary to me, I guess.' Will
thought as he stopped walking at about the halfway mark across
the interlink from the train station to Riverside to look at the nearly
twenty-six-year-old complex, he felt nothing for the dilapidated
place anymore. It was in serious need of its own refresher to say
the least. It had already needed a bit of freshening up when he had

first set foot in it all those years ago to meet Ashley in 'The Restaurant' which was now gone. In its place was another overflow or Upstairs Cafe' to compliment the bigger Downstairs Cafe' after the management had approved a complete top to bottom whole Store Refurbishment Program back in mid-2013. It had taken a good four to six months of continuous construction work while working around keeping the Store open to trade, so it didn't lose custom or footfall in the process but one of the things that had been ear-marked for one of the biggest overall changes was the ground floor Cafe'. It had gone from a rather modest seventy-five covers to a staggering two hundred and fifty total covers complete with a total change not in just capacity but design as well. Will had been there throughout the whole experience. Another thing to remind him of how much time flew by when you had a steady job over the years as this particular day was reminding him to no end. Letting out a somewhat frustrated sigh he stopped looking at the Complex that had become a secondary home to him on the interlink and continued on his way to start work, he took the stairwell rather than the lift since they were also sorely in need of being renovated entirely, he saw a group of people waiting to get in so they could get off on floor three which was the ground level they needed for the Complex but he knew he could make it by easily walking down the stairs as the lift doors were always the slowest to open and close. Yet the management of Riverside still had it on the backburner despite the ever-growing list of customer complaints about it in the last year alone. Sure enough Will got down to the ground level before the lift had barely made it to floor four, he felt sorry for the people stuck in the metallic box as he made his way through the House of Fraser entrance. Being a Saturday the place was just picking up the pace with customers, he was starting his shift at twelve then he would be working straight through till nine tonight and he hated his Saturday night shift on with a passion. It was a late one he had not asked for but had been lumbered with when he had transferred over to become a proper In-House Department Store Staff Member after having to reapply for the company way back in October twelve as for the first two years he had been contracted to *Orbit Group* working almost consistently every weekend there under the sun unless he took it as holiday, with lower pay, no discount to be seen ever and fed up of being told by every Manager arriving to put their signature stamp on the place who had come to run 'The Restaurant' with their new convoluted ways, that made sense to them but not the workforce he was a part of that he wasn't allowed to apply for a transferral between companies because the *Orbit Group* simply wouldn't accept it. Rather than continued to be intimidated by the latest Manager who was some middle-aged female Canadian whose marriage she was in had clearly left her more than a little sex starved, Will had bit the bullet and re-applied for the Downstairs Cafe' anyway and not a single person had tried to stop him. He had even re-done the entire two-stage interview process in his work uniform. His last day working in 'The Restaurant' had been on November 2nd with a start date in the Downstairs Cafe' on November 6th after an induction course firstly. The Canadian Manager had demanded his letter of resignation anyway after she found out and had practically screamed at him for it, Will had just laughed at her pathetic posturing, handed the letter over with relish and rejoiced in the act she wasn't his boss anymore. She had soon left after that in the April of 2013 as the *Orbit Group* had all of a sudden to everyone's shock decided to withdraw their Contract they had in place with the company as it was deemed to not be working for them anymore, the Canadian Manger had stayed with them while the workforce in 'The Restaurant' were absorbed into the In-House Staff and the rest was resigned to the history books. Will though had just made the jump six months prior to the upcoming change and had benefitted mostly by receiving London-weighting on top of his pay and working no Sundays at all. Except for this dreaded Saturday shift of twelve till nine which fell on his six-year anniversary today. That was not the consolation he had been hoping for but at the time he had begrudgingly accepted it since he had no more Sundays to work. You win some, you lose some.

He made his way out of House of Fraser, confirming his suspicions that the kids were indeed out in force today before school started back up for them again. Mostly teenagers who thought they were

too cool for their parents anymore, Will had remembered that
feeling of being able to go out and not be chaperoned anymore, he
missed it from time to time but not much now that he was twenty-
five. He smirked as he walked past a small group of teens who
were clearly walking around Riverside thinking they owned the
place then they all started behaving more nicely when a member of
the on-site security team made their presence known, they of
course made themselves look busy on their smartphones instead.
*"Kids today, who would they even be without those bloody
mobiles?'* Will asked himself as he walked past the Topman and
Topshop joint unit. There were some parents out with their
younger kids but not many as of yet, they would arrive later
probably after midday which would mean Will would be swamped
at work. *'I can just hear the moaning and groaning about how
their extra dry cappuccino is too frothy and not hot enough'* he
squirmed at the scenario he knew would more than likely happen
today. He wasn't looking forward to it. Will still couldn't believe
six whole years had elapsed since he had started working at
Riverside all thanks to dear Ashley. She was long gone now
however, after only nine months of working on the job at the time
she had more or less thrown the towel in when she continuously
bumped heads with the infamous Canadian Manager when she had
arrived in the first six weeks of her being there, rather than putting
herself through any more of it Ashley had resigned to go work at a
plush office job Monday to Friday in the City and hadn't looked

back as she made her escape, she barely visited ever again after she
left as well much to Will's dismay. The Canadian Manger had
gloated for a good two weeks about her departure if not more at
how she was glad Ashley had quit rather than her getting to sack
Will's beloved college friend for some entirely fake reason she
clearly made up on the spot. From then on Will hadn't warmed to
her at all but then again she made disliking her almost an art form.
She was quickly forgotten about when the Contract concluded with
Orbit and she departed for pastures new. Will swore that someone
from 'The Restaurant' had floated the idea to him of having a big
drinking session to celebrate she was gone and not coming back
but nothing had come of it and like all good ideas, it was very
quickly another thing forgotten about and life moved on for the In-
House team. Pondering the many events he had witnessed or heard
of in his time at Riverside still made him laugh but he had to stop
his current nostalgia trip for now. He was back outside the
Department Store after successfully navigating the many youths
loitering within the Complex and was walking up to the Staff
Entrance. A pair of blue double doors that were badly in need of a
lick of paint just like everything else at the Shoppers Complex, he
now had a reason to enjoy this day a bit more before his shift
would begin, the reason being was a person standing near the doors
like she was waiting for him. Standing at four foot twelve with
vibrant red hair to match her fiery personality the person may be
on the small side; she was one not to be messed with. She was also

one of Will's actual rare best friends he had made on the job whilst working here. Her name was Kym Harrison and she had been aptly nicknamed 'Firecracker' by Will because she was just that, a fellow Leo like him their birthdays fell only a day apart and she took no prisoners if you got on her bad side. It was one of the reasons why Will had becomes friends with her in the first, she literally embodied all the traits of the perfect *faghag* any Gay man could ask for; that and her infectious personality to boot. She was just finishing her cigarette as Will approached her with a smile only she knew was really meant for her and no one else. A true friends smile.

"Oioi Willyboy! How's things Mr? Just starting your shitty late ah?"

"Oh you know my shift pattern scarily well my dear '*Firecracker*', dare I ask how your early shift has been?" Will sidled up next to his best friend after giving her a quick side-cuddle in greeting. She snorted at the question because Will knew what was coming.

"Ha, you know how it goes? I end up being chained to coffee pod one all morning while *them lot* do what they always do..."

"...Do their normal routines and the Manager or Supervisor looks the other way obliviously?"

"Spot on Mr, like always."

"Typical of them I guess" Will shook his head as he laughed softly "you working till two o'clock then 'Firecracker'?"

"Oh yes then I am *outta here...*" Kym responded as she moved towards the staff entrance "...you ready to face the music?" She looked back at her best friend with a cocky grin in place blatantly egging him on. Accepting the bait Will joined her as she entered the building, *'here we go then'* Will thought ominously. He went up the first flight of stairs with Kym and got his swipe in card and put himself into the on-site board so he was now subject to the whims of the company to whatever torture they would more than likely subject him to today on his late shift.

"Sucks don't it when you move your name over right?" Kym asked him as they made their way up the eight flights of stairs to the separate female and male staff locker rooms as Will grimly nodded, "trust me you have no idea how much it does suck, and it will be so much better after nine tonight when I move it back" he answered despairingly as Kym laughed at him as she patted his back trying to cheer him up. "Someone's got to do it Willyboy, and you drew the short straw evidently, I'll see you down there in a moment?" Kym said as they she left him at the male locker room door. "Yep, see you down there Firecracker." Will nodded and swiped himself in to drop his coat and bag off. The male locker room paled in comparison to the female locker room, the Store itself had a large contingent of women working that far outnumbered the men, the Cafe' alone had a team of twenty to twenty six team members at one time on the rota all working shift work and that comprised of about six men with the rest all women, the scales were definitely not in their favour but it didn't matter as all did their respective jobs well or some of them liked to do certain jobs their way because they just could at least. But the male locker room was a simple small rectangle shape while the female one was at least an easy three times the size of their male counterparts. After all these years working at the Store Will had changed lockers a total of three times, the first time because the locker the HR Team assigned him was quite old at the time, the second someone had used their steel tipped boot to kick in his locker door due to its low placement near the floor in either frustration or as a cruel joke and now he was on his third one which was serving him the best so far. He placed his backpack in, took his coat off, and checked the time on his phone which was eleven-fifty-five am before stowing it away in his backpack then placing his coat over it then locked the door. Will did his normal routine of locking and unlocking his door to make sure it was properly secure before he made his way downstairs to begin his dreaded late shift. He exited the locker room and swiped the electronic box that would pay him for while he was there on-site then trudged down four flights of stairs to come out of a side entrance for staff only on the first floor of the two floored Department Store by the public toilets for customers which was a part of the Ladies Wear section. It was starting to fill up with more of the mature generation which the section catered for, young teens or new mums for that matter didn't seem to be the primary demographic the Store was aiming for even though both categories screamed tonnes of profit to Will as he made his way to the escalators, he got on them and let it take him down to where he was looking forward to his not so wondrous day of work. There it was, the Cafe' like it was waiting for him, he saw the place abuzz with activity, he saw Nat in the open plan kitchen with only a small wall separating them from the shop floor keeping everything under order even if she wasn't a Supervisor anymore, Will caught her gaze and waved at her which she acknowledged with a quick wave back in return, she was obviously in the midst of preparing an order. *'Some things change yet some things don't.'* Will watched Nat hard at work and admired at how welcoming she had been to him on his first day at Riverside all that time ago which truly felt like a small lifetime had passed since, he didn't think he would still be working here after all these years, yet here he was still plodding along in a Hospitality Department for better or for worse. Sighing but masking it as if he were happy he looked around at the Cafe's which was on the brink of starting to get busy, there were two separate coffee pods with two till points and two coffee machines to each pod so four in total for the downstairs unit while the upstairs one had two tills, two coffee machines so that was six for the whole Store. In the early days just after the Store refurb it had been considered quite normal to have all four stations open to serve customer footfall that would be very busy, but after all these years the footfall had fallen off a little so it was more rare to ever have all four running at once but three was genuinely considered the normal if it were extremely busy, which judging by the looks of things to Will it was going to be very soon if not in the next few minutes. Will looked at the station closest to the large entrance and saw Kym had been plonked straight back on coffee pod one with one of the younger members of the Cafe' team, Aaron Connors. He was sixteen years old, but he was far more mature than most for his age group, he had thick back hair which could go curly at any given time if he didn't look after it along with a matching set of eyes to boot, he had a good strong physique on him due to his love of football and working out, he was a proper one of the lads but him and Will had always gotten along well despite Will being openly Gay which could sometimes unnerve young heterosexual guys coming into their prime but not Aaron. Their working relationship had progressed well when Will had put him forward for an Employee Showcase Award when a couple of customers had tried to get extremely aggravated with another co-worker he had been working with at the time and he had stunned Will with the way he had professionally dealt with the sticky situation. Needless to say he had received the Award from the Management Team with great affection, and they had developed a good friendship. "Hey Aaron, you keeping well Mr? Will called him from the entrance;

he nodded enthusiastically in response, "yeah boy! You ready for your late? I'm on till eight tonight so I can keep you company." He responded then gave the one-minute finger gesture to Will as he started serving an approaching customer. Will let him carry on as he made his way over to the kitchen area where his Supervisor Coralie Casper was waiting with the days rota on a clipboard, she had her lips set in an almost semi-pout, awaiting Will to come to her. "Are we ready to begin your shift at your own leisure today then Will." she said it dryly and it wasn't meant as a joke either. Will stood there and willed himself not to roll his eyes, he didn't really want to get on Coralie's bad side today. Keeping his voice restrained but polite he responded in kind.

"Coralie, your hilarious as always, how are we today?"

"Annoyed and for once not with you..."

"Uh oh, dare I ask what's happened?"

"you won't like it, two have called in sick today."

"Don't tell me Judy has called in sick *again*?"

"It's worse than that. She's got *another* sick note from the Doctors. I swear she must be bribing them to give her time off." Coralie went back to studying the rota openly frustrated as Will stood there in some disbelief himself. Judy Howard was the resident member of the Cafe' who always found excuses to try and get time off, she had begun working in 'The Restaurant' after Will had transferred over so he hadn't met her for a time until the staff upstairs were absorbed into the company after the conclusion of the *Orbit* Contract. Once he had come across her Will secretly wished he could have taken it back. All in all Judy was a complete piss-taker of epic proportions. She was a lesbian plus a butch one too; she was also a single mother seemingly bouncing from one relationship to the next, everyone in Cafe' was convinced she only went through these relationships not out of her desire to be loved by someone but out of a need to feel wanted by whatever poor woman would give her the time of day and then they would in turn feel sorry for her being a single parent and help her out with the raising of her daughter. Through all of that in her personal life she was a well-known unreliable employee who was forever trying to manipulate the system so she could get more and more of what she wanted out them, Will didn't understand why they hadn't tried to sack her from the job already when she had a multitude of employment sins that could be listed against her at a disciplinary hearing. Shaking his head with his eyes closed for a second Will tried to steer Coralie on from the new yet repetitively tired situation that swirled around the enigma that was Judy Howard.

"So that's one down, who else called in sick?"

"Oh one of the early-shift starters, she was meant to be finishing around two-thirty anyway, but we've been ok on that front since it's been a quiet morning but..." Coralie paused as she eyed Will up in a look he knew all too well, he wasn't liking it one bit.

"But what exactly Coralie?"

"Well it would be doing me a favour..."

"Don't say it. Whatever it is."

"It's just, well can you cover some breaks upstairs later on for me?" She finished asking Will and seemed to be holding her breathe. Will wasn't best pleased like he knew wouldn't be, he hated going up to the now Upstairs Cafe' which Coralie knew he wasn't a fan of. Sensing his frustration she offered him a sweetener. "I'll let you go up when a few of them have finished their shifts, that way you won't cross paths with *you know who*?" She had kind of gritted her teeth as well as trying to smile at Will which just made the Supervisor look a bit freaky to him. He openly sighed again as well as eyeballing her then he relented simply because he was a nice person.

"How long and how many break covers do you need me to do up there then?"

Coralie beamed at this, she could change like the wind at any given moment which was why Will was wary of her and tried not to annoy her as much as he could.

"Oh excellent thank you! it's just two covers you'll need to do, they're both thirty-minute breaks so only an hour or an hour and a half tops, your experienced since you've been here for years like me so that's why I was hoping you would do it for me..." She was perking up nicely towards him now. Will gave her the once over after this, her blonde hair was always done up in a meticulously tight bun despite the staff not needing to wear skull caps anymore since the business deemed it was a rather bland look for the customers to be seeing on the shop floor of the Cafe' from their workforce. For the girls it meant that they could finally do something with their hair rather hiding it, for Will it meant having his receded hairline on show for the world and its mother to see. For Coralie though she still maintained the same hairstyle after the uniform change, she always seemed so concerned about being a tough Supervisor with only a few friends she chose to socialise with out of work. Her dark brown eyes betrayed nothing to anyone either, she had a job to do and cracked the whip nearly every day, but if you did her favours well and right she would be on your side so Will did what was asked of him despite not being fully happy about it.

"So what time do you want me up there then? I'm assuming close to three o'clock?"

"Yes, yes that would be actually perfect timing..." she was looking back down at the rota on the clipboard she refused to ever surrender if she was on shift "...for now can you go help Sarah on tables until I let you know it's time to go on up." She finished by moving off to inspect the two queues that were now forming on coffee pod one and proceeded to get coffee pod two opened up. Will knew it wasn't a request but a simple instruction she had given him, so he went to the tables which were getting busier as the minutes passed on by. Sarah Bailey was another one of the younger members of staff falling into Aaron's teenager group in the Cafe' at the tender age of seventeen, she was in the cleaning station closest to the kitchen with a trolley full of used trays of customers left over orders sorting out the odds, the relief was obvious on her face as she flung her arms around Will for a surprise bear hug. "Oh boy am I glad you have arrived Will, I'm starting to get it right in the neck here being on my own!" She was a little bit out of breath, but she also seemed ready to spring into action as well. Sarah was probably about an inch or so taller than Kym so she was neat, petite with a wonderfully mixed-race skin tone, black straightened hair in a ponytail and pair of prescription glasses she would near enough be blind without if she didn't wear them. Will smiled at her in amusement as he took a cleaning spray with a cloth to go hunt out any further tables that needed clearing. "What are co-workers for right? Started picking up before I arrived today then?" He was speaking to her but looking out at the shop floor as near enough every table in the general vicinity of the cleaning station was full except one errant two-seater; today really was going to be hellish for everyone working. She nodded with vigour, "oh yes, I hear nothing but good stories about the opposite Saturday shift always having a nice, relaxed afternoon whilst us lot...", "Get thrown into the deep end when our weekend swings round, it's a complete shit show if you ask me." Will finished her sentence which got a laugh of agreement from his younger co-worker. "Oh Will..." she turned back to the trolley full of trays that still needed to be cleared out and sorted appropriately "...just knowing your here makes this day all the more better!" She knuckled down double time with the trolley as Will wandered off having spotted a table with a dirty tray waiting to be cleared which was already being partially claimed by a family of four, customers always plonked their sorry behinds quickly on a table even with a dirty tray like it was the most luxurious thing they have ever seen on their exhausting day of shopping, the fact that it still needed to be properly cleaned down didn't seem to register on their common sense scale surprisingly however. "Hello there!" Will chimed in promptly "if you don't mind just giving me a moment I will get this table of four all cleared up and cleaned down for you if you don't mind waiting while I do my business in two shakes of a ducks tale for you all" he beamed at the family of four, a husband and wife with two teenage boys who were more engrossed in their smartphone's to even look at Will. The husband was smiling at him kindly while the wife in her all-in-one tacky pink jumpsuit with her bad dye job looked like she had just smelt something quite odious at Will's arrival. In fact she looked like she was really put out by the offer of Will's timely help.

"Well as long as you won't be too long with it at all." the wife practically sniffed at him.

"Oh no not at all Madam..." Will began by spraying his cloth "you won't even notice me!" he smiled for all his worth, while his mind spoke a different language, *'listen bitch. Wait there like any normal person would and don't get the fuck in my way or I'll just take longer to spite you.'* The thought made him focus and he cleared the contents onto the waiting tray left by the last customer in no time then began wiping the table with his cloth while balancing the leftover tray expertly with the right hand, the bottle of cleaning liquid sat tucked nicely under his right arm causing him no trouble, the husband who was a rather impressive looking fellow with a fine pair of toned muscled arms plus excellently looked after grey hair was impressed by his technique.

"You've done this before; you can serve us any time mate!"

"Oh thank you sir, it would be my pleasure."

"Well if your all done here then, boys?" the wife instructed her two sons who sat down ignoring everything going on around them, Will then intentionally wiped the table some more, "excuse me boys if you don't mind..." Will got both of the boys to look up quickly from their phones as he wiped down their side of the table thoroughly "don't want you to get dirty now do we?" he asked his voice laced full of innocence as the boys thanked him when he was done then he finished the other side in less time, he could see out of the corner of his eye that the wife was annoyed he was still there while the husband clearly had the patience of a saint, Will was enjoying being near the husband in all honesty.

"If your quite done thank you!"

"Oh yes madam all finished, I didn't want any leftover food to get on your lovely purse you have there or potentially wet either, is it Chanel by any chance?"

"Err..." the wife's thin mouth shut quickly then opened again promptly "...why yes it is in fact." she almost stroked her purse which was very much a fake piece of Chanel, she even raised her nose to the air like she was the most important customer Will had ever served. The husband though clapped Will on the back with his sexy arms in thanks grinning as he took the seat. "Luv" the husband was looking at wife "give him a break he just served us all really well and made our table spotless! You take a tip mate?" the husband asked Will who shook his head at the question "ah no sorry sir the company doesn't allow us to accept tips I'm afraid. But, we do have an online customer service form you can fill out if you like? The Supervisor will definitely feedback any nice comments you leave?" Will countered the offer of a tip with something else and the husband was game for it straight away, "oh perfect! If you could get us one in a bit I will fill out on my phone for you, you've made my day a little bit more bearable with this lot already..." he side-eyed his family as the wife threw her husband a disapproving look then folded her arms showing off her badly done acrylic nailed manicure while Will suppressed a little snigger and just focussed fully on the husband smiling from cheek to cheek with gay abandonment. "Oh thank you very much sir, I'll go get you one and bring it over while you enjoy your lunch together..." Will then had a clever idea about what to say to the wife "...you're a very lucky lady I must say" he finished making sure his customer service smile never faltered, the husband took the compliment well in his stride as a Gay man paid him a nice compliment, his two sons actually stopped whatever they were doing on the phones to glance up at their Mother who just harrumphed in the direction of Will and he made his escape from the awkward woman and her poor family. Will was now smiling for his own personal amusement as he walked away, there was nothing like making a customer feel put out on his own terms. He dropped off the used tray to Sarah in the cleaning station who was smiling at him.

"What is it Sarah?"

"I saw that over there Will" she raised her eyebrows at him.

"I don't know what you're talking about..."

"Uh-huh ok then, whatever you say Mr." She used her eyes to look him up and down.

"Oh that reminds me..." Will turned to walk away quickly from her "I have to go get a customer service form for that *lovely husband* over there."

He glanced back over his right shoulder at his young co-worker and table-cleaning buddy for the next few hours, she was smirking with her arms folded shaking her head as she giggled at him, Will then chose to strut like his life depended on it as he continued away from her and he swung his pert ass from side to side for good measure. He looked over also at the family of four; the husband was queuing at coffee pod two waiting patiently in line while the rest of his family sat at their clean table, the two sons were still on their phones while the wife, well she was looking around vacantly like she was permanently bored. *'Ungrateful snotty ass cow.'* Will thought as he conjured an image in his mind of the wife slipping over a banana skin ruining her pink jumpsuit and making a complete idiot of herself in the process, it made him smile and the rest of the day seemed to become a tiny bit more bearable for him despite it being his dreaded anniversary. He went off in search of the customer service form he knew the rather cute husband would fill in for him.

*

1:34 pm.

It was a good hour and a half later now and the Cafe' was heaving, every table was occupied, three till and coffee stations were firing on all cylinders, the ticket machine was pumping out order after order like crazy in the kitchen, Coralie have conversed briefly with Nat and both had jointly agreed on a minimum twenty-five-minute wait for all hot food orders regardless of the easiest ones that could be made at the press of a button since a good ninety percent of the menu was just that, ping food. The two runners on the hot pass with the plush marble counter were doing the best that they could though, they each had a huge tray each and were carrying close to eight toasted sandwiches at any one time but it had now tipped over into not being quite good enough, there was a lag starting to develop somewhere in the great machine that was the Cafe' and customers were starting to get very opinionated or even aggravated in having to wait for their toasties, of course Will and Sarah were starting to receive the brunt of these complaints even though they weren't running any food orders out themselves. According to the all-knowing, all-seeing customers however they didn't want to hear excuses, they just wanted a miracle of some kind to drop out of the sky and give them their food order now because they were the ones so aggrieved at the end of the day. Will had other ideas, however.

"Young man? I've been waiting exactly *twenty-six-minutes* for my order according to the timecode on my receipt, where is it? Since I was told only a *twenty-five-minute* waiting time..." an elderly woman asked him.

"Oi, you there with the spray. Yeah you? My latte has *a lot of milk* in it and its barely warm, sort me out a new one would ya..." a bald-headed man was tapping his coffee cup impatiently.

"Err excuse me? My Cappuccino has a lot of *froth* in it but not a lot of *actual milk,* what exactly are you going to do about that?" a young lady with too much time on her hands was being extra for the sake of it.

'Ok. Breathe deeply Will you can do this.' Will told himself taking a sharp breathe inwards, and then he jumped into action. "Right let's see here..." he took the receipt gingerly from the elderly woman still waiting for their toastie "...ok, ah yes that wasn't the *actual time* you ordered if you see here my dear?" Will pointed out the actual time; the woman peered at it with narrow eyes which then went wide at her mistake, she looked up at Will still convinced she was the one in the right and he was wrong, but Will saw her off before she could form a response. "Now since this was

the time you actually ordered, that means you have been waiting approximately *ten-minutes* for you order so you have a good amount of waiting time still to elapse but..." one of the runners, it was Coralie as it happened was passing him with a tray, he caught her eye "...one of the runners here will go see where your *order twenty-two* is won't they?" He gave Coralie a wide-eyed look who was at the ready, "*Order twenty-two* did you say Will? I just saw that going in the oven so it will be about 90 seconds at most, I'll bring it straight to the customer over soon as its done" then Coralie was off in a dash with a load of toasties on her still full tray to deliver for other customers. Will looked at the elderly lady who looked back at him like she had well and truly been rumbled, Will smiled, and moved on to the bald man with the supposed cold latte by not evening acknowledging him but took his latte and called out to his 'Firecracker' at coffee pod one as he approached.

"Kym!"

"Yes Willyboy? Cold coffee?"

"Yep, do us a favour also?"

"Name it?"

"burn the roof of his *fucking mouth* since the cup is still nice n warm as it is please." He made sure he muttered this naughty part.

He had intentionally lowered his voice at this, but Kym had gotten the message loud and clear, she warmed a new cup up from the tea urn which dispensed water at 85 degrees minimum temperature, she got the double shot of coffee in no time then made the latte milk a searing 210+ degrees hot, standard milk was meant to come out either 150 or 160 unless requested by customers otherwise. Will thanked her and asked her to do a wet cappuccino for the young lady who didn't have much to do with herself. He took the latte over to the bald man who went to feel the side of the cup immediately.

"Hmm seems warm enough I guess..."

'just drink it you annoying twat.' Will thought as he smiled at the man. The man took a sip, and his eyes went wide with shock as Will expertly moved off to go retrieve his wet cappuccino from Kym, as he departed he heard what the man said to his companion.

"that almost burned the roof of my *fucking mouth*!"

Will snorted quietly and sent Kym a silent thank you, she winked back at him in kind. Proceeding with the wet cappuccino he placed it down in the front of the young lady who was then all of a sudden surprised.

"Oh I wasn't expecting it *that quick*..."

"Oh we aim to please if you're not happy with your initial coffee madam."

"Oh well let's see shall we..." she took a delicate sip like she was a connoisseur of coffee all of a sudden then she was nodding her head like a happy puppy dog. "Oh that's fabulous, good amount of milk in there!" she was almost clapping her hands as Will took her old cappuccino away which was as light as feather, exactly how that type of coffee should be. "Glad to help madam, just know that for future reference cappuccinos are an espresso shot with a tiny hint of milk and three-quarters of *froth* only as their meant to be light as feather and not filled with actual latte milk, have a *lovely day* now!" Will smiled walking away leaving the young lady with a strangely wonky smile on her face, the realisation then sunk in for her and she didn't make any more diva demands whilst she enjoyed her caffeine fix. Will nearly hit the ceiling in delight when she left the Cafe'. He got back into the hustle and bustle of tables with Sarah who seemed to be permanently trapped in the cleaning station sorting out dirty trays. "Never-ending right? What time you hear till tonight Mrs?" Will stole a quick moment to lean on one of the interior walls inside the small three-quarter enclosed cleaning station with Sarah who seemed to be in a daze, she looked at him like he had spoken a foreign language.

"Oh me? I'm off at seven tonight, I'm gonna need a good stiff alcoholic drink after this day Will..."

"Stating the obvious, I aim to get a bottle of wine and Chinese for one on the way home tonight Sarah!"

"Ooo *Chinese*, you bitch, I'm so jealous right now!"

"Are you two quite finished?" Coralie then appeared out of nowhere with an empty tray on her way back to the hot pass where more hot food was waiting to be run out, Will snapped to attention.

"Yep, sorry about that Coralie, I'll just go..."

"Change of plans now Will. I just had a phone call off of upstairs..." Coralie held up the portable work phone each department had assigned to them, since there were two Cafe's they each had one to communicate whenever they needed anything. Will was staring at the phone like it was kryptonite, *'oh god please don't say it.'* he was desperately hopeful it wasn't what he thought it really was. Coralie was simply nodding however.

"Yep sorry, need you to go up now, their busy."

"But you said I wouldn't have to see..."

"Nothing I can do about that; you'll just have to avoid them."

"But...what about Sarah? She'll be alone on tables?"

"Got it covered. Someone from one of the other Departments is already on their way." Sarah groaned loudly at this, Will stood there pleading silently with Coralie who just deadpanned him with that same fixed look; there was nothing to be done.

He was going upstairs now whether he liked it or not.

"Off you go Will, don't dawdle either or I'll know!"

Two

The Upstairs Cafe'.

Formerly known as 'The Restaurant'.

Five Minutes Later.

1:57 pm.

He hadn't even had the chance to say goodbye to Kym his 'Firecracker' before she finished at two. That sucked the most out of this whole situation more than anything. By saying goodbye to Kym he could mentally prepare himself for the rest on his crappy Saturday shift. The Chinese was already calling to him later tonight. Thanks to Coralie he was heading to the one place where didn't want to be, the place where it had all started for him all those years ago and had now been taken over by a group of people who Will quite frankly didn't want to interact with at all, he even made it a habit not to come up here since 'The Restaurant' scheme had been completely abolished from the Company entirely along with the roots as of it as well. Now it was a hundred cover overflow Cafe' to help with if it ever got busy downstairs, and it had been heaving. Now they were busy up here too, so that meant Will had been selected to work with this group of people for the next few hours, he really didn't want to be around any of them for as long as possible. He had an apt nickname he had dubbed them all a long time ago.

He had named them *'the Clique'*.

They were the Old Guard of Riverside still fighting their so-called good fight in their eyes, to Will it looked more like a lost cause as each year went by since he had been employed at the Store. Coralie had told him not to dawdle on his way up, but he was in fact taking as much time as he could. Will was known for being a faster than the usual walker in the Cafe' but when it came to this group of people, well Coralie could be damned for all he cared. *'Christ why me? Oh, I know why really. Because I'm known as the reliable one in this place that's why. That or I have the word mug written across my forehead.'* he thought to himself as he got off the escalator back again at Ladies Wear Department then began walking slower than he normally would towards the Kids Wear Department. The second floor was comprised of three different sections in total, Ladies, Lingerie and Kids. Despite a total store renovation though every department always felt like everything was crammed in without much chance for any leftover space, it just showed the way the designers had a very narrow vision for what they thought was good on their level but not at all useful from a customer perspective. When a sale always came up each section allotted a space and it always resulted in utter chaos for customers who almost ended climbing over each other in search of that bargain they wanted to get their little grubby hands on at any cost. Each section barely left any space left to breathe for customers and staff alike since there was so much marked-down stock squeezed in to whatever space they had chosen which made Will feel slightly more grateful he worked in a Hospitality Unit of the Store, the only downside was the customers would come storming in to the Cafe after making their purchases acting like ravenous beasts who hadn't seen a cup of coffee in a good decade at least, it made every upcoming sale a highly unpleasant experience. Will was now in the Kids Department and he saw the Upstairs Cafe' fast approaching him, he had dawdled at least a good five minutes more than he should have, he asked a passing member staff putting clothes back on their hangers what the time was and it was almost five minutes past two now which meant we had dawdled more than successfully than he first thought he had. He looked in at the Upstairs Cafe' and he could tell it was busy just by the tables, he was standing a good ten or so feet away from the entrance/exit, but every table was full with them all using every seat available. *'Well this is gonna be shit for me then, let's go face those bitches plus the customers too.'* Will psyched himself up by shaking his body in readiness, straightening his shoulders; he then marched through the staff entrance at the side straight into the Dishwasher Area tucked neatly outback. Breathing in relief none of the group he despised so much were there, they were all out front for the time being so hadn't noticed his arrival, but he could hear them all pottering about like nobody's business.

"Lucy you got jacket potato order on the way? Make it two more on top of that now..."

"Jan add a hot chocolate on with that latte please!"

"Sherry do you need me to jump on the other till? No? Ok then..."

"Trudy how are you on tables, you need anyone to help you out? They must have sent someone up already by now..."

"I will do soon Josie, its murder out there; I'll call down again..."

The two-way revolving door Will had gone through countless times in his first two years of working when it was 'The Restaurant' swung open violently and out came none other of than

Trudy Harrie, one fifth member of *'the Clique'*, and she looked flustered more than anything as she plonked down a single tray loaded with cups, saucers and toastie plates onto the waiting Dishwasher. She had her severe looking spectacles on, and she unclipped them from the front at the bridge section, her hair was forever pushed up into a short ponytail that always looked like it hurt more than it comforted her dark brown hair with a few whispers of grey on show meaning she was due to colour it again soon. She always walked around with the attitude of a strict old-fashioned schoolteacher from the moment she started her shift right up until the very end of her working day, it made Will feel on edge around her constantly. Trudy looked up only just noticing Will had arrived, she eyed him some more with her severe teacher-like look she always had permanently in place then shouted round to the front.

"No need to call down! *The help* has finally arrived at last."

"Hi there Trudy..." Will really didn't like the way she referred to him as *the help* "...busy is it?"

"Understatement of the week Will..." she began busying herself on the dishwasher "...can you get on tables; I've certainly had my fill of them today I'll crack on with this lot here." She then got on with the lone tray she had brought out, but Will was already noticing that was the only tray she had brought out, the rest of the

Dishwasher Area was otherwise pretty clean. *'Oh here we go;
they've basically been waiting for the lapdog to pick up the flack
which is me. Thanks a lot.'* the grim thought became an even worse
certainty as Will stepped out onto the shop floor leaving Trudy
with her convenient one tray she would more than take her time
with now that he was to be the dogs body for the next few hours.
Sure enough he had been right; every single table of the hundred
covers was taken by customers, some of them even sat at tables
with leftover trays from previous occupants. Will truly couldn't
understand the customer mentality when it came to coveting a
table. After six years of working here he had never gotten his mind
around the fact that customers became inherently more stupid
when they visited the Cafe' for whatever they might be purchasing,
they would sit at a table with a dirty tray left, take one look at it
and then continue on with what they had brought themselves. Will
would have sooner moved the tray out of his vicinity if he had
been a customer rather than sit on a table with someone's leftovers.
'I'll never understand these people I serve daily' he thought as he
started with the first few tables closest to the revolving door,
wiping them down as he went, in just over ten minutes of being up
there he had successfully taken out no more than eight trays of
used stuff from customers who were done and had plonked it on
the empty stands right next to the Dishwasher Area as Trudy was
unsurprisingly to him taking her sweet time with her singular fully
loaded tray Will saw she was being intentionally slow about

finishing it too but she was watching him out of the corner of her eyes as he loaded up the stands with more trays.

"On a mission out there Will?"

"Ah Trudy you know how it goes, just gotta bash it out then move on to the next!"

"Yes but I am the *only one* on dishwasher you see currently..."

"Yes I do see currently..." he was letting her know he was blatantly mimicking her "...I am also the o*nly one* on tables now since you took the dishwasher duties on just like that" He snapped his fingers on his left hand in a camp flourish as Trudy stared at him with a beady-eye look planted on her face over those hideous teacher-like specs she always wore. "So I think it's a good idea if we keep up the pace, what do you say? Those tables aren't gonna clean themselves after all..." he called out to her not bothering to wait for her response as he dashed back to the shop floor, she had no authority of any kind to tell him what to do since she was the same level as him, a Customer Assistant, the lowest of the low in the hierarchy that existed in the structure of the job, yet these people here operated on their own entirely set rules that the Management Team simply looked the other way at and did nothing to do what was needed to sort them out despite many more people than just him calling out their bullshit work politics over the years. Split them all up and teach them all a valuable lesson in getting along with other people they didn't normally associate themselves with. That was Will's ultimate fantasy at the end of it all, he had tried it many moons ago when he had first transferred down to the Cafe' full of renewed hope and optimism along with the more money he was getting plus the discount he would get in a fortnights time when he officially started. As he cracked on with more tables farther afield from the countertop whilst trying not to look at any of *'the Clique'*, he let his mind wander back to that time he first went down to work in the Cafe' after his two-day induction in the In-House HR Department with the Mentors. Sometimes if felt like only yesterday when he thought about those first few days working properly for the company.

'It all seemed like it was such a welcoming place at first despite their attitudes. If only I had, had a bit more authority backing me up at the time I would have been able to let these women know that they were lucky to be gaining a hardworking, reliable yet loyal person joining their team. All they had to do was be a little bit kinder that very first time when I came down after the induction. Heck it could have been such a different Working Relationship entirely if they had met me at the halfway point. I still remember it to this day so clearly almost 4 years ago...'

*

November 6th, 2012.

Tuesday.

4:00 pm.

Excitement. Nerves. Giddiness. Adrenaline. He felt all of those
feelings and more. He could start referring himself as proper staff
now that the days of sub-contraction with the *Orbit Group* were
officially resigned to the history books for him. *'I just can't believe
I am gonna be on £8.00 an hour with a discount card arriving for
me in no less than two weeks and no more Sundays for me. Ever!'*
that thought made him happiest of all as he arrived on the shop
floor at the Ladies Wear Department. He had just finished up the
last of his induction training which was near enough a two-day
course on the history of the company, where it wanted to go in
terms of its ambitions and what it was doing to make itself better
financially to last longer in the economic sense. That bit had been
the most boring, Will had been trying extremely hard to fight his
eyes that had become a bit heavier than usual at the time,
thankfully no one had noticed he had drooped a little while the two
female Mentors had prattled on. He had known the two trainers in
the time had had been here, he couldn't believe over two years of
working in the Store had gone by for him. When he had done the
interview with the lovely duo that consisted of June and Dianne he
had been equal parts grateful whilst equals part a little bit on edge,

he knew they were a formidable pair when it came to hiring for the company, but they were both lovely women with hearts full of love and patience for not only the process but the candidates who they gave each their fair due to sell themselves whomever they might be. So when they had interviewed him they had treated him the same as anyone else despite his uniform he already wore for 'The Restaurant' at the time. The role-playing exercise done by June was exquisite while Dianne had sat in the corner scoring him, what hadn't been scripted was when all three of them had looked at each other and burst out laughing at the predicament they all found themselves in. It was the best unscripted moment in Will's life thus far. He sailed through the rest of the interview process with ease, then he had been offered the job by June and Diane, met the Manager for the Downstairs Cafe' for a quick meeting then the rest as they say had been history. He became full time staff with shifts spread across four longer days rather than five since they had tweaked his shifts just a bit so he was taken out of working on Sundays ever again which had floored Will to no end. Their reasoning behind it though more than made sense for them to do it though, all the current staff worked Sundays on either time and a half or double pay due to their old Contracts they clung onto fiercely. Times were changing in the Retail Sector however and the new company mandate was to cease giving these incentives to work Sunday shifts with those types of pay so they had been phased out over a length of time. One of the things that had been given to Will by pure luck of the draw was the London-weighting however. The Store had been a viable candidate for it for many years since it was located in close proximity to the M25 Motorway but in the last few weeks the Store had been chosen to lose its location premium bond as when it came down to the technicalities of its actual location was about something over five hundred feet outside of the Motorway so that was in the midst of being phased out too. Not in Will's case though as he had applied in the time frame they were in the midst of losing the bond, they had to officially honour giving him London-weighting in his pay, so he was awarded it. He felt like he was the cat who got the cream really. Now here he was, induction completed, and he was on his way down to the Cafe' to do the last few hours of his second day with the company to get his hands truly stuck into the Cafe' way of working. *'I know it's an all women team, but I can't wait to work with them, they'll love having a Gay co-worker to bitch with about customers, that and I love to bitch in general.'* the gleeful thought filled him with more happiness as he walked down the escalators. The Cafe' was just off to the side of the Food Department in its own little corner. It was just gone four in the afternoon so it wasn't that busy anymore which meant Will would be meeting some of the team today and getting to know them for a bit, he still couldn't wait for it though. He got off the escalator then walked into the smaller seventy-five seated area. Just as he suspected only about eight or so tables were filled at this late hour of the afternoon. All was calm so he wasn't about to be thrown under the bus by any surprises thankfully, he took a good look at the place and was instantly thinking one thing. *'This place needs serious refurbishment; I feel like I've time travelled back to the Nineties in the space of a few short seconds'* he assessed the decor along with the tables. The floors had probably started as a nice, pleasant cream colour but years and years of people pummelling it with their footwear had reduced it to what could only be described as a pale yellowish hue. It wasn't pleasant to look at. He made his way to the back area of the Cafe' where he knew they all escaped to from time to time and it was beyond small, *'how in the world do they all fit in here?'* he asked himself then it hit him like a tonne of bricks. It was intentionally designed this way so they all couldn't fit in here at any one given time, a shrewd but effective decision on the Manager's part he was sure of it. Some of the team were out front but there was no queue or customers to be served, they were all talking in their own little group, Will observed them and took notice of how physically close they were all standing to each other, as if no one else could encroach upon the conversation at all, it was a strange thing to be doing on the shop floor of all places. *'If this was a busy bar or pub I would totally get why they are all standing like that, but this is work after all, no need not include anyone else like say, me?'* He was waiting for them to still take notice of him, but they hadn't yet in fact he was sure they didn't even know he was standing there waiting patiently to be acknowledged.

"*Ahem.*" he let out a quiet cough.

The group of women kept on talking none the wiser to the ripple of disturbance.

"*Ahem...*" he made the cough louder now.

One woman with her back to him raised her head at the sound of the cough he made but then resumed her conversation with the group as if it were nothing.

'You have got to be kidding me with this right?'

He looked at them all with wide eyes then just decided to go dive off into the deep end for the hell of it.

"Hello there ladies! I'm Will your new co-worker from 'The Restaurant'" He chimed in overly loudly plus he planted a smile to please anyone on his face, half of the group then jumped while the other half had looks of extreme annoyance.

"Who on *earth* was that?"

"Disturbing our chat, who would *dare*?"

"They'd better have a good reason for the interruption, which was *our time*."

Will continued smiling as the group of women all turned to face him at once slowly in an eerily fashion, each looked at him like he wasn't the new boy but a new thing, all had a different set of narrowed eyes, one of them even had some serious looking teacher-like glasses on. *'Well, this is a bit of a tough crowd.'* He approached them slowly, none of them made any move to get closer to him, oh no they were waiting for this new person to come to them. He kept the smiling going even if he felt out of sorts around these women who were now his new co-workers for the foreseeable future. "Hello again ladies, so sorry to interrupt your chat I just wanted to introduce myself again, I'm Will Hardley and I'm going to be working with you all from now on as your new employee" he finished by offering his hand to the one with the serious looking glasses, *'definitely getting a teacher vibe off of you.'* Will thought as the group of women all looked at his outstretched hand waiting to shake anyone's hand who would take it. The woman with the glasses stole a quick look off her friends then took Will's still waiting hand, *'whenever you're ready ladies, you can't catch Gay anymore in case any of you are worried about that still...'* Will kept that thought firmly to himself; he dared not alienate his new work team having only been there a precious few minutes.

"Nice to meet you Will, I'm Trudy Harrie." Trudy shook his hand firmly and finally gave a smile to him, but it came off of her in waves like that smile was in fact coming from a very forced place, she was about the same average height same as him as well. Will still smiled back thinking of one of the eternal lessons he had been taught by his mother at a young age that he carried with him to this very day, good manners cost nothing.

"Trudy, lovely to meet you. I like your glasses…"

'I hate them really. They freak me out.'

"I'm Sherry Michaels, hello there..." Sherry had black hair barely shoulder length and was clearly not far off of retirement age, her handshake was weak and minimal, like she didn't really want to touch anyone else until she was ready. She stood about a good foot taller than Trudy.

"Sherry, a pleasure."

'Two down, two to go.'

He turned to the other two left out of the four. Next was another close to retirement buxom blonde who stood probably another good half a foot taller than Sherry was, she was literally looking down at him from her slightly wrinkled nose. "Hi, Lucy Cricker here..." her handshake was firm but one shake only then it was back to being folded as she continued to observe Will like he was something not to be entirely trusted.

"Lucy, good to meet you. And last not but certainly not least...?"

Will faced the final woman in the group of four was the only one to give him a half smile, quite frankly he was elated to see some politeness at all of any kind. "Nice of to you to introduce yourself to all of us battle-axes there Will..." her group looked at her in surprise then they all seemed to let out a restrained laugh at the joke as the last member shook Will's hand the firmest but seemed to be the most welcoming so far.

"I'm Jan, Jan Betty. How's your induction been?"

she was actually asking him a genuine question of inquiry; her group Will saw out of corner of his right eye were looking at her judging if she might be unwell. Will however kept the niceties going for as long as he could. "Oh you know how it is Jan, a bloody big information dump! My brain feels like a new form of soup that Heinz will be quick to snap the rights up too if their lucky..." Will grinned as Jan let out a laugh full of humour that felt real; even the rest of the group consisting of Lucy, Sherry and Trudy gave a small unique laugh but only allowing themselves the one again. "Have you seen Josie yet Will?" Trudy took hold of the conversation again, arms folded, she was still inspecting him over with her glasses Will did not like them the more he saw them with each passing moment.

"Josie? She's the Supervisor right?"

"Yep that she is, she's in the office, you'd better go introduce yourself..."

"Ah I will do just that; office is just there right?" Will pointed at an unmarked door right next to the Cafe' hidden in the corner, Trudy nodded then moved aside to let him pass as did the other three. "Well nice to meet you ladies, looking forward to working with you all once more" Will moved past them and then he felt it. The staring, the judging, it was coming off all of them in waves, each doing it differently, but he still felt it as he walked to the office door. *'Am I really just saying that to appease them?'* the question sat in his mind and he decided to put it down to first day jitters, before he knocked on the office door he looked back over his shoulder briefly and saw the group of four still looking, all assessing him, chatting about him, narrowed distrustful eyes boring into his back but there was something else as well. It was the talking; they were clearly talking about him while he was still there in the immediate vicinity of them. *'They've got some nerve I'll give them that'* Will thought about the group of women. He turned his attention once more to the waiting door and he knocked confidently again hoping this Josie was anything but different from the others he had just met. Well he hoped she was at least a little bit different. "Come in..." a soft-spoken voice called at last from the other side, Will took a calming breathe and entered the office. It was an unremarkable place that was filled to rafters with stuff.

Lots and lots of stuff that didn't really need to be there probably was Will's first impression. There was just one too many computer terminals for the space as well. Three would have been a nice round number to slot into this small office but it had been decided by someone that four would be better, it was clearly too much for the space as it gave the sense of a claustrophobic interior, Will hoped he wouldn't be spending to much time in here while he worked in the Cafe'. Sitting at one of the terminals furthest away from the door was the room's sole occupant; she had her back to him as she was clearly engrossed with something on the computer.

"Just a moment please, I'm finishing up here, will be right with you..."

Will stood there silently not saying a word till she was ready if he was using any of his previous encounters with the group of four outside was evidence to go by. *'This lot clearly like doing things a certain way around here, the difference between 'The Restaurant' up there to down here is quite jarring and I've only been here five minutes at best.'* Will thought to himself as he took up to looking at the one of the many notice boards adorning the walls filled with old bits of paperwork attached to them making the already cramped space even more tighter than it needed to be, he was not a sufferer of claustrophobia by any stretch of the imagination, but he made the judgement call that he didn't want to use this office unless it was absolutely necessary.

"Right..." the back was now turning to face him. "...You must be Will, our new starter?"

And Will Hardley met Josie Sybille for the first time.

Josie stood up giving Will her own once over as she went, she didn't any move closer to him, but she folded her arms to inspect him just like some of the group had done outside. Will felt like he was something to be put on display and this woman was letting him know that through her guarded body language. If the group still outside were the followers then Josie here, she was the ringleader which she knew by wielding that status accordingly. *'Looks like this new job placement is going to be one very interesting experience for all of us involved.'* the thought kept him on his feet which he needed to be, so far these women definitely came across like a formidable force to be reckoned with, he didn't know how that made him feel truthfully. Josie wasn't a tall woman, she clocked in about Will's height with maybe an inch or more to her than him; she had chocolate brown shoulder length hair she kept up with a band at the back, a set of dark eyes that might as well been black which bore into him, she had a thin mouth that had a very dark shade of red lipstick well painted on as well which meant she enjoyed colours to signify authority or control, her shoulders were set in a power pose conveying she was in charge despite being only a Supervisor, if Will had been slightly unsettled but the group of four out on the shop floor, in here in this cramped office he was absolutely being thrown off kilter by this new woman before him. *'No wonder I'm Gay, I feel sorry for whatever boyfriend or husband that has to put up with her in the bedroom department of a night-time the poor sod'* Will kept on smiling however different his thoughts were currently, he wasn't prepared to show weakness to Josie having only just met her, he extended his hand outwards hearing his mother's lesson at the back of his mind nurturing him to keep it up until all other options were exhausted. "Josie it's nice to finally to meet you face to face, June and Diane had told me about you but considering I have worked here for over two years sub-contracted under *Orbit* it's amazing how you don't really meet or come across someone properly until you actually start working on a Department" he chuckled to ease any tension there might be, she hadn't initially taken his hand but she took it politely shaking it but Will still couldn't get a full read on the women yet, he had noticed one very small discrepancy in her demeanour before he shook his hand however, she had looked down at the it in a very quick fire movement with her eyes only in the same tradition as Trudy had done earlier but far less noticeably. *'Trudy needs to take lessons in subtly if this ringleader is anything to go by'* Will made a mental note to try his best to get on with Josie even though she wasn't one to give anything away on first impressions, she practically wore it like battle armour. "So how was your induction training Will?" she was finally asking a question in his direction much to Will's internal relief.

"Oh crikey I don't feel like I could take any more new information if I tried..." Will chuckled noticing she now gave the barest of smiles, like she was only relaxing by a mere fraction of a point being in his company. "Yes those Mentors up there..." she looked off in to the distance like she was reminiscing "...it's a lot of hot air if you ask me but the business requires a near two-day course for all new employees, *well* not so new in your case but a little bit of a refresher." she had closed some of the physical distance between them but there was still that noticeable divide Will could see.

"So, your all done now? I take it your day ends at 5:30..."

"Yep Josie that's correct, anything you would like me to do now?"

"Well let's go out and see shall we..."

She moved passed him now with an almost cat-like ease about her. She also spoke only in quiet soft tones, but Will could feel something lurking underneath, just lying below the surface of the water, it was absolute authority with an edge of conviction. *'Christ, I'd really better go out of my way to get in her good books.'* the ominous thought made Will feel like he was being judged for any minute detail or flaw that could be found out, he still had over an hour to go with these new co-workers of his until he finished for the day. They both walked back out in single file to the shop floor, the small Cafe' space was more glaringly obvious if you looked at it from the angle of the office, it was screaming out to be renovated. *'A fixer upper for sure.'* he thought, all the fridges were louder than they should be, the coffee machine's automatic wand was being used by Trudy as they had come out of the office and it was like someone had set of a police siren at close range, it went right through you just by the sounds it was making. "Oh my, that sounds hits the spot and not in a good way either doesn't it?" Will held one of his hands to his ears that felt sensitive at the jarring noise, Josie though remained the same, impassive, unflinching with only a slightly pinched nose; her own way of registering the sound. "It's become like background noise to me now, we all get used to it down here don't get we girls?" She called out the group of four still on shift who all laughed at Josie's statement as if like clockwork, Trudy on the coffee machine sniggered as the auto wand ceased its awful noise, Sherry was over by the small dishwasher smirking with a good shrug of her shoulders, Jan a gave toothy laugh whilst serving a customer and Lucy on the tables created a nice round movement with her mouth pointing at Josie with a wink and Will, well the joke was lost on him but he saw the look that was now passing over her face. It was the power she had in here, she was smiling but it was all because these women she worked with were conditioned to her way of thinking, her way of working, her way of conducting the days schedule, her type of atmosphere that she wanted above all else. *'If I didn't feel welcomed earlier, then I certainly don't feel welcome at all at the moment.'* he felt this unpleasantness feeling almost pouring out of his body in waves upon waves, he didn't know how to act around any of them as Josie found something for him to do. "Ah yes here we go..." she handed him a bottle of cleaning spray and a roll of tissue "...Lucy goes home at five, just like me, Sherry and Trudy do as well so just keep cleaning tables until your done at five-thirty then you can head off" Josie turned to head back into the office, but Will was alarmed all a sudden. The Cafe' didn't close until ten pm tonight so who was going to left once his shift ended at five-thirty and it was now four-forty-five, so they were all leaving in fifteen minutes time. Not wanting to let her leave he grabbed Josie's elbow quickly.

"Err, Josie so sorry, one quick question..."

He stopped what he was saying as she looked back at his hand on her elbow then she looked at him with only the same movement of her eyes again. They were alight with curiosity but also a fire that she fully controlled; Will let go of her elbow slowly as he eyeballed her not meaning to do it in the first place.

"What is it Will?" she made her voice sound like she was bored of this already.

"It's just err..."

"It's just what?"

"Well you said you're all leaving at five and I'm only here till five-thirty? Surely there are others coming in too close up right? Stupid question I know but it is my first time being down here properly..."

She was now catching on, realising her small infraction she filled him in.

"Oh yes, you're quite right about that..." Will saw Jan and Trudy looking at Josie oddly out of the corner of his left eye at her admission "...don't worry there are three late-night starters all coming in at five before we *all* head off, it's been a tiring day right ladies?" she didn't look at Will, but she looked at her posse who all caught her wavelength.

"Oh yeah it's been a trying day..." Trudy called from the coffee machine.

"Yes indeed!" Sherry called from the dishwasher.

"I can hear the wine calling me since it's been so busy." Jan sniggered again from the till.

"Oh you're telling me Jan; do you remember that one Tuesday where..." Lucy struck up a chat with Jan from the tables on the shop floor and they all got involved with one another again, all save for Will who was still stood off to the side with Josie who merely glanced sideways at him now satisfied Will was clued up in

where he stood in the status quo. "Now that's all been sorted..."
Josie nudged him with the cleaning spray and kitchen roll, he had
been staring at the dynamics of the group of four, "you can go help
Lucy on tables, cheers for introducing yourself today. Will." Josie
finished by not waiting for his response, but she re-entered the
office, closing the door with a decisive snap. Will stood there
holding the cleaning products feeling even more out of place
amongst these new people. *'Guess I'd better just clean tables
then.'* he set off around the counter to join Lucy who was chatting
away once more with Jan, Sherry and Trudy, they paid him no
mind as they had an animated chat about a past Tuesday that had
been busy, well busy to their standards anyway. Will was
perplexed in all honesty; part of the induction training required
them all to go on the shop floor twice over the two days, once for a
shopping exercise, the other for a fire tour. The fire tour had
happened today, and the Fire Health and Safety Officer had them
walking past the Cafe' briefly earlier around lunchtime and Will
had seen it had not even been remotely busy, it had in fact been
rather quiet. *'So their already trying to bullshit to me about their
so-called busy day down here, well that's just great isn't it?'* Will
wiped a table down as Lucy didn't help him, she was too wrapped
up in her chat with her girlfriends. Will was more than content to
keep it that way for now since there was only ten minutes left until
they all finished their shifts; he was more than aware that Lucy was
now going to be speaking to her friends rather than help him out.

Thankfully there only about a dozen lone customers all wrapped up in the own individual stuff who were causing no fuss, he wiped done one of the highchairs when there was only less than five minutes left on the clock for them and he heard a new voice all of a sudden.

"Oh well hello there, is this the new person I heard about the other day?"

He turned to the cheery voice like it was an alien. He stopped his one eighty degree turn to come face to face with a slightly taller lady than him with a grin in place and lovely blonde hair with a few strands of brown in it, and she was offering her hand to shake Will's before he had a chance to do it himself. "Hello there, I'm Daisy Davidson and who might you be?" she shook Will's hand with eagerness but full of affection, Will had never felt more welcome in the Cafe' until this moment. "Wow, Daisy so nice to meet you! This is a lovely welcome I must say..." Will was openly surprised at how nice she was being as they continued the handshake, her hand was warm just like she was coming off as and Will instantly liked her on the spot, he felt like he had someone he could get along with in here at last.

"So you started today then Will?

"Well I finished my induction around 4 so then we all came down to finish our days on our set Departments..."

"Oh god I remember those induction days, nightmare aren't they?"

"Like you wouldn't believe, June and Diane are great but it's just *so much* information to take it in one long sitting!"

"Oh I remember so well I tell you; I still have nightmares about those two days from time to time..."

The both laughed openly on the shop floor at the inside joke, Will had never felt so good to meet a member of staff who was making him feel truly at ease. Their little moment was cut short as the group of four along with Josie leading the pack walked past them. It was like the weather changed instantly whenever they all appeared as a group.

"We're off now Daisy, all the best." Josie half-looked at her as she didn't stop walking.

"Yep, see ya later darling!" Lucy patted her on the shoulder as she left too.

"Bye love." Jan said not far behind.

"Adios amigo!" Sherry acknowledged her on the way out.

"Bye for now." Trudy spoke at her not to her trotting to keep up with the others.

The all filed out in the group like no one else could touch them, not one of them had uttered a single word of goodbye to Will on their way out, he watched them all the way until they got to escalator to head upstairs to the safety of the staff level and the sanctity of the female locker room where he was sure they would be cackling away like witches at his expense. Will shook his head in quiet disbelief then realised he was being watched by Daisy, she was smiling a little awkwardly at him, but he felt something else coming off of her. It was empathy.

"I take it I have blended into the fixtures today then!" Will winked at her which made her laugh loudly.

"Oh Will I know I've only just met you, but you seem like you're a right laugh Mr, come on let's get to the till and coffee station since it's just us for now!" She moved off to the back area and he followed her, but he was following more so because he was enjoying her company, the first person to actually treat him like a Human Being and not like an object. They entered to the till and coffee area devoid of anyone but them then Will saw the time on the till.

"Bloody hell!" He was surprised "it's only *4:56 pm*; they've gone up a bit early haven't they?"

Daisy was now giggling to herself again at Will's surprised nature.

"Am I missing something here?"

He was genuinely confused but Daisy placed a reassuring hand on his shoulder, she still had that look of understanding on her face, but she wasn't doing it out of pity, it was even more empathy more than anything.

"Oh Will, how long are you here till?"

"five-thirty, why do you ask?"

"Oh excellent! That's a good half an hour to give you a quick crash course about how the Cafe's is run..."

"What about the other two closing with you?"

Daisy looked back out at the escalators, sure enough it was now bang on five pm in the afternoon and there were two other women with skull caps making their way into the Cafe'.

"Nothing to worry about, they're here. It'll... I mean we will be fine." Daisy smiled as she appraised him.

Will felt like he was about to make his first real friend in this place.

"So Will, are you ready for your crash course in the politics of the Downstairs Cafe'?"

"Honestly, Daisy? Not really. I mean what I just experienced is something not many people ever expect when they start somewhere new, I know I've been working upstairs for two years but I already feel like this is a new can of worms I've opened by transferring down here and I don't know where to start with this lot."

"Excellent then. This is an easy solution to your problem..." she clapped her hands excitedly "...let's start at the very beginning of it all shall we!"

From then on for the last half an hour of his day Will hung off of every word that came out of Daisy Davidson's mouth.

He had never been more grateful to meet a kind person like her.

She taught him the ways of the Cafe' and all its intricacies, especially when it came to 'the Clique'.

It was as good a nickname as any.

Three

Back To Now.

The Upstairs Cafe'.

September 3rd, 2016.

3:16 pm.

'They were welcoming but they let me know straight from the off that, that was their territory. You were more right than you give yourself credit for Miss Davidson. I do miss you.'

He never forgot that first day with Daisy; it had helped him more than she could have ever realised for him in the ensuing weeks.

Will still missed her incredibly after she had taken a new
Administrative Job working in a Hospital in Essex at the beginning
of the year. After the Store refurbishment he and Daisy had been
regular Saturday-Night closers together, they always knew how to
get each other through those shitty shifts. *'Now it's just me, myself
and I.'* he thought to himself as he continued with his table
clearing while *'the Clique'* kept well away from him. Since those
early days things had changed significantly between them and he
didn't want to think about them today any more than he had to on
his Anniversary today of all days, they could be in his thoughts
another day or time when he deemed it worthy of their petty
politics to take up his valuable thinking time. For now it was
slightly more calmer but the sheer amount of customers that were
still occupying the upstairs Cafe' was more than he could handle, *I
just hope I'm not closing up here tonight.'* Will hoped as he
crossed his fingers to make a silent wish to karma or fate if any
higher purpose that existed was listening to him on this busy shift.
Most of *'the Clique'* weren't there anymore, all save Trudy who
seemed to be keeping to herself now that her pathetic little group
had concluded their own early shifts. Like always Lucy, Sherry,
Jan, and Will's personal favourite Josie *'not in a million years if I
can help it.'* he almost said the thought out loud but had stopped
himself at the last minute for fear of looking a crazed loon by the
customers still around him, all of them said their goodbye's to
Trudy as they filed out bang on at the two-thirty pm mark. He

didn't know how all of them had done it but after the Store
refurbishment every single member of them had been able to keep
their extremely plush and desirable early shifts. With the Cafe'
having had one of its most radical face lifts since its creation the
Store had gone to every Department and had chosen certain staff
member's to be put into the Cafe' to increase the numbers so it was
better staffed overall. Of course there had been some that said they
didn't want to be transferred and of course the Management told
them point blank they didn't have a choice in the matter, it had
been made for them no ifs or buts to be added. It was also in every
Employee's Contract that they had to work where the Business
required them too; it was a clause many had come to openly
despise. What Will had found most surprising of all was all the
new people being pulled from every Department had been told
their shifts were changing to accommodate the need for some staff
to be on this late or that late whenever necessary, the new staff
asked why their shifts had to be changed but it was again in their
Contracts where it clearly stipulated that you needed to be flexible
for what the Business expected of you. The original lot: however,
not a single one of them had any shift touched or modified even by
the smallest of degree. Will had sussed this out after the first
fortnight. The very first few other weeks of getting to know all the
new staff who weren't exactly enjoying being in the refurbished
Cafe' Will had done his best to make them all feel welcome, all
except *'the Clique'* who didn't go out of their way for anyone else

other than checking to make sure their own friendship group was still very much intact despite such a change to their work environment, but heaven forbid that they were the ones who missed their old haunt. Everyone else could clearly play second fiddle which just added to his mutual disgust towards their elitism. The years following the Refurbishment Will had gone out of his way to any new member of staff joining the Cafe' team feel like they weren't the new person on the block but a new addition to a very convoluted family with all its ridiculous dynamics. He adopted what Daisy had done for him, be a force for good in the Cafe' and certainly not act like he was above anyone else just because unlike some he didn't become untouchable for the amount of years he had been working there. No, he left those attitudes well alone, but it of course made him a lone ranger when he had to work in the vicinity of *'the Clique'* today. It was almost over much to his delight when Trudy came out to join him on the shop floor.

"Will I just had Coralie on the phone a moment ago asking for you..."

"Oh? Everything alright?

"Yeah all fine, she just told me to tell you're back downstairs at three-thirty that's all."

'Well that has definitely made me feel a lot better already.'

"Thanks for that Trudy..."

Too late for her to hear him, she had disappeared back into the Dishwasher Area to escape the many tables he still had to clear by himself, *'why do I even expect her to help when I know where her allegiances will always lie.'* he shook his head looking at the ceiling as he got on with the job at hand. The customers were different breed up here; they were less demanding, less annoying, less anything really. Downstairs as it was such a huge space to be filled by bodies it seemed to fester the worst traits in people who walked in, impatience, rudeness, arrogance, they all came flying at the staff downstairs like nobody's business. Up here everyone seemed not happy but simply content to just form a single file queue, get whatever coffee or snack they wanted, find a seat then they were off in their own little escapist moment. Will just couldn't work up here often, not with the Employees at present. *'What I wouldn't give to have a hot chocolate and toastie right now.'* he was thinking as his stomach grumbled for sustenance.

"Will! You ready to head back down?" a voice spoke out of nowhere.

Will turned and saw Sasha Chase walking on to the shop floor to relieve him. Sasha was a mother to two young daughters, brown haired with a nice smile alongside a set of deep green eyes but a fiery can-do work ethic whilst being another short person, she was also one of the few close friends to Coralie so Will knew never to bad mouth her around Sasha, she also had the distinction of working in the original Cafe' alongside Will himself but like him she had never been in with *'the Clique'* when she began working there too, no they treated themselves like the elitist club they really were which Sasha made abundantly clear she wanted nothing to do with that sort of closed off work style so she made her feelings known about it very early on. Shockingly *'the Clique'* had shown her more respect when she had aired her views to them yet when it came to Will, he might as well have been public enemy number one to that lot; it was no skin off his nose either way.

"Sasha my love!" Will smiled giving her a high five in greeting "How are the girls keeping?"

"Oh their both little tearaways I'll tell ya, but they are my *tearaways* all the same" she smiled at him as he happily relinquished the cleaning spray and cloth to her.

"Bless, whenever you bring them in it's always a pleasure to see them. How's Coralie coping down there so far?" He asked her as they both began clearing a table together, Sasha shrugged but answered anyway.

"Oh you know, she's stressing cause its busy and she's not getting the help from the Managers on duty for the weekend yadda, yadda and more yadda..."

"Ha, I know to avoid her for the rest of the day when she's like that."

"Oh yeah everyone knows that and she's my actual mate too!"

They both laughed at the irony of this, some friendships didn't translate into certain others getting treated differently from the rest in this place, Coralie happened to keep it professional when it was all about the work and Sasha knew that it wasn't ever personal, it's a shame the same couldn't be said for the certain crowd up here. *'If only they took a leaf out of Coralie's book.'* Will wished they would but knew they would all sooner quit or retire than do that, then again he would have jumped for joy if this option had come to pass also.

"Oh also Will..." they were both out back now "...Coralie said she had a message to pass on from Bianca but it's nothing to worry about, she said she'll tell you more when you come back down" Sasha said over her shoulder as she went back out of the revolving door to the shop floor. Will watched her leave, his curiosity peaked now. *'What on earth could that be about I wonder? Unless it's really about...?'* Will stopped his train of thought as he felt like he was being watched. Sure enough the Dishwasher was all of a sudden rather silent at the moment, he looked over his shoulder as he had his back to it, and as soon as he looked he saw Trudy then suddenly started busying herself with the dishes she still had to put through the machine. *'Nice try there Mrs, fat chance I'm letting you get any details of my personal goings on in this joint.'* Will had wished now that Sasha had told him that piece of information on the shop floor rather out back where a member of *'the Clique'* was listening in, alas it wasn't her fault she had just been passing the message on to him after all.

"You alright there Trudy?" he turned to look at her as she kept up her rather weak pretence of being seriously busy; he even kept his voice relaxed but controlled.

"Yep, all hunky-dory here." she acknowledged with the most politeness she had ever shown him in all the years they had worked together as she scrubbed hard at a toastie place with a scouring pad.

"Oh goody good, I'll be off then downstairs..."

"Ah leaving so soon? guess I won't see you till next week sometime, since I only two days now what with all my social engagements and the house being done up."

"Again? Thought you were happy with just the *eight bedrooms* you already had in your house?" Will moved towards the side door to head back down, Trudy though hadn't noticed the sarcasm in his voice, if she had then she didn't let on to the fact.

"Oh no, nothing like that but I think that some of them need a good redecorating that's all. What was that about then with Sasha just now may I ask?" Trudy kept on scrubbing the same toastie plate with the pad not even glancing at Will, but her demeanour was clear, she wanted some fresh gossip to tell her friends about as soon as she finished her day shortly. Will could just visualize her dashing into the locker room, grabbing her phone and typing away furiously into their joint WhatsApp group he was sure they all had set up to bitch about everyone when they weren't at work together. *'Nice try Trudy, but you can kiss my very pert ass before I tell you anything that's going on with me.'* he thought as he judged her up and down from the door disapprovingly.

"Oh that with Sasha? Nothing important."

"Really Will? It *sounded* like it was..." she kept on scrubbing the same toastie plate, but Will had heard her tone all too clearly, she wanted some kind of dirt on him at any cost.

'Christ lady. Give it a rest you nosey cow!'

"Hmm, let's see shall we..." he'd had his back to her as he was about to leave, his hand was on the door handle in fact. *'You want something from me? then here you go Mrs'.* He turned back to face her without moving from the door, she kept on scrubbing but was half glancing at him now with those bloody awful glasses he really still did not care for once in the entire time they had known one another.

"You really want to know what that was all about with Sasha?"

"Well only if you're willing?"

"Hmmm...good thing I'm not *willing* then!" he marched out of there without a backwards glance at Trudy letting the door swing shut of its own accord, *'god that felt good.'* he was smiling satisfactorily as he marched through Kids Wear confidently, his held high, just for a small pause despite it being his Anniversary plus his crappy late shift Will let himself go for a moment, savouring the look he had left on Trudy's face seared into his memory, complete shock. *'One of the best things I've ever done in all my time here.'* he got back on the escalators heading down, he was back in the main Cafe' in no time, he didn't even mind that it was still rather busy, not after leaving Trudy high and dry as she deserved to be. Coralie was dashing about making sure everyone was at their assigned stations, Will knew she was more stressed than ever when he had left her as a few strands her scraped back blonde hair had escaped her tight bun. Will felt just a tiny bit sorry for her since she was the only one in charge today, if she wanted a Manager to assist her she had to call one of the other Departments since the manager for the Cafe' worked the opposite weekend to her. "Oh thank goodness your back, was upstairs ok?" she said it like the wind had been knocked out her sails, "oh yeah despite being around that lot I coped, I got your message from Sasha. Trudy was listening though when she passed it on to me however..." Will rolled his eyes but not in Coralie's direction so she knew it wasn't aimed at her.

"Trudy was listening in you say?"

"Oh yes, she was trying her level best to get some gossip out of me!"

"Well I hope you didn't say anything to her?"

Will then didn't care if she was his Supervisor; he eyeballed her in shock which answered her line of questioning.

"Ok! I believe you" Coralie actually held her own hands up in mock surrender this time which satisfied Will.

"Anyway, what is it you wanted to tell me from Bianca" he asked her as they both headed to the back area of the Cafe' to both have a breather from what was sure to be more customers bugging them with tedious tasks as the day wore on. Will was in fact referring to Bianca Fray the current Manager for Cafe'. At one time the senior Management Team had insisted the Cafe' be run by two Manager's until otherwise stated or the policy changed so one could work each weekend that way one weekend wouldn't suffer or be worse off from the other, simple enough. Bianca had transferred in from a Store well out of the way close to the Southend region as this was seen a promotion for her since she had worked there for quite a few years. All Manager's in the company eventually get moved around after a few years to keep the idea's fresh and so no complacency doesn't s develop in one particular Store at any given time. It's also a clever political tactic to move Managers who aren't up to scratch or skill either, ruthless yes but highly effective also. Bianca had arrived when fellow veteran Manager Joyce Cooper was unexpectedly on the way out to everyone's surprise; no one had seen it coming in fact not even Will who kept an eye on most things in his time at the Store as best he could anyway. Joyce had originally been a part of the In-House HR Department upstairs which didn't deal with any customers but only staff related issues, enquiries into holidays, sorting out tax codes for Employees, sabbaticals or maternity leave, stuff like that. Over the six years Will had been there the company had made a Business decision to remove their Switchboard and HR Internal Units to centralise them for the sole purpose of saving as much money as possible and it had worked out wonders for the people at Head Office for the cash they recouped, the Store though wasn't best pleased about the decision but had no say in the process at all, they had to grin and bear it which meant the staff who worked in these Stores Unit's either took paid redundancy or returned to working on the shop floor as much as they probably disagreed with it. Of course some of them were at a level considered the same as a Manager on the shop floor so Joyce had been chosen to lead the Cafe' just before it received its big renovation which made her look good of course, then because they had two Cafe's and a big team that needed staffing, the trainee Manager under Joyce at the time Emily Arms, a young eager girl in her early twenties with a cheery disposition who had worked with Will in their 'Restaurant' Days was deemed not to be ready for a such big task ahead so she had been swapped out with Bianca from the Southend region on the down-low. Emily had risen through the ranks of Customer Assistant then on to Supervisor then last but not least entering the Management Scheme as a trainee, the team had all such high hopes for her but as time went by everyone saw the way she approached the job was not what was needed or wasn't even right at all so one day it was announced she had been sent off permanently to Southend, out of sight, out of mind and not making any more rookie mistakes. In came Bianca who now had sole control of both Cafes' since Joyce had then unexpectedly resigned from the business due to certain ongoing health reasons with her back near the end of last year and Bianca was just about muddling through with the help of Coralie ever since. Joyce had helped her initially for the first few months before her leaving then when she went Bianca had been left to pick up the pieces, but Bianca was really only a nice face with not much or if any backbone to her character. She was more interested in playing nice with everyone, plus Will had heard some gossip on the grapevine that the company might end up shifting her out because she wasn't delivering the standard the Senior Management wanted or expected themselves, it was a known fact the Store Manager avoided her calls until they were out of all options before they had to talk or even deal with her. But through it all she was still the Manager he had for the time being and he had needed her to do something, now all he was wondering about was what news Coralie had to tell him that she had gotten from Bianca. *'Please let it be some good news at least.'* Will had his fingers crossed which he kept behind his back, so Coralie didn't see that he was doing it.

"So…" Coralie took to leaning briefly against the wall near the downstairs narrow Dishwasher Area, "nothing major to tell you Will, but..."

"But what Coralie?"

"Basically, Bianca wanted me to let you know that you'll be getting some news of what you asked her to look into for you s*oon*." she finished by folding her arms and closed her eyes to relax for just a moment, today must of really taken its toll on her, she never showed this side of herself especially at work. Will wanted to know more though than the vague message she had just relayed to him.

"That's it? I'll know *soon*? How soon?"

"Honestly, that's all she messaged me on the Management WhatsApp Group."

"No indication or timeframe per say?"

"Seriously Will, it could be a few weeks till you get some *concrete* news."

"But it's moving in the right direction for me Coralie?"

"As far as I know, *yes*." Coralie looked exhausted now from everything, this conversation, this job, this day in fact. Will laid off her with the twenty questions.

"Ok cool I'm happy with that for now."

"You should be, can you go back on tables for now, and I've plotted your break at five, so you've just got over an hour to go ok?"

"Cheers Coralie, are you ok Mrs?"

"I will be. No Managers are helping me so it's down to me like always..."

"I don't know why you put yourself through this Coralie; I couldn't do what you do."

She laughed at this, it felt good for her to laugh, then she looked at Will who patted her arm sympathetically which made her feel better, then she stopped leaning and got herself ready for the shit storm still swirling outside in the Cafe'. Turning her back to Will a she headed outside she stopped then look back at him for just a quick moment.

"Hey Will."

"Yes Coralie?"

"Thanks for that" she smiled at him in real appreciation "...I'll double check with Bianca about your news ok?"

This time Will smiled back at her which told her he knew he appreciated the small olive branch she was extending to him. Then she snapped back into Supervisor mode.

"Now get on those tables, no one else is gonna clean them!"

Will did what was expected of him and he did it with no fuss at all, he would have to wait for the news he wanted to hear a little while longer yet.

*

Just over an hour later.

4:55 pm.

He'd been on his own when he had returned to the table's downstairs, young Sarah had needed to have her forty-five-minute break, so he was left to sort them out himself, it seemed he was cursed with them on this fateful day. Sarah was back now, she was running in trays of discarded orders while he sifted through them as efficiently as he could, his break couldn't come soon enough. He was counting down the minutes left. Mopping his slightly perspiring forehead he took a quick breather to check back in with Sarah who seemed perkier after her respite from the unrelenting nightmare that was called work.

"You're in a better mood?"

"Oh am I? I think its cause I'm counting down the last few hours..."

"Yes, *few hours* for you. Still got four left for me remember?"

"Err three once you factor out your break time Mr Will..."

"Huh, that's true I guess. *Oh shit*, do not turn around Sarah!"

Sarah froze on the spot, wide eyes, a full tray in her hands, she looked at Will in the cleaning station and no one else. She dare not too.

"What's the matter?" Her voice went up an octave higher as she stared at him slightly horrified through her prescription lenses.

"It's them..."

"Who's them?"

"Oh you and everyone in the Cafe' knows who this certain *couple* are Sarah Bailey..."

"*Fuck off! You're not telling me it's actually them...*" she had resorted to whispering at Will as she turned around which he really wised she hadn't, but it was too late now, she saw them with her own bad eyesight. It was the Couple. Now Sarah was wishing she had really followed his instructions in the first place as she looked back at Will with a truly mortified look for them both and everyone else on shift. The Couple were a retired married duo who without fail always cut a peculiar yet infamous path whenever they appeared on the horizon to shop at the Store, they were well known in all departments for being notorious freeloaders who actively went out of their way to get anything free of charge out of the Company by any means necessary. At first it came across like they were a bit hard done by in some circumstances then Will noticed a pattern emerge in their behaviour early on when he first laid eyes upon them, it was the frequency of how much they tried to get anything of worth to them out of the store in each visit. A free meal, a free food shop of the larger than normal variety, refunds on their purchases because there was some extremely small insignificant minute details they didn't particularly like about that certain product they had ordered which was always the free additional item that came with it. Will had taken an item left in the Cafe' to the lost property desk on an odd day which was right next door to the designated Refunds Desk just off of Ladies Wear only to see the wife literally shouting the Department down for attention and pointing repeatedly at the poor hapless Manager that had to deal with them at the time while the husband stood a foot away from her leering like he was some toughened bodyguard when you could literally blow him over with an air kiss at his slightly advanced age. Neither of them were attractive anymore. They were both a sight to behold as well; there were not many or any people who looked similar to them either, both looked like they still believed the voluminous hair of the eighties was still very much a thing of today's society. The husband had a huge white afro that was thinning more rapidly as every year went by while the wife sported a red afro that never seemed to change style or move as she did. After every meal in the Cafe' the wife would always pull out three different shades of lipstick to apply to her thin lips when she shouldn't even be wearing that much heavy makeup in the first place. The husband always watched her admiringly but to Will it came across as so creepy. He hated serving them, with a passion. He remembered all too vividly when the husband had ordered his usual round of two pots of decaf tea's with two extra teapots of hot water that were to be as hot as possible for him and the Mrs so they could both top them up after the first teapots worth, so they were essentially getting a free rounds worth without having to fork out on the extra £1.85 for the pots of tea in the first place, they were taking liberties every single time they knew they could. He had everything on his tray, the four teapots along with the teacups then Will had saw him do the smallest action intentionally. He was just about to start on to the next hot drink order, then the husband had leaned ever so delicately on the tray out of the corner of his eye and the whole tray of tea and hot water went falling down to the floor with an almighty crash. Everyone, customers, and staff alike had looked round at the loud disturbance, the very first thing any normal person would do when hot water spills onto your trousers would be to yell out in surprise then hoping they weren't burned at all. Not the husband though, no he simply stood there unmoving with a wistful look planted on his smug face, but it was those eyes of his, his eyes were alight with the gleeful opportunity he had created to rob the Cafe' blind out of something free, Will was even waiting him to lick his truly loathsome lips in tasty excitement. That day he had not only milked the Store out of a free new pair of trousers, but he was also even trying to get the Store to pay for the

dry-cleaning of his surprisingly barely wet trousers. Will had
watched the Store Manager practically doing a battle of morals
with the couple outside on Men's Wear once they had completed
their business for the day much to the relief of the staff who were
more than glad to see the back of them. The Store Manger had won
out that day without offering them to dry clean his trousers so they
had left with the tails between their legs in defeat, but Will had
seen their faces from inside the Cafe' on the coffee pod as they
went, they were formulating their comeback for the next dreaded
visit for what else they could get for free with their hands
entwined, looking at each other in deep concentration. They were
vultures of the worst kind the pair of them and their hunger was
never sated. Will looked at them from the cleaning station over
Sarah's right shoulder as she turned back to him with a sickened
look.

"Do you have to go on your break Will?"

"Err let me think about that...YES!"

He flung down the cloth he had in hands onto the side in the
station, he made a beeline outside to wash his hands in the
dishwasher area then he peeked round the corner cautiously, the
coast was clear for the moment. Sarah was half hiding herself in
the cleaning station as it had calmed down even more on the tables
now. Risking it for a biscuit he came back out on to the tables

waved silently at Sarah that he was leaving the shop floor then turned left to walk past the kitchen, only to almost bump into the wife of the Couple. *'Fuck me sideways, this is not my day at all.'* Will raged internally as he had his service smile back on before he would have had a look of pure dread plastered on his face at the sorry state of the wife. No one on the Cafe or Store knew their first or last names and Will was determined to never learn them but the Couple as part of their grand master plan always went out of their way to learn specific names to curry favour or sympathy among the workforce even though they had no idea how much they were disliked by all throughout. The wife had the signature red hair all hair sprayed to death in her afro along with a matching cream outfit with the blazer along with a pair of high heels that were simply too high and not suitable for lady who clearly pushing over seventy know, he ankles must be killing already, the whole ensemble looked like it would be better on her if she was in her fifties no doubt but since she was twenty plus years older than that easily, it wasn't the right look at all, yet she didn't seem to care. In fact she seemed to flaunt it in front of Will which had him even more secure in his homosexuality. *'God the poor husband. I shouldn't feel sorry for him, but I do contrary to the fact the he probably likes her this way.'* Will continued to smile politely but he was already looking around to see if there was any way he could sidestep the wife, there wasn't however. "Well hello there my dear Will how are you today?" she spoke in a high-pitched nasally tone with a very light Scottish twang as if to draw attention to them both, this made Will feel even more put on the spot. "Oh just fine thanks for asking, is the other half doing his usual bit?" he asked but he didn't know why he had, he saw Nat watching the exchange unfold between them with a rather amused expression on her face, she hadn't moved to come pry Will from the wife yet either. *'Come one Nat, help a lad out would ya?'* Will was trying to get her to move from her spot, but she teased him more by simply folding her arms and not moving a muscle, the wife was still talking at Will like he really cared what she had to say when he really didn't.

"...just another productive day, you know us regulars. Lots to do!"

"Oh good to hear like always, well I must be..."

"Well we had to go to your refunds desk again you see..."

'Fuck me be quiet would you, I really don't give a toss Hun.'

"Oh yes, these trousers the husband had a free belt with them..."

"Oh right?"

"Yes well the belt wasn't going well with them so him and I wanted to money back from the trousers so we could get a better pair of trousers for free without spending *more money* you see!" Her overly mascaraed eyes widened as if it was the most shocking thing Will had ever heard.

"Sorry, what was that?" Will couldn't quite understand or believe what he had in fact heard.

"Oh yes, we're rather thrifty you see..." she then moved off to a table looking at Will like he understood her without saying goodbye to him, like she was casually placing him on the shelf to finish the chat he had hoped wouldn't have happened in the first place, he saw her find an appropriate table then did the normal routine she and the husband did. She got out her own anti-bacterial wipes despite the table already recently having been cleaned by Sarah, wiped it down almost too meticulously then got two napkins out, unfolded them as far as they could go placed them down on opposite sides then got the knife and fork set she had picked up from the cutlery station then placed them down for her and the husband neatly. She then double-checked the cutlery to wipe them down as if dissatisfied with their overall appearance. *'Love, this is a bloody Cafe'. If you wanted a fine dining experience go to a bloody upmarket London restaurant, except you and that wretched husband can't afford it really now can you.'* Will walked away from her as quickly as his feet would carry him, the husband was still getting their decaf teas at coffee pod one so he knew he could make a lucky escape on that front. He was passing Nat who was chuckling at him.

"Did someone get caught in a spider's web then?"

"Nat, you could have come to save me you know?"

"Then what? get caught up in her sorry state of affairs? You're alright on that front Will." she chuckled some more as Will looked at her with a power pose.

"And I thought you had my back *Nat Hardley...*"

"Yeah I do...just not when it comes to the Couple!" Nat was beside herself now so took herself off to let the laughing run its course, Will rolled his eyes and left the Cafe' for his break. He successfully made it out without the husband even noticing him. He knew was fully safe when he made it back to the staff entrance to head up to the staff canteen. He was glad to be off the floor, five hours down and less than four to go until this dreaded day could resign itself to the history books. He stopped off to get his phone and wallet then made it in quick time to the canteen; it was quiet as well which was a welcome reprieve from the mayhem of the day down on the shop floor. What little staff there was there they all kept to themselves on their own tables. Will made himself a nice cup of builder's tea then went to canteen fridge to see if they had anything good to offer. It was always a much of the same when it came to the canteen, lots of bread items, very few salads, lots of sweet treats with yoghurts or fruit, all spectacularly bland. *'The business always knows how to look after their employees.'* he sniggered sarcastically as he chose a random sandwich because it was just there. He paid up and plonked himself on to an empty table taking a moment to enjoy the fact he had stopped for the first time. The silence really was a nice touch; he took a sip of his tea enjoying the strong taste with the one sugar he always had in it. He was hoping he could close the Dishwasher Area down without having to deal with any more petty customers, give him the dishes and leave him be. He was going to try and twist Coral's arm before she went home tonight. His mind made up his tucked into his sandwich enjoying the peace; he hoped it wouldn't get worse for him today.

*

Just Over Ninety Minutes Later.

6:35 pm.

'I could kill Coralie.' Will thought with determination as he handed the change to the waiting customers hand as they moved to the back of coffee pod one to collect their hot drink being made for them. Turns out Coralie had plotted out all the roles for the closers tonight and Will had missed her when he returned to the shop floor. She had rather conveniently headed up a few minutes earlier than normally yet if Will had ever been caught out by her doing that she would have given him a bollocking for bad time keeping right there and then. *'Yet if you go on up early Coralie its fine for you, the Clique could use a new case of young blood after all.'*

He had folded his arms imagining that scenario happening then instantly regretted ever thinking it into existence, he knew Coralie had her ways, but she was not a fan of them lot upstairs, not by any stretch of the imagination. *'Just get on with it Will, nothing you can about it now.'* He unfolded his arms then readied himself for the rest of the rest, only a few hours to go. Nat had clocked off at six pm as well, so she wasn't there to entertain him either. His luck wasn't all bad though, he had Aaron as his coffee maker to cheer him up till eight pm anyway so there was always a silver lining to every bad situation when working in this place. With no customers to serve he turned around to his young co-worker who was handing over the hot drink to the waiting customer who took it without thanking him, he didn't let it phase him though. *'That boy is a true pro if I ever saw one, he defies his age demographic.'* Will was impressed by Aaron's continuous maturity, his only downside was he could be led astray with silly joking sessions by the other young teenagers who worked part-time in Cafe', Will kept him focused on the job whenever they worked together but allowed some good banter and chats to occur between them. The place was trying enough as it is; having a healthy but fun work relationship to help you through the day was always a bonus which is how Will viewed Aaron as such.

"You have no idea how happy I am your on coffee with me Mr Connors" Will patted his broad back as he cleared the auto wand then wiped it down for any excess milk residue. Aaron looked at him with one of his cheeky grins.

"Yeah boy, it's always a laugh a minute if you're on with me."

"But which one of us is making the other laugh?"

"Well isn't obvious Willy?"

'He's one of the very few people I allow who can get away with calling me Willy. Kym calls me Willyboy yeah, but Aaron is the only one who I'll allow that.'

"Enlighten me then Aaron..."

"It's clearly me!" He flashed that boyish grin then flexed a bicep muscle to show off because he could, and he knew it. Laughing Will rolled his eyes and turned away as another customer came up to the till point, Will dealt with the order in quick succession as Aaron made the mocha they had requested in no time. With a perfect hand off they resumed their banter. "So let me guess what you're up to tonight after work Will..." Aaron folded his arms looking at him inquisitively, this amused Will more that a sixteen-year-old was really trying to suss out his evening plans after work.

"Go on Aaron; give it your best shot."

"You Will..."

"Yes?"

"You are going out clubbing!" He made a pistol motion with his left hand at Will as if he were hitting the bull's eye, he was way off.

"Wrong! Chinese takeaway for one with a bottle of Rose for me Mr" Will held his hands up in surrender without making eye contact as Aaron gave him a dumbfounded look.

"You're winding me up right Will?"

"Nope, sorry."

"But your twenty-five right?"

"That is quite correct Aaron".

"So why stay in when you're still young?"

Will was back at the till looking at the sandwich fridge on the other side when Aaron said this to him, it made him think of other times not too long ago when he would have headed out to go clubbing right after work. He would bring a change of clothes in his backpack on his Saturday late night like today, finish his shift, get changed then dash to the train station to head into London for a night out in Soho with friends which would then in turn end up with them going to Heaven night club right by Embankment

Bridge for what would be an extremely late night out, get the Night Bus all the way back to Romford from Leicester Square then make the rest of the journey home to collapse in his bed to recover the most of Sunday since he didn't work those days then returning to work on Monday somewhat recovered. Will laughed at the few times he had done this routine and how exhausting it had made him every single time. He liked to have some adventures from time to time like any other Human Being. Aaron was still waiting for his response as Will was still staring at the sandwich fridge reminiscing about these times, they had been fun, but they took a toll just like other things did in life. "Oh my dear sweet Aaron..." Will turned to him at last "...when you're my age you'll understand" he smiled admiringly as always at Aaron who seemed a bit lost on his words. "I'm sixteen, that's only nine years difference mate."

"Maybe so but there are some things you're made for and other things you're not made for all the same."

"Like clubbing?"

"Exactly *like clubbing*."

"I can't wait to be able to go clubbing when I'm eighteen."

"Trust me Aaron, I loved it too. Especially from eighteen to twenty-two. Then I kind of grew out of it."

"Really? You think I will as well?"

"Oh no, no. Listen I am my own person, I did it, I'm glad I did it also. But I just know I won't be doing it when I am in my thirties. It's not for me. You though, go enjoy it but just do me one thing..."

"What's that Will?"

"Make sure your careful Aaron."

His young co-worker smiled at this advice, Will was just glad he was looking out for him, but he knew he didn't need to do it, he wanted too. *'That young man has got a really bright future ahead of him.'* Will turned to another customer approaching the till who had a bit more than just a sandwich on their tray, they had a full load that needed putting through along with at least four coffee orders on top. He and Aaron operated like a well-oiled machine all the way up until Aaron's time to go home when eight pm swung around, then it was just him all by himself on coffee pod one. Aaron bid him goodbye before he made a dash upstairs and Will watched him go, he was the next generation down from him. *'Guess it wasn't all such a bad day on this bloody Anniversary after all.'* he went over to the sign to let people know that the Cafe' was now closed, him and the closers had an hour now to clean down what was left. There was four of them closing, one on coffee which was Will, the other three machines had been closed down as Coralie made sure that got done before Will had come back from his break. One for tables, young Sarah had left at seven pm so someone else was on there now, one for kitchen and one for dishwasher. A team of four for the final hour to make sure a two hundred and fifty seated Cafe' got closed down to a degree of success. Sometimes it worked, sometimes it went tits up. It had been a busy day and Will was sure they had probably hit their target goal for takings for the week; all he knew was come nine pm he had a takeaway to order on the way home. The hour passed without anyone really checking up one another, they all knew what to do. Then after what seemed like a small eternity, the team of four were done for the day. They knew they were properly done as they all chucked the full bins into the blue skip they would then wheel out at the end of shift to the Loading Bay for the Operations team to deal with. They got in the staff lift in the Bay and headed up to floor two all mostly silent as it had been a long arduous day. Will saw Sasha up ahead in the corridor with the other closer to from the Upstairs Cafe' they had finished in good time as well. Everyone got their stuff from their lockers then hit the electronic box that paid them for the day's work with decisiveness; made their own way down the eight flights of stairs again, moved their names into the off-sight section and they swiped out the dilapidated blue doors that were still in need of a paint job. They are all parted with final goodbyes, Will was the last one standing by the blue doors looking up at the sky, being an early September night the last vestiges of the Summer season was still clinging on, the sky was gloriously going from red to purple meaning it would be a fully black night in less than an hour. After the long shitty Saturday Anniversary shift with no Daisy Davidson to get him through it anymore, Will was at his wits end with Riverside after all these years. He hadn't told anyone, not even Kym his 'Firecracker' or Nat that it was his dreaded Anniversary today. It didn't seem like an actual thing to celebrate in a place of work that would rather fester arrogant egotistical attitudes over actual decent work ethics.

Will did know of one certainty however.

'I can't stay here in this routine for much longer. It's gonna do me in if I give in to the complacency any more than I already have.'

He looked at the darkening sky as it soothed him; the thought gave him clarity, he let out one final very tired sigh then made his way back through the Complex to head home with nothing but Chinese and wine to occupy his thoughts.

It had been one heck of an Anniversary to say the least about this day.

Four

September 9th, 2016.

The Downstairs Cafe'.

Friday.

12:56 pm.

It was Will's once a fortnight short shift.

He started at twelve-thirty in the afternoon and finished up at five. He always liked this shift best as he did four long days followed by a short one to top himself up to thirty-seven and a half hours a week or what was classed as a standard working week in the UK these days. To make his day even better, he and Kym were on coffee pod two and they were performing their Husband-and-Wife skit for all their customers who always enjoyed it. This was always guaranteed to go down a treat for the customers every time they ended up working together which these days was a rare occasion since for some reason the Management seemed to almost enjoy keeping the pair of them apart whenever they happened to both be in work at the same time. It was always pissed both of them off equally since there were others who always got what they wanted but that was always down do the unspoken arrangements in place but when it came to Will and Kym, no they were the ones who had to be made an example of whilst suffering for just being best friends with a great work relationship on top of that. Another thing Will added to his extensive list of what he disliked about working at this Store after all this time. Not today though, for now he would lap up every second of being able to sell marked-up coffees, sandwiches, overpriced-cakes, toasties, and everything else it with his 'Firecracker'. They were on particularly fine form today as it happened.

"So my *wife*, if you could just stretch to the making two extra cappuccinos I might cook dinner tonight for you."

"Ha! My *husband* if I wanted you to cook I wouldn't contract food poisoning off of you in the process!"

The two customers were watching their exchange occur with open surprise. Will was going over the top while Kym kept her performance sarcastically dry as much as it could be for effect.

"Well now my *wife* I was going throw in one of those deserts you liked so much…"

"Now see here my *husband...*" Kym paused eyeballing Will for some more dramatic effect as the customers waited, they were glued to the spot wondering what was about to happen, "...if you had started with desert I would have said go full carte blanche!" Kym finished as she cracked on with the coffee order while Will threw his hands up in the air for a camp finish turning to face the patient customer duo who were sniggering at their little double act as it came to a close on the payment with one of their debit cards at the ready. They collected their coffees from around the back still sniggering their thanks at Kym and Will as they went to take a close by table waiting for them. Will and his 'Firecracker', they were both smirking then high fived each other on a performance well done. "Now that never gets old I tell ya Willyboy." Kym wiped the coffee machine down as he watched, "oh of course it doesn't, just a shame this lot don't seem to want us working in close proximity together." Will looked around the Cafe' on what should have been a busy Friday lunch rush, but it was anything but that. The huge marble cake table was still full of this morning's cakes that had only had a few of their slices removed by paying customers, if it were normally a busy lunchtime the second round of cakes from the delivery would already be out on display by the designated baker/certified stock re-filler Tonye Patricks. Tonye was another one who had been transferred in from the Food Department against her will and she had been one of the more vocal ones who didn't want to be in Cafe' from the immediate off. She was in her mid-fifties and she let everyone know from that she was one who liked to do what she wanted to do when she was ready in her own time unless whatever Manager decided to intervene, of course she was an approachable lady with a pleasant enough personality with simple brown hair always in the same hairstyle, she never let it down ever for any occasion, always up in a short ponytail at the back with a set of deep blue eyes that never missed a trick or beat, she was a pistol that's for sure. When she joined the team after the refurbishment she was able to procure a job that ticked her very few boxes she already had what she classed as her own hard work to her standards. Another one who came in on all early shifts with zero late shifts never be seen of her, she turned on the baking oven, got all the pastries plus the scones ready for the morning open along with whatever cakes came in on the delivery, put the cold sandwiches and toasties in the display fridge then only bringing herself out from her nice little hovel corner where the Baking Oven was situated out back to check on stock levels when they needed some rather minor re-filling so she was seen to be doing some actual work for the day, she had manipulated the system more than to her advantage then treated the whole thing with great indifference. She was very much cut from Joyce Coopers Management Styled-Cloth which everyone knew. Joyce when she had been still Manager at the time saw that certain people worked well doing a particular thing or set routine they liked that was then deemed 'their specific job' and no one else's. Forget anyone else wanting to learn how to do a morning bake or how to operate the oven if they found themselves opening on a rare occasion for some holiday cover. Will had once asked Tonye why she never jumped on a till once or do another task in the place and the look he had received in return was enough to never try and ask her the question again, she was one person who did not want to be put anywhere else so worked the situation again to her advantage and that was where she stayed always. It was a rather plush but highly easy part-time job she had well and truly in the bag. Will saw Tonye come out from her corner but not exactly putting herself on the shop floor, she kept herself firmly placed in the small walkway between the kitchen and shopfloor, so she saw the cake table, get on her tippy toes for a quick moment gave a curt singular nod of her head then she was off back to her corner, no one else looked at her or acknowledged her presence which obviously made her more than satisfied. Will shook his head which Kym saw him doing as she stood beside him at the till. "Tonye doing her normal routine I see?" his best friend asked him without looking up at his face, nodding at her question he replied.

"Ooohhh yep, doesn't it just piss you off sometimes?"

"What do you mean exactly Will?"

"I mean 'Firecracker', the ones who get to do their nice little jobs whilst the rest of us all suffer being pushed around from pillar to post is what I mean." Will folded his arms still looking at the empty spot where Tonye had been standing a moment ago. Kym shrugged her shoulders at the situation; Will knew what kind of response he was going to get anyway.

"Will, you know what it's like, old Managers putting their mates in the plum jobs while all of us play second, third or even fourth fiddle, why do you let it get to you?"

"Because it's simply not fair Firecracker."

"When has this place ever been *fair*?"

"I know that Mrs, but still, when it all changes again..."

"...me and you will hopefully won't still be working in this dump ah Will?"

Will looked at his best friend as she moved back to the coffee machine to give it another quick wipe. She wasn't looking at him, but he was looking at her, *'god I do love your blistering honesty.'* he appreciatively thought of her as she kept herself busy even though the day was anything but that. Turning around he sighed then he saw a new customer approaching him at the till. The customer was blatantly gay like him and he was rather easy on the eyes to Will's tastes. A little bit taller with a jaw line for days, he was dressed in gorgeous charcoal grey suit with a wonderfully crisp white shirt which meant he worked at one of the jewellery shops in Riverside, he had black spiky hair with the same eyes to match, broad shoulders plus some arms Will imagined would happily pin him down onto a bed or anywhere he desired so he could have his wicked ways with this absolute stud muffin. Will felt his face go hot and the guy knew he had Wills interest as he gave him a cocky grin.

"Well good afternoon *sir*, how may I help you today?"

Kym looked at Will then saw the customer just about over his right shoulder, she suppressed a laugh at was unfolding between them.

"Just a latte to takeaway please." the customer asked without looking directly at Will as he inputted it into the till.

"Would that be a nice *large one sir*?"

The customer now took notice of Will with his gorgeous black eyes, they flashed in recognition at the naughty innuendo, he was now properly looking at Will who was only using his eyes to look him up and down, and he let Will know he was enjoying the attention.

"Yeah, a *large one* would be great in fact..."

"Kym, a nice *large* takeaway latte please!"

Kym got on with the order as Will flirted with the sexy customer who kept allowing him to do it, he paid then came round the back to collect his coffee which Kym handed over, he then intentionally went back round the front to sip his coffee and get a good side look at Will's ass in his work trousers which Will made sure was noticeable. He looked at it quickly without moving his head; he brought the latte up to his lips.

"Nice. *very nice* indeed."

"Please do come again *sir*."

"Don't worry..." the sexy customer walked off with his back and his own rather pert ass in his suit in full view for Will to admire some more "...I'll definitely *come again.*" the customer left the Cafe' and Will felt rather thirsty all of a sudden. Kym was just laughing at her best friend. "You need a cold shower after that encounter I see" she teased him as Will still looked out the entrance of the Cafe', he was fanning himself with his left hand.

"I tell you 'Firecracker', he could have done anything he wanted to me honestly."

"Ha, you used to think the same about *Jim*."

She went back to the coffee machine as Wills head snapped around in her direction in surprise. "I did not think about Jim like that or in that way thank you very much!" he retorted but Kym was laughing at him again.

"Oh come off it Will! You had a big ol crush for Jim when you came back up to 'The Restaurant' when the team were all made proper staff from the *Orbit Group* all those years ago. Be back in two shakes of a ducks tail Mr..." Kym took the coffee grout tray out of its slot then headed off to go and empty it into food bin in the Kitchen Area leaving Will alone in coffee pod two with his mouth slightly agape in more surprise at the accuracy of his best friends statement, but some other old thoughts were starting to rattle around inside his head from yesteryears gone by. He could feel them bubbling to the surface, even more of a revelation to him was how much he hadn't thought about these times in so long.

'She's not entirely wrong about that; Jim was a definite easy on the eyes sort of guy too...'

*

April 11ᵗʰ, 2013.

Thursday.

9:05 am.

'The Restaurant'.

The first day after everyone was formally transferred over from *The Orbit Group* Contract.

'Those two-faced bunch of basic ass bitches downstairs in that grotty little hovel of a Cafe'.' he thought bitterly to himself as he stalked back into the Restaurant. Will was not pleased in the slightest. Two days ago, he had been working in the Cafe' minding his own business when the newish Manager from the Restaurant who had replaced the now departed Canadian had come up to him in the Café' when he was working on hot food, the news he had brought along with him had shook Will to his core that had come out of nowhere. He was returning to 'The Restaurant' and he had no say in the matter at all. It had all been delivered with an overall sickly presentation to it as well which made him feel even worse thinking about it. So here he resided after his once a fortnight Wednesday off to try to cope with the unexpected announcement and now here he was, back to where it had all begun for him. *'That Josie Sybille had nothing to say to me about this transferral either, that was very convenient on her part, that skank.'* Will dragged his

feet some more as he walked through the staff entrance into the
Dishwasher Area, no one was there to greet him which gave him a
moment to compose himself. He could still see the events
unfolding in Cafe' on the Tuesday just gone.

It had been a busy lunch rush with the queue out the door and it
had stayed that way for a good two solid hours with no let up. Will
was putting the toasties in as fast as he could despite the oven in its
old sorry state not being able to toast more than three at once, but
he was able to manage four into the available interior space with a
quick booster setting after the first pre-programmed sequence. He
had done well despite the odds being against him for the whole
time, yet customers had all been pleased with how quick he had
got their orders out to them. During all of it though, *'the Clique'*
had been making some odd comments in the vicinity of him but
not elaborating further on it, such was their vague nature. Will
knew it was something to do with him as the majority weren't even
talking to him directly throughout the lunch rush, but they were
always talking amongst themselves like they always did. Just one
of their ways they were still letting him know ever since he had
first arrived the previous November that this would always be their
safe space to be their own wretched, uncaring inner circle no one
else could be a part of.

"So Josie when is it happening?" Sherry called quietly from the
dishwasher.

"Yeah, is it today or tomorrow Josie?" Trudy enquired mutedly over her hideous teacher spectacles.

"Yeah, can't be long now right?" Jan asked muttering from the till.

'What the fuck is this lot on today? New prescription drugs?'

Will wondered from the old, overused oven, it pinged as its latest batch of toasties came out nice and hot for the waiting customers in the queue who all took them with impressed looks. "If anyone needs their toasties boosted I'll happily oblige it's no trouble!" Will called down the long line snaking around out into Foods, he got more looks of thanks with some thumbs up plus a few appreciative nods from the waiting customers. He saw Josie who was for once on one of the two tills doing some work by helping Jan out give him a quick side-glance seemingly forever dissatisfied that he was providing a good level of actual Customer Service to the crowd which he was contractually obliged to give, that and he knew it pissed her off to no end when he did a good job on shift. As always, Josie tried to pull rank on him without caring if the customers witnessed it. "Will, you'd better slow down a bit there; their toasties will be cold before they even get the coffees." Josie kept serving on the till without looking at him; she had said it very nasally too which didn't go unnoticed by him. "Well yes that's a good point Josie..." she half-glanced at him again when he used her name "...but as any of the customers will know as their just about to be served by you and Jan in the queue that I will happily heat *any or all* of the toasted sandwiches up for them, or better yet I'll replace them, and hand deliver them myself which will of course keep you happy that I'm providing such an *exceptional* level of service today. After all everyone..." he intentionally walked closer to the two till points but kept a respectable distance since Jan was physically in between him and Josie as he looked at all the customers waiting in the queue still rather than looking at his decrepit co-workers, "...I'm here to serve you all as best I can!" he then flashed the best dazzling smile he could muster which got a lot of awes and more appreciations as the customers fell hook line and centre for his performance. He could see out of the corner of his eyes that Jan was looking back and forth from him and Josie like it was a vicious round of tennis, Josie looked like she had just smelt something rather odious more than anything. *'Go on bitch, do your worst. You don't scare me.'* he half-glanced back at her with a smile that he made over the top for appearances sake, Josie just fixed him with her usual uncaring sour face.

"Carry on then Will." she added with tone of finality to her voice.

She went back to serving the next waiting customer while the rest of *'the Clique'* along with the ever-patient customers in the queue watched the pair of them, almost as if they could smell the tension coming off of them both. Will didn't care anymore as he went back to cooking more toasties, which was when the Manager came down from 'The Restaurant' with his unpleasant news for him. Fast forward to two days later and he here was again, standing back in the bland Dishwasher Area having been ejected from the downstairs Cafe' with every ounce of power or persuasion tactics Josie had, had at her disposal to get rid of him. He hadn't missed out on the fact after he had received his transferral news she had not said one single word to him the rest of the entire day, in fact she looked right past him a few times like he was dead to the world and her. It sickened at him how a woman in her early forties had conducted herself throughout her life operating this way to people she worked with simply because they didn't get on, her age was irrelevant to Will, but her pettiness spoke volumes to him. It was a disgusting work mentality to have which made Will vow to himself he would never assume a position of authority in a place like this while he worked here. *'I think I might just quit right now, I never wanted to come back to this, but someone thought differently about that and saw me carted off anyway.'* he folded his arms looking around the area hating every square foot for all he was worth. Daisy had text him before his shift had started today which had cheered him up somewhat, but his predicament was unchanging. The two-way revolving door swung open and in walked Nat Hardley, always there to greet him with him with a welcoming smile along with a look of understanding.

"Ah Will there you are! Welcome backs are in order or is that not a good idea just judging by your face at the moment?"

"Why wouldn't it be a good idea Nat?" He approached her in greeting along with a hug; it was always good to see her regardless of circumstances.

"Well..." she paused uncertain what to say at first "...your face is telling me another story all together Will, no offence. I know you're not happy about being back up here under the current circumstances."

"Yes about being brought back up here also Nat..." he interrupted her as she stopped, he didn't see no option but to just lay it out on the table for her. *'Sorry Nat I know this is gonna cause you no end of trouble but its best I resign for my own piece of mind or sanity even. I know when I'm not truly appreciated.'* he readied himself with his mind made up.

"Well Nat, there the thing is..."

"Yes Will? You sure you're ok?"

"Well, this isn't easy for me to say but..."

"NAT!"

An unfamiliar voice rang out of nowhere from the Kitchen Area followed by some quick footsteps, that's when Will laid eyes on him for the first time.

Jim Hendrickson.

He swaggered confidently into the Dishwasher Area like nobody's business interrupting Will's moment. Will stood there speechless as he looked at this new man standing before him. This new gay man in fact, you could tell he was so by a clear mile off and he didn't hide it, he wore it like a badge of honour, and you could tell he didn't give a shit if anyone else didn't like the fact he was gay, he just simply was. Will instantly on the spot liked what he saw.

"Nat! There you are...this the new boy?"

'New boy?'

"Oh Jim, glad you came round..." Nat made a triangle between them all so everyone was included, "Jim I would like you to meet Will Hardley here. He's not related to me in any way, but we share the same last name. Will's been working for the Downstairs Cafe' for the last five months but now he's transferred back to re-join the team in 'The Restaurant' up here."

"Not through my own choice bear in mind Nat." Will pointed out, Jim eyes flickered at him with their rather penetrating greenish colour, and Will was captivated by them. Jim was probably only a couple of inches taller than him but not by much, he had some dyed spiky blonde gelled hair but dark brown roots on show, he held himself with some good posture, but Will noticed something else. He wasn't just confident; he had an abundance of sass just lying below the surface waiting to erupt from him. *'I wonder what else is waiting to erupt from him.'* Will used only his eyes to check him out, if Jim saw him doing this he didn't pay attention, Will had the distinct feeling he had done the same thing to him, but he couldn't be entirely sure. *'I bet you're a force of nature in the bedroom department Mr Hendrickson. Well I hope you are.'* Will hoped as Jim trained his gaze fully on him now, he didn't want him to stop looking either. "Well it's their loss and our gain if he's back here, it's another more body to bolster the workforce in 'The Restaurant' which is always a good thing" he was talking about Will, but he was now looking at Nat instead, *'no don't do that, you haven't even seen my rear end yet.'* Will was willing him internally to draw his attention back on him but alas it wasn't to be, he needed Nat for something.

"What did you want from me exactly Jim?"

"Yes, right. That lady wants a refund, she says her food was cold, yet she's eaten most of it already, must have been some crap food she had!" Jim was looking at Nat with both his eyebrows raised, he didn't suffer fools lightly. Nat rolled her eyes at this "Christ. Let

colour, and Will was captivated by them. Jim was probably only a couple of inches taller than him but not by much, he had some dyed spiky blonde gelled hair but dark brown roots on show, he held himself with some good posture, but Will noticed something else. He wasn't just confident; he had an abundance of sass just lying below the surface waiting to erupt from him. *'I wonder what else is waiting to erupt from him.'* Will used only his eyes to check him out, if Jim saw him doing this he didn't pay attention, Will had the distinct feeling he had done the same thing to him, but he couldn't be entirely sure. *'I bet you're a force of nature in the bedroom department Mr Hendrickson. Well I hope you are.'* Will hoped as Jim trained his gaze fully on him now, he didn't want him to stop looking either. "Well it's their loss and our gain if he's back here, it's another more body to bolster the workforce in 'The Restaurant' which is always a good thing" he was talking about Will, but he was now looking at Nat instead, *'no don't do that, you haven't even seen my rear end yet.'* Will was willing him internally to draw his attention back on him but alas it wasn't to be, he needed Nat for something.

"What did you want from me exactly Jim?"

"Yes, right. That lady wants a refund, she says her food was cold, yet she's eaten most of it already, must have been some crap food she had!" Jim was looking at Nat with both his eyebrows raised, he didn't suffer fools lightly. Nat rolled her eyes at this "Christ. Let

me go sort her out, Will I'll sort things with you when I get back."
Nat left them both to go deal with the awkward customer waiting
for her on the shop floor; it was just them two in the Dishwasher
Area now. Jim looked at him folding his arms, Will felt like he was
being probed but he welcomed it, he liked having another gay guy
around on the team so far. Was nice to not be the only one for a
change.

"So I'm speaking to a fellow *Queen* then Will."

"Well if you're asking Jim?"

"No I wasn't asking, just stating the obvious right in front of me."

Jim appraised him, he even walked around Will quickly to judge
his height then his posture, Will happened to noticed he walked
just a fraction slower when he was behind him. *'That's it, check
out my ass please.'* he thought the wicked notion whilst remaining
ramrod still as Jim came back round to face him directly, he
brushed his right shoulder to his left one but again Will couldn't be
sure he had done it intentionally to tease him.

"So, how long you worked here for Jim?"

"Just a couple of months so far, it's not bad here..."

"Relentless work though right?"

"Oh yeah, I'm use to some *relentlessness* in my life however Will."

'There's that sassy undertone again. Is he doing it to get me excited or is he just like that normally?' Will noted of him as they both judged each other. Just then one of the chefs slaving away in the Kitchen round the corner broke the small moment happening between them.

"*JIM!* You've got about three new coffee orders come through the ticket machine mate..."

Jim's eyes widened in surprise and he did a U-turn marching away from Will with purposeful intent who looked at his ass as he left him standing at the Dishwasher, as he went round the corner on the left through the Kitchen Will swore he saw him looking back at him for a second, *'did he just wink at me?'* he hoped but his thoughts were distracted again as Nat re-joined him again. "Will come on out here, I know it's been a while since you've worked up here, but we will have you all clued up in no time on the menu and how we run things again" she indicated to follow her so Will did. The breakfast rush was starting to pile in. Nat showed him the ropes from scratch while successfully keeping all the customers happy, she made it look like an art form really. Will ran out the coffees and cleared tables keeping an eye on Jim who worked the coffee machine like it was his property, after less than an hour and half of being back in 'The Restaurant' which he said goodbye too only a few short months ago Will was back in the thick of it like he had never been away despite only a singular floor separating the two Units. Nat knew he would pick the whole routine back right up like nobody's business as she came over to him around the ten-thirty mark. "Well Will your back to exactly how you were before you left us." she patted him on the arm which he smiled at, "oh you know what they say Nat? Some things never leave you really right?" Will folded his arms inspecting the half a dozen tables left that were tucking into their breakfasts with aplomb. Jim was making sure the cake display was nice and full to temp more customers in from the walkway, it was working.

"He's not bad behind there I noticed Nat..."

"Oh you saw him working like a worker bee did you Will or did you look at something else as well?" Nat had said it with a playful tone, her eyes were glistening with humour as she looked at Will with a cheeky grin, he feigned ignorance.

"Yes I noticed he works very hard behind that counter."

"Is that all that was *very hard* Will?"

"*Natalie Hardley*! Go wash your mouth out with some soap young lady." Will stared at her genuinely shocked as she laughed openly at her own joke; Jim was none the wiser to what their conversation entailed about him. He busied himself with another coffee he had to make. "For your information Nat…" Will kept his tone even only because he knew she could read him like a book "…he is quite efficient with those coffees I must say." he didn't look at her, but he could feel her smiling at him still; he chose to ignore it by sorting out the menus which he decided needed tidying then and there. The revolving doors opened again, out walked a new person to help Nat and Will on the shop floor. "Ah Kym there you are!" Nat beckoned the short lady over with vibrant red hair who joined them both promptly, she was a bit flustered. "Oh Nat sorry I'm a few minutes over, parking was bit of a nightmare this morning, the main car park outside the store is chocker block already so I had to go in the multi-storey can you believe it!" Kym threw her hands up like it couldn't be that busy at Riverside for a Thursday late morning. Nat shook her head in disbelief "you're kidding right? That means we're gonna get it right in the neck shortly...yes madam how I can help you?" she moved off as a customer had signalled they needed her help leaving Will and Kym to introduce themselves. They both looked at one another not sure to make of either. Kym short but full of character with Will being taller but camp which you could spot from miles away.

"Hi there." Kym said.

"Heya." Will replied.

"So your that boy who used to up here then he went downstairs? I heard that lot down there aren't the most welcoming bunch in this place?"

"Ha! You don't know the half it trust me, nice to meet you by the way, I'm Will" he stuck his hand out and she took it with confident firmness. *'Ok I think I'm gonna like her, she's got a good grip on her.'* Will gave Kym a smile as he returned the firm shake in kind which she seemed to appreciate, "likewise Will, I'm Kym Harrison. How you finding it being back up here then?" she asked as they both released the handshake. Will at first didn't know how to respond to her question, it had felt like a lot of things to him in this last hour and half. Sure it was like putting on an old t-shirt you hadn't worn but it sure was comfortable to wearing it again, yet he also felt like it was something he had resigned to being at the back of his wardrobe for a long time or even to never be disturbed again. *'Truthfully, I feel really out of sorts, I don't know if I even belong in this Store after working here all this time. Especially how I was discarded from downstairs like a bad afterthought.'* "Well I am little nervous really Kym..." he began with some of the truth as they both made their way over to Jim who had a coffee order each for them to take. He and Kym greeted each other as Will and her took their individual orders, "your nervous? Whatever for, you worked up here for a couple of years?" Kym asked him as they made their way to customers waiting for their orders. They delivered them then made their way back to Jim at the counter, "well for starters I'm meeting new people like you and Jim here..." Jim waved at the sound of his name absently from the coffee machine even though he had his back facing them, Will was staring at his ass again unintentionally which Kym saw him do and she laughed out loud. Jim turned around at this to look her like she was mad.

"What's so funny Kym?"

Will was staring at her with his eyes wide in shock at her as she looked mischievously from him then to Jim. *'Bloody hell she has sussed me out with my horniness factor after only knowing me five minutes, she's a fiery one for sure.'* Will was slightly trembling hoping Kym wouldn't give him away to Jim, she didn't however. "Oh nothing Jim…" she winked at Will which Jim didn't take notice of "…it's just funny how someone like Will here can be *so nervous* after only leaving a place like this a few months ago, know what I mean?" She looked back at Will having covered for him. Jim looked at Will again with that same look he had given him earlier which nervously excited Will even more. *'Oh my he is an attractive one.'* Will melted inside a little as he stole another quick glance at his behind while Jim continued busying himself on the coffee machine, Kym didn't miss a beat of this action however. "Ha-ha Will, you're a funny one aren't you." she moved off to clear a table a customer had left in disarray, Will went to help her.

"Am I that obvious then?" he answered feeling his cheeks flush a little with embarrassment which Kym laughed some more at.

"Well put it this way Will..."

"Yes Kym?"

"the *International Space Station* could spot what you were doing from space!"

She took some of the leftover stuff on the plates from the customers that they hadn't touched to deposit into the Dishwasher Area out back laughing some more in amusement at Will's poor moves when it came to checking out Jim behind the counter. Will watched her leave; she was an impressive woman no doubt even if she was as short as Peggy Mitchell in EastEnders. He looked at her back as she disappeared out back then at Jim's back who was still busy making coffees and not even paying him any attention. Will had come back to 'The Restaurant' not even under his own volition but by force, he had to start again from scratch with some new working relationships. He had met one heck of good-looking guy who was now his co-worker who may or may not be interested in him and he had met a woman who was onto to him from the first moment they had met with her own brand of fiery but infectious personality. *'A new sexy gay guy and a little 'Firecracker' of a lady on the block, guess it could have been far worse for me. Fuck the Downstairs Cafe' that's for sure.'* he thought as Nat called for him to sit some new customers waiting to be seated at the designated stand from them, he saw them and rushed over apologising for the wait then seating all that were waiting. The rest of that day passed in a blur for him, he served food and drinks, he got reacquainted with Nat like they hadn't been apart for more than five months, something brewed other than the milk from the coffee machine between him and Jim who seemed to make a habit of strutting around him whenever they were in close proximity to one another, and Kym just laughed at the both of them every time as they made her shift all the more fun with their blatant sexual tension. When his day was done Will felt like he hadn't left at all. He felt something completely new was beginning again, he didn't know where it would lead him exactly, but he would definitely be hanging on to Kym who he came to like a lot that first day back. Without or without Jim being there to begin with.

*

Back To Now.

1:26 pm.

'You see 'Firecracker'; it wasn't all about Jim that day. It was more about you and the friendship that has blossomed between us ever since that first day we met.' He smiled at his now best friend as she returned from throwing the coffee grouts out of the tray into

a food bin in the Kitchen. She saw him smiling at her as she walked back over to join him at coffee pod two.

"What you smiling at then Mr?"

"Just you 'Firecracker'."

"O-k then..."

"Bet you can't wait for four pm to swing round?"

"Trust me; I'm out of that staff exit later faster than a speeding bullet!"

"Superman would be so proud of you."

Kym laughed at this as she put the coffee tray back into its slot, it really was turning out to be a very quiet Friday for the Cafe'. They'd been to lucky to serve a half dozen customers in the last half an hour, *'roll on five pm and my weekend off.'* Will tried to motivate himself by jumping up and down on the spot. Tonye came out from her designated corner again to poke her head as far it would reach from the Kitchen to check the cake table, then if Will had blinked there and then he wouldn't have even noticed her as she was off like a shot back to her hovel. "God what a sad little job if you can call it that she clings on too." Will gave a tut as he folded his arms at the little set up Tonye continued to get away with day in, day out on her part-time hours. "You know what I'm gonna say Willyboy." Kym called from the coffee machine she was cleaning again even though it was basically spotless as it was. *'Yes 'Firecracker' I know, it's just not fair that it goes on. You can only keep looking the other way for so long until it becomes simply unbearable.'* Will thought as stared at the spot Tonye had been at a moment ago.

"Don't you think all this pathetic behaviour just grates on you after a while?"

"I guess it sometimes does Will" she joined him at the till again "what can we do about it though?"

"We can shout from the rooftop about it? Oh could you just imagine that for a second?"

"Ha! With a big flashing neon sign to any thinking about wanting to work here..."

"Warning. Don't do it, *it's a trap!*" Will opened and shut his hands looking up at the ceiling as if he were the sign, Kym rolled up at this slapping his arm in approval. Will smirked at the visual image of him and Kym operating a big sign above the place telling the world over that working in a Store like this could either make you or completely break you. *'One day this lot won't be working in here anymore, it will be a brand-new team, a brand-new work ethic, a whole new load of egos to deal with.'* he paused his thought as Bianca Fray the Manager for both Cafe's came walking into the place in her usual slow like manner, she was never in a rush for anything but had that same fixed pleasant smile in place as if she were about to greet a bunch of her friends rather than employees. *'Hopefully, I won't be here to see that new team set up in the future.'* he finished his thought as another idea took hold of him, asking Kym if she would be ok on her own for a few minutes which she gave him a thumbs up to he made a beeline for Bianca in quick succession as she casually inspected the cake table but didn't seem to be that bothered about anything. She was tall girl Bianca, she was another one who wore thick rimmed glasses which seemed to a recurring theme for some in Cafe', bright blonde hair sat atop her head which was never curly, she clearly straightened it too much for its own good, she always wore one of the Managerial knee length black work dresses that didn't really accentuate the female figure in fact it was a rather uninspiring thing to wear but Bianca wore it every time. She most certainly wasn't a trouser wearing kind of person which translated to her personality well. No authority to her but a nice enough person to stomach either way yet never a mix of the two, Will was forever wondering how she had ended up in the position of Manager. *'I bet she had to be strong armed in to assuming the role just so they could shift her out in in the hope she would leave Southend to never return to the place.'* Will kind of pitied her since he wasn't the only one who knew she got walked all over but it was another known open fact *'the Clique'* had taken one look at her then treated her like they had treated him in the beginning, like some sort of inanimate but annoying object they could easily assert their will over so they got their way, it had worked in their favour like always since they all worked upstairs now with no one to disturb them unless in extreme cases. It just made the case of Bianca that little bit sadder so Will always wanted to treat her with kindness even if his own internal thoughts of her style of work left a lot lacking or to be desired. For now as he finished walking up to her at the cake table, he needed some news to make his short but slower than normal Friday shift to pick up a gear for the better. "Bianca!" he chimed in beaming from ear to ear "How goes everything today? Get all your stuff sorted upstairs?" he made polite conversation as she took notice of him.

"Ah Will, yes not bad. Was just a meeting with the Managers from all Departments but nothing serious, I just sat at the back listening in."

'Oh dear you poor cow, bet no one acknowledged you either.'

"Was there something you needed from me at all Will?" she asked as she adjusted a cake label with the clearly marked up price on it by a fraction, but it was more just out boredom than anything else. *'Here goes, hope she's heard some news at least by now.'* he hoped as he prepared himself. "Yes there was in fact Bianca, you see about *the thing* I mentioned to you a good what was it? Must be six weeks ago if I have my dates right? Well Coralie gave me your message last week, then I've hardly been able to catch you since you've been up in the offices a lot this week…" it was true as well, he hadn't known her to be much of a Manager who did any of the strenuous administrative tasks that was expected of her job role, she delegated to Coralie do all that while Bianca made her presence known on the shop floor more than anything she did, a nice person but also one who skirted some or most of her responsibilities, it was a wonder how she had lasted here so long. "Ah yes I do have some news about that…" she began but she wasn't at the same really giving Will her full attention. She was holding some cake slices up to the harsh fluorescent lighting to inspect some obviously non-existent smear marks. *'Bianca come on love, you're a nice enough person if a bit on the lazy side but I need you to be Managerial right now in this century if you can pretty please.'* he willed the thought in her direction even though his posture was relaxed his mind was racing in anticipation. "Yes the news is…" she put the cakes slices back down seemingly satisfied with them.

"Yes Bianca?"

"Well don't get too excited now Will."

'Oh great, I'm not gonna like this am I?'

"I'm just waiting on a phone call and an *official email* for confirmation but come this Monday the 12th if my dates are right? Then I will have the news you've been waiting to hear, that ok with you?" She finished this time giving him her full attention, but it was only for a moment, he could see her already turning her focus towards the cold sandwich fridge which had some noticeable gaps that needed re-filling. "Tonye! You able to replenish the cold sandwiches please?" Bianca called out to as Tonye seemed to march out from her hiding place with some frustration visibly on show at being disturbed by her Manager of all people. Tonye looked at the fridge then back to Bianca weighing up her options, anyone who had some common sense in the general area knew that Tonye wasn't in the mood to want to top anything up, but Bianca just kept on smiling at her totally oblivious to her mood swing. "I'd really appreciate it if you stocked it up a bit more please?" the Manager smiled sweetly as if butter wouldn't melt, Tonya Patricks stood there unmoving but cocked an eyebrow. "Well I was just in the middle on cleaning some baking trays as it happened Bianca..." Tonye even made her voice sounded like she was being interrupted from one of the most important tasks of her day, Will knew better though. *'Are you kidding me with you bullshit excuse Tonye? If your cleaning those baking trays then that's got to be the fourth time you've done them today you cheeky cow.'* Will couldn't believe how incredulous she was acting over a simple re-fill, then he had an idea he knew would definitely rile up Tonye some more.

"Listen Tonye..." he stepped in intentionally, so he was between Bianca and her, "I'll happily help you out with the cold sandwiches if you like? It is quiet today after all." he finished as he could see Becky's face light up impressed he would put himself out but then Tonye all of a sudden had another mood swing that changed her attitude entirely.

"Oh no you're alright Will, it's just a couple of sandwiches after all..."

"Well as long as you're sure Tonye? Don't want to keep you're from you tray wiping?"

"Nah you're alright, only had a *few* left anyway!" she was off out back to collect refill stock in the back fridges, Will saw Nat watching the whole incident happen from the relative safety of the Kitchen with that same amused face she always had whenever Will got himself involved in these kinds of situations, he winked at her and she laughed softly to herself cracking on with whatever she was doing at the time. "Will that was very generous of you to help Tonye out." Bianca patted his arm as she moved past him, she was heading for the sanctity of the small office that had been left over from the old Cafe' before the refurbishment.

"So don't forget, this Monday ok Will?"

"You got it, *boss*!" he called out to her which she smiled at, she kept on walking through the tables and disappeared through the office door which she wouldn't come out of again until her shift finished at around after five pm, she would cover with some excuse of being busy like she always did when everyone knew she would probably be playing solitaire on her laptop. Tonye came back out with the bare minimum of cold sandwiches in one very small crate, Will could tell she had a stroppy attitude swirling around her like black thunderous storm clouds, Will decided to jump in at the deep end for the hell of it. "Need any help there Tonye?" he asked in a sickly-sweet voice batting his eyelids as he went, she slowly looked over her left shoulder at him with a pointed stare. "I'm good. *Thanks*." She said the last word like it was a shard of ice that could pierce anyone's heart right there and then. *'Aww, isn't Karma a bitch Tonye.'* he chuckled to himself at the amusing thought as he walked away from her, he could hear her chucking the few sandwiches she had into the fridge without any care or consideration to it then he heard her stomp off back round to her still pathetic hovel of a corner which one day wouldn't be her domain anymore, *'I wonder when that will be?'* he asked himself internally as he re-joined Kym on coffee pod two. "Everything all good with Becky Mr?" she asked without looking at him from the coffee machine as she finished an order for a lone customer, that made seven that been served in the last half an hour. Today was going to be a slow one indeed.

"Yeah, yeah all good Firecracker, nothing to worry about." he looked back up at the ceiling lost in his thoughts.

'Monday can't come quick enough that's for sure Kym. I think I now know how Jim was feeling when he got his news all that time ago as well. One thing is for certain come Monday. Everything is going to change.'

Five

September 12ᵗʰ, 2013.

'The Restaurant'.

Thursday.

2:05 pm.

They were now sharing the Dishwasher Area with the Downstairs Cafe'. Nobody was even remotely happy with the situation at present. He could see the looks passing between the two groups, *'the Clique'* and the New Arrivals, regardless of the fact that 'The Restaurant' team had now been official In-Store staff for over five months now, staff discount included as well. Will was happy seeing Daisy or Sasha; he got along with them just fine, the rest however were something else. They could all do him a favour by not existing. *'We have to put up with this shitty predicament for god knows how many months.'* he thought ominously as he came out to the Dishwasher Area in the full knowledge knowing one of the Cafe' lot would have already commandeered it so their crappy stock could go through first, they were like a bad stain that simply wouldn't go away. The worst about the whole situation was the looks of contempt. It frustrated Will to no end; 'The Restaurant' team were now starting to pick up on how they were muscling their way into their space that the majority of them had been working in for well over three years now all except him, who could forget his little excursion downstairs to not made to be welcomed much or if at all. He stopped by the racks to drop what he was carrying only to see Lucy Crickers busying herself with what was blatantly more Cafe stock while all of their items needed washing remained relatively left on the racks without being touched. "Lucy, how goes it on the other side today?" Will asked politely as he tried sorting out what space was left for his addition which was wasn't much, Lucy glanced back at him. "Ah Will, yeah you know us, need our *precious* stock to keep going like always" she was back to concentrating on what cups, saucers, and plates she had. She was as per what was normal for her group taking her sweet time causally putting them through like they were her property, not that it was the Company that really owned them. *'Christ Lucy you're what? In your early sixties now? Just do me a favour and retire already.'* he thought as he watched her continue with her slow work. Will knew she was doing this on purpose. He remembered all too well in his first few months working with her she was the one with the most self-entitlement issues amongst *'the Clique'.* They all embodied different traits that added to their collective whole which made them all the more pathetic. It had been a busy Saturday shift in mid-January earlier this year, the sales were going strong so of course the masses were all the more hungry or thirsty or both, he and she were doing the best they could on the tables, but it was tough going, relentless in fact. As soon as a few tables were cleared there were at least another half a dozen to take their place, to be fair they were both working flat out, he had never seen Lucy move with such speed for someone who got away with whatever she wanted whenever she wanted but today he had seen her really putting in the work to keep the tables as clear as possible as they could be. He had almost been impressed by her performance that day until they had both gotten a quick breather from the immensity of tables only for him to start talking with her. Then Will in that moment had cracked beneath the surface of what Lucy Crickers considered were her true priorities for the job she clung onto. "My, it has been a bit intense today hasn't it Lucy? I still have left seven hours to go until I finish as well" he rolled his eyes away from her in despair whilst adjusting his black skull cap at the thought of finishing at nine pm on another busy day, Lucy was chuckling slightly under her breath at him which he took note of.

"Something funny?"

"Oh, only a little bit." she quickly stopped chuckling.

"What did I do this time?"

"Oh it's nothing really. It's just I don't do those kinds of shift anymore Will." she was now inspecting her uniform for any errant dust when there was none to be seen. *'Hmm, let's see where this is going shall we?'* he asked himself as this feeling in his gut started tugging at him, it was uncertainty.

"Do you mean you found it funny that I was on a late Lucy?"

"Oh yeah but again, someone's gotta do these crappy Saturdays right Will?"

"That's true I guess, what late shifts do you do then? Weekdays obviously I'm sure?" he kept his voice intentionally light with curiosity; he wasn't trying to ruffle her feathers in the slightest let alone her pride, he wasn't that brave or audacious.

"Well you know what it is really Will…" she was now looking at the lights as if they had become really interesting.

"Don't think I follow you Lucy?"

"Well you know how it is, we've done our years of closes, we're *exempt*. We've got *grandchildren* to look after." She finished the sentence without saying anything else as a customer signalled her over for help with their dirty table. Will was left standing there staring at the space she had occupied only a moment ago, he couldn't quite believe the amount of extreme casual arrogance and self-entitled bullshit that had just flown out of Lucy Crickers mouth, yet he had seen it and witnessed it in all its horrifying fascination. He felt numb from it all but he presented a calm exterior to any customer who might be staring at his unmoving figure currently. Yes he had never forgotten that small moment with Lucy that probably meant nothing to her on that busy Saturday shift, but it had meant something else completely to him. He was on the losing side working down there with that lot, no wonder he had gotten shafted back up to 'The Restaurant' as soon as humanly possible. He continued watching Lucy slowly put her stuff only through the Dishwasher when Nat appeared from the Kitchen. "Everything alight here Will?" she stopped talking for a moment taking note of the racks were pretty full with their personal stock that still needed washing while Lucy was only focusing on what little Cafe stock was left. Nat side-eyed Will but didn't say anything, she didn't have too. "So Lucy, are you going to crack on with our stuff sitting here? It won't wash itself after all?" Nat stopped as Lucy opened and closed her mouth a few times searching for any sort of reasonable response to come back with an active defence, then like fate itself was playing a cruel trick on both Will and Nat, in walked Josie Sybille like she was Lucy's fairy godmother. She took one look at Lucy then used only her eyes to look at Nat, she ignored Will. "Lucy love, why don't you go on your thirty-minute lunch break darling?" Josie continued her staring competition with Nat as Lucy scarpered out of the Dishwasher Area like her life depended on it, Nat wasn't one to take it lying down however. "So Josie..." she took a step forward showing zero fear, *'go on Nat, go pull that bitch right up.'* Will internally egged on his Supervisor "who is going to clear all this stuff of ours that has been all too *conveniently* left?" Nat let the question hang there between her and Josie, they were both the same grade so they couldn't really question the others authority, but they could definitely play the game to no end. "Well *Nat*, all my girls are occupied, and we have queue, so I have to jump on to the other till you see. We're just so busy…" she walked off to the other side the Cafe were occupying a small section on Kids Wear while their former seventy-five seated space downstairs was now a ripped-out husk of a shell of what it had been before. Nat didn't say anything as Josie was already gone; she had as per usual manipulated the situation to her advantage, it made Will bubble with anger. "You know Nat, Lucy went on a *thirty-minute break* this morning, but they always cover their own backsides and say it's their *fifteen-minutes* however, Joyce always says fuck all to them. In fact, she partakes in the same shite with them" Will said into Nat's ear as she moved over to the Dishwasher clearly pissed at what she had been left to do. "What's gets me is how they all get taken for their word at face value" she said through slightly gritted teeth "it's like they would rather just hear anything then they will just let em all get on with their shit" Nat folder her arms letting out a tired sigh, Will was a bit concerned for Nat now so walked over to join her at the sink placing a comforting hand on her arm. "Hey, you alright Mrs? I know they're the world's worst but..." he stopped talking as Nat was shaking her head with her eyes closed. "It's not that Will. I think I'm being manoeuvred out of being a Supervisor when the refurbishment concludes." she glanced at Will who always had her back and she had his, *'please, please don't let that be true.'* Will was worried for his co-worker now. "You're kidding right? Someone as hard-working as you Nat? Surely not?" he was saying it to actively encourage her, but his gut was once again telling him that he was very wrong, Nat's days were numbered, they both knew it but they were the ones fighting the losing battle this time. How the 'Powers That Be' got away with it was anyone's guess. "It's the little things more recently Will..." she began then took a quick breathe to elaborate further while he stood next to her in solidarity "It's the missed messages or the last-minute meetings I'm not invited too about anything to do with the refurbishment of the Cafe, you know there's talk of them getting rid of the Restaurant scheme from within the business right?" she looked worryingly at Will as he stared back in shock, it was the first he was hearing it from her but he didn't interrupt. "Yep that's right, you watch. This will be another Cafe' up here and you can bet they will rule the roost in both Units no questions asked. It's all just so..."

"So what Nat?"

She gave laugh along with a tut, she looked up at the ceiling like it was amusing all of a sudden, "It's all so tiring. Trying to be included when you're not welcomed from the start." she stopped speaking as she started to sort out what cups needed to be put through the Dishwasher, Will however just looked at his Supervisor knowing all too well how she felt. He gave her a half hug with his left arm and rested his face against hers which she allowed. "Welcome to my world Natalie. You don't know the half of it from what I've had to deal with down there…" he didn't finish the sentence because he knew she knew exactly what he was talking about; it didn't need to be further elaborated on.

"I guess that makes us public enemy number ones then!"

A voice then rang out from the staff entrance. They both stopped what they were doing looking at each other then turning in unison to the new voice. It was Sasha; she was leaning against the open-door frame smirking at them both. "To what do we owe the pleasure from the other side then Sasha?" Will folded his arms whilst looking her up and down but she wasn't there to play games with them, she wasn't in with *'the Clique'* after all. "You know me Will, come in, do my shit and I go home." she moved to join him and Nat by the sink, "besides, I don't give a *toss* what the majority of them lot back out there think" she used only her head to indicate the loud chatty lot on the other side where the makeshift Cafe' was set up for however many months it was there for. *'Good girl Sasha, I've always liked your stance.'* Will approved of her can-do attitude; she was someone who Nat could come to trust in time he hoped. "Now let me guess, Lucy was on here doing only their shit and she didn't even bother with your stuff" Sasha used her head to acknowledge all the leftover Restaurant stock that still needed to be cleaned on the racks.

"That obvious is it?" Nat asked dryly.

"Yep I'm sorry to say." Sasha began by clapping her hands together "that and that lot out there are bitching about the fact you were gonna try and tell Lucy what to do until *St Josie* herself intervened. Look Nat you can count on me, I ain't *one of them* and I don't plan to ever be either." Sasha made sure she was looking Nat directly in the eyes as Will watched her extend the Olive Branch to his Supervisor. "What I am is a *friend* and I am gonna crack on with this crap they've left you in and Will can help me out, how does that sound?" she finished waiting for Nat's response who was immediately more relieved she had someone offering the help rather than having to do it herself or go pull someone from another job to cover. Nat smiled and then hugged Sasha "thanks Mrs, I really appreciate that" Nat released her from her hug, but Sasha was now shooing her away "go on you, scram! Will, let's get this *shite* put through and cleaned down in double time ah?" Sasha flung herself into the dishes as Will moved to the end of the Dishwasher to collect the stuff once it was all cleaned from its cycle inside the machine. Nat moved off back around into the Kitchen happier than she had been all day thanks to Sasha's help, her and Will then had the Dishwasher Area in a much better state no more than twenty minutes later, they both stepped back for a second to judge their handiwork. "That was a team effort Mrs if you don't mind me saying so?" Will high fived Sasha who returned it in kind, "yeah I gotta say your spot on there Mr, we did good!" She put her hands on her hips pleased the Dishwasher and the racks were less of a state, it was only bound to get worse again with two Units both needing use of a working Dishwasher. Sure enough Sherry Michaels came in with full tray, "sorry people but it's gonna be a new wave of incoming stuff rather shortly from *our side*" she dropped off the tray without waiting for Will and Sasha to respond, she was off like a shot. "Will if it gets busy I'll give you a shout" Sasha got on with the new dishes "you sure? I can stay..." Will offered but she shook her head in assuredness. "Na, go on they probably need you out there I bet, right Jim?" she asked Jim over Wills right shoulder who came in with his own tray, he was huffing as well. "Oh yeah Will I could use your help in fact,

I've got some bitchy customer moaning at me, could you clear her table while I deal with her? She does not wanna pick a fight with me since she's the reason I need a cigarette right now!" Jim disappeared back into 'The Restaurant' side in a flash without waiting for Will; he looked back round at Sasha who had her signature smirk back in place. "Better you than me buddy" she raised her hands in mock surrender then busied herself with the two new trays of leftovers she had to sort, Will turned around then headed back out on to the shop floor. Sure enough it was still sort of busy but manageable enough, Jim was talking to a short female customer with shoulder length brown hair and a pair of glasses just perched on the ridge of her pointy nose, she was looking up at Jim like he wasn't anything but a man servant she could use at her beck and call, little did she know that Jim gave as good as he got. He was dealing with her well despite the fact she was aggrieved by something that was clearly a matter of life and death in her eyes; to Jim she was just another inconsiderate customer punching above her weight to score points. "Madam, like I said if you take a seat back at your table I'll bring the bill over to you..." Jim kept his cool exterior up, but Will heard the tone of steel emerging in his voice, the customer hadn't taken note of it yet. "Well yes you did say that, but I have something more I wish to say to you young man!" the lady was now raising her voice like she wanted to be seen making a fuss, *'uh oh here we go. Hun you shouldn't have raised your voice at Jim like that.'* Will stayed where he stood, he saw the odd customer starting to look their way at the drama unfolding between the two on the shop floor, Jim was as still as a statue however. "What is it you wish to say to me madam?" his voice was raised by a fraction but not by much.

"I think you have been quite rude to me and my daughter today as it happens!"

"Really? I well I do apologise if I have been Madam..."

"That doesn't excuse your behaviour TOWARDS US!" she was shouting now, and she had also stepped into Jim's personal space, he was more than holding his ground however. "Don't shout at me!" Jim looked down at the short woman as her eyes grew wide in shock at an actual member of staff speaking back to her. He hadn't raised his voice any further, but he had made sure the short statement wasn't lost on the aggravated lady. "YOU WHAT?" she fired back as she held her own ground, but he didn't let up, it was a battle of egos. Most people in the general vicinity of them were watching the heated exchange now. "Are you going to take a seat so I can bring the bill over to you Madam? Or are we both gonna stand here defending our bruised egos?" Jim asked as the lady didn't move, "I want to speak to your Manager; I'm a *loyal customer* you know!" the lady brought out the statement like it was the best thing she had ever said, Jim just blinked at her uncaringly. "Really? Then how comes in more than half a year of me working here I have never served you once and I work full time here Madam." he kept his voice level but loud enough for other customers and staff alike to hear him say it, Nat made a quick dash out back to get to the shop floor as quick as she could. *'Bloody hell Jim, you're braver than me. You've definitely got some balls on you.'* Will was scared for him but was also admiring his tenacity. The lady just looked like she had been slapped around the face with the unflinching truth. "HOW DARE YOU SPEAK TO ME LIKE THAT? Who you do even think you are!" The lady was getting more red in the face by the second, but Jim just judged her casual attire up and down like the nobody she actually was.

"Who me a Madam?"

"YES, YOU!"

"*I'm a Human Being*! Has that thought ever occurred to *once* the entire you think you have *the right* to stand in my space speaking so rudely to someone who is doing his best just serve on tables to make a living? Well, do you? I bet you think you can waltz in here with here with your designer bags that clearly have the *Primark price tags* sticking out of them to think that any member of staff deserves to be spoken to like that!" Jim was now leering over her as she for once looked afraid to try say anything more, she was being put in her place and she knew it. *'I hoped she wouldn't have tried it on but oh my she is getting served up on a platter rightly so*

by Jim, give her hell mate.' Will was secretly super proud of him,
customers seemed to think they could vent their frustrations
without fear of consequence in a place like this, especially when it
came to the gay members of staff like him and Jim, now the
reckoning was upon them all. "Now I will say this clearly
Madam!" Jim's voice was raised, it was full of conviction, he was
not to be messed with. "Go sit down and I will happily let my
Supervisor take over from me because sweetheart guess what?" He
was now in the woman's face; her bottom lip was starting quiver
just a tiny bit. "wha...what?" her voice had lost a lot of its
loudness; she seemed to be getting smaller under Jim's withering
gaze by each passing moment.

"Because *sweetheart*, I have no time for rude, insignificant,
hateful, egotistical, no good for nothing, inexpensive, low-priced,
timewasters *like you*!" Jim then marched off the shop floor without
looking back to gasps from some customers, another couple
laughed but there was something else, a couple of other tables
applauded Jim as he left followed by the odd cheer of "hear, hear"
which the lady turned around just as shocked by. "Oh you can't be
serious? You heard what he just said to me! I'm in shock as it..."
she was walking slowly back to her table looking for the other
table who cheered, they didn't make themselves known but another
table spoke up anyway. "If I were you *madam*, I wouldn't say
another word. You goaded that poor young man, and you should

be ashamed of yourself!" this statement got an even stronger round of applause meaning 'The Restaurant' customers were backing Jim up all the way. Nat walked pass Will; she was floored by the response Jim was getting from other customers.

"I've never seen anything like it Will..."

"Telling me Nat, is Jim ok?"

"Yeah, yeah he just went for a cigarette. Listen I'll deal with that lady, but can you cover the coffee station while I get things straight out here?" Will accepted the task grateful he now didn't have to clear the aggravated customers table, he walked past them on the way to the station and saw the daughter staring at the floor like she praying for it to swallow her so she wouldn't have to share in the embarrassment that was her Mother. All the prays in the world couldn't help her at the moment. *'Poor kid, fancy having an angry person like that for a Mum?'* He looked at them as the Mum was now trying to convince her daughter she was the one in the right, the teenager just looked like she wanted to leave as soon as viably possible. Nat dealt with the mother and daughter accordingly but in a much more civilised way than the lady had been a moment ago with Jim. ten minutes later after the whole debacle they both left 'The Restaurant' and Will hoped they would never grace the place with their presence ever again. *'Thank fuck their gone, good riddance.'* he watched their backs as they walked off up into the main part of Riverside as he placed a double order of cappuccinos on the clear glass serving hatch which Nat took to a waiting table. Jim then appeared from the Kitchen Area calmer plus being perkier from his obvious nicotine fix.

"Hey Jim."

"Hey Will."

"You ok? Or is that too soon to ask?" Will looked at him a little nervously as he got on with the next order of three large lattes to make, Jim seemed to be still off somewhere in the recesses of his mind rather than focusing on the task at hand. "I don't think I've ever spoken to a customer like that before Will…" he began after a short pause "…I mean I defend myself sure because I am a fiery person, but I've never responded *like that* before" Jim was now looking at Will explaining himself as Will made the latest coffee order. Rather than standing there still slightly numbed Jim decided to help.

"Want me to get the saucers ready?"

"Yes please Jim."

He did so carefully, still processing what had happened with the lady a short while ago. "I see they've finally left?" Jim asked as he continued scanning what customers remained in 'The Restaurant', "yeah they have, and I think it's safe to say that's a blessing for everyone working today" Will placed his first two lattes on the saucers Jim had readied. "Thank fuck for that then." Jim said quietly as Will retrieved the last latte left at the machine, the milky top glistened on top like good latte milk should do, Nat came over to collect them noticing Jim had arrived back. "How you feeling Jim?" Nat asked genuinely concerned, it seemed to relax Jim somewhat knowing Nat had his back. "Yeah fine I guess the cigarette help...I just hoped it hasn't messed up my chances with, you know..." he stopped talking as Nat waved whatever he was going to say away. *'What chance has he messed up then I wonder?'* Will's curiosity was peaked again as Nat alleviated Jim's concern.

"No, no Jim. Don't worry about *that* at all."

"Are you sure Nat? I mean that woman was gunning for me, what if I don't get it..."

'Don't get what now?'

"You will I'm waiting on the Manager to call me today about it, shouldn't be too much longer in fact, aha! Here he is ringing me now on the portable phone." Nat walked off to the side of 'The Restaurant' nearest the exit so she wasn't heard by anyone eavesdropping, especially Will. Jim watched her as she chatted away on the work phone, he seemed almost nervous now which

surprised Will even more. *'Since when does Jim ever get nervous?*
This is turning into a strange day all together.' Will went back to
the coffee machine to make a medium mocha that had just printed
from the machine as Jim looked some more at Nat on the work
phone, he didn't say anything until Nat beckoned him over,
without saying a word to Will he was halfway over to Nat as she
held the phone out to him patiently before Will turned around with
his fresh mocha applying the complimentary free whipped cream
top the customer had requested. Will saw just in the nick of time
Jim take the phone and hold it to his ear with his back to 'The
Restaurant' Nat seemed to be watching him with baited breathe. *'I*
seriously need to get in on what's going on with them.' Will
thought as he noticed his milk jugs were in dire need of a clean
along with the leftover coffee cups that needed to be put through a
Dishwasher to be cleaned within an inch of their life. He took them
all on a spare tray and walked through the Kitchen turning into the
Dishwasher area where Sasha still had everything very much under
control. "Well you have certainly made this place your own today
Miss Sasha." Will looked at the area as she was just finishing it
wiping it down, there was only one tray to do from the Cafe' side
but the place was remarkably more clean than it had been in a long
time. "Well you know how it is…" Sasha chucked the cloth she
was using in the bin to get herself a new one "…if you got it, you
got it!" she shrugged her shoulders innocently, but her eyes were
alight with how impressed she was herself, Will dropped his new

tray of stuff off but she welcomed the work. "So what happened out there with Jim then Will?" Sasha helped him unload the cups and milk jugs into the warm soapy water waiting in the sink, Will however didn't have the strength repeat himself. "Trust me Sasha, it's a *long story*" he said then a voice disturbed them.

"Will, come over here please."

It was Jim, he was by the two-way revolving door, he was once again standing still as a statue looking at Will. Sasha eyed them both up curiously. *'O-k, what does he want from me?'* Will didn't know whether to be nervous or excited judging by Jim's look as he approached him, he didn't make any sudden moves, but Will noticed he was breathing faster than normal. *'Oh god is this it? He's gonna tell me how he feels about me truly then we're gonna kiss and start something that will change the both of us for the better.'* Will mind was racing with delight at the thought if this was the moment to be for them both. He closed the distance between them. Rather than ask, he waited for Jim to speak.

"Will, I have something to tell you."

"Yes Jim?"

"Well it's pretty important...."

Oh Jim, you really do like me the same way I find you bloody sexy!'

"It's something I have wanted to say for so long but couldn't Will..."

Sasha's eyebrows were raised in surprise at this from the Dishwasher.

"Go on Jim, I am more than ready to hear this!"

"Will the thing is..."

'Just take me right here, right now Jim, I don't care, I just want you so badly!'

"Well, I just received my transfer date Will. I'm transferring to Stratford Store at the end of the month, Ha!"

Jim finished with a huge ecstatic smile on his face, he opened his arms to Will for a hug, Will was speechless dropping his jaw as he reciprocated the hug. Jim then started squealing so Will mimicked him, then before he knew it they were both jumping up and down on the spot like two overly excited school kids. Sasha was still at the Dishwasher staring at the pair of them dumbfounded, she had clearly been expecting something else to happen in the same vain as Will had. Will saw her staring as the jumping hug continued with Jim, he had only one thought left to spare for the moment as the realisation sunk in.

'Jim's transferring? He's leaving me to rot here with this lot at Riverside. Fuck me indeed! Guess it wasn't the scenario I really wanted to happen. Oh bloody hell, I'm really gonna miss Jim now!'

*

Exactly Three Years Later.

The Downstairs Cafe'.

4:59 pm.

Monday.

'One hour to go.' he thought motivationally.

It had been another long and drawn-out Monday; the lunch rush had been a one-hour hit around the midday mark then after that hour it had dropped off like a stone. Will could not wait for the six pm finish, but he was also still waiting on any news from Bianca who had yet to approach or call for him. He was hoping that with his last hour to go he might get the news he was more than ready to hear. *'Come on Bianca, just stop being your lazy self for five minutes and tell me what I want to know.'* he was going through the motions of crossing and uncrossing his fingers, the waiting was always the worst part. Sure he had, had the weekend off to do what he liked, and he didn't pay work anymore attention when it was his time off, but he had come back after a lovely weekend away in the hope he would get some news promptly, of course he had been wrong again. *'I bet their just gonna drag it out some more to keep me forever in some form of suspense.'* the miserable thought felt like the most likely outcome. It was eerily quiet in the Cafe' now, the parents had picked the kids up from school and were now more than likely getting their dinners started, that left the footfall drastically down in places like where Will worked. The Cafe' also didn't stay open till ten pm like the rest of the Store anymore, a few months back the sales figures had been analysed extensively by the Management Team and they worked out by having the Cafe' now close at eight pm along with the workforce to finish at eight-thirty not only saved on staff costs it also showed the sales they took in the final two hours of trading were negligible to what they made in the daytime. It was a win, win situation all round, the store benefitted, the team benefitted. The rest of the Departments however weren't pleased at all, especially the ones who had been working in the place for years on end thinking they were the ones who had it good, Head Office had authorised the decision then it was all out war of words for a time, Will remembered anyone who had been told to come help out on tables from another Department that the looks they gave the staff as they helped were nothing short of murderous, it was just beyond stupidity really. They had a job, and they weren't unemployed which should make them grateful but no, their pride was the most important thing first then the job second. Will had come to not like a lot about the job working here after all these years but he was forever happy in the knowledge he did his best when on duty every day he was there, for however long that would last. He served one couple who had an easy order request of two coffees, they paid, he made, they collected. One big conveyer belt of routine then it was onto the next. Kym walked back into coffee pod one where he was situated to join him. "How was your break 'Firecracker'?" he asked his short best friend as he wiped the auto wand for any leftover milk, "you know Will, never long enough." she replied as she scanned the till quickly for any item that had been removed off the menu for the day. "It's funny really 'Firecracker'..." Will looked up the ceiling in thoughtful amusement.

"What is Will?" she looked over her right shoulder in his direction.

"Me and you stick to our allotted break times, but others here get away with blue ass murder when it's their breaks, taking extra time all cause their mates with the right people" he shrugged as he wiped down the surface of the coffee machine with the proper cleaning solution. Kym gave quick snigger from the till.

"You know what that is don't ya Willyboy?"

"What is it?"

"It's called *sods law*!"

This made the two best friends laugh aloud at their predicament; they behaved or kept well within the boundaries of their workplace rules set up for them while others just didn't care, it was another stab of arrogance that bit them both on their backsides. *'How long will this continue for me I wonder? I mean six years of working in here and it's not like I haven't tried to leave or get another job in that time that I've spent working here.'* he finished the thought as he inspected the pristine work counter he had wiped down, it looked practically brand new if you didn't inspect it closely. *'Another job well done with no one to appreciate it, not that this place would even do that.'* the thought sobered him as checked the time on the till over Kym, five-ten pm, less than an hour left yet the time was dragging like it always did at the end of his nine till six shift he did four times a week for the place. In all the times he had worked in the Downstairs Cafe' since the refurbishment Will had never even been asked to come in on an early shift, not even if one of *'the Clique'* was on holiday or one of their dreaded group holidays they always seemed to be able to take together. The Company Policy stated that only three members of staff from one Business Unit could be off at any given time, the maximum allowance could not be modified any further to accommodate other members of additional staff also working in the Unit at the time or

date of a specified holiday. *'The Clique'* however had been able to
have a total of all five of their group off in one time while Will had
gone to Joyce when she was still Manager practically to beg that he
and one of the other members of staff be allowed the same time
off, Joyce had of course acted like what Will was asking of her was
one of the most time-consuming tasks he could ask of her but she
had somehow magically found a way for them to both be off while
making it sound worse than it actually was at the time. This was
before Will had decided to inspect the Company Policy himself
with a fine eye for the details to discover how far and how much
these women were being piss-takers with their Employment, just
another reason how he was treated differently from the in-crowd.
"God this last hour is driving me nuts!" he folded his arms in
frustration, only five minutes had passed by since he last checked
the time. Kym looked at him like he was having a break down,
"Someone had a bad Monday then?" she nudged him with a
cheeky grin in place; she knew he would calm down in a moment
anyway. "It's not that, I just wanted to speak to Bianca before I left
but she has barely been seen today. It's like *come on* I've got less
than forty-five minutes to go, and I am certainly not waiting
around after work tonight for her when I just want to get home."
Will kicked a rubbish bin in more frustration; Kym didn't try to
stop him when she knew this was how he operated. "It will be
alright Will; you know what kind of a Manager Bianca is anyway"
Kym gave him one of her probing motherly looks which did calm

him down right away, he knew he was acting like an impatient idiot. Coralie then appeared in the entrance looking around the Cafe', when she spotted Will she made a beeline for him. "Will just passing on a message, Bianca wants to see you upstairs in about less than half an hour so just before you finish your shift." Coralie delivered the message but kept on walking past the coffee pod to go check out the furthest away cleaning station on tables to make sure it was shut down properly for the day. Will stood there watching her walk away, the news he wanted to hopefully hear from Bianca was now in touching distance. He could feel it. His frustration became instant anticipation, *'ok relax Will. Half an hour then you'll get the news you've been waiting to hear for last few months.'* he took a calming breathe closing his eyes, but he felt something else. He felt Kym, his 'Firecracker' had her eyes narrowed in on him; she wanted to know what was going on. "Kym, I know what your gonna say Mrs..." he looked at his best friend so she wouldn't be even more suspicious of him than she was already. "Well are you gonna fill me in or you just gonna keep it from me then?" Kym asked but her tone was pointed enough to put Will back on edge, *'oh my 'Firecracker', as soon as I know the full truth I'm gonna tell you everything.'* he thought lovingly of her, he hated withholding anything from her, he had to wait to see what Bianca had to tell him, he came up with a compromise solution. "How about this? Once I've spoken to Bianca I'll come straight back down with my stuff and tell you immediately what news she had for me, deal?" he opened his arms for a hug from his best friend who probed him some more, but she accepted the hug in good will. "Hmm ok, but you better be down after you've finished or me and you are having *words* Mr!" she gave him one of her deadly looks in his eyes just so Will knew she meant business. He nodded his head vigorously in agreement. They continued on with their work or what work they had from the still low intake of customers; the time seemed to be intentionally teasing Will to no end, he was forever checking the time as it ticked down to when he could reasonably head up to see Bianca in the In-Store Admin Offices. *'Ugh, get me out of here please.'* he was willing whatever deity might be listening if they even existed. Coffee order after coffee order came his way and he made them with restrained frustration whilst presenting his pleasant exterior to the waiting customers, it was the most annoying waiting time he felt like he had ever been a part of. When he had made what must of the been the six or seventh latte in a row he almost slammed down the milk jug but stopped himself from going there so when it made contact with the surface of the coffee station it sounded like a loud bang rather than a slam. Kym however looked at him from the till sensing he wanted to get upstairs in a timely fashion. "Don't get your knickers in a twist Willy, guess what?" she asked from over her shoulder at the till not looking at him, she knew he would come over anyway. "What 'Firecracker'?" he came over like she knew he would, she smirked at his routine behaviour.

"It's time."

she looked up at him as he looked at the time on the till with
widened eyes, his breathing had gotten quicker, he even felt his
heartbeat flutter a touch. The time on the till was five-forty-six,
more than enough time for him to race upstairs for his news with
Bianca. Kym continued smiling up at him "go on Mr." she nudged
Will which seemed to make him realise he needed to get moving,
nodding he moved out of coffee pod one with purposeful intent
gathering his thoughts. He walked over to the entrance then
stopped for a moment, he turned back to look at Kym who was
watching him leave. "I'm coming back down after, ok?" he told
her like it was a question, but he knew that she was fully clued up
in their commitment to their friendship they had both equally
moulded beautifully together. Nodding that she was satisfied Kym
didn't say anything but motioned with her right hand to shoo him
away as another customer came up to place an order with her,
smiling a bit more at his best friend Will took a moment to watch
her work then did a full one eighty turning to face the escalators
awaiting him. He took a sharp breathe in then made his way
upstairs. He thought he would almost run up, but he found his body
operating a different way, slowly but with ease like it knew a
change was now dawning on the horizon. *'Ok, whatever happens,
happens. If it's not the news I want I will just do my best to accept
it either way.'* he mentally prepared himself as his slow walk

upstairs went on, he found himself naturally breathing in and out deeply as if he was expecting the worst. He didn't know how to feel as he swiped through the exit to the staffing level on Kids Wear, the double doors swung open for him to the flight of stairs leading up to his fate. He made his way up still not gaining anymore speed but taking calming steps as his anxiety climbed, he maintained his breathing to level himself from all out panic, the unknown could be a frightening prospect depending on the particular situation. He swiped through another set of double doors where the staff canteen entrance was waiting for him on the right; it was eerily quiet in there with no one to be seen as fair as they see-through doors would let him see, he made his way past the canteen to walk down the long corridor towards the Admin Offices, there wasn't a soul to be seen as he made his way, only the sound of his footsteps reverberating off the walls which strangely made him feel a little better despite being alone. He stopped at the open window that looked into the Offices and he saw Bianca on a work phone with an open computer terminal chatting away without a care in the world. *'Here goes nothing then.'* Will gave himself one last shake in the empty corridor to muster up some courage he wasn't feeling, he knocked on the door the Offices and poked his head in while still half out in the corridor, Bianca turned around at the sound to see his expectant face. "Ah Will, excellent timing..." Bianca held the work phone away from her ear for a quick moment "...if you could go wait in one of the interview rooms I'll be right

with you in a couple of minutes ok?" she brought the work phone
back to her ear not really waiting for his response, but Will nodded
his head a little too vigorously as he closed the door to the Offices
then made his way round the corner to the interview rooms. They
had four of them, all rather small with a bland cream colour that
needed to be painted over soon since it evoked the old cream
colours Will had grown up seeing in his Juniors and Senior School
classrooms. They also gave off the vibe that they were also rooms
you could detain an employee in to have them fired from their job
as well, they even had a solo window with blinds to offer privacy
but it all of a sudden held a double meaning to Will. He entered the
one closest to the long corridor, a simple table with two chairs
occupied the already small space, and rather than sitting he leaned
against the table too unnerved to sit on a chair to be still. When it
came to imminent news he was a bit of a fidgety mess which is
exactly what he was right now. The silence in the small
interview/detaining room was deafening, the waiting seemed
endless even though it had probably only been a minute at best,
Will folded his arms exhaling his frustration which didn't help his
nerves. Then he heard a door open and close from out in the long
corridor followed by slow footsteps, now was the time and he felt
it approaching. *'Whatever happens, happens.'* he told himself
again internally as Bianca came round the corner with her usual
simple cheery smile which gave nothing away. She entered the
small room to an anxious Will who tried to not fidget but was

failing miserably. "Sorry to keep you waiting in here Will, are you ok?" Bianca asked she shut the door looking at him with some genuine concern.

"Oh, me Bianca? I'm a little nervous I won't lie to you."

"Ah Will there's nothing to worry about".

"There isn't? Does that mean you have the news I've been waiting to hear about?"

"Yep, I do indeed Will; I know you've been waiting over a good six weeks for this..."

"Seems like a small eternity either way..."

"Ha! Yeah these processes take their time unfortunately. However I won't keep you in suspense any longer Will..."

Bianca gave him the news he had been waiting close to two months to hear. Will listened intently not interrupting as she spoke, once she was finished he doubled checked he had heard her correctly which she verified. He even asked her a third time just to make sure he wasn't being hoodwinked which Bianca laughed at. She conveyed the rest of the news Will needed to hear, they shook hands professionally and Will thanked her and they both exited the small room. Bianca went back to the Admin Offices to finish up whatever she needed to do, and Will began a slow walk down the long corridor which was still devoid of any people except him. He swiped himself into the male locker room and went to his designated locker in a numb state. Bianca's new was still sitting heavily in his mind, he couldn't believe it.

'Whatever happens, happens. And boy did it happen.'

He slowly took out his locker key and opened it up to get out his coat and bag. He put them on slowly still processing his news, he closed the locker door locking it then leaned back against the lockers behind him. A date was now swirling around in his mind. It was an important one to not forget.

'October 22nd. My final day working at Riverside before I formally transfer to Stratford Store.'

He couldn't quite believe it still. He was leaving Riverside after all these years. Who would have thought he would have lasted here all this time, certainly not him at first when he had that fateful conversation with Ashley after his trial in 'The Restaurant'. Will stopped leaning against the lockers and shook himself again, pulling himself out of the stupor he was in. He looked at his locker realising now it had a real fixed-term time limit on how much longer it would be his then it would be someone else's. It was a small insignificant thing, but it meant his time was really coming to an end at the Store, he turned and left the locker room to swipe out of the building down the eight flights of stairs he would definitely not miss. He had to go see Kym to tell her the news now and he didn't know what to expect of her reaction. As he walked down the stairs with this new information practically wanting to burst out of him he did feel something inside of him. It was déjà vu. He had been in this position once before where he had considered transferring to Stratford when Joyce Cooper had still been ruling the Cafe's with her narrow-minded iron fist.

He remembered all too well near the beginning of Summer last year when he had approached her about it.

She hadn't been exactly over the moon about it either.

'Feels like only yesterday when I first tried to leave this place...'

Six

June 10th, 2015.

The Downstairs Cafe'.

Wednesday.

11:32 am.

"You want to *potentially* transfer stores Will?" Joyce Cooper asked of him as she looked up from the staff rota which she never surrendered to anyone. Not even Coralie. Will stood somewhat nervously in Joyce's presence. She was just a fraction shorter than Will but only by a minuscule, she had blonde shoulder length hair with a couple of whispers of brown at the end of a few strands representing she dyed it regularly and she kept it in a bang style. She sported some small no-nonsense black glasses that she used to inspect everyone whenever she arrived at the Cafe'. All with the exception of Josie Sybille and her posse, however. When they were all around one another no one else got a word in edge ways and they let the whole team know it from day one of the refurbishment, it was a pathetic work setup that was begrudgingly accepted by the majority, well most of them anyway. Will was one of the very few to push against it from time to time, he was certainly not about to be bullied into submission by a bunch of women who used not only their ages but also their so-called *years of service* under their belts as excuses for the creation of a partial toxic work environment or elements of one for that matter. Quite frankly this wasn't Seniors' School and Will had no intention of ever going back to that way of life, especially when it came to attempting to do a good honest day's work in the Cafe' for staff and customers alike. Will still felt awkward standing in front of Joyce with his specific request, Joyce was appraising him up and down meticulously, like there was some ulterior motive hidden deep beneath the surface for why he really wanted his transferral. He was unsettled by her continued studying of him. "It's not that I am not grateful for my position here at the store Joyce, it's just..." he stopped as his Manager raised a hand to silence him, it wasn't a quickfire hand movement of course but it was slow yet full of purposeful intent behind the actual way she conducted herself, Will found himself waiting with baited breath at what might happen next. Joyce lowered her hand slowly to symbolise that she was now taking full control of the conversation Will had begun with her, she would not be surrendering control of it either. Joyce Cooper wasn't an unreasonable women or Manager, but she was another of the Old Guard who liked the role she had carved out for herself in the Store having been employed with the Company for well over a decade now. "Just what Will?" Joyce tucked the staff rota neatly under arm and clasped her hands together loosely, her inspection of him carried on. They were just off to the side of the Kitchen between the space where there was an opening to head out back to the narrow Dishwasher Area and the small tucked away corner of the bakery section that Tonye Patricks claimed as her own personal hovel where she made herself look fake-busy each shift she was on, today was her day off however so for the time being so it was just Joyce and Will. The chain of command was asserting itself between the pair, the Manager, and the Customer Assistant, Will knew whatever Joyce was about to say he wasn't going to appreciate or accept at all. *'Looks like I've cracked open a can of worms.'* Will thought ominously as Joyce took one measured step to close the distance between them, she hadn't changed her facial features either, that in itself must have been some sort of art form to maintain for a such a prolonged period as they had yet to even get into the details of why Will wanted to transfer out of the Store. "I think I know what's really going on here Will." Joyce continued as he remained silent "you *just want* to throw the status quo we all play a part here in keeping right up in the air, don't you?" Joyce was asking but she was throwing it to the ground like a gauntlet at Will's feet, Will was just more confused by her question, *'where is she going with this? I don't want anything to do with her co-called status quo. I want to try working at another store it's as simple as that.'* Will kept his facial expression completely confused just as his own thoughts were equally puzzled by Joyce's probing question. "Oh, come now Will I'm not that naive. I know this is just another ploy because you don't get on with some of the people who conduct themselves in a certain way in here..." she gestured back out to the hustle and bustle of the Cafe' as the staff went about their business serving customers none the wiser to Will and Joyce's rather specific chat unfolding. "Is that really what you think I'm trying to accomplish by asking about transferring to a *different store* Joyce?" Will asked his Manager who returned her gaze to him seemingly unconcerned by the question he had aimed back at her, it was like a very carefully toned war of words between them or some convoluted game of chess that was becoming tedious very quickly. "Please Will; I'm your *Manager*." Joyce almost leaned in as if trying to intimidate him on the spot "it's my job to know these things about my staff. I know you and Josie don't see eye to eye but then again, everyone knows that don't they." Joyce stopped as Will scoffed at this which caused her eyes to widen is surprise at the supposed infraction he was committing in front of her. Joyce had a few tendency's she did not permit her staff to do if she was ever on the shop floor, one of them was leaning of any kind of surface at any given moment and the other was scoffing openly at something she was saying purely because it got her back up practically immediately. "Now your *scoffing* at me Will, are you?" Joyce made her tone of voice switch from light and airy to cold and menacing like it was the easiest trick in the book, Will however gave her a bug-eyed look in return. *'Joyce sweetheart let's get some facts straightened out, shall we?'* Will internally asked himself as he then did something he knew would rile his Manager some more, he started looking her and up down which she saw him doing whilst she folded her arms. She was not going to let someone beneath her in the hierarchy of this place even dare try to undermine her authority right now. "Right Will listen here..." but Will had had enough so he cut her off growing tired of the tediousness of the situation "No Joyce. You *listen* to me now rather than making some more utterly ridiculous assumptions that are taking me and you around in circles." Will stepped further in so the space between them was barely there, he was taking a bold risk, but he wanted what he was originally going to say be heard whether Joyce liked it or not. "Now I want to transfer stores Joyce. You wanna to know why? I will tell you. I've spent nearly five years working in the In-Store Department of Riverside and it's time to switch things up, it's time to push myself into a new adventure. Yeah sure I may be trading one Store for another, but you know what? It's in the City and its a new challenge with new kinds of customers which actually excites me believe it or not if you like, now you're a reasonable lady..." he stepped back to give them both some comfortable breathing space this time satisfied she understood how serious he was about this "...so how about you tell me you will *consider* my request for a transfer and I'll get back to work?" he finished by folding his owns arms to match her stance refusing to back down. Will was going to be heard by his Manager. Joyce hadn't moved when he had gotten into the personal space, but her face was set in a stone like feature as he had widened the gap after he had finished his statement to her, she was breathing only slightly heavier than she normally did. "Will, I will say this once and once only..." she unfolded her arms like was getting ready to attack "...don't ever get in my space like that *ever again*. Do I make myself clear?" she was asking but it was only to retain an air of politeness if anyone happened to be watching them close by, Will wasn't about to be put in his place though. "Then with respect since you are my Manager and it's *your job* to know how your staff feel Joyce..." he unfolded her arms appearing to relax but his voice remained pointed "...don't start making assumptions before you have all the facts presented before you then I suggest? After all you are a Mother yourself so you should be able to understand others all too well. Not just your close personal friends here in the Café'." he cocked an eyebrow at her as she looked him up and down again like he was an insignificant bug, they were both at a stalemate in their convoluted game of chess and they were both fully in the knowledge of this. Shaking her shoulders just a fraction to relax the tension she surprised Will by planting a half-smile on her face then responded to Wills loaded question "good idea Will, I'll keep that in mind. If that is everything…" she turned to move off, Will still wanted some reassurance from her "so you'll consider my transfer request then?" he called out to her as she continued moving off to the shop floor, he followed in her wake. She didn't look at him but looked at the cake table absentmindedly, she moved a cake slice a fraction intentionally making him wait for her reply just because he knew she could play this game of work politics for all its worth. "I will, *think it over. I'm off upstairs now.*" she spoke over her shoulder again as she departed the Cafe' in the direction of the escalators without looking back, like it or not she was the Manager, so she had a degree of freedom to do what she wanted, when she wanted. Will stood near the cake table having watched her leave and he let out a frustrated sigh at the games that played out on an almost daily basis at his employment these days, he really didn't care for them at all anymore. *'No wonder I enjoy a few glasses of wine after a couple of shifts in here during the week.'* he turned to look around the Cafe'. It had become quiet somewhat, coffee pod one was open and ready for action but there was little need for any of the others to be active for now. Kym was on the coffee machine at the ready finishing off a cappuccino for a waiting customer as Will headed over to her to tell her his news about the somewhat tense exchange between him and Joyce. "Oioi 'Firecracker' you causing trouble as always." Will stopped on the other side of the coffee station where there was a gap between the coffee grinder and the machine so Kym could see him, she grinned at his arrival. "You know me Willyboy, always do!" she winked at her best mate who felt better just being around her especially with everything that had occurred between him and Joyce. "So, I spoke to Joyce about *you know what*…" he began but Kym interrupted "don't tell me. I don't wanna know Mr." she then made it look like she needed to vigorously clean the coffee machine, Will wasn't giving up though so he went round the back section where customers picked up their coffees so Kym couldn't avoid him this way. Will wasn't looking forward to this, but he knew that she needed to be told about his potential transfer, he had tried to broach the subject with Kym only the other day and she had given him the same response as she had now, it was more than obvious she didn't want him to leave.

"Listen 'Firecracker'."

"I'm busy Will."

"No, you're not."

"I could be?"

"Well then I won't tell you about what just went down with *me and Joyce* then..." he turned to leave hoping his best friend would take the bait.

"Hold on a second!"

She called out to him which stopped Will dead in his tracks, he smiled to himself at Kym when she wanted to be clued in on the latest drama he had for her because he knew she lived for it as much as he did in this place despite his current feelings about his Employers. Turning back around to face her he saw her expectant face practically buzzing with curiosity. "So, you do wanna know what went down then hmm?" Will didn't move any closer just to tease Kym some more, but she placed her hands on her hips and gave him one of her mothering looks that could crack anyone. "Ok, ok enough with that face your pulling will you!" Will walked back over to the station then promptly filled Kym in on what had happened a few minutes ago, her attention never wavered from him as he explained away, luckily there were no customers waiting to be served by the Sasha on the till who was also keeping herself busy by filling up the tissue dispenser. Once he was finished, she was shaking her head in shared annoyance with him, "I'll tell you. I don't know what it is but them lot including Joyce seemed to have it right in the neck for you I swear Willyboy." Kym wiped the surface down again to make herself look busy as they both awaited the lunch rush to hit the Cafe', they only had about five minutes to go then midday was upon them all. "I know, it's like I'm asking for the moon or something right?" Will threw his arms up in exacerbation.

"More like blood from a stone Willyboy."

"Tell me something I don't know 'Firecracker'."

"Think she'll say yes?"

"Lord knows; bet you any money I have she's consulting with *'the Clique'* about this right now about it all."

"You think they'll try to change her mind?"

"Ha! Firecracker, it's *'the Clique'*. The unseen hand, the ones behind the Managers, the shadow behind the crown and all those ridiculous bullshit politics that go with it." Will finished as his arms dropped with a thud to his sides, he was at a loss as to what Joyce might say to him later or if she would say anything more about it at all. He knew that when it came to her and *'the Clique'*, they were the ones who had her ear plus her confidence; they held her in their grubby manipulative hands and clung on tightly for all their worth. They kept her close because Josie clearly played the friendship angle up even though for appearances sake Joyce had to look like she was the objective one when once again the majority of the Cafe' staff knew otherwise, the unspoken rules reared their ugly head to bite anyone in defiance which happened to be Will more or less since he questioned their motives on the odd occasion. After all these years here, he was nearly at his wits end though, he wasn't sure how much more he could take from all of it whilst just still falling short of full-time hours on his contract. Kym looked at her best friend's crestfallen face with sympathy; she decided to extend an Olive Branch to him. "You know I don't want you to go right? Purely for my own selfish reasons of course, that and your my friend Will." Kym spoke to him quietly as she leaned over the station on her tippy toes to pat him on the arm which got a smile of thanks in return, "I know 'Firecracker', you know it's because I need to do this otherwise I might not ever leave right?" Will tried to make it sound like he wasn't being unreasonable which Kym fully understood all too well, "I know Mr. I guess for me I am being a bit selfish, you do keep me going in this place after all..." she tried to raise his spirits some more. "You do the same for me, but that's not reason enough to stay." Will countered with the logic that he knew Kym would not be able to work around. Their friendship was as solid as anything between them but there were a few differences with their lives outside of the job. Will was in his early twenties and had the opportunity to go on to do other things, Kym was twenty years older than him, a single parent with three wonderful kids to provide for, two were adults but one was still a teenager, so Kym had this job to provide primarily for her family who came first always in her life. Will had this job because an old friend had helped him out all those years ago. Two vastly different reasons but through this job their friendship was a truly strong one that defied their ages or time, they were of little consequence to him or Kym. All that mattered was they loved their friendship fiercely yet deeply, they would both equally do anything to maintain it. Even if they didn't end up working together in the future anymore. "Who knows if she will even give my request the time-of-day 'Firecracker'?" Will shrugged his shoulders in mock defeat but a part of him was still holding out hope for anything, he was a staunch optimist at the end of the day. "Well, if she doesn't then you could explore the proper channels about fulfilling her job description? She cannot just fob you off. Throw it back in her face but do it the *right way*?" Kym had a new coffee order as a customer was ordering with Sasha at the till; she went to the machine so Will caught her eye to let her know he was heading off to clear some of tables. He busied himself with the furthest away cleaning station, so it was just him and his thoughts for companionship, he needed the time alone. Rather than worrying about what might not happen he gave in to the routine of work then got into a good groove of sorting out the leftover tray's customers brought him or left discarded on their tables. He forgot the time; he forgot about most things, he let his mind become a blank canvas that allowed him to relax. He didn't ponder the tense exchange between him, and Joyce any more than he had too which soothed him all the more. Before he knew it, he was well into the tail end of

the lunch rush a few hours later with most tables in the vicinity of
the furthest cleaning station full with customers all mixed up in
their own goings on, he heard out in the Food Department from the
smaller exit next to the cleaning station the throng of other
customers going about their daily excursions as well. He stood on
the shop floor amongst all of it for a few moments simply soaking
up the sights, the sounds, the activity, the atmosphere, the many
different people some regular, some not, all of it and Will for a
very small moment despite the underhand political side that came
with job let himself be truly at peace. But as always it only lasted
for a moment as he felt someone join him from behind, he felt their
presence approach as if trying to catch him out, but he was ready
for them and he turned, only to come face to face Joyce one again
entering through the smaller exit/entrance from Foods. *'Ok here
goes, round two is underway. Ding, ding.'* Will heard the wrestling
ring bell sound off in the deep recesses of his mind as he plastered
on a pleasant smile for his boss. Joyce had a smile on too, but Will
could tell it was all for show, she had something to tell him as her
shoulders were set. "So Will, I've been thinking about what you
asked of me a few hours ago." she wasn't looking at him now, but
she was doing her usual inspection of the tables smiling at some
customers she noticed as she went, she even gave another table a
casual wave who waved back at her. *'Yes you do that Joyce,
reminding me you're the one in charge I get it, I'm sure 'the
Clique' must have given you a good pep talk while you were*

upstairs shoring up their utterly twisted moral support and listening to their sweet nothings in your ear.' Will could see the visual of her airing her frustration about him to them, he didn't let the image stay in his mind for long, it made him feel queasy enough of them all conspiring and gossiping or a mixture of both. "As I was saying Will..." she now turned to look at him after her veiled table inspection, he waited patiently with his fixed smile still firmly in place "I think if you really want to transfer stores to Stratford then there's only one thing for it." she paused looking at him like it was obvious, Will was now none the wiser to what she was implying, he waited for her to elaborate some more "if you want to transfer, then I guess you're going to have to go and do a few hours work there. Of course you would have to go on one of your days off to do it *unpaid* if you're that serious about this idea of yours..." Joyce finished maintaining her casualness as she went to inspect the interior of the cleaning station behind him while Will was now rooted to the spot at what she had just stated as a simple matter of fact. It wasn't that she was suggesting he used up some of his day off or that it would be unpaid, but she was actually saying she might let him transfer if he was happy about working there, *'I can't fucking believe it.'* Will let the dumbstruck thought ground him in the moment as he turned to look at Joyce who was still inspecting the cleaning station. "Do you really mean that then Joyce?" he asked her as she walked past him without making eye contact, "oh yes Will." she called from over shoulder "Jim

Hendrickson works there as a Supervisor now so if you get in touch with him I am sure he will arrange something. I know you two had somewhat *special bond* when he worked here until he transferred to Stratford if I'm correct in my assessment?" Will had heard her tone of voice shift when she brought up Jim, he didn't like the insinuation at all, yet he refused to be goaded or poked by it on the shop floor by his designated boss of all people, it was beyond petty, it was a cheap shot if anything. It was callously meant on Joyce's behalf that much he could definitely tell. "So, you want me to text Jim then and arrange it Joyce?" Will asked as casually as he could, Joyce kept her back to him still acting like she was looking over the still rather busy Cafe' with her hands clasped firmly together behind her along with her shoulders still set. "Oh yes you do that by all means Will but one more thing also..." she then surprised him by doing a full one eighty turn to face him in a deadpan stare full of powerful intent along with a lowered voice with a clear hint of intimidation to it, "if you do end up transferring to Stratford *Will Hardley*. Don't ever think you will be welcome to return to Riverside. As far as I'm concerned once you're gone, you're out for good." Joyce then re-enacted her one eighty turn without a backwards glance at him marching off leaving Will truly shaken to his core. *'You absolute cold-hearted bitch Joyce Cooper. Quietly threatening a member of staff on the shop floor full of customers surrounding us? That's a new low even by your standards.'* Will retreated with his shocked thoughts into the sanctity of the furthest away cleaning station to gather himself, he breathed in and out deeply letting his partially shaking body calm down as one handheld onto the interior wall for support, Joyce certainly knew how to put the fear in her employees that's for sure. *'Guess I'd better get on the phone to text Jim about my news. Clearly my bridges have been burnt for me here.'* he thought to himself as he came out of the cleaning station to get on with the tables trying to forget about Joyce's crystal-clear threat. They may have stalemated earlier but Joyce had won this latest battle between them with extremely efficient yet decisive action, looks like that transfer really was Will's only viable option out of the Cafe' now.

*

Five Days Later.

Monday.

8:58 am.

Will stepped off the escalator with an unusually positive spring in his step. He was happy. Truly optimistically happy for once in an exceedingly long time. He felt like he even had renewed hope coursing through his veins instead of blood, which was how elated he was feeling. He walked into the Downstairs Cafe' with the continued bouncy spring and a beaming smile despite it being

Monday morning when he would normally be craving his bed rather than being in work right now. He scanned the surroundings of the Cafe, Coralie was trying to peek over Joyce's shoulder at the staff rota as the Manager ignored her while talking to Emily the young trainee manager from Will's Restaurant days, Nat was just leaving the Kitchen Area to make her way over to coffee pod one with Sasha so they could be ready to receive customers when they opened in a few minutes, and Will's all-time favourite person Josie Sybille was in the Kitchen chatting away to her trusty lieutenant Trudy who was unclasping her school spectacles from the bridge of her nose like she always did, Tonye was taking her sweet time adjusting the cake slices minutely along with the tongs like she couldn't find the right place for them even though she was obviously done baking now so she had nothing else actually meaningful workwise to do. It was all in its tired repetitive routine that Will usually loathed seeing first thing on shift that would normally annoy him immediately for most of the day, but not today. Quite frankly nothing could spoil his jubilant mood after the weekend he had just had. After the threat from Joyce last week he had gotten in touch with Jim at Stratford Store and Jim had come through for him. Saturday came up and Will had found himself doing a three-hour unpaid shift at the In-House Store in East London. Jim had been on a day off, but Will had mucked in from ten am till one pm helping the staff out and he had loved every second of it. The staff were more than welcoming, the customers were varied yet delightful and he had not seen a single regular from Riverside on a day out up in the City to change their routines a little. The coffee grinders may have been a different design, but the work was the same, but it had been much more fun than here which had helped persuade him that seeking a transfer was right for him despite having to pay more for a daily train commute into the City instead of out. The Cafe' today would have a hard time trying to kill his mood as he made his way over to Nat and Sasha on the coffee pod. Nat was already staring at him with her curious eyes knowing there was something going on with her more than cheerful co-worker this morning. "Either one of two things have happened to you this weekend Will." she was folding her arms as she continued looking at his still smiling face with more curiosity, "and what would these *two things* be exactly my dear Natalie pray tell?" Will winked at her willing to play the guessing game; she unfolded her arms with a wagging finger in his direction as she attempted the challenge before her.

"Ok, number one. You either had a shag this weekend..."

Will laughed loudly whilst shaking his head at this first guess that was very much incorrect. This only egged Nat on more whilst Sasha was observing them with amused fascination.

"Number two..." Nat paused with her forefinger and thumb on her chin as she tried to think of a good guess, Will waited but was bouncing up and down of the spot very much enjoying the moment occur between them both.

"What's number two Nat?"

"Bear with."

"You're certainly no Tilly from *Miranda* the sitcom now are you Nat..." Will teased his co-worker some more just because he could; she ignored him while Sasha's head went back and forth between. Then at last Nat had a number two guess for him.

"Number two you...got absolutely plastered on booze?"

"Wrong on both counts I win!" Will clapped his hands eagerly as Nat became annoyed that she had lost the guessing game, Will offered her some form of consolation, however.

"Nat my darling. I paid a visit to good ol Stratford Store you see..."

"And how did that exactly go for you *Mr Hardley*?" an all too familiar voice chimed in behind him all of a sudden causing Will to nearly jump out of his skin in fright, turning around he came face to face with Joyce who wasn't as severe looking as she had been last week when their last tense exchanged had occurred. "Ah good morning Joyce." Will began then stopped abruptly, Josie was lingering about a foot away behind Joyce like a bad smell as he found her eyeing him up in her usual manner, all posturing like she could do what she wanted as always. Will refocused his attention back on their Manager rather than pay the manipulative bitch any more attention. "Joyce, Stratford was quite an interesting experience I must say. Everyone was really welcoming as well so I think my minds kind of been made up for me after Saturday if you catch my drift?" Will finished as the first trickle of customers started entering the Cafe which him and Joyce both took notice of. "Well I think that does *indeed* change things up for us all then doesn't it Will." Joyce was looking at the amount of customers piling in for the breakfast rush rather than giving Will her full attention, she was talking in his direction regardless, "either way…" she now looked at him somewhat passively "…I think there are things we both need to discuss when Niall pays us a visit later today." she had moved to leave the Cafe' with Josie about to follow but Will hot on her heels at the mention of Niall. The fact that she had mentioned or even brought up Niall at all gave him reason for pause in his mind. Niall Rogers was their Regional Manager for the South-East Region of England, the In-Store Company utilised them, they had to look after a certain number of stores amongst their assigned Region. Niall was a well-known entity of course who was likeable man, but his status affords him considerable sway, he was the top boss really in these parts. The Store Manager reported to him whenever he visited which was every couple of months when it fell in his schedule by contractual obligation. When he did visit however he always made it his first priority to stop in Cafe' to catch up with Joyce which then became a full on over an hour chat that was probably less about work and more about their social lives, another thing everyone knew that went on but never bothered to rock the boat, not when it came to Joyce and her iron grip. "Why is Niall here today then Joyce?" Will kept his voice level whilst ignoring Josie's probing gaze still on him as she folded her arms with mock impatience, Joyce just cocked her head strangely at Will like it was obvious. "Well you know his visits normally fall at the beginning of the week and I think I need to explain to him how you're jumping ship Will, I know he is rather interested in your placement here after all. Now, if you'll excuse us, me and Josie here have our fifteen-minute breakfast break to attend too." Joyce finished without waiting for a reply as she joined Josie who hadn't changed her facial expression in Will's direction, but she followed Joyce out of the Unit as the breakfast rush hour got well underway. Will watched them leave not knowing whether to be nervous about Niall's upcoming arrival today, *'what's she going to do now? Utilize every dirty trick she knows in the book to throw at me?'* the thought unnerved him as he could really do with Kym his 'Firecracker' being by his side right now, she was on her day off however. "Will..." a voice came from behind him which he turned to find a fidgety Coralie who still didn't have the rota, "sorry Will it's just that I need you on tables this morning if that's ok?" she asked him cautiously, Will shrugged his shoulders uncaring about what the day might bring now that he knew Joyce was stirring her witches cauldron once again. "Yeah, yeah I'll do them...it's not like people want me around anyway." he cast his eyes to the ground giving in to whatever predicament was coming for him later today, he went to move past Coralie when all of a sudden she grabbed his arm to stop him walking off, he looked at her hand then to her face and saw something he hadn't seen before. Her eyes were ablaze with a fire, widened and full of purpose. "Will listen to me right now." She stared right into his own eyes and he could not tear his own set from hers, he dared not too since he was all of a sudden fearful of whatever repercussions might spill out of Coralie's mouth. "You need to understand something. Joyce may be giving you a hard time recently, but she wants to you to stay believe it or not. I will be sitting in on this meeting today with Niall at his request from the message we got from him, we will be discussing a few agendas and you are one of them, that does not mean we are ready to cut our losses with you, you just need to know Niall probably doesn't want you to go, so be grateful that there are forces in this place that want you to stay despite whatever people or co-workers you don't get on with." Coralie finished by letting go of his arm. *'Damn, you're gonna be one fierce Supervisor once you've found your footing Mrs.'* he thought respectfully of her doing what she had just done for him with that searingly honest statement, he'd never known Coralie to lay her cards on the table before ever until now. "Coralie, I don't know what too..." but she stopped him with a raised hand similar to what Joyce did, she was starting to learn very quickly now. "Don't say anything but just turn around and get on with tables." she indicated by turning around herself to see Emily pouring over the rota that Joyce had relinquished to her like it was toy and almost marched over to pry it out of her hands if she could. Will was still surprised by her admission to him gave a soft tut then went to the cleaning station closest to the Dishwasher Area to set it up as some of the customers had started settling down on their tables with their breakfast orders. The rest of the morning passed by in quick succession, no customers disturbed him, and he didn't disturb them, in fact he was left alone to his own devices without a care in the world which suited him fine. Joyce didn't return after her fifteen-minute breakfast break with Josie who probably escaped to her little kingdom in the Upstairs Cafe' so that was one less thing to worry about. Nat tried to catch his eye once or twice, but she was equally too busy with constant coffee orders on the machine to get much more of a conversation in with him, Will knew she had more than likely observed what had gone with him and Joyce plus Coralie too but there was no time when work was getting busier for them both as the minutes of the shift ticked on by unabated. He had lost track of the time until it must have been midday as Coralie was looking at Emily who had just received a message on the work phone, he picked up their conversation as he walked past them with a dirty tray of leftovers.

"You'll never guess what." Emily was incredulous.

"Don't tell me…" Coralie responded.

"Oh yes. Judy Howard has got *another* bloody six-week sick note from her Doctor!"

"Again? I know she is a lesbian but what on earth is she even saying or doing to her Doctor to get these sick notes even!"

"Trust me Coralie, it's probably better we don't know, you ok there Will?" Emily asked him as she hadn't noticed he had stopped walking to eavesdrop on their chat about the constantly off sick and unreliable piss-taker that was Judy Howard. *'Woops.'* he thought mischievously then he turned around with a big smile in place to cover his naughty behaviour. "Oh yes sorry about that, just giving the legs a quick breather you see" he started picking up each leg to give them stretch hoping it was enough of a cover story, Emily smirked at him while Coralie just looked like he was being weird for the sake of it, laughing it off Will turned around and walked away from the two ladies before they could suss him out further. *'That was a close call, but bloody Judy not coming in again, she needs to be sacked already.'* he thought to himself as he dropped off what felt like his one millionth tray of discarded food and cutlery for the end of the morning. Breakfast rush had come and gone but lunch rush was now beginning, Mondays were always the days the other workers in most of the shops in Riverside always came in to get their pick me ups readying themselves for another hard slog of a week selling whatever products they sold in their shops to the thousands of people who came through Riverside's doors day in, day out. Today the whole work force of the Complex seemed to be descending upon the Cafe' or the adjacent Food Department next door to them, for Will it was about to step up another gear with probably little or no help on the way. The first hour between midday and one went by like a shot, he was starting to get hungry, but he knew that two was going to be his break time more than anything, he checked with Emily who confirmed his suspicion's so he went back to tables to do what he could, then Will saw him. It was Niall Rogers the man himself. He was a tall one in his late forties with a completely bald head, an easy smile but always wearing a crisp suit that didn't have a crease in sight, today he had gone for a charcoal grey suit with a deep red button shirt with a matching tie, and he cut a fine path as he saw Will making a beeline for him from the tables. "Well if it isn't my favourite table cleaner." Niall teased Will dryly with an outstretched hand, Will couldn't help but laugh aloud at this as he took the hand being offered and found a strong firm shake which he copied, Will had always liked this feature about Niall when he started with a joke as an introduction rather than keeping it formal, it was unconventionally comforting. "Niall, always a pleasure to see you at Riverside, how's the rest of the Region doing?" they released the handshake as Niall scanned the Cafe' quickly before responding to Will's question, "oh you know Will same old, but I run a tight ship as you well know of course. Now I see Coralie over there so I'd better grab her for our meeting with Joyce..." he moved off in the Supervisors direction leaving Will to the tables, he watched his back walking away now all of a sudden feeling nervous. His fate was being left in the hands of three people for all he knew, and Will didn't know what to think or feel so he decided to switch off and knuckle down with the ever-increasing workload. Luckily, Emily came and gave him a hand so that made it easier, but Will found himself watching as Coralie and Niall chatted while clearly waiting for Joyce. When she arrived back on the floor Will could hear his heart hammering in his chest. This was it. They were about to begin their meeting with him on the list and there was nothing he could do to stop it now; they all took a booth further away from the cleaning station so as not to be disturbed and the talking began in earnest. What was worse was he couldn't even make out one bit of what they were saying to one another. It was torture just watching. "Fuck me sideways, this could go south really quickly and it's all my fault!" Will murmured to himself as he stared at the talking group whilst he sorted through the trays Emily was bringing him in and he was getting slower with each tray he attempted to sort, Emily brought a new one to him in the cleaning station and she snorted at his slow pace plus how he was now ignoring her presence then followed his gaze to the chatting threesome. She looked back at Will then did something she normally would never do, she poked him hard in the arm to draw his attention away. "Ouch Em! What the bloody hell did you do that for?" Will rubbed his arm vigorously as he looked at the now laughing Emily who covered her mouth not even trying hide her amusement.

"Sorry Will it's just…"

"Just what?"

"Well it's just, you, really." Emily shrugged her shoulders and stepped into the small cleaning station with Will who looked at her enquiringly but at a loss as to where she was going with this. "What about me Emily then?" he joined at the sorting table with three holes in it, two for recycling, one for glass bottles only. "Oh Will, you really need to chill out you know." she gave another small chuckle as she sorted the tray on the side as he looked at her some more still none the wiser to the train of thought. "Ok Emily, you wanna fill me in? Cause I am pulling a real blank right now." Will rubbed the back of his neck as Emily got a new tray from the trolley stack and began sorting that one without looking at him, she shook her head tutting with a smile like he was missing the most obvious punchline ever. "Will, Joyce doesn't want you to go, Coralie told me that she told you the same thing, but you really do have to understand Joyce's position amongst all of this…" Emily stopped as Will made an overly loud noise as if clearing his throat out, but it was to stop her dead in her tracks as to where she was going with this, Will would certainly not be pulled in the sympathy direction by the trainee that much was certain. "Oh Emily, seriously…" he began as he folded his arms looking at her in the small space they occupied, the customers on the tables were all engrossed in their own goings on as well. "Not you. I can handle Coralie giving me the blunt truth but your gonna play the little miss innocent act to get me to behave and then fall back in to line like a good little schoolboy? I left school nine years ago also for your information." Will stopped for a second as Emily turned to face him having finished the tray off in quick succession, she was still smirking at him, it wasn't from a condescending place, it was from her own genuine amusement at his forthrightness.

"Will I only mean…"

"Oh, I know *exactly* what you mean Emily Arms. Your still just that precious little girl who is now a trainee Manager who wants to do her very level best to not be a trainee anymore and Joyce has told you about me wanting to transfer out of here as soon as possible so she weaponised you to butter me up and here you are right now doing just that." Will stopped for a moment unfolding his arms as Emily's humorous smirk became a wide-eyed face of silent shock as Will then exhaled before going in for the kill "let me be frank now. You, Joyce, Coralie, damn even that sly *bitch* Josie Sybille cannot or will not threaten me into staying if I am not happy. I will do what is necessary for my own peace of mind, I will do whatever it takes to make a progressive change in my life for the better even if that means quitting this job and making myself an unemployed hot mess in the process. five years of loyalty to this place had gotten me *jack shit* and now…"

"And now what Will hmm?"

The voice stopped Wil dead in his tracks. Will didn't want to turn around, but he knew he must, so he did. There was Niall in all his imposing glory along with his still sharp suit standing just outside the cleaning station his arms folded regarding him with an almost quizzical look. "Will…" Niall unfolded his arms "follow me please." he finished by setting off in the direction of the Food Department without a backwards glance, he turned the corner and Will knew he would be waiting patiently for him out there. Turning to look back at Emily who now smirking at him again, but it wasn't as if he was in trouble with her, it was the sympathetic look she was also giving him. "Will, I was just gonna say…" she started to exit the cleaning station as Will stared at the floor willing it to open up and swallow him whole "I don't want you to go either, and Niall is about to convince you of why you should stay as well." she finished by giving a soft laugh and shaking her head at the ceiling as she moved off away from him, he watched her leave then called out to her.

"Sorry for my outburst Em!".

He was making his way to where Niall would be waiting just round the corner, but she just waved in his direction with her back to him, Will knew they were cool. She was probably enjoying this far more than she let on. Will shuffled out into the Food Department round the corner and found Niall standing there waiting patiently taking a phone call on his mobile, he acknowledged Will with a quick one-minute gesture, so he nodded and waited nervously on the spot. *'Come on floor, swallow me up now. I deserve it.'* he looked down again as the floor did not yield to his request remaining firmly closed, *'fine, fuck you then floor.'* he cursed it with his thoughts as Niall finished his call. "No, no I told that poxy manager where to stick it last week! No that is a definite *no* from me. Oh really? Well as the *Regional Manager* for the South East I will be making some Managerial changes if they don't like it. End of discussion." Niall put the phone down without a goodbye then pocketed it in quick succession then turned ninety degrees to face the still nervous Will, Niall once again folded his arms eyeing him up and down. *'Great here goes, I'm fucked either way. And not in the good way I normally like.'* Will readied himself for the dressing down he was about to receive from the top dog, then Niall surprised him.

"What exactly as we gonna do about you then cheeky?"

Niall casually asked him without a hint of steel in his voice, Will was speechless. He was sure Niall was having him on.

"Aren't you mad at me right now Niall?"

"Why would I be Will?"

"Well, what I was just saying to poor Emily in the cleaning station…"

"Was a lot of pent-up feelings that just happened to come out like a word salad." Niall waved his hand as if he could wave the whole situation off like a magic trick, Will still wasn't fully convinced however. "Niall, seriously. I spoke to her like crap, and *I knew* I was as well!" Will almost began pleading to be formally told off, Niall simply wouldn't go there. "Will Hardley listen to me now, I've spoken to Coralie and Joyce…"

"Oh, joy to the bloody world…"

"And I have smoothed things over with them believe it or not. I like you Will. I may not be here that often, but I like you and what you do here. Now Joyce and you may have had some words *exchanged* quite recently, correct?" Niall made sure Will noticed his pointed look this time which made Will reply with a silent curt nod of understanding, satisfied Niall pressed on. "Now listen well Mr, you are liked here, furthermore you are *wanted* here. You have a good relationship with your customers and their going to make you stay put young man, stay, and show us all how good you can, stay and they will sort you out. Stay and just pay the people you don't get along with no mind and they'll do the same." Niall finished as he took out his phone to answer a text, Will had one thing to say however.

"That's easier said than done Niall…"

Niall was walking past him to head back into the Café'. He stopped at Will's latest comment, he looked up from his phone and out into the days happenings outside the Store whilst placing his right hand on Will's right shoulder without looking at him. "Sometimes in life Will, we come across people we will never be friends with, we will never know their lives out of work, we will never know their comforting gaze or their ways of thinking. But we will have to work with them I'm afraid regardless of our age, race, gender, orientation, or background. That's one of life's great cruelties that we have to learn to live with, it's not easy and its certainly never simple." he let of Will's shoulder to adjust his tie that didn't need adjusting in the first place, "but we learn to live with it either way. You'll be alright mate, now stay. That's an order." Niall didn't even glance at Will as he walked briskly back into the Café' the way he came leaving him standing there silently as customers and staff alike went about their own business. Life went on for them as it went on for him. Breathing in sharply then exhaling slowly Will turned promptly on his feet and walked about into the Café' as well to find it still just as busy as he had left it. Niall was collecting whatever he had left on the table he had sat at with Coralie and Joyce as he chatted some more Joyce while Coralie sorted the tables. Will watched them chat some more then Niall bid his goodbyes without even trying to find him, Joyce looked around the busy Café' until her eyes fell upon him, she made her way over not too quickly, she didn't dawdle either way. She came to stand next to Will and they both observed the busy place of work before them, they both remained silent for a moment soaking up the place and its energy.

Joyce was the one who decided to break the tension between them.

"I take it Niall and you had a good chat then?"

"It was certainly, a *chat* of sorts yes."

"I can only imagine with a character like Niall".

"That he is and then some".

"Will?"

"Joyce?"

This time they both looked at each other in unison then they stopped to look away laughing quickly before getting down to the honest conversation they were about to have. "Ok I'll start then." Joyce shook her shoulders turning to face Will on the floor of the Café' "I, may have said some things to last week that could be considered *out of term* shall we agree for arguments sake?" Joyce gave him a look that all too well said she was allowing herself to admit in a small way that she may have overstepped her boundaries as Will's Manager. *'My, my Joyce. Letting your guard down? Out of guilt or because Niall told you too? Probably both I bet.'* Will looked her up and down quickly again letting his Manager know that he was doing as such and she didn't say anything or look at him in a certain intimidating way to stop him from doing so as well.

"You definitely made you feelings very clear to me last week that much is clear to the pair of us Joyce."

"Yes, well I feel like I went a touch too far Will."

"Good to know we agree upon something for once. What are we going to do about my predicament then?"

He said it bluntly with no emotion behind the wording, he went for the jugular without being goaded, surprisingly Joyce didn't react negatively to his bluntness, she maintained the neutrality between quite well in fact. Now she looked Will up and down briefly which he let her do then she clasped her hands together and twiddled her thumbs, she didn't have the staff rota on her person either which surprised Will internally. "Here's what we are gonna do Will" she began as she looked around the Café' again "I'm going to head up to the Admin Office later today and get on the system to m*odify* your Contracted Hours, how does that sound to you?" she looked back at him directly in the eyes, but it wasn't a challenge, it was a real question to him rather than her putting him in his place. "That depends on…" Will took a step closer and folded his arms as he looked her in the eyes as well "…what exactly are you modifying them for?" he asked without any tone to his own voice, he wanted to come across as calm as possible. Joyce stepped closer to him as well.

"Well, we will be upping hours essentially Will."

"You don't mean?"

"Oh yes indeed I do, congratulations Will. You will be *officially* classed as a Full-Time Employee after today, wanna shake on it?" Joyce extended a waiting hand to him as he looked at it then back to her, he took her hand and found a firmly confident handshake plus a small smile which he reciprocated. "I guess there is a condition to me becoming Full Time staff however?" he asked as they released the handshake equally, Joyce was nodding her head at his line of thought.

"Quite correct, this mean Stratford is off the tables for you. Understood?"

"Understood completely."

"Good, your gonna have to text Jim back about this latest development then." Joyce walked away then stopped to quickly turn back to add something further on "oh, also about Jim?" she raised a finger to the air trying to find the correct words. "What about Jim, Joyce?" Will asked his Manager as she seemed to find the correct words she wanted "Tell him…" she began then paused again, Will was ready for whatever snide remark she was about to make however, *'come on, let me have it. Keep it to just a small casual homophobic remark though bear in mind Joyce.'* the thought flashed through his mind, he squashed it quickly.

Joyce was ready now with what he had to say. "Tell him, that I am sorry we couldn't let Stratford Store poach you, their missing out on a good worker I guess." she finished with a simple shrug as Will's mind seemed to implode that his Manager had paid him a compliment, a veiled one yes but it was still a compliment regardless. "I will, *absolutely* pass that along to him thank you Joyce. Just one more thing though…" Joyce had started to turn away then stopped in her tracks looking back at him again, "what is it Will? Make it quick as we are busy after all." she gestured to the still full Café'.

"What about Josie, Joyce? You know exactly what I mean as well".

He waited for his reply and kept his arms calmly at his sides rather than folding them even though he was desperate to do so, Joyce however did not keep him in suspense for long at all. "Don't worry about her Will, leave it with me. Now get back to these tables with Coralie please." Will's Manager then ended the conversation by marching in the direction of the Kitchen Area and promptly picked up the staff rota to inspect it meticulously as if nothing had transpired between them both a few moments ago. Will could not believe it, Full Time hours, a sound vote of confidence with some sage advice from the Regional Manager and his own co-workers wanting him to stay too. It all seemed too good to be true as he walked to the cleaning station to find a rather flustered Coralie trying to deal with a lot of trays.

"There you are, give us a hand. I'm well back logged here!" Coralie loaded him a full tray of leftovers and Will knuckled down to help his Supervisor out. The next forty-five minutes flew by for the them both as they probably did a few good circuits of the tables together, but they managed it and it calmed down as well as customers departed to spend their hard-earned money, Will didn't even realise all the breaks were delayed including his own until they both physically stopped to take stock of what was left and to both their equal surprised, not much was left to actually deal with. Coralie looked at Will then placed both of her hands on her hips seemingly satisfied they had done a good job together, but she knew what was else was on his mind right there and then.

"So, you got what you wanted, and we got to keep you ah Will?"

"Yeah, I guess you did, that alright with you Coralie?"

"You know me, do your job right and it's all good…"

"…Unless your name is Judy Howard right?"

Will looked at her with a funny look as she returned it with a bug-eyed looked of her own. "Oh, do not get me started on that *lazy cow*!" Coralie began as she launched into a full-on ranting session about the ever absent lesbian co-worker. Will listened to her rant as a smile began to spread from one cheek to the other as he looked around his place of work as it was calming down some more, he may well have almost left this place but for now, he was staying.

And that wasn't such a bad thing today.

Seven

September 26th, 2016.

The Downstairs Café'.

Monday.

1:33 pm.

It had been a full fortnight since the news had broken amongst the rest of the Staff about Will's official transfer to Stratford Store. The questions he received on a near daily basis from most of his co-workers since the news was announced were persistently repetitive. He had answered them in equal measure as repetitively as possible in kind to the point he was ready to walk over to any available wall and slowly start hitting his head against it, such was the mind-numbing nature of the same questions asked of him in a different way each time, he was essentially over it and wished all the others would just stop now. He was leaving Riverside Store for a new start. Nothing more, nothing less. *'If I don't leave now, then I'll never leave. I can't become that person or worse, one of 'the Clique' who stay because it's simply all they want to know and be.'* Will kept reminding himself repeatedly as he made an extra dry cappuccino for one of his regular customers. One of the things that had warmed his heart was the reaction of his regular customers when he announced to them that he was transferring. Each and every one of them had all reacted uniquely every time much to his own amusement. Happy, sad, surprised, numb, perplexed. Some had even surprised Will further by not being the least bit surprised at all but simply shrugging their shoulders, wishing him all the best for the future then going back to whatever business they were conducting. Those kind of reactions kept him grounded yet also reminded him that for some people who you serve repeatedly over the years, not everyone has certain attachments like others do. It was refreshingly human of them and made Will look all the more forward to his late October end date. Kym had more or less come round to accepting that he was leaving for his own sanity which made things easier between them that they had now progressed to the point that they were starting to joke about what he would or wouldn't miss at Riverside. "Your telling me that you're not gonna

miss making her *extra-extra dry* cappuccino Willyboy?" Kym
teased him in a lowered voice from the till point with a cheeky grin
fully in place as she readied herself for more customers
approaching them. "My dear 'Firecracker', are you kidding me or
actually being serious?" Will asked in his own hushed voice so the
regular couldn't hear they were discussing her as she used a
teaspoon to inspect her extra dry frothy coffee. The regular in
question was a stalwart of the Downstairs Café', she was known
for even requesting only a few select people to make her coffee the
way she ultimately liked it. Curiously over the years she was very
vocal about having a lactose problem so she couldn't have milk,
yet without fail her coffee order had never changed once in all the
years Will had served her, which was an extra dry cappuccino, all
froth that Will had to physically spoon from the milk jug into the
cup along with the espresso shot. The froth, however, was of
course dairy milk based every single time without fail which she
insisted was fine despite her lactose dietary problem. "Oh yes, this
is lovely as always Will, thank you!" the regular customer gave a
curt nod of approval as she walked off to find a vacant seat whilst
Will smiled in acknowledgement as Kym sniggered overtly from
the till point which he tried to ignore but couldn't help but grin
back at her. "The answer to that question my dear 'Firecracker'…"
he began wiping down the surface of the coffee machine in
preparation for the next order incoming as Kym glanced over at
him again "…is hell to the fucking no! I will not miss making her

thoroughly messed up coffee order." He finished his brief clean down as Kym inputted the next order from the batch of new customers at the till as she suppressed a much louder laugh at Will's remarks. He listened in on what they were ordering silently, then got to work on the two decaf lattes, surrendering himself to the routine of coffee-making as he looked around the Café'. Everything was ticking along in what was surprisingly a low-key lunch rush for a Monday. Everyone was in their place, undisturbed like the well-oiled machine it was, all were playing their role adequately. For just a brief moment it was a routine Will quite liked despite the passive-aggressive politics that very much went on behind the scenes that he was now itching to leave behind come late October. As he poured the hot milk into the cups to mix in with the rancid decaf coffee, he saw some movement all of a sudden at the entrance of the Café' in the form of a co-worker who had been keeping their distance since he had dropped the news of his imminent departure from the Store. It was Jan Betty with an empty crate from the Upstairs Café' clearly in search of some more stock that she was going to take without even asking Coralie if it was alright to do so. Such was the arrogance of 'the Clique' and their ways of conducting themselves. As Will handed the two decaf lattes over to the now waiting customers at the back of coffee pod two he couldn't help but have some old memories creep up on him that he hadn't remembered in a long time. The emergence of them made him physically shiver just for a quick moment. Kym being the ever observant one spotted his reaction almost immediately. "You alright? What's up?" She folded her arms as she looked at him uncertainly as Will joined her at the till nodding his head slowly without looking at his best friend.

"Oh, I'm fine 'Firecracker'."

"Yeah? Then why you acting weird all of a sudden?"

"Oh, it's nothing really…"

"Looks like something to me Will?"

"We have a visitor from upstairs Kym." Will used his head to indicate Jan Betty going about her business of taking what was clearly now far too many sandwiches and toasties from the fridge as Coralie watched her from afar with the clipboard in her hands as Jan ignored everyone around her then promptly left the Café without a backwards glance, Coralie put the clipboard down in frustration and marched out towards the back fridges to replenish the stock Jan had taken without even doing the courtesy of asking in the first place. For Will it was just one of those small things he would not be missing when he finally departed Riverside. Kym looked up at him then back to the entrance where Jan had just left confused at what Will was alluding too.

"Am I missing something completely obvious? Or am I just plain stupid?"

"Nah its ok, its nothing really."

"Well, I'll say it again, it looks like something to me Will."

"it was a long time ago after all 'Firecracker'."

Will went back to the coffee machine slowly and began wiping it down absentmindedly, but Kym was now looking at him with her still folded arms, her eyes narrowed then they widened in surprise as she started putting two and two together. She looked at the empty entrance Jan had departed from only momentarily ago then looked back at Will who was still wiping down the coffee machine again for no reason as he was very much lost in his memories. "God I should have realised when you shivered all of a sudden." Kym unclasped her folded arms and place them on her hips as she addressed Will directly, he looked around at her having been pulled out his stupor.

"Sorry?"

"You."

"Me, 'Firecracker'?"

"Yes, you. I just figured out what all that was with Jan."

"Oh god. You're not referring to…"

"I definitely am referring to that *incident* Will Hardley. How could I forget when I was actually there for it…"

*

August 4th, 2015.

Tuesday.

11:21 am.

Summer had been a hot and muggy affair which meant the Café'
wasn't much of a hub of activity during the week besides what was
guaranteed to be busy weekends as it was the annual six-weeks
holiday for the majority of school children in the UK. They
descended on Riverside like a plague pretty consistently when each
weekend came around in packs unless their parents were able to
take them off for a sunny holiday in Europe or wherever they
chose to jet off too. Come Monday when it was a quiet one, the
rest of the staff had to keep busy in the Café' which is what Will
was trying to do currently on Dishwasher when very little washing
actually needed to be done. "Fuck me, it's a so humid today!" Will
was wafting his work shirt to get some air circulation going as an
unexpected hot flush overtook him, the steam emitted from the
Dishwasher after a standard cleaning cycle did not help matters in
the slightest. Still wafting his shirt as much as he humanly could
Will found himself still with a sweaty forehead and a sticky back
that for once he was not appreciating at all in work, in his personal
life that would be a different more enjoyable tale all together. But
work was not the place to be perspiring in this August humidity.

Jan Betty all of a sudden entered the Dishwasher Area disturbing his attempts to try and cool down. "Ah Will, I see your burning up in this muggy weather just as much as the rest of us I see." Jan chuckled to herself as Will turned to face her, "Oh yeah Jan tell me about it! This Dishwasher has got me sweating in places I'm normally not accustomed too I tell ya!" Will tore off some nearby kitchen towel to dry his still sweating forehead as Jan continued hovering in the doorway between the Kitchen and Dishwasher Areas. "Sorry was there something you needed also?" he asked her as he binned the used tissue, "Oh, yes sorry could you bring me and Kym out a full trolley of crockery when you've got a second?" Jan asked earnestly as Will nodded his head with a simple thumbs up, "Oh cheers Will, see you shortly on pod one." with that Jan left to return to the coffee station leaving Will to it. He couldn't help but smile to himself a little as he got a crockery trolley ready for Jan. After his less than six months of working in the old pre-refurbished Café' with the controlling ways of *'the Clique'* he had found some sort of common ground with Jan Betty, granted she was a well-entrenched member of that group having worked with most of them for many years, but she had always near enough consistently shown Will some form of kindness plus an ease of chatting to him as they had worked together in that close-quartered environment. Even after the refurbishment she had always had time to acknowledge him whereas others of her conceited friendship circle chose to not even fully see him or give him just the barest of hellos when he came in to start his shift at nine in the morning when they had all been probably meandering together because they could on their cushty six till two early starts that no one else got an option to have those kinds of shifts as they had all secured them well in advance because they could manipulate people like Joyce Cooper to their hearts content almost too easily. It had gotten to the point that Will would rather stay away from them at this point, except for people like Jan. She was probably one of the very rare exceptions he could allow in these circumstances. Having double-checked the trolley was ready, Will wheeled it out of the Dishwasher Area passing Nat being ever diligent in the Kitchen as she filled in some paperwork to keep herself also busy as it was still more quiet than usual, they both nodded at each other silently without needing to say anything to one another as Will carried on wheeling over the crockery to coffee pod one where Jan and Kym were chatting away without a care to be had as no customers were in need of their services as of yet. "Here we go ladies, one very full trolley of crockery." Will politely interrupted the chatting ladies who look around at the sound of his voice.

"Ah thanks Will".

"Little star you are Willyboy."

"Aw shucks girls, stop you'll make me blush!" Will got a smattering of laughter from the twosome as he took their spare empty trolley away back to the Dishwasher Area. He deposited it back in the vacant spot waiting for him then looked down the narrow area that was still his designated job for the next hour if not longer. There was absolutely nothing needed of him, no cutlery, plates, or kitchen dishes in need of a good scrubbing, he was at this moment a floater without a purpose. *'Ah sod it, I'll go join in on the chat with Jan and Kym.'* Will decided internally turning an ever purposeful one-eighty then almost marching out of the Dishwasher Area in search of a better conversation with two people he knew he got along with. Joining them promptly they were well into their chat, the few customers in the Café' already were seated to their hearts content, it was a thoroughly dull Tuesday morning. "Oioi ladies, mind if I join you both?" Will announced himself as he entered pod one to the softly laughing duo who both turned to smile at him.

"Ah, no problem Will, we're keeping ourselves entertained here."

"Why am I not surprised your joining us Willyboy? It's really bloody boring so far right?"

"God tell me about it 'Firecracker', I have zero things to do on Dishwash, so I thought I'd come see what we're all chatting about?" Will folded his arms and leaned slightly against the till point area just relaxing a touch, "oh nothing to serious are we Jan? We're just comparing how different it was for us lot in 'The Restaurant' to the girls when they were down here in the old Café', before we all became one team anyway." Kym was labelling up all the bottles of open syrup flavours as Jan watched her whilst nodding in agreement.

"Oh yeah it was laugh in that old Café' set up I must say Kym, I'm sure your lot upstairs had a good time as well though?"

"Oh, well, Will would know when he re-joined us from you all downstairs, right Mr?

Sensing the opening to engage by his ever-faithful bestie, he jumped into the conversation smoothly as if on cue. "Oh of course. I won't lie, I'd gotten used to working in the Café' by this point with Jan and the others but after a few weeks it was like getting back on that old bicycle you haven't ridden in a long time. Kind of felt like no time had even passed at all really." Will had released his arms relaxing further then he stopped allowing himself to go further, Jan had his full attention all of a sudden. She was still smiling, Kym had her back to her, Will however was part facing her from the till point, so he saw her shift in her posture, in a split second after he began speaking about his time back upstairs Jan had her shoulders almost stiffened, her smile had faltered just a touch and she was shifting her weight from side to side very slowly as if she had almost become uncomfortable in the direction the conversation was heading. As soon as it had happened Will had blinked and she had reasserted herself to how she was, relaxed with poise, almost like Will had imagined it yet he knew fully well in himself he had not at all.

'Now what was that about?'

He internally noted of Jan as he chose to ignore her awkwardness. "…once you settled in upstairs though Will it was a good time right?" Kym gave him a quick smile across her left shoulder as she was finishing up her labelling, she brought him back into the here and now.

"Hell, yeah Mrs, we had some memorable times up that place, didn't we?"

"Ha, that doesn't even cover it Willyboy, some of the customers we had though were something else entirely! Bet you had a good reliable crowd of regulars down here as well Jan?"

"Oh, we definitely did Kym, they weren't too put out when this whole place got refurbished as they knew all the old Café' lot would be staying, even the ones who had left before the refurb like yourself Will…"

"Sorry, I don't think I quite follow you Jan?" Will asked of his co-worker.

Jan had all of a sudden begun checking the milk fridge opposite Kym to make sure their dates were correct, whilst also not facing Will in the same instant. *'Where's she going with this?'* Will thought as he instructed himself to forcefully stay relaxed, Jan didn't at first respond to him until she couldn't keep her face in the fridge any longer than necessary then she closed the door and got back up facing him and Kym who was done with her labelling as well.

"Jan?"

"Yes Will?"

"What did you mean exactly when you meant when 'I left before the refurb'?"

Will's probing question received Kym's attention briefly as she flashed a look of confusion his way, but she stayed silent waiting for Jan to respond. Jan had paused, as if she were trying to form some sort of appropriate response.

"Well, everyone has their time and leaves after a time as you know Will…"

"Yes? Well, I guess most of the old Café' lot wouldn't know about that right Jan? Since you've all worked together for a minimum ten plus years. But that goes without saying obviously."

Kym didn't move but she was looking from Jan to Will with her eyes in quick succession. Everyone was silent, Will oozed his relaxed nature like he was pro, Jan kept her cheery exterior intact this time without faltering and Kym felt the intensity levels rise up on the spot. "Ha-ha Will! You know how it is, we've all had our part to play, you were always welcome as you well know." Jan smiled at this alleviating any sort of tension which seemed to vanish whatever had been between them both only a moment ago. Will seemed to agree as he smiled along with Jan as well, Kym joined with them by smiling then jumping in to further help. "I'm sure Will was disappointed to be taken out of the Café when he was, but I can assure you Jan that he was well looked after by us Restaurant lot upstairs at the time." Kym offered to be a little of bit icebreaker as Jan and Will seemed to the let any of the previous remaining tension dissipate all together. "Well, that's more than alright then Kym, isn't it Will? Jan kept her toothy smile up.

"Oh yes of course Jan…" he stepped towards her wrapping his arm around her shoulders in a reassuring way.

"Besides. Back when I was down in the Café' before I went upstairs, I was sure you lot wanted to *bully* me cause you hadn't bullied anyone lately, but I knew most of your lot including you as well Jan ended up *loving* me instead!"

Will squeezed Jan's shoulder whilst laughing innocently at his own joke, Kym ended up joining him in the laughter as well.

"Ha-ha-ha Willyboy! You do crack me from time to time, you cheeky little joker." Kym turned around to give the coffee machine a quick wipe down to keep busy as Will went back over to the till point that still had no customers waiting to be served, Jan was still in the same place as she had been, arms folded, her posture relaxed, but she was still now. Almost too still for a normal person. Her smile was in place but she it seemed to have become almost forced as she looked off in the distance, her arms were crossed but they were tightly wound. Still keeping her forced smile in place Jan then came to life once again, and Will had not missed a second of it. "Right then…" Jan turned around to look out there tables "…if you don't mind you two there are a couple of tables that need clearing so I'm gonna go get those sorted." And without even waiting for acknowledgement from Kym or Will, Jan was off in a quick-march fashion as fast as her legs could take here away from coffee pod one. Will watched her leave in her hurried manner, he couldn't help but wonder about her unusual stillness he had watched unfold before his very eyes a second ago. *'Now what has got her knickers in a twist I wonder? She is definitely not acting herself.'* Will made another mental note on his departed co-worker as she sorted out the few tables that needed clearing.

"Now that's strange…"

"What's strange Willyboy?" Kym turned to face him from the coffee machine.

"Jan's acting weird all of a sudden Kym."

"Is she? I didn't notice, that joke you made was an absolute cracker I must say."

"Ha, yeah I did try to make it as funny as I could. Well would you look at that 'Firecracker'? We have actual customers!" Will indicated by turning around to face the till point as a new queue of thirsty customers began to form. Will and Kym for the next ten minutes got the customers served, everyone was satisfied then it was back to silence with no customers in need again, all the while Jan Betty seemed to now be stomping around on the tables, very much keeping her distance from coffee pod one. Or anyone else for that matter. Will was confused as to why she remained on tables when officially she was went to be on the pod with Kym. He spotted a tray of leftovers near pod one that needed clearing, so he took the initiative. "Kym, I'm just gonna run that tray over to Jan ok. You'll be alright for a few minutes on your own won't ya?" he called out to his best friend as he left the pod, she gave him the thumbs up for the all clear. Will picked up the leftover tray then made his way over to the farthest cleaning station that Jan had set up shop in, he stood out in the opening as not to disturb her until she turned around and was facing him, he held out the tray innocently to Jan, but she was looking at him then at the tray then back to him with a completely differently way about her. Jan was not happy in the slightest about something and she was letting Will know from the immediate off as she turned her back on him to continue with the leftover trays she already had to sort out without taking the tray still waiting in his hands. *'Ok, what the hell is going on with her? Less than fifteen minutes ago we were all chatting away happily in the pod together, now she's giving me the silent treatment? She's old enough to be my mother yet she's acting more or less like a spoilt teenager right, I don't get it?'* Will thought to himself as he took the plunge and stepped gingerly inside the small three-quarter enclosed cleaning station to put the tray down next to Jan as she sorted her own one out. As he place it next to hers, she stopped what she was doing to barely glance sideways at Will whilst making herself still looking busy, she was wiping the now empty tray with extreme vigorousness that could tell anyone she had an underlying issue right now, especially to Will as he watched her wiping it almost aggressively.

"You ok there Jan?"

"I'm fine."

"Are you sure Jan?"

"Absolutely."

"*O-k* then. I'll just go bring you some more trays to you then?"

"You do that Will."

Sensing that he was being stonewalled he decided to back out of the small, enclosed area carefully. That all changed as Jan started muttering away to herself well within earshot of Will before he left the cleaning station.

"…and watch what else comes out of that *mouth of yours* as well!"

Will stopped dead in his tracks, turning around slowly to look at Jan, she still had her back to him, but her aggressive wiping of the same tray was now slowing down to a stop as she felt his eyes burrowing into her. "Thought you were gonna get me some more trays and leave me be." She stated it as a matter of fact rather than a question, Will had frankly had enough of her tone of voice by this time, *'fuck it. Here goes nothing.'* he braced himself, inhaled a quick, sharp breath, then he went straight for it. "Let's just cut through it shall we Jan? What's going on with you?" he folded his arms, set himself on the spot and waited for her reply. She stopped what she was doing entirely, she looked up at the wall with her back still facing him but still didn't turn towards him, she wasn't going to give in that easily.

"Nothing. I'm fine."

"So why the catty remark under your breath just as I'm about leave Jan? Or did I imagine that…because *I know* I didn't."

"Well…"

"Well? Please feel free to indulge me Jan, I'm all ears and I'm most certainly not going anywhere."

He had practically called her out without needing to explain it, this got her attention as she turned to face him, her face set in an angry glare, her eyes flashing, her nostrils were flared, her breathing had quickened. Jan was most definitely ready to share. Keeping her voice level but pointed Jan let rip into Will. "Will, I'm going to say this loudly and clearly. I have worked in Riverside Store for well over two decades. I have never, *ever* been accused of being a *bully* once in the entire time I have been employed here. That is until today with you in the coffee pod. I am a dedicated and well cultivated member of staff here who has more than earned their place plus the ability to be able to do what like they like within reason as Management know they can trust me get on when the job requires it. I am part of a *Friendship Group* that has deep and lasting ties in this establishment that affords certain privileges that *certain* people such as *yourself* can only ever envision about in their minds. I have never been so insulted as I have today!" Jan finished by exhaling yet losing none of her fire in the process. Will could not believe what he had just heard. He was floored not only by the fact that Jan was upset with him personally, but she had in one fell swoop laid out in the open that being part or a member of *'the Clique'* afforded you immunity from any sort of Management interference of any kind. Jan had essentially put in Will in his place because in her mind she had the 'absolute privilege' to do so whatever she wanted, whenever she wanted without fear of repercussion. It not only chilled Will to the bone, it also lit a fire from within him, and he knew only one way to respond in kind. Keeping his posture relaxed, his voice cool, he let his hands open outwards showing Jan he meant nothing malicious in his movements, he began to respond.

"*people such as yourself?* What exactly do you mean by that Jan?"

"I think I explained myself well enough Will."

"Yes. You most certainly did. Now it's my turn."

Will put his left hand over his heart and took a step back in to the small space of the cleaning station so it was just him and Jan, he wanted her to be aware that he meant what he was about to say to her.

"Jan, I cannot tell how genuinely shocked I am that I offended you. Honestly, what I said in the coffee pod was an off-the-cuff joke, nothing more, nothing less. You were right there and saw Kym laughing at the joke I made, you stood there and said nothing to even insinuate that you were upset. If my joke made you feel that way, then I sincerely apologise to you right now for making you feel like that." Will paused for a moment as he lowered his left hand away from his heart, Jan was still standing in front of him unmoving, her arms still folded, her angry face had taken on a pinched quality to it. She was still expecting more of him. *'What does she want from me? Blood?'* Will was still stumped as to what else he could do, he had offered her as true as any apology for his joke yet as it stood, Jan wasn't ready to accept it.

"Is it ok to ask if we're gonna be ok Jan?"

"Will…I think its best we leave it there don't you!"

She walked out of the cleaning station now, as she left she had to brush past Will on his right and the nudge he received was definitely more than a harmless one. He felt exactly what she was doing now, exerting herself because she knew in her eyes that she could. And Will was not going to let that one slide. He walked out of the station as well in pursuit.

"Ok, Jan. Stop right there. That brush off is something I will *not* tolerate."

Will asserted himself in the moment which got the desired affect he wanted, she stopped, turning to face him once more.

"I made myself perfectly clear didn't I Will?"

"Yes you did. But did I make myself *perfectly clear* as well?"

"Very well. What is it? Be careful of how you word it *exactly* also."

'Don't rise to it Will. Your better than that.'

"Ok, I'll just lay it out as politely as I can. You've known me close to three-years now Jan. In at all that time we have gotten on, today of all days you just *decide* to take offense to a harmless joke? And it was a harmless joke as you well know, you weren't born yesterday. You're an intelligent, assertive lady with a strong work ethic as you well reminded me a second ago in that cleaning station after all."

Jan glanced sideways at this remark which Will didn't miss a beat of, *'ha. You don't the like truth when its explained in a way that doesn't benefit you, do ya Jan.'*, he pressed on. "Now, granted you were offended by my joke which I just profusely apologised for. But just rewinding a moment to my previous comment. You're an *intelligent person* Jan? You would really react this way after all these years even if it were unintentionally meant? Yet your so upset by my joke that you just can't see past your own anger? I think your far better than that personally. Come on Jan, I am truly sorry I upset you!" Will implored with her, trying to bridge the divide she clearly wanted to make it far wider between them. "People change Will…" Jan decided to look at him again, her fire on show for all to bear witness.

"…and this time you went a step too far!"

Jan then left through the Café side entrance out into the Foods Department without a backwards glance at him, Will watched her walk away speechless at her audacity and ignorance. With nothing left to be said or done, he turned around in a daze and began to walk slowly back to the coffee pods. He was numbed by the whole experience with Jan. *'After all these years of working with me, she's willing to throw all of the good working relationship we've developed away because of a silly little joke she simply chose not to take. All for the sake of her pride? Or is it her standing with 'the Clique'? Or all even of it in fact.'* He stopped at the back coffee pod one where Kym was filling in the coffee shot paperwork for the day having been none the wiser to what had just unfolded between him and Jan. Will stood there on the outside of the pod, he couldn't even bring any kind of words to form coherently. He felt completely desensitized from everything currently. Kym stopped what she was doing with the coffee shot paperwork when she felt his presence behind her. She turned around and saw Will's face and knew instantly something was amiss with him. Like any concerned friend would do in any serious situation when a fellow friend was upset, she went in gently so as not to alarm him any further than necessary.

"What's up Willyboy…?"

*

One Week Later.

August 11th, 2015.

2:15 pm.

After the debacle between him and Jan. Will had seen an almost
immediate shift in the energies of both Café's almost overnight.
Then he noticed more as well how *'the Clique'* conducted
themselves around him when they ended up in the vicinity of one
another, it wasn't exactly pleasant, but they didn't go out of their
way to make life any more bearable for Will either. Lucy Cricker
ceased any sort of conversation to be had with him when he
crossed paths with her, she'd even removed him as a Facebook
Friend in the preceding days after Jan and Wills altercation, he was
surprised yet not in the same instant a person like Lucy would take
a stance like this. It reeked of petty loyalty Will simply could never
understand. Sharyn Michaels had gone from short chats with him
to bare-boned basic one-worded responses if he needed to ask her a
question. Trudy Harrie not only kept her teacher stance up in his
presence, but she also more or less doubled-down on it by giving
Will severe looks over her ridiculous forward detaching spectacles
whilst making the conversation purely worked based without any
let up. And Joe Sybille, well she didn't acknowledge him if she
happened to be walking past, as far Will was concerned, that was
just fine for the both of them. Throughout all of this Will had relied

heavily on Kym to keep him going. From trying to end up working together on shift to talking about how best to conduct himself on shift over their many WhatsApp texts they exchanged. "Just keep that chin of yours up Willyboy, me and you both know their just being their usual pathetic selves, what else is new ah?" Kym gave him an encouraging squeeze of her hand on his right shoulder as he made a mocha for a waiting female customer who was more concerned about her Twitter page than to be paying them any attention. "Oh, I know Firecracker. It's just…here you go madam, one *extra-hot, decaf, wet mocha with less chocolate and an extra shot of decaf.* Can I get you anything…?" Will stopped even asking as the social-media obsessed customer with her overly specific mocha gave him the barest of glances in acknowledgement yet she somehow managed to seat her herself at a vacant table without running into anyone or even notice it was available as her eyes continued to be glued to her phone screen. "Rude-ass bitch." Will muttered under his breath as he wiped down the auto-wand for any residue milk that might be left on it, he began wiping it up and down firmly, then he went at it almost angrily using it to vent his frustration, all under the watchful eyes of Kym. "If I did that to some bloke I had over mine what you're doing right now to the auto-wand Will, I think it would raise some serious alarm bells about if I was more of an S&M sort of bird wouldn't you say so?" Kym teased him from the till point, Will stopped his aggressive up and down motion as a fit of uncontrolled giggles and sniggering overtook him all of a sudden. His best friend really knew when he needed to just laugh for the sake of it.

"Oh 'Firecracker', that was a really good one. Thanks Mrs."

"Your most welcome Willyboy. Now, how are we going to deal with…"

"Ahem."

Will and Kym stopped talking as their attention was drawn elsewhere. They both turned around at the sound of the noise to find the always cheerful trainee Manager Emily Arms standing just outside the entrance of coffee pod two, she seemed to be dancing on the spot today for some unknown reason. *'What exactly is she doing here I wonder?'* Will thought to himself as Emily stepped into his and Kym's space. "Well, hey there you two! How's my favourite couple today?" Emily's cheery disposition came through, she also wasn't one just to drop by and start a random conversation amongst staff.

"Hey there Emily."

"Heya Ems, all good?"

Emily always seemed to get overly excited that Kym and Will were asking how she was as her voice went an octave higher than it usually did. "Oh yes, yes! All good here. Lots to do like always, don't know how I fit it all in, in one shift I must say." Emily loved exaggerating about what she did without going into specifics of what is was she actually did up in the Admin Office, these days even seeing her seemed to be less of an occurrence. Will had heard people like Aaron Connors who was employed part-time were surprised she still worked here. Will swore he had heard Coralie mentioning to Sasha that Emily might be going elsewhere, not that Emily knew that currently of course. "So Kym, have we been upselling side-salads with our toasties today?" Emily asked as she folded her arms with her still innocent smile in place. Kym never missed a beat though.

"Of course, Mrs, what do you take me for?"

"Jolly good! Will? Are those coffees being made to your excellent high standards?"

"Wouldn't have it any other way. You knew that back in 'The Restaurant' anyway Ems?"

"Ha-ha-ha! You know me *Willy*. Have to ask as its possible I'm gonna be more than likely signed off and Managing both Units someday soon now as it happens..."

'You are? Not what I've heard on the grapevine dear. Also, Willy? Aaron is the 'only one' who gets away with me calling me that in a pinch at best.'

"…Anyway. I decided to swing by and make sure your all getting on ok here? Kym if its ok with you I need to borrow Will for like ten minutes if you don't mind? After your both done with those new customers that are about to order of course." Emily finished by leaving the coffee pod two promptly not waiting for Kym to respond to her request which for once was out of character for her. Normally she would without fail wait to hear what the response to any request she gave would be, her unusual cheery departure had Kym and Will both looking at each other thoroughly confused.

"*O-k*, that was ten levels of weirdness wasn't it 'Firecracker'?"

"Your telling me. She never leaves without an answer, plus, what does she even want to talk to you about I wonder?"

"Beats me Mrs?"

New customers had arrived now forming a short queue. The two best friends sprang into action like it was second nature to them. They smiled, processed orders, coffees were made, money was exchanged, delicious cakes were upsold, it was all part and parcel of the routine. All the while Will looked over his right shoulder to look for Emily who had found a vacant table; she was typing away on her phone patiently awaiting Will to join her. She looked up from the table she had grabbed, she smiled reassuringly at Will whilst he returned the gesture in kind. Then, he saw where she was sitting exactly in the Café' now. On a two-seater table. Right next to the furthest cleaning station.

"Fuck me sideways." Will muttered to himself.

"Sorry? What was that?" Another female customer asked Will as they waited for their latte.

'Shit.'

"Oh. My apologies madam, I was just wondering if you wanted any caramel or vanilla in your latte?" He quickly deflected, thankfully the customer hadn't heard him swear. They answered no to the syrup request then left satisfied they had their coffee fix in order. Kym and Will finished with the small queue they had then Kym turned to face Will who was still staring at Emily who was engrossed in her phone. He was anything but relaxed now. Kym saw him staring at her then she looked back at him judging his facial reactions accordingly.

"Your putting two and two together Willyboy."

"Am I though 'Firecracker'? Or am I about shit my bollocks out?"

"Your fine, she doesn't look like she's got any bad intentions. Not that she would know what the term *bad intentions* means exactly. Most people know what Emily is, a mouthpiece with far too much positivity for any one person to actually have. That and she clearly isn't a good trainee Manager which we are all acutely aware of here in the Café but we all keep that to ourselves as you well know of course." Kym finished as she came to stand next to Will who hadn't taken his eyes off Emily. He didn't trust what he was about to walk over too. He didn't want to walk over to her at all, but he knew he had too at some point.

"Go on Will. I'll be fine over here whilst you two speak".

"Are you sure?"

"No time like the present is there?"

With a careful nudge, Kym sent Will on his way. He found himself walking over to Emily with the speed of a snail it felt like, then before he knew it, he was standing at the table as Emily stopped typing on her phone to look up at him with that same overly happy smile. *'Crikey, I wouldn't trust you as far as I could throw you Emily.'* he thought to himself as he stood there without sliding into the waiting seat. "Ah Will, please take a seat." Emily had her hands clasped together now so she used her eyes to highlight the available chair opposite her, Will didn't take the offer of the seat yet which caused some confusion to flash across Emily's normally happy face.

"Everything alright Mr Hardley?"

"Oh yes all good, I'm just standing cause I feel like it might get busy, and Kym may need me."

"Aww. Kym will be fine, don't worry about that…"

"I feel better standing all the same Ems…"

"Will. *Take the seat.* You'll be glad you did."

Emily's tone had changed all of sudden to something Will had never heard from her before. Assertiveness and conviction.

It had all been laced with her cheery tone like she normally used on a daily basis, but this time she had made sure he understood that he was being told to sit by a member of the Management Team regardless of if he wanted to or not. He complied with her veiled request, settling himself into the chair. Emily's face had reasserted itself into her usual happy exterior.

She stared at him and he stared back.

"Will."

"Emily?"

"First off, how are you lately?"

This comment threw him off entirely.

'What on earth does she want with me?'

"I…err…I'm fine for the most part I guess? Yourself Emily?

Her body language seemed to shift on the spot as Will asked her the same question in return. It was almost like she instantly became uncomfortable yet kept her smiling face intact throughout.

"As well as can be, that brings me to why I asked to speak with you today Will…"

'Here we go. Bring it on.'

"Well, Will, I need to discuss with you about a *conversation* that occurred between yourself and Jan Betty in this cleaning station next to us a week ago today." Will noted how Emily used the term 'conversation' to describe what had really gone down between him and Jan last week. A conversation, it was not. Her blatant overreaction along with her refusal to accept his genuine apology was seared into his memory and may never leave anytime soon. Now here he was, with his trainee Manager who wanted to talk to him about it. Will was not impressed in the slightest where this was heading, all the while Emily kept her truly grating happy smile firmly in place as she probed him with her dark green eyes.

"A *conversation?* Is that what we're calling it then Emily?"

"Well, I think that's an appropriate thing to call it wouldn't you?"

"I seem to remember it being more than a simple *conversation.* I remember it all too well in fact. But if that's what we're gonna coin it then by all means lets discuss this so-called *conversation*. It was anything but polite as well."

Will was annoyed and he wasn't hiding it. If Jan Betty were truly so offended and put out by a harmless joke that her ego simply couldn't take it then Will was most certainly going to give as he good as he got.

"I see. It would probably make more sense if I showed you this then as well." Emily then produced two single sheets of paper Will hadn't noticed as of yet, she unfolded them, placing one in front of her and one in front of Will with three words emblazoned on the top of it:

'Personal Dialogue Report'

Will looked at the sheet of paper not knowing what to think. He looked back at Emily who seemed more relax than the she should be. Sensing his confusion, she elaborated.

"In regards to your *conversation* with Jan Betty taking place on the 4th of August a week ago, she approached the Management Team quite distressed and explained her version of events to us." Emily stated it as if she were reading from a script, she pressed on as Will sat there silently still listening yet prepping himself for the inevitable punchline. "She went into detail of course but we found ourselves in a predicament as how best to broach this subject with you Will. We thought it was appropriate to let a week rollover, so we could gauge what the mood was like in both Café' Units. So far as I can tell it's not been too bad, but I did need some guidance myself as how to approach this matter in regards to the original *conversation* that occurred between you and Jan. Now, just to put you at ease. You're not in any kind of trouble firstly. I have decided to go down the route of a 'Personal Dialogue Report' or a 'PDR' for short which is essentially a 'Note' that will stay in your Personnel File for a set amount of time before it is then formally removed from your File after the stated time period has elapsed and it is destroyed. It does not affect your rate of Pay; it is not a formal Reprimand or Warning and it is most certainly not a reflection of your Conduct or Misconduct depending on the severity of the situation. It's simple a Dialogue me and you are having right now, we discuss what happened, I note it down in an abbreviated form, declare that we both agreed on a simple course of action I also note down so a *conversation* like that doesn't arise again in the future. You go back to your duties with Kym, and they rest they say is History. How does that sound to you Will?" Emily finished and began jotting down the time and date on the PDR form as Will sat there letting the situation sink in for a moment. He wasn't in trouble, but he wasn't entirely off the hook. Jan Betty had purposefully gone out of her way to try and enact some form of repercussions just so he could be put in his place. All because she couldn't take a joke after less than three years of working with him plus knowing the type of person he was, humour included.

'Has it really come to trivial matters like this? Are people like her and 'the Clique' so used to their convoluted existence of getting away with doing whatever they like, whenever they like that nobody can even question it anymore. Why do I honestly put myself through these situations anymore?'

Emily looked back up from the PDR From and saw that Will was mulling things over, for once her cheery disposition altered into something else. It was concern for her Employee. "I know this probably wasn't what you were expecting today Will…" she began then she stopped dead in her tracks, Will was now looking her directly in the eyes, his own set were alight with a fire she hadn't witnessed before. Her concern vanished, only to be replaced by something new instead. Fear. Not waiting for her to continue talking Will started speaking, his eyes may have shown how he was feeling but his voice came off cool yet calmly controlled. They were both on the shop floor in the presence of nearby customers, pretences had to be maintained which Will understood all too well after all the years he had been working at Riverside for.

"Your absolutely right Emily. This isn't what I was expecting at all today. Come to think of it, after almost five years of working in this cesspit of bruised egos, stiff upper-lips, elitist attitudes, and blinding arrogance you'd think I would have developed a bit more a thicker skin when dealing with the utter *shite* politics you and I deal with on a near daily basis these days. Yet here we both are, fighting the good fight like we always do. You have to admit, we were never dealt with this level of utter crap when we were both in 'The Restaurant' together. Even under the *Orbit Group* contract. This company wanted nothing to do with us when we weren't *officially* their staff. They certainly didn't help us out when we were overrun like hell with not enough staff to deal with how busy we were. Especially if *'the Clique'* of all people could have helped. Not that they help themselves bear in mind. But now look what fate has dealt us, we've been integrated with a bunch of people who have *decades* of working together and they still don't want us here Emily. You know that and I know that." Will stopped by taking a deep calming breath even though he had never once raised his voice at Emily. In the time he had spoken, she had put down her pen and had actually listened intently to him. He looked across from her and she looked back at him, he saw another new thing he had never witnessed from her before in her eyes. It was the look of understanding. She then did something she had never done openly to Will before; she reached across the table and placed her right hand on top of his, patting it in comfort.

"I know it's not been the easiest of experiences Will…"

"I really don't want or need your patronization Emily."

"Good, cause you haven't got it either."

Will looked her in the eyes again, he instantly felt ashamed at making such a brass assumption when for once in a blue moon she was trying to make a conscious effort to understand how he was really feeling about the sorry state of affairs he was currently in.

"I'm sorry Ems."

"Don't be. For what it's worth, I do know how you feel. But Will, I am a *trainee Manager* now. I have to do these things regardless of if I like them. It's part of *my job*. Jan came to me about your *altercation*. Yes it wasn't an exactly a pleasant *conversation* for the pair of you but here we are right now. There's not much to done other than to get on with it. Now you really are not in trouble Will, after listening to his her I realised what would be the point of disciplining you? I know you and your humour. She's the one who took it out of context and that's her issue to deal with. Granted *yes*, her affiliations with certain people in here are somewhat of a nuisance. But I can manage them, and you Will…" He hadn't taken his eyes off her as she released her right hand from his "…can most definitely carry on as well. Your better than them and you know it, don't give them the satisfaction or time of day. Just be polite, stay away from them. I'll even have a word with the appropriate people, so they end up working upstairs most of the time. Ok?" She finished by reclasping her hands back together and wating on him to reply. Will closed his eyes, took a breath, and exhaled, then looked back Emily again.

"Ok Ems. Let's do this."

So they did. Will recounted what happened with him and Jan, his version of events anyway. Emily jotted down the necessary events that had transpired in the first box of the PDR Form then moved on to the second box of the Form about what actions were required. It was a simple yet harmless procedure that everyone got to walk away from knowing that it had at least been addressed. Emily signed by the Managers Signature and Will did the same for the Employee Signature. He got back from the table as Emily pulled out her phone to make a work call and Will went back over to coffee pod two to re-join Kym who was serving a couple at the till. He jumped back on the coffee machine, made the coffees, handed them over then he got to giving the machine a quick wipe down even though it didn't need it at the time. Everything was quiet for a moment now, lunch rush had come and gone, the Café was in a normal routine, Emily got up from the table she and Will had occupied, waved at him before leaving through the Food Department entrance that Jan had stalked out of only a week earlier. Will now made himself accept that, that whole entire affair between him and Jan was a thing of the past now. Yet he couldn't or wouldn't forget about it. Not anytime soon anyway.

"So, you gonna tell me what you two spoke about or am I gonna have to play the guessing game?" Kym's voice pulled Will back to reality all of a sudden as he looked over his left shoulder at his

'Firecracker' who was watching him with folded arms and an impatient face about her.

"Ah, my dear 'Firecracker'. Where do I even begin."

"Easy Willyboy. The beginning. Off you go, and don't scrimp on the details either…"

*

Back To Now.

1:55 pm.

"…I mean, how on earth could we forget that whole sorry affair. I still can't get over the fact was you made a harmless joke that she took the wrong way then accused you of things for no reason other than she could cause she knew when she stalked out of here in a huff to probably go bitch about it to her mates. I've looked at Jan in a completely different way after that Willyboy I tell ya." Kym exhaled annoyed at the memories of what had transpired between him and Jan over a year ago. Thankfully, events hadn't repeated themselves since, but his working relationship with Jan had never been the same and now it never would. Not when Will was officially only three-weeks away from leaving Riverside for good.

"Do you think anything will be said between now and when you leave Willyboy?"

"What? Between me and Jan or *'the Clique'*?

"Both really?"

"Who can say Kym? I know very little about what is said between any of them these days. Other than not one of them has even bothered to ask me why I'm transferring."

"Well, they've enquired to other people about you leaving…"

"I'm not surprised. Remember, that insidious little group live, breath and thrive off the gossip in this Café' despite claiming our old haunt upstairs as their own. Yeah I know, everyone else does the same when it comes to gossip. But at least me and you are nice about it 'Firecracker'…"

"Oh, I know Willyboy, why do you think I'm friends with you after all these years?"

"Exactly Mrs!"

They both laughed in unison at this. When Jan had come in earlier to take too much stock without asking, the memories of her and Will's animated but dreaded *conversation* had reared its ugly head like a bad smell. It had surprised yet also reminded him to never try and end up in a situation like that again when his transfer to Stratford Store would commence all too soon. *'I can't let that happen again; I will not let that happen again.'* Will set the personal rule in his mind as a standard he had to maintain when he arrived at his new Store. Lessons from the past had to be learnt, the good, the bad and the ugly plus everything else that went with them too. It was another quiet day in the Café', Summer was very much over and the nights were just starting to set in earlier as each day ticked down to October. Every day that went by in the lead up to October 22nd felt a like another day of memories Will had to hold on to them before they really did become a thing of the past. It was a strange sensation when it had never really happened to him before. Leaving for somewhere new. Yes with the same Company but new friendships to be made, new encounters to be had, a new way of conducting yourself in a strange place. *'Better start trying to act a different way now. Time to starting cutting the...'* the rest of his thought eluded him as he saw another new individual enter the Café' from the escalators. It was none other than Josie Sybille herself, head cheerleader of *'the Clique'*.

"Oioi Will. Have you seen?"

"Yes I have Kym. Can't miss that face if you even tried."

If Josie felt eyes on her as she entered the Café she never showed off that she had, she walked in as she always did, like the place was hers and nobodies else's despite not even being a Supervisor anymore. *'Now there's one person I will never be sad to see the backside of. The bitch.'* the grim thought flashed through Will's mind as he continued watching Josie from coffee pod two with

Kym. She had entered the Kitchen to talk to Nat who cooking something, they exchanged words for a few brief moments then moved to the back area, all under the watchful eyes of Coralie who was stood frozen on the spot with the clipboard in her hands as their encounter happened. Kym and Will were speculating about what was going to happen.

"What do you think Firecracker?"

"Got no idea Willyboy, oh hold on a second. There goes Coralie…"

Coralie had slapped down the clipboard on the wall separating the Kitchen Area from the rest of the shop floor. She marched off in the direction of where Josie and Nat had gone out back disappearing from view as well.

"Bet you a coffee this isn't gonna end well Kym."

"Deal, shake on it?"

They did so with firmness then waited for all three to emerge from out back. Whilst they waited Kym and Will got to serving another customer. As they finished up, they both heard a sound from out back. It was clearly a fridge door being closed far too loudly than it needed to be from the Backstage Area. Then out of nowhere came Coralie and Josie. Both were talking at the same time.

"I'm just saying Josie, that your staff could just simply *ask* rather than *take*."

"I'm not sure I follow you entirely Coralie? I don't have any staff under me since you're the Supervisor of both Café Units.

"Really Josie? We're gonna play that game are we? You and I both know I don't get a look in with *your lot* upstairs and your fully aware and in the knowledge of this."

The Downstairs Café team was silent as the conversation unfolded between the ex-Supervisor and the newer one. Nat had appeared back in her place at the Kitchen Area watching them both nervously. Tonye had stopped restocking the fridge as she glanced at them from over her left shoulder. Sasha was on coffee pod one with Aaron who both tried to not look while Kym and Will were transfixed in coffee pod two as both women squared off.

"My lot? I'm not sure what you mean there exactly Coralie?"

Josie was turning away from her to try and make a quick escape, but Coralie wasn't that much of a pushover as she may have been in the past. Not anymore anyway.

"You know *exactly* what I am talking about Josie. So, let's be honest about one very simple thing here. You're not the Supervisor anymore, *I am*. Therefore, if you need something, call with the work phone and I will try to accommodate you as best I can. Do not send one of your *lackeys* to do you dirty work for you, do I make myself perfectly clear?" Coralie took a step closer towards Josie who had turned back slowly to face her. She looked like she'd just been slapped across the face. Hard. No one in the Café moved a muscle accept the customers who were immersed in their own goings on.

"I think I understand you Coralie. Now you can hear what I have to say…" Josie took a step towards Coralie now closing the gap between them, Coralie was younger than Josie by a good two decades, but she was taller than her, yet Josie was senior in age to Coralie drew herself up to her full height. She wasn't a woman to be easily put in her place, not after all these years of manipulating the system at Riverside to her hearts content. "You Coralie, you're not a bad Supervisor. But you've got nothing on me dear. My place here is something that can't be simply wished away or excused as sleight of hand, I know people who will back me up *all the way* and you can only hope for that kind of support if you go the distance young lady. I hope I made myself clear on that matter." Josie turned to leave without what she came for, but Coralie wasn't done. Not just yet.

"Are you threatening me."

Josie stopped dead in her tracks right at the entrance. Nat looked back and forth quickly between Coralie and Josie unsure of who would come out on top of this, Tonye looked at her reflection in the fridge, Aaron and Sasha suddenly found the light fixtures extremely interesting whilst Kym and Will dared not look away due their own horrified fascination.

'Get her Coralie!'

Will egged her on from his thoughts as Josie turned around again to face her, her calm exterior always in place.

"Not in the slightest sweetheart. Just a friendly reminder, know your place. You might not like the can of worms you open as other people have very well found out in the past." Josie finished by not even looking at Coralie this time. She looked over at coffee pod two directly at Will, just for a split-second. Then as soon as it had happened, it was over. Josie went off in the direction of the escalators and the sanctity of *'the Clique'* waiting for their imperious leader to return to them in the Upstairs Café. Coralie stalked off to the back Office to vent her frustrations in peace, Nat made herself busy in the Kitchen, Tonye all of a sudden sprang to life as she went off to her hovel by the Bakery Section out back, Sasha and Aaron began serving a new customer that had just entered while Kym and Will were shocked at the events that had just taken place.

"Well, that just happened."

"Telling me Willyboy! I hope Coralie is ok..."

"Yeah same here..."

Will went back to the coffee machine lost in his thoughts as Kym served the regular customer who came back up as she wanted another extra-dry cappuccino.

As he got to making it, he couldn't forget when Josie had looked at him dead in the eyes for that moment just before she had left.

It had deeply unsettled him to the very core of his being.

'October 22nd really cannot come quick enough by the looks of things...'

Eight

October 1st, 2016.

The Men's Locker Room.

Saturday.

11:38 am.

'Twenty-One Days to go.'

Will thought to himself as he started to deposit his coat and bag into his locker that could never fit anything properly. He was not going to miss his small locker that's for sure. It was his dreaded late night Saturday shift, and he didn't want to be here. Hopefully, his shifts would change for the better at Stratford. As he closed his locker then did the normal routine of opening and closing it to make sure that it locked securely he realised after finishing that his mobile was still in his work trouser pocket, he fished it out, frustrated that he had to go through his routine again to store it in his bag even though he hated leaving his phone upstairs and not on his person. As he was about to open his locker door again he stopped and saw he had a message notification come through all of a sudden on his phone. He stopped what he was doing to concentrate on who was messaging him before he started work, he unlocked his phone, then went to his Facebook-Inbox for his private messages. Once he had opened the App he was smiling at the person who had messaged him. It was none other than his ex-co-worker Sarah Harker who was still online currently. Delighted to receive a message from her he opened their private chat:

1 OCT AT 11:42

Oioi Will you cheeky slacker! I hear your leaving Riverside? This is news to me and the Mrs out here...

Sarah! Bloody hell, it's so great to hear from you. How's life in sunny Spain? Yes, you are correct, I am transferring from Riverside at the end of this month my love. End of an Era indeed!

1 OCT AT 11:44

Blimey. So you're doing a me then? Up and off outta that place like the rest of us 'Restaurant Lot' then. I thought you were gonna be part of the furniture in that place for the long run...

Ha! Me Sarah? No Mrs, it's time to move on. Six Years I've
been here and it's time to go. Had enough of the attitudes and
bitchiness in this place to last me a small Lifetime.

I get that completely. But aren't you just trading in one Store
for the same sort of thing in another with just new people Will?
I mean, hats off to ya an all for finally jumping ship, but still?

1 OCT AT 11:46

Honestly, I understand exactly what you mean Mrs. But I need
this Sarah, for my own sanity really. Complacency can make
you or break you. It's breaking me right now I swear. I mean,
remember your last day here at Riverside? It was only less
than a year ago…

*

October 28th, 2015.

Wednesday.

The Downstairs Café.

3:59 pm.

In one hour it would all be over. Another dear friend was leaving
for pastures new and there was simply nothing Will could do about
it but smile, try not to cry and wish them all the best for the future.
Which is exactly what was happening for his co-worker Sarah

Harker right now. From five o'clock she would be bidding adios not only to the Store and Riverside, but the UK as well. Sarah and her Partner-in-Life Janice were jetting off to the sunny Costa Blanca in the Alicante Province, specifically living only a ten-to-fifteen-minute car journey from the very popular tourist hotspot that was Benidorm. The sudden announcement that Sarah was moving had come to a shock to the entire team of the In-Store Café', both Units in fact. Will and Kym were particularly not enjoying the final hour, it meant that Sarah really was leaving for good, it didn't make it easier on them both.

"God, I am really not liking this Willyboy."

"Don't 'Firecracker'. I know exactly how I'm gonna be when five swings round, a mess!"

Will and Kym were on coffee pod two, Sarah had been on her usual place which was the Dishwasher Area. As it had been her last day however she had been flitting in and out of there to see her regular customers who had come to say goodbye but also wish her the best of luck in her new upcoming adventure moving out to Spain. As each hour had crept down, Will had gotten more and more sad to see that such a good co-worker and friend was leaving. Sarah had deep roots between him, Kym, and Nat. She had started out in 'The Restaurant' with them all so they were closer than other members of staff when the refurbishment had come around plus the abolishment of their old haunt all together. Of course rather than sending any members of *'the Clique'* from Upstairs, Joyce Copper had come in their stead with Managerial pleasantries well in place along with a smile that Will was definitely more on the forced side of things. The fact that after Joyce wished Sarah all the best, no sooner than five minutes had elapsed after she had done so, she had shot off back Upstairs faster than her crisp black Manager's skirt could carry her. Sarah being the typical South Londoner that she was took it only in her stride as she always did. She was not one to let many things affect her outwardly, in fact when it came to Will and his many run-ins with *'the Clique'* she was always the one to offer some tough honesty about how he should behave around them or staying well out of their way. Nothing got past this lady who was proud to be from 'South of the River'. Will definitely was going to miss above all else going her many put downs of him, when she didn't see him working she put him in his place, but it was all very much from a place of love and respect. Such was her Londoner way of being.

"…what are we gonna do?"

"Sorry 'Firecracker'?"

Will had been in his own world when Kym brought him out of it and back into the here and now. He had been staring off vacantly wondering how best to conduct himself when the time came round to give Sarah that final goodbye. Right now she was having to give the younger Sarah Bailey another hug as she was just as upset as Will that the older 'Sarah' was leaving soon.

"I said, what are we gonna do without her? She keeps me going in this, just as much as you do."

"I know, but clearly her visit to Spain last month has very much changed all of that for her and Janice, I mean I was never expecting her to just up and move like this so soon all of a sudden..."

Sarah and her partner Janice had been in Spain at the start of September when Will had also been holidaying in Benidorm with his own friends as they held their annual week-long Pride event in the tourist attraction City as part of the official end of European Summer Closing Pride. Will remembered how he had, had to grovel to Joyce about him and Sarah having to be off the same time, thankfully it had all worked out well for them both. The holiday had been a blast to say they least, walking along the long stretch of the Costa Blanca in the New Town soaking in the humidity, sunny climate and friendly people who lived in Benidorm permanently in the day, then royally living it up in the Old Town in the small but cute Gay Bars located down the side streets where the spirits had no official measures to due Spanish Law, and the atmosphere was electric. Yes it had been a fun week for all involved, then like all good holidays it come to an end and reality harkened Will and Sarah back. Will had come in the day after a late-night flight back to the UK. Sarah had flown back with Janice the day before. Will came in to work the next day a little more than tired than he normally would be due to his late-night flying, he had met his good friend Johnny Michaels who worked at Debenhams in Riverside for a quick catch-up coffee before starting his shift at work only to have Sarah walk out from the Dishwasher Area with a frog in her throat from all the drinking and her own travelling home to declare that next week she and Janice had another spur of the moment flight booked to take them back out to Alicante much to Will's genuine shock. After their week out there having a brilliant time, the Benidorm-Bug had very much taken hold of them both, so they were seriously considering about moving out to there. Fast forward less than two months later, Sarah and Janice had a property waiting for them in the town just next door to Benidorm, their pet cat was already on its way out there so it would be ready to greet them when it came for them to get on that waiting plane to ferry them away from the UK, permanently. Will was so glad that Sarah and her partner were taking the leap into the unknown together for their own happiness as the wonderful couple that they were. It inspired him immensely, yet no one could replace anyone like Sarah with her cockney charms. The Café' would certainly be a lot more quiet and a hell of a lot less fun without having her stomp around in the Dishwasher Area. Will watched as she hugged young Sarah Bailey for what must have been the fifth or sixth time since she had started her shift, Will was desperately in need of one of her hugs as well currently. He came to stand next to Kym at the till on coffee pod two as they both stared at the older Sarah giving the younger one some encouraging words. Within a moment young Sarah was nodding her head in agreement then she was heading back to the cleaning station closest to the Dishwasher Area with more of a spring in her step as she adjusted her prescription glasses. Older Sarah disappeared out back to finish off whatever she had left to do. Will still didn't know how he was going to control himself once she came to say goodbye for the final time. "Your right 'Firecracker'. I have no clue as to what we will do once she's gone." Will admitted to his best friend as she looked up at him.

"Oh I know, it's all well and good that she will stay in touch with us while she's living out there Will, but…"

"…But you're wondering how long that will continue until it doesn't anymore correct?"

Kym looked away from him this time and decided to top up some of the tissues in the dispenser despite it still being nearly full to the brim. She may have been silent; however she was also nodding her head in agreement with Will. The truth was neither one of them knew what would happen once Sarah settled into life in Spain over there. Would she forget about them and all their shenanigans from 'The Restaurant', would she close this part of her life for good and never look back. Not a single one of them had the answer to those situations. All they had was their collective faith that Sarah would still want to stay in touch. Truthfully for Will it was even more difficult to see her go than he was letting on to Kym. Sarah was not only a goof friend and co-worker; she was also someone who backed him up every time when it came to any moment that gone very sour with *'the Clique'* or Joyce for that matter. Sure, she may have assumed the role of Devil's Advocate on more than a few occasions, ultimately she would do what she could to try and make a shift more bearable at work for him. To be losing a co-worker and friend like that while all your enemies were still going to be working in some proximity to him filled Will with an increasing dread at the coming days ahead. He didn't like it for one second at all. So the fact that his goodbye to Sarah was fast approaching was something he didn't want to have to ready for himself, but he knew that he had too regardless.

"We're gonna be ok you know 'Firecracker'?"

"Yeah I know."

"I mean it. Sarah is taking a big life-changing opportunity. She's moving to somewhere for a better quality of life and that's to be applauded above all else. Granted yes, we aren't ever going to get those days back of us lot knuckling down to another day of backbreaking work in 'The Restaurant' where we all cracked jokes or bitched about Judy Howard taking herself off for *another* toilet break when we all know she went for a cheeky ciggie outside instead…" Will placed an arm around Kym in reassurance, "…but the memories we will remember will be the best ones once Sarah is gone. She'll always be there as a reminder in our hearts of how good it can be to come to work and have a good laugh 'Firecracker' rather than having to fight a battle with another member of staff!" Will gave Kym an encouraging squeeze as she nodded her head again in agreement.

"Your right. Your absolutely right Willyboy…"

"Of course that *slacker* is right you complete pair of silly idiots!"

The unexpected voice of Sarah Harker had them both turning around in surprise. There she was smirking at them from the back opening of coffee pod two with her arms folded, she shortish sandy blond hair done up in a loose ponytail, her cockney Londoner grin fully in place as she looked at the two of them trying to psyche themselves up before she left the Café' for good at the end of the hour.

"You two do make me giggle I must say."

"Well *excuse us* for feeling sorry about the fact that your leaving us Sarah."

"Spot on Willyboy, you Sarah are leaving us and the UK plus its unpredictable weather for sunny Spain. I mean, there's no competition to be had…?"

Will and Sarah both looked at Kym slightly confused as she looked back at them like it was obvious.

"…You should be staying here in the UK for us clearly!"

Kym let the answer hang there in there as she deadpanned both of Sarah and Will, they all looked at one another, then they burst out in uncontrolled laughter.

"I know, I know. I just had to put that one out there just for us three!"

"Oh 'Firecracker, you do know how to drop a quality joke when we least expect it…"

"Telling me Will, you had me going there for a hot minute Kym!"

Kym, Sarah and Will all laughed a bit more at the joke. It was rare moments like this that you couldn't replicate again once one of them was truly leaving. But they all would remember it fondly without question. They all looked at each other smiling in respect.

"Oh sod it, come here you two!"

Sarah marched quickly from back of coffee pod two into the space of Kym and Will and got them each in a successive bear hug and squeezed them each both hard. They both returned the gesture in kind whilst savouring the fleeting moment for their memories.

"What are we gonna do without you Sarah Harker."

"Kym, you'll be alright."

"I sure won't be the same without you my lady Sarah."

"Will Hardley…" Sarah turned towards him "…your just gonna be even more of a *slacker* than you are already once I'm gone. For one thing your gonna come out and visit me and we will have a riot! Plus Benidorm is only next door after all? Point is, this isn't the end you two. It's simply the start of something new for all of us." Sarah finished by looking at them both sternly yet with great affection in her eyes. Will all of a sudden felt his eyes growing up and he started blinking fast to stop himself from crying on the shop floor, Sarah missed none of this however.

"Aww look, Will's tearing up!"

"Shut up Sarah…" Will was now fanning his face dramatically.

"Need a tissue Will?" Kym offered him the tissue dispenser in full on tease mode.

"Oh sod off!" He finished abruptly then departed coffee pod two for the Dishwasher Area as Kym and Sarah began cackling at his lack of emotional control. Finding sanctity in the empty Area that

Sarah normally occupied he found it organised yet utterly spotless as well. Whoever took over from Sarah on this had big shoes to fill considerably. *'I pity the fool who comes in here after my mate departs…?'* Will looked at the clock time at the far end on the narrow area *'…in less than twenty-five minutes! Ugh, you never fully appreciate something or someone until their gone.'* He was dabbing his eyes with some kitchen towel as he got his emotions back in check. Satisfied he pivoted to return back to pod two and found Sarah standing in his way having been spying on him with great amusement as her face told him so currently. Feeling his cheeks flush in embarrassment he ended up laughing nervously as she cackled some more at him.

"Cor blimey Will, you really are going to miss me aren't ya!"

"Like that's even something you have to say out loud you clever lesbian."

"Don't break a nail now Mr, now come here, one more time you silly sod!"

Sarah took him in another hug but this time it was laced with more love than a bear hug squeeze. She then whispered gently into his ear.

"Don't you worry Mr, sometimes I could give you a good clip round the earhole like any good mother would do to her Son, but other times you have made this job just a bit more bearable

whenever we've worked on shift together. Thank you for that."
She released Will from the tender hug they shared and this time
there was no tears to be had from Will. Only smiles of gratitude,
then Sarah went back into full Londoner mode.

"Now…get back on that pod with Kym, double-time!"

She clapped her hands in rapid succession together and Will half-
jogged out of the Dishwasher Area as he left her chuckling at his
behaviour. Will was back with Kym in no time who watched him
return. Inquisitive as always, Kym studied her best friend with just
her eyes from the till. "Sarah came and made sure you were alright
didn't she?" His 'Firecracker' asked of him as Will got back to
wiping the surfaces around the coffee machine to a good standard,
Will glanced back at her on his left shoulder with a half-smile on
his lips.

"Of course she did, she's not that cold, she's just…

"A South Londoner I know."

"Your gonna miss her just as much as me 'Firecracker'."

"Oh, that goes without saying Willyboy."

The last twenty or so minutes flew by, then before they knew it
Sarah came back out from the Dishwasher Area that would no
longer be her station anymore. Keeping a brave face on, she wasn't
prepared for what she saw next. The staff on duty had partly

assembled to clap her off as she left the Café' for the last time. Will, Kym, Nat, Coralie, Sasha, young Sarah, Aaron and even Joyce had appeared just before she left and they all cheered, whooped, applauded as passionately as they could. Sarah, ever the tough one as she left through the large entrance for the final time turned around to look back as they kept up the rapturous applause. Even the customers were enjoying the spectacle of it all. Sarah stood there, her time done, her new adventure and life in Spain awaiting to begin with her woman Janice, and she smiled with eagerness plus a few dignified tears in her eyes. Being the typical Londoner she was, she bid goodbye in the only way she knew how.

"See ya!"

Then Sarah Harker gave the peace sign to the Café' staff and sauntered off to the escalators as her now former co-workers applauded until she was well on her way upstairs. Everyone went back to their assigned roles. Nat on Kitchen, Sasha, and Aaron on pod one, Kym and Will on pod two, Coralie inspecting the Café', young Sarah on tables and Joyce observing all with the clipboard tucked as always under her arm. As one Employee left the Company, life reasserted itself placing everyone back in what they knew. The routine went on as it always did. For Will, he would always go forth now realising that there was no one quite like Sarah Harker. As he got to work on a coffee order Kym was processing through the till by a new customer, he overheard Joyce speaking to Coralie as the Supervisor joined her by her side.

"Aww, I'm gonna miss Sarah. No one kept Dishwasher in order quite like her right Joyce?"

"Huh…?"

Joyce looked up from her clipboard then realised what Coralie said "…oh yes, quite right about that Coralie…" Joyce wasn't completely focused on the here and now Will noticed as he finished the coffee as the customer picked it up from the back. Coralie and Joyce were just on opposite side of coffee pod two, well within earshot of him, they weren't even attempting to chat quietly either.

"Are you sure you alright Joyce?"

"Yes, yes all good. Just my back has been playing up again recently that's all Coralie. Your right, there wasn't anyone quite like Sarah. However…"

"However? Joyce?"

Joyce was now looking at Coralie, but her focus still wasn't fully on her. As Will saw out of the corner of her eye she seemed to be rolling each shoulder individually very slowly as if she were working out a kink she had going on in her back.

"Oh, it's just that yes Sarah is gone for that new life in Spain, good for her…" Joyce stopped her shoulder rolling as she seemed to kickstart her assertiveness back into motion, then like always Joyce Cooper floored Will once more with her cold Managerial mentality.

"You watch Coralie. Less than a week later no one will even blink twice at someone like Sarah. Sure, she'll have the odd mention down the line in future, but no one will even remember her properly in the end. She'll just be another sorry Employee who did a good job for the time she was here, yet no one will be able to even name her off the top of their head in a few short years. She'll simply disappear off into the ether. Forgotten. It's always been the way of this place. Some of us don't even blink about it anymore truthfully after all these years. The ones who stay, well they know how to work the system *just the right way…*"

Will blinked hard whilst taking a quiet yet calming breathe, his Managers comments still very much ringing in his ears. Truthfully, he shouldn't have been fazed by what he had just heard, yet Joyce Cooper had that way about her regardless. *'When it comes down to it, you really know how to just cut someone out of your life, or the workforce don't ya Joyce? I certainly won't be forgetting Sarah Harker anytime soon. That you can be sure of.'* The thought gave him focus as he wiped the auto-wand down as he always did, his posture was relaxed, he kept his back to Coralie and Joyce as they both moved off after Joyce's select words about the recently resigned Sarah. He was quite glad that they had. He watched them over his right shoulder as they left through the Food Department exit and for once, he had never been more grateful to see the back of both Coralie and Joyce. One of his friends may have just left, someone who he could rely on, but they had gone off to pursue their own personal happiness. But Will's enemies were still very much circling in the air above.

You always keep your friends close yet your enemies closer.

Especially in Riverside.

*

Back To Now.

The Men's Locker Room.

11:49 am.

1 OCT AT 11:50

…Will as long as your happy with your decision then who am I to judge you for it? Your still a slacker though.

How am I a 'slacker' exactly? Cheeky cow like always aren't ya Sarah, that Spanish temperament hasn't dulled your senses one bit has it?

Not for a second, can't believe in November me and Janice have been out here almost a year!

I know! That blows my mind honestly Mrs. Listen, I'd love to chat, but I start work in less than ten minutes so gotta put the mobile away. Speak soon?

Of course baby, no problem. Proud of you even if it's weird your just going to a different store. But you're doing it for you which is all that matters. Talk soon, love ya...slacker! Xx

Will closed the Facebook-Inbox chat with Sarah grateful he had his former co-workers support all the way from the sunny Costa Blanca. Some people really always had your back regardless of where they lived in the world these days. As he went to stow his mobile back in his backpack, Will then had another message come through, this time from a WhatsApp message. He opened it wondering who was contacting him and he received an unexpected surprise. It was his good mate Josh Sullivan.

Hey Will. You all good? 11:53

Well hey Josh! I'm good, you ok? 11:53

Yeah not bad, not long till you leave your job now right? 11:53

That's right. Only three weeks to go! Which is kind of mad to think about... 11:53

I bet, fancy celebrating before your all done at Riverside then? 11:54

Now that's a thought actually, what you got in mind? 11:54

How about we have a night out at The Precipice? 11:54

Well there's another thought... 11:54

What's that? 11:55

I probably haven't been to The Precipice in about less than a year actually. 11:55

Damn. You're not missing much really. 11:55

Good point, it is out of the way I guess. Here's an idea...why don't I bring my shy friend Johnny Michaels along as well? 11:55

Oh the shy one? He's cute in a geeky sort of way I guess. He's never been though right? Sure that's a wise thing to bring him along Will? 11:56

Yeah why not Josh? It'll be a good night out for him. 11:56

Fine, Johnny can come. You can both crash at mine then head home Sunday morning if you like? 11:56

Great! I'll run that by Johnny, I know he'll say yes to a night out with alcohol involved more or less. What date we going then? 11:57

Cool. Say two weeks' time today? That'll make it October 15th. I'll pick you guys up from Basildon Station? I'll bring my mate Joe as well. 11:57

Great, a night out at an out of the way Gay Bar in Southend, what could go wrong! The infamous Joe ah? Young twenty-one-year-old Joe ah? Naughty, naughty Josh... 11:58

No comment Will. See you on the 15th. 11:58

See you then Joshy! Your still a naughty boy though. 11:58

Will finally stowed his mobile back in his bag, properly secured his locker then dashed out of the Locker Room tapping the swipe in box so he could start getting paid then ran down to the shop floor. As soon as he made it on to the Ladies Wear Department he stopped running but kept himself going in brisk power march. Before he knew it, he was in the Downstairs' Café' bang on two minutes passed midday. Thankfully, Coralie was too busy sorting out an issue to notice he was only two minutes over the time he was meant to start his late shift. He slipped past her and walked through the side entrance of the Kitchen and went out back to wash his hands in the Dishwasher Area. It wasn't mental with thirsty customers yet, but he could feel the oncoming business of the Saturday. '*Just Twenty-One Days to go Will. That's all, then you can say goodbye to this reductive place once and...*'

"Excuse me would you?"

The voice was like a shard of extremely sharp glass that pierced him whenever he heard it near or around him. Looking over his shoulder from the sink he was still using, he saw her in all her imposing glory. And in a split second he was instantaneously on edge, his posture was stiff, and he raised his chin upwards in a defiant manner. Josie Sybille had that effect on him after all these years as it was. He continued washing his hands as she stood at the entrance separating the Kitchen from the Dishwasher.

"Are you quite done there Will?"

"Yes. Almost."

"Well I need to get around you to get to those fridges you see…"

"Did you officially inquire to Coralie about any stock you may need however Josie?"

He had been drying his hands slowly just to make her wait longer than necessary then as soon as he brought up that she needed access to the fridges, Will knew she was in search of stock without showing Coralie the curtesy she deserved by asking out of politeness. He had now turned to face her, he found her quintessential poker face already fixed onto her unpleasant face along with her thin lips always painted in that same dark shade of lipstick.

'God I hate you with a passion.'

The thought gave him clarity as she did her typical look of making him feel less important than she was despite the fact she had no authority whatsoever anymore.

"Well Josie?"

"Well what?"

"Did you go through the proper channels and ask Coralie if you could take whatever stock you so needed for the Upstairs' Café?"

"That's none of your busy really…"

"…Somehow I think it is since it may have a knock-on effect in the smooth *operational running* of the Downstairs' Café today. And that greatly concerns me I must say…err, do you mind!"

Josie had decided without saying so to walk right in Will's path which caused him to intentionally jump out of the way as she got to one of the back fridges opening the door then began rummaging through it with total disregard to Will and his objections.

"Josie. I will tell you this only once…"

"I really could care less whatever comes out of your mouth Will."

"*Excuse me,* but who the hell…"

"*Mum*?"

Josie and Will both froze on their respective spots as the new voice interrupted their near heated exchange. Josie pulled her head out from rummaging in the fridge, Will turned a one-eighty slowly at the new arrival. Standing in the doorway between the Kitchen and Dishwasher Area was a young man standing a little shy of six foot tall, thick blonde curly, and strong jawline. It was Henry Sybille, Josies Son. He was staring back and forth with his eyes between his Mother and Will uncertain of what was happening.

"Harry my love…"

'My love? Whose this person I'm hearing all of a sudden?'

"…aren't you supposed to be on tables dear?"

'Dear? She's genuinely freaking me out now.'

Harry hadn't moved from the doorway still; he was still looking between both Will and Josie. Sensing the tension, he decided to help alleviate the situation.

"Yeah I am Mum, but…"

"But what?"

'There it is. That immediate questioning of why she gets to do what she likes when she likes.'

"It's just Coralie wanted to speak to you outside Mum…" Josie had begun to rummage again in the back fridge for stock she was still trying to pry away from the Downstairs' Café, Henry wasn't quite done yet however.

"Yeah Mum!" Henry got his Mother's full attention now as she looked at him like he was being intentionally annoying, Will just stood between the two silent as a mouse.

"What is it Henry?"

"Coralie wants to speak to you…*before* you take any stock. And she has Bianca waiting with her too." Henry stopped to look at the floor all of a sudden as Josie pulled one of her classic pinched looks of annoyance. Will took this opportunity to look back at Josie who closed her eyes for a brief second to calm her nerves. Snapping them back open with intent, she closed the back fridge door loudly still cleared annoyed, then marched out of the Dishwasher Area to the front without a backwards glance leaving just Henry and Will to themselves. Henry looked at Will sheepishly.

"Sorry about her Will, you know how she can be mate."

"Henry…" Will began, then exhaled a long tired breathe, "…its ok. She is your Mum after all."

"Yeah I know. Doesn't excuse her behaviour though. Oh, Coralie told me to tell you that your on Dishwasher ok?"

Will nodded his acceptance as he looked down the narrow Dishwasher Area that was now his for what was probably the next few hours. He had two full crockery trolleys waiting to be cleared, a sink full of dirty cutlery, plus the Dishwasher still needed to be unloaded from the current clean cycle it had just completed. Sarah Harker Will was most definitely not. *'What I wouldn't give to have my lesbian with me right now helping. I wonder what the cheapest flight to Alicante is at the moment online?'* Will thought to himself as he moved to get started on his washing up duties. Henry was still loitering in the Area with him he noticed.

"Was there something else you needed to tell me Henry?"

Henry looked Will in the eyes this time and Will saw something he hadn't seen from Josies Son before until now. It was pity. Henry had gotten a part-time job in the Café' only a few months ago at the end of August since he was a full-time College Student. Of course his Mother being the former manipulative Supervisor that she was had essentially made him apply for a job in the same place she worked. Henry had flown through the two-stage assessment as his Mother had clearly fed him all the necessary information he needed to succeed, and he was an Employee just like Will. Will thought he would have ended up hating the kid just like his Mother, He had been pleasantly surprised to find Henry was cool, confident, and approachable sixteen-year-old who was nothing like his cold-hearted and removed parent. It had been quite refreshing to work alongside him Will had found. Henry stopped looking at him in the eyes silently to respond to Will's question now.

"Yeah, it's just…"

"Just what?"

"Well. I wanted to say sorry to you Will."

Will had not been expecting this at all.

'What on earth does he want to apologise to me for?'

"Yeah look, I wanted to say sorry to you about my Mum. I know she can be a handful at times and I also know you two haven't seen eye to eye, especially in this Dishwasher Area as well. But yeah, you're an alright guy and I felt like you deserved to hear that from me." Henry stopped as Will studied him in total surprise. Josie and Will were not friends, but to have her teenage Son apologise for her behaviour was extremely telling of the kind of Mother Josie was in her Working Life and her Personal Life. Will had been truly eye opened by Henry's apology, so he did something he thought he would never do to the kid. He extended his hand waiting for Henry to the return the gesture. Henry looked at the outstretched hand then back at him surprised as well, then he took Will's hand and clasped it firmly shaking it.

"Thank you Henry. I really appreciate that."

"No worries mate."

"Yeah there is actually…" Will paused, inhaled a quick breathe then just spoke his mind like he always did, "…me and yout Mum are not friends Henry. We never will be. He actions speak for themselves after all these years I've worked here. One of the reasons I'm transferring is partly to get away from her and her way of working. She isn't inclusive or respectful of others and she only likes things done her way or else. That's simply not how you conduct yourself in a place of business. But you, Henry? You're the only good thing to come out of her, and what you just said there…well it really meant something to me ok?" Will finished as he released the handshake, Henry was nodding along and smiling with him in acknowledgement now.

"I know my Mum basically gave me a handout with getting me this job but working with you isn't all that bad as she has made out to me in private Will. It's been really fun working alongside you in fact and these next few weeks you have left here, let's have a good ol laugh you and I, ok?"

Henry finished, Will looked the tall kid up and down and smiled at him. They both fist pumped then Henry set off for tables to get them sorted. Will turned around and found all the Dishwashing he had still needed to be completed. He still wished Sarah Harker were working here to this day. Friends like Sarah may leave their jobs eventually while enemies like Josie stay and toil to their hearts content purely because they could. Work was a never-ending cycle of emotions day in, day out. As he got down to the business of sorting out the Dishwasher, Will remembered not too long ago how a previous run in with Josie in the Dishwasher Area had set them both on the opposing sides of their ways of being. This time however for both Josie and Will, it had been permanent with no way back or reconciliation to be had.

'Thank goodness Henry intervened between me and his Mum today. If only he had been here last year to sort out our last rather explosive confrontation. Now that was something else entirely...'

Nine

December 23rd, 2015.

The Downstairs' Café.

Wednesday.

3:00 pm.

It had been hell on earth. Literally. Christmas Season at Riverside truly exposed human beings at their most vulgar baseline impulses. Tis the season to be jolly, it was not. Will had quite frankly had enough of all of it. The constant stream of customers had been never-ending in the Café'. The customers in turn were stressed to high hell about their last-minute Christmas Shopping and they took their pent-up energy out on the staff before quite literally collapsing into any vacant table that became available, they then demanded with no politeness to be seen or heard for it to be cleared by whatever member of staff they could eyeball, that staff member happened to be Will who was slowly but surely losing the will to live. Any chance he got he escaped to the Dishwasher Area for a quick respite from the onslaught out on the shop floor. Since Sarah had now been living over in Spain for almost two months, Kathy Bailey had assumed most of Sarah's duties as the person who enjoyed doing Dishwasher the most. She was Sarah Baileys Mother as well having worked at Riverside for about a good decade, she had never worked in the Café' before until the refurbishment had commenced. Then like all unsuspecting employees, she had been hand selected by her Manager at the time on the Lingerie Department to find herself working the Café' all of a sudden without any choice in the matter. She was a kind woman who was just as short as Sarah was, mixed race with pixie cut brown hair plus a smile that could melt butter, she couldn't hurt anyone with her words if she even dared to try. Her and Will had gotten along easily when she had come down from Lingerie, whenever she got the chance though she would without fail as if like clockwork moan about how truly horrible it was to work in the Café'. This was one of those days for both of them. Will was trying his best just to keep himself sane whilst trying to comfort Kathy who seemed to be chained to the Dishwasher today. "Oh Will, it is ever going to physically stop being busy today? My feet are killing me." Kathy said as she cleared the Dishwasher of what must have been its millionth clean cycle today, under both of her eyes dark circles had started to appear and her bodily functions had become more and more laboured as each hour ticked on by. Will was leaning against the wall to give his ever-increasing aching back a rest, he had his eyes closed, his head was raised upwards, so his forehead plus vastly receded hairline was reflecting the harsh fluorescent lighting a little. He didn't know where up and down began anymore. "Kathy my dear, I feel like six o'clock can't come quick enough, I feel like all the dirty plates, dishes and cutlery I give you will just overflow with no end in sight!" Will opened his eyes to look at his petite co-worker who was finishing clearing the last clean cycle of crockery into a waiting trolley. She stopped back at the sink as she began the routine of starting anew with the small mountain of dirty dishes leftover by the customers.

"It does feel like there is no end in sight Will, I dare not even look out on that shop floor…"

"You really don't want too Kathy; a bombsite is an understatement for the hell going on out there. Speaking of which, I better get back out there with what little energy I have left."

Will left Kathy to her Dishwashing as she knuckled down. Will steeled himself then marched back to the nearest cleaning station where he knew he had more trays to sort, before he made it, he stopped to take in the literal ocean of people all seated. As far as he could see, every single cover in the Downstairs' Café was occupied by someone with a bag or at least a dozen bags of shopping. He saw a young Mum with two toddler children who looked like she was about to lose it as she tried to keep her kids entertained whilst downing what must have been a lukewarm coffee by now. He saw a lone gentleman staring vacantly off into the distance surrounded on each side by bags of shopping with gifts with what was also far too many different colours of wrapping paper he was bound to be using on the floor of his living room on Christmas Eve only a day later. Will saw two teenage girls chatting happily away with a few bags of gifts that could only be for themselves and not their family members as they inspected something new on each other's phones that must have been of extreme importance as they were practically bouncing up and down in their seats as he walked past them making it into the sanctity of the three-quartered enclosed cleaning station. His welcome loneliness didn't last long as three different individual customers decided to disturb him all at once each with a tray of leftovers they wanted to get rid of immediately. *'Lord give me strength.'* Will thought bitterly as he dealt with the three customers who dumped him their trays then stalked back off their tables without evening thanking him, *'people have no idea on this planet today how they really are the worst when it comes to Christmas Season here in this place do they?'* he internally asked himself as three of the customers collapsed back down at their respective tables without actually relaxing, it mirrored how Will felt right then. Tense yet wound up like a tight piece of string, done up in so many knots that there was no discernible way to untie it properly. With less than three hours to go, he got on with the sheer amount of leftovers he had to sort. It wasn't pleasant or pretty in his cleaning station, being alone on the floor as well he had to run out every few minutes to give the floor a sweep, he always came back with more trays each time without fail. All the coffee stations were open and taking orders, the kitchen under Nat with Tonye of all people having to help her make orders as well was a sight Will simply couldn't get used too. He ran out two more trolleys full of to the brim to Kathy on the Dishwasher, as he wheeled back the empty trolleys waiting for him, customers started to signal him to clear their dirty tables not caring one bit that he was currently busy, they just expected it now or else. It wasn't that they were demanding him to serve them right there, it was the looks they were giving him when he would just apologise or try to reassure them that he would be a few minutes as he tried to sort or finish what he was currently doing.

"Err excuse me? I just asked you *less than a minute ago* to clear my table…"

"Hello there, yes you? I need that gone *right away* if you can hurry it up!"

"Could you just *stop what you're doing right now* to assist me, thank you…"

'Seriously. Every single one of you. Just go fuck off a cliff, right now!'

Will more or less slammed the trio of trays he had somehow manged to clear from the customers in one singular hit who were being short with him just because they could, in the cleaning station then let out an angry sigh, this was too much for just one person to manage on their own, he needed help and he knew he wasn't going to get it anytime soon. He sorted the three trays quickly then added them to the trolleys that were almost full again that he would have to take out to Kathy soon knowing that she would groan as more was brought to her. He didn't like it, but he had to do it since no one else would be able too at this current time.

'I literally hate the lead up to Christmas. Give me the actual day and I'll be sitting in a corner drinking all the Prosecco I can get my hands on, but the actual leading up to that one day? No thank you. Next.'

He began wheeling the first trolley towards the entrance of the Dishwasher Area, as he was passing the Kitchen side entrance he stopped to take stock of how Nat and Tonye were getting on in their pulpit. Nat was rushing backwards and forwards from oven to oven while Tonye seemed to be physically trailing in her wake taking toastie after toastie from her to plate them up, Nat was perspiring from underneath her skull cap she always wore when she was in the Kitchen. "Keep it up Nat, you're doing great Mrs!" Will called out to her, she didn't look at him directly, she managed to give him a prompt thumbs up that she had heard him, then Tonye stopped following Nat to take orders to look at Will, she was looking at him oddly as if expecting a compliment for her, like she earned it for simply following Nat. *'Not on your life Tonye. Following someone to assist is good an all but you aren't actually doing the orders dear.'* Will kept on wheeling the full trolley as he chose to not bother with Tonye and her so called work ethic. He certainly didn't to see whatever filthy disapproving look she gave him either, he didn't have the time nor patience for it on today's chaotic shift. He wheeled the first full trolley into Kathy who was just about finishing up with her empty trolleys waiting for him, like clockwork he heard her groan as she moped her forehead with some kitchen towel.

"Still no let-up then, or is that a stupid question to ask Will?"

"That's a stupid question to ask Kathy."

He departed quickly to fetch the second full trolley for her, in quick succession he was back in the cleaning station with two empty trolleys and a very full Café' of overly annoyed customers that were going nowhere anytime soon. He was trying to not think

of the volumes of people out in the Complex barging past one
another as they frantically searched for those last bits of shopping
that they needed before Christmas Day swung round in less than
forty-eight hours. *'Oy, the amount of Christmas wrapping I've got
to do when I get home as well is not a welcoming thought.
Definitely gonna need a few bottles of Rose to get me through that
ordeal.'* he thought to himself as he knuckled down to more of the
trays he was about to collect. He stepped out of what was
becoming his sort of sanctuary from the onslaught that awaited
him, he looked around the Café' taking in the sights he saw. Both
pods were still going at full strength, each of the four tills had a
small queue with a co-worker processing the orders through as fast
they could, Will noticed how much Aaron was concentrating on
the till screen as he put an order through while the customer he
served seemed to just be talking continuously not allowing
themselves to pause to take a breather or let Aaron off the hook for
a second. Once Aaron had bid them what must have been a very
welcome farewell, Will saw his chin dip and he exhaled a long
calming breathe himself, his shoulders even sagged a little as the
brief moment was over then Aaron snapped back to full attention
as the next customer started sprouting their order in his direction.
One relentless customer after the next, it was gruelling work every
single one of them was conducting today. All except for one Josie
Sybille who seemed to walk in without a care in the world into the
Café at that very moment, she never stopped walking, yet Will saw

her eyes overlooking the chaotic scenes of Christmas shoppers, she never gave anything away which Will kind of envied of her despite their general animosity towards one another. *'Now what does she want?'* He observed of her as she disappeared out back towards Tonye's personal hovel in the Baking Section. All of a sudden Tonye scarpered out of the Kitchen to meet Josie leaving Nat to her own devices rather than being her unwelcome shadow. Will continued watching as Nat seemed to relax more now that she didn't have anyone following her in her space despite the small help it provided. Will hadn't missed a beat of Tonye heading off to meet Josie in her hovel. *'Lord knows what their discussing. I never trust her motives when she is down here these days.'* He got back on with his work and tried to get on with whatever tables he had to deal with, for a little while the tables became more manageable as it crept into the late afternoon, customers seemed to be taking their time plus the queues remained, they were all small for each till person to be able to get the orders through without worrying about how many more customers were waiting in line behind them. Will before he knew it had one full trolley of dirty dishes to wheel out again to Kathy while his second trolley awaited to be filled, rather than filling the second one up before taking both to her, he decided to get the first full one out so as not to overload her in one hit like had been doing earlier. He passed Nat again who had settled in her own groove with far less tickets of orders to be made, she was taking a very much needed gulp of water before getting on with

Billy Harding © 2021

what orders she had left to do. Over one of her shoulders though, Will saw Josie and Tonye nattering away to one another in hushed tones. Their body language was almost timid with a few glances over their own shoulders in case anyone happened to be listening in, Will too far away to make out what their conversation was, not that he even cared. He still wasn't entirely comfortable with Josie being down here. *'If Coralie hadn't called in sick today she wouldn't stand for their chatting while everyone else is working currently. No sir.'* He had stopped wheeling out his full trolley to glance at Josie and Tonye still talking in their cagey manner, before he got back to getting the trolley out to Kathy in Dishwasher, Josie glanced again over Tonye's right shoulder to look Will dead in the eyes, he stopped in his tracks as the former Supervisor stared at him, he did not like the blatant judgemental look she was giving him right now. In fact, he was incentivised by the look she was still giving him. *'Really bitch? You wanna stare me down just because you can, not gonna happen on my watch Mrs.'* Will let go of the trolley, set himself on the spot as Josie still tried her level best to unnerve him, he put both his hands on his waist, assuming a power pose then stared her right back down with an ever so slight tilt of his head to the left. Tonye and Josies conversation had stopped mid-flow as Tonye turned halfway to look at the unspoken moment occurring between her friend and Will, she looked from her to him very slowly unsure as to what to do so she stood there gormlessly. *'You may have your certain ways about you, but you will never, ever frighten me into submission.'* The defiant thought gave him more focus as Josie never missed a beat of their staring match. Who would outgun the other, no one knew. Nat was now getting in on the action, so she did something to alleviate the tension.

"Come on Will, let's give you a hand with that ah?"

"I'm fine thanks Nat."

"I insist, no excuses."

Nat stepped directly into his line of sight breaking the stand-off between the two of them, she did however turn around with one of her hands on his hips and gave Josie her own unimpressed glance. Sensing her moment to jump back in Tonye got her hand and physically pulled Josie's attention back to her re-starting their hushed chat. Nat knew the moment had passed now as she looked at Will with her own motherly glance about her as she physically guided Will with the full trolley to the Dishwasher Area where Kathy was cleaning down two empty trolleys that awaited Will.

"Care to explain what that was all about Will?"

"You tell me Nat? She started it."

At the sound of their unfolding conversation, Kathy looked over them both with concern.

"Everything alright guys?"

"Oh yeah Kathy, Will decided to get into a staring contest…"

"Er, I did not *decide*, it just happened thank you!"

Nat looked at him with her mothering look still in place, she then patted him on the arm reassuringly, "don't let her get under skin like that Will, it's really not worth it." Nat put her thumb and forefinger under his chin and raised so he held himself up tall with confidence, then as soon as she had done she was marching off back out the side entrance to the Kitchen leaving Will and Kathy to their devices. Breathing out loudly to relax and forget about Josie with her unnerving ways, he turned ninety degrees in Kathy's direction who waited patiently at the sink for him.

You alright now Will?"

"Yeah, yeah all good here Kathy, those for me?"

He indicated the empty trolleys that he knew were for him, he was simply asking out of politeness given the craziness of today's shift. Nodding her petite head vigorously they swapped trolleys, one for her, two for him. He took them out to the cleaning station then he saw the second one, he filled it with a few errant bits which were loaded onto it that he had then wheeled it out promptly to Kathy, he folded his arms then leaned against the wall for another quick break. Kathy got down to what Dishwashing she still had to do, she stole a glance or two in hid direction.

"Tired Will? I'm feeling the same way myself…"

"Let's just say I *cannot wait* for six to roll round my dear."

"I bet, shame about Coralie being ill today isn't it?"

"Oh yeah, I think she'll be ok though, Christmas can do that to you though…"

Will had stopped leaning against the wall to join Kathy at the sink as she knuckled down to some cutlery in serious need of a good cleaning, their chat was a harmless one between to mutual co-workers enjoying one another's company in the moment. Then as if it were by magic, Josie Sybille came round the other corner separating the Dishwasher Area from the Kitchen and Baking Sections with purposeful intent in her walk and everything changed with the next statement she uttered without any fear of provocation.

"Oh Will, are you gossiping again? There's enough *shit-stirring* going round this place as it is!"

Time seemed to stand still suddenly. Will felt as if everything had become extremely distant whilst he appeared to be moving in slow-motion in the direction towards Josie. Thoughts, emotions, feelings, and bodily function seemed to elude him all at once for a split-second. He even forgot where he was. Then as cruel as the passage of time could be to some, it asserted itself in its all its ugly manner. He didn't know he was even speaking again until he then heard back what he was actually saying in response.

"Excuse me? What did you just say?"

He was now facing Josie fully; she couldn't have been standing less than three feet away from him. She stood there as if soaking up her own defiance simply because she knew she could, it was the epitome of arrogance. For Will, something within him caused an explosion of intense feelings he had briefly been numbed too. Now, the red mist had settled all around him, like a storm that was made up of all the unreleased explosion he held within him, he simply released into the wild that separated Josie and himself.

"Excuse me, who the hell are you to interrupt a *private conversation* between to co-workers? First off, you have zero right to do that, secondly it is beyond rude its downright an invasion of privacy, then again someone as *insidious* as you wouldn't give a damn whomever your feel like interrupting and don't get me started on your pathetic group of lackeys Upstairs' as well…"

Josie had raised her overly pencilled on eyebrows up in surprise, her eyes widen just a fraction in shock as well while Will continued his angry speech.

"…You really know no bounds do you Josie? For that fact you really are a nasty piece of work and from day one you've never liked me!"

Will finished exhaling hard as the vitriol escaped from him. Josie was frozen on the spot, her arms folded tightly, her awful eyebrows still raised, her probing eyes were narrowed. Who was this person to scold her, in her eyes she could never be punished for anything she did, so she responded the only she knew how.

"*That's got nothing to do with it*!"

Will's jaw went slack as the statement came out of her mouth, the red mist all around him seemed to grow in intensity.

"Who the *HELL* do you think you are? Do you have any idea…"

He stopped short of finishing as he had begun to step forward in retaliation of Josie's loaded statement, he was now being pushed back forcefully by none other than the petite Kathy Bailey who he had forgotten had been stranding more or less between them. Before he could protest anymore at Josie's blatant goading of him he saw her marching off in the opposite direction while Kathy successfully pushed him out of the Dishwasher Area entirely and back onto the shop floor where there were still customers all going about their own Christmas craziness. None in the immediate vicinity of the Dishwasher entrance seemed have any idea of the fiery confrontation that gone down between Josie and Will a second ago. He was breathing heavily, his heart was thumping loudly in his ears, he didn't know where to look or what to think, all under the watchful yet worrying eyes of Kathy.

"Will I know what just happened was awful, but you need to calm down Mr."

Kathy had her left raised in his direction as if providing herself as a human barrier between the Area she worked in and the shop floor to stop him from entering, Will had other ideas though.

"Oh don't worry about that Kathy. This is most definitely not the end of this…"

Will set off in his own march rounding the corner sharply so he was on the other side of the Kitchen with the wall that separated it from the rest of the floor. He stopped dead in his tracks as he saw out of the large entrance as Josie was heading up the escalator in full retreat of the Downstairs Café' as fast as her work shoes could carry her. She didn't turn around at all which Will was grateful for as the look of pure filth plastered on his face could have disturbed anyone, he was standing still but he used both of his hand to cling on to the wall that separated the Kitchen, he found Nat staring at him hard, her eyes full of concern, she knew something had happened out back.

"What went down Will? I heard raised voices…"

"Trust me Nat, you don't wanna know what I'm feeling right now."

"You ok there Will?"

The voice was full of uncertainty yet curiosity also, he turned his head with his filthy look still in place to see Tonye standing at the edge of the Kitchen shuffling from side to side. She was looking at him trying to convey some form of sympathy that Will did not believe for a second, not when Tonye herself was an ally of Josie and *'the Clique'*.

"Am I ok? Tonye, I'm gonna say this once. I will never tell you anything again how I am feeling exactly right now since your pathetic little friend will want to know all the details won't she? She'll probably be texting you the second you leave work in fact if I know her motivations after all this time. So if I were you, *Tonye Patricks*. Turn around and go back to your ridiculous corner and *leave. Me. Alone.*"

Wills statement got him the desired effect, Tonye shuffled off to where she always went without looking back at him or Nat, she dared not too. Nat was still very concerned about Will's state of mind.

"Will perhaps you'd better…"

"Better what Nat. I am so not in the mood for anything right now."

"Will. I was gonna say, leave the floor and take a moment or two to collect yourself. Your of no use to anyone with the angry state you're in right now."

She had said it with care to him but also a firmness she knew would get through to him. As if she were the lightning rod he needed right now, he finally felt as if some of the red mist that been swirling around him was at last dissipating. *'She's right. I need to get out of here and fast.'* The thought gave him something to focus on other than his anger which continued to ebb away, he was now nodding his head without looking at Nat.

"Your right. Your absolutely right."

"I know I am, now get out of here and I'll get someone to cover you on tables. Go."

He didn't need to be told twice, so he departed out of the large entrance of the Café' without looking back. He walked, not anywhere in particular but he found himself walking faster than he normally would be, he still had some unworked energy he needed to get out his system and quickly. He was aware that he had walked into the Food Department, which was alight with activity, every isle was filled with people getting the things they need for their upcoming Christmas Dinners they were going to make or to whosever's they planned on going too. Will knew he needed to get off this floor as fast as he could. So he headed for the Operations door that would get him away from any customers that might try and draw his attention with unnecessary requests. Once he was through the Operations door where no customers were allowed to venture except for staff he felt only a fraction better, it was something at least. *'God she got under my skin in the worse kind of way possible.'* He made his way through the Operations Hub of the Store as staff went about their business too busy themselves to pay him any mind which he was silently grateful for, he wasn't ready to interact with anyone, at least not normally yet. Will made his way to the staff lift and pressed the button a little too sharply, as he waited for the lift to arrive he found himself tapping his left foot repeatedly, his impatience telling him he still needed to calm down, there was only one thing for it. *'Better go tell Bianca everything that happened. Only way I'm going to get this anger for Josie Sybille processed in a way I know how, tell my Manager the whole story.'* The lift arrived and he got in punching the button for the staff level of the Store, the lift doors closed, then the metal box was ascending. Once upstairs, he exited the lift his strides long and full of purpose as he made his way to the Admin Office where he knew Bianca would have set up shop to finish whatever she was doing. After the shock of Joyce Cooper resigning only very recently along with the swapped-out Emily Arms who was ensconced in the Southend Region, it was just Bianca as the sole Manager for both Cafes'. So far she was just about muddling through whilst simultaneously not impressing many with her style of work. Will had no idea what he was about to walk into and unloading the whole sorry affair that had happened between him and Josie, he had no choice in the matter, Bianca was the Manager he had to report too so she would just have to sit there, listen, then make a decision as to what exactly to do about it. It was the only logical course of action available to Will presently. Entering the Admin Office, he found Bianca typing away at a computer, she turned at the sound of the door, when she saw that it was Will she had what was becoming her well known trademark smile in place as if butter wouldn't melt. *'Oy, this is gonna be an interesting conversation to say the least.'* Will psyched himself up then went for the jugular.

"Bianca, I wouldn't be smiling if I were you…"

The next ten minutes seemed to fly by as he recalled the entire sordid ordeal that went down between him and Josie. He left no stone unturned. Bianca went from her pleasant smile that she used to get away with for doing very little to a sort of wonky downward curl with her eyes widened in surprise. As Will finished retelling what had happened, he finally stopped speaking to allow any kind of response from his Manager as to what should be done. He waited a full minute as the events sunk in for her with a few open and closing of her mouth as she pondered what to say, then words were finally formed then they were vocalised to him.

"Will…I think for the time being…we'd best wait until Christmas is out of the way."

Bianca finished by clasping her hands together then placing her usual smile back in place as if this was a satisfactory outcome, Will however was stumped by what Bianca was suggesting.

"Your saying to *just wait*?"

"Yes, that's right. At least for now."

"Are you absolutely sure about that Bianca?"

"As clear as I can be. Not a lot can be done at this time so close to Christmas Day. Its best to wait until we get past Boxing Day then take a look back at the whole situation with more fresh eyes. Tempers can run a little high in retail anyway. Feel free to come back to me afterwards, take all the time you need to calm down right now if you do."

Bianca finished by giving Will another smile as if what had gone down between him and Josie was simply a matter that could wait for another day. For Will, he wanted something done now or a more firmer course of action to be suggested then taken as soon as it possibly could be. He wouldn't settle for less, yet his own Manager was simply deferring the issue to an undisclosed time or even for it to maybe be forgotten about entirely. *I'm gonna have to take this beyond Bianca now. Beyond this Store in fact. My only option available to me right now might as well have closed the proverbial door in my face permanently.'* The sobering thought didn't fuel anymore anger from him, he just felt completely as cold as it was outside the Store in the wintery climate. Will didn't know what to do so he decided to leave Bianca to her own devices, making a swift exit, he was back in the long corridor alone with only his thoughts for company. *'I had one of my co-workers near enough admit she has never liked me, accused me of being a shit-stirrer in front of another member of staff and she still got to walk away from me thinking she can still do what she likes, when she likes. This place of work has literally been its own kind of enabler for her to be that nasty person that she truly is for years. I present the case to the suitable person I need too, and they want me to basically wait so then it can be brushed under the carpet. How is any of this fair and equal treatment in a workplace?'* Will found himself in the staff canteen without fully remembering the walk down from the long corridor from the Admin Office. He was standing in front of the tea and coffee section for staff, so he made himself a strong builders-tea with extra sugar than he would normally put in it. He felt the need right now. He found the staff canteen thankfully empty for the time being, he sat at any table closest drinking his strong tea. He was at a loss with his employment. Five years of loyal, backbreaking, committed work all felt like it was for nothing after his and Josie's encounter, demoralized didn't even cut it. He finished his tea, walked over to the kitchen to drop his empty mug off to be cleaned, then he had an idea. The only viable one he could think of right now, he turned away from where he had deposited his empty mug then left the staff canteen with his stride returning to him. He walked back off down the long corridor in the direction of the Men's Locker Room. And the idea he was now committed too completely helped him refocus with the task at hand he had to deal with, at all costs.

*

The Downstairs Café'

5:05 pm.

Nat saw Will return through the large entrance having disappeared for what must have been a full forty-five to fifty minutes of being upstairs. It wasn't that he had been gone all this time it was the fact that she was concerned for his well-being due to the circumstances at play. Will marched back over to the tables that were still somewhat busy to help the person that had been covering him. It was Aaron who nodded at him in acknowledgement, Will indicated to him he was going to clean and shut down the furthest away cleaning station, Aaron gave him the thumbs then got back to sorting out the leftovers he had at the moment. Nat saw Will disappear into the furthest station then made a decision. As Tonye had left now she got Sasha to cover her in the Kitchen then made her way over to Will. Arriving she observed his behaviour. His posture was calm as he was getting on with closing the station down. Almost too calm after how Nat had seen his anger coming off of him in waves earlier. She wasn't convinced he was fully over it or would ever be over it. With no time like the present, she made herself known to him by asking him the obvious.

"So what's the verdict then?"

Will glanced over his left shoulder at the sound of her voice but he kept working as he did so.

"Bianca said to wait until *after Christmas* then look at it with a fresh pair of eyes."

Nat had a confused look about her as Will remained working while she absorbed what he had said. She wasn't fully satisfied with what she had heard from her young co-worker.

"What else did she say or offer though?"

"Oh that was it in a nutshell. A member of staff calls me a *shit-stirrer* and a *gossip* but sure, let's all wait till Christmas is over with then hope that's all just a thing we imagined by all means!"

Nat was surprised by this now, yet in the same instance she wasn't. This place was almost notorious for sweeping things under the rug on more than a few occasions if it suited the right person in the wrong predicament.

"So I'm gonna take a wild guess you weren't best pleased with what Bianca suggested?"

"Not for one second Nat."

Will had turned to face her now, he had a dustpan and brush in one hand while he held some cleaning spray in the other. He wasn't angry anymore, he was tired. Will just wanted this shift to be over with so he could walk away from the Store today, grab a bottle of chilled Rose' and forget about the whole thing. He knew that wouldn't be the case, yet he could damn well try, especially after the course of action he had decided to take. *'Being angry for long periods of time really does take it out of you I guess.'* He continued to stare wearily at Nat, his ever-loyal co-worker. Their working relationship after all this time had always been an honest one, they always knew where the other stood. The could count on each other when the time was needed. It certainly was not like his friendship with Kym, their relationship went far deeper, Nat was a real support to him when Will least expected it. Today of all days had proven that to him most of all. Putting her out of her misery he elaborated on his state of mind.

"Bianca's entire *suggestion* on how to deal with what happened, I completely disagree with it Nat."

He got back to shutting down the cleaning station while Nat kept staring at him.

"So what can you do about it now Will?"

Will didn't look at his loyal co-worker this time, he had his back facing her again, so he looked at the interior wall instead. He still gave a short response to her question though.

"I took matters into my own hands Nat. What else could I do…"

Nat was slightly confused for a moment, she looked down at the floor thinking intently. Then it dawned on her what Will had done. It was all rather obvious if you took the time to think about it.

"You don't mean…"

"Oh yes I do Nat. I had too. Not after what Bianca was proposing, that's *do nothing* then hope it all *goes away*. Well I'm not sorry when I say it that I…

"You're gonna get burned Will. And it won't end the way you want it too either."

Nat interrupted him with her sobering statement. She had said it to warn him not scold him as such. Will knew what risks he was taking, after what had happened today, he wasn't afraid of much anymore. That included thoroughly entitled people like Josie Sybille as well. He turned around again to face Nat, he put the cleaning spray down, then removed a full big bag of rubbish, tied a secure knot in it then came to stand beside his co-worker once more. She was looking at him with pity in her eyes. He didn't blame her though; it was just her way.

"I may end up burned Nat your quite right. I may even end up in a situation that won't be too my liking. But I still have the sheer *bollocks* to do it in the first place as it is. I've got nothing to lose."

Will looked out at the Café' as it staff worked, customers drank their overpriced coffees, they were none the wiser to the day's events of Will and his enemy. Nat place her left hand on his back and rubbed it to reassure him, he looked at her, smiling in appreciation.

"Are you ready for what's next Will?"

"Am I ready…?"

He looked at Nat then cast his eyes once more around the still busyish Café'. Will knew how he felt right then and there.

"Am I ready for the email that I sent off to Head Office whilst upstairs filing a formal grievance against another member of staff?"

He folded his arms, his shoulders were set, his co-worker offered her moral support to him by his side.

Will had never been more sure of anything in his life thus far.

"…You bet I'm ready Nat."

Ten

October 15ᵗʰ, 2016.

The Men's Locker Room.

Saturday.

10:52 am.

'Seven Days left.'

How he had ended doing extra hours on his day off he had no idea at all. All Will knew was that he could not wait to be drinking a good alcoholic beverage later tonight when Johnny, Jo, Josh, and himself arrived at The Precipice Pub in Southend. *'Five o'clock needs to seriously hurry up and pronto.'* He thought to himself as he shut the door is his locker. He had one week left at Riverside then it would all be over. On to the next adventure. The mere thought of this place becoming a thing of the past to him was a truly baffling concept to wrap his mind around. As he departed the Locker Room he swiped the box that would pay him like normal then he made his way down to the shop floor not pleased in the slightest that he was still here in this place on his day off, he was too nice for his own good. Kym wasn't in and neither was Coralie as it was her weekend off yet here Will was doing her the ultimate favour. She had found out only yesterday that as Will came in for his once a fortnight short shift that they were a person down for the next day. That person in question being the ever-missing Judy Howard who Will could not even remember the last time he physically saw her in work doing an actual honest day's work. *'No wonder Coralie asked me to come in, least I know I'm the reliable one.'* Will was now making his way through the Ladies Wear Department; he saw the escalators waiting to take him downstairs for his sixth unplanned day of working then he stopped dead in his tracks at the sight of Josie Sybille getting on the escalators before he made it to them. She didn't see him as her back was facing him fortunately, one of the reasons he much preferred doing his opposite weekend was knowing the majority of *'the Clique'* all worked the opposing one to him so that limited his contact with them significantly. Seeing Josie on this bright if a bit on the chilly side mid-October day didn't make him feel any better about being at work. He could practically hear the double doors of The Precipice calling to him as he finally stepped on the escalators to take him down to this awaiting shift. He walked through the large entrance of the Café' into a quiet atmosphere with only one till open, Bianca was standing by the wall separating the Kitchen looking at the rota then around the Café to see who was working on what, Sasha was in the Kitchen this time as Nat also worked on his weekend, so she was off as well. There was one consolation for him to enjoy as he looked at coffee pod one to see Aaron Connors with his cheeky grin and black curly hair in full view, he gave Will a thumbs up of greeting from the till point.

"*Willy*! This isn't your Saturday to work normally mate? What gives?"

"*Aaron*! How's it going Mr? I know, I know it's not my day in, but a certain individual with the name of *Judy* decided not come in today, or should I say *ever* for that matter." Will came up to stand next to Aaron on the coffee pod as he received a firm clap on the back from his young co-worker who was pleased as punch to see him.

"Oh *Willy* mate, don't mention Judy these days seriously, I'm hearing things about her…"

"Oh? Don't keep in suspense all of a sudden Aaron?"

"Well, between you and me, it looks like this time her days really are numbered now…"

"Your bullshitting me aren't you? Your actually having me on for a laugh right?"

"I wish I were mate, but nope. From what I've heard it really is only a matter of time now before Judy Howard gets the boot from this place!"

Will still wasn't completely happy about being in when it should be his Saturday off to do as he pleased. Yet hearing the news that Judy Howard, the ultimate piss-taker of epic proportions in this place could be losing her job for the right reasons made him feel a hell of a lot better about being here. Sure this place he was leaving in only a weeks' time had, had its fair share of storms that he had weathered, but when it came to being dedicated to a job, Will took that to heart and Judy Howards conduct or lack of spoke great volumes to what she clearly thought of her Employment, it really was a case of when she would no longer work for the company. The way she always used a doctor as an excuse was starting to clearly wear thin on the Management at last. It made Will feel ready to seize the day whilst setting him up for a night out as well. "So you're on pod one, whose your coffee person then Aaron?" Will asked he folded his to look up at the taller teenager.

"That would be me I guess…"

The new voice broke their conversation, Aaron and Will both looked forwards to find Henry Sybille standing awkwardly in front of them as Will saw out of the corner of his eye that Aaron's face started to fall in disappointment, he'd clearly been hoping it was Will that would have been his coffee person. Today was not that day for them by how the look of things that were about to unfold.

"Good morning there Henry, so you on coffee with Aaron then?"

"That I am, and Bianca asked me to tell you that your on tables with Sarah Will, Moring also."

Henry went round the opposite entrance of pod one as Aarons face became more and more crestfallen. Him and Henry were practically the same age yet for some reason the two boys never really saw eye to eye which surprised Will, he thought most teenagers got along with one another these days. These two obviously had personality clashes whilst maintaining their professionalism at work as they should it. It was another thing that baffled Will about the next generation down from him.

"Guess I will be seeing you later Aaron."

"Yeah…guess so mate. Laters."

Will gave Aaron's right arm a gentle squeeze to encourage him, he found that it didn't really have the desired effect that he wanted as Aaron put his concentration fully into the till so he could best ignore Henry who was starting to set up the coffee machine to his liking. *'Boys will be boys I guess.'* Will wondered as he left them to their own devices, they'd just have to work it out as best they could. Will hoped that they would anyway as he joined young Sarah Bailey on the cleaning station closest to the Dishwasher Area. She always looked relieved whenever she laid eyes upon Will. Bouncing up and down on the spot she gave him a quick hug in greeting.

"How goes it miss Sarah?"

"All the better for seeing you Will, I see you got roped into working today?"

"Yeah Sarah the less we talk about the *why* I'm here, the better!"

Sarah laughed at Wills predicament as she got back to work sorting out the leftovers she had. Will observed the Café', it was still relatively quiet, being a Saturday just gone after eleven in the morning he was more than ready for it to change anytime soon. As he continued scanning the floor he ended up stopping dead in his tracks for a second time, Josie had reappeared from out back of the Kitchen carrying some stock for Upstairs, what got Wills back up wasn't the fact that he was seeing her again, it was how she barely acknowledged Bianca who had clearly just tried to get her attention. Before he knew it, Josie had left the Downstairs Café with the stock making a decisive beeline for the escalators. Bianca had watched her leave, shook her head then returned her attention to the staff rota. *'Poor cow. She really needs to just grow a backbone and stand up to her one day.'* Will felt sorry for Bianca, alas that was up to her to change how Josie treated her with contempt. Forgetting about what he had witnessed, he left Sarah in her cleaning station then headed over to the furthest one by the Food Department entrance to set it up. It was crazy that only a week remained for him at Riverside, then after that he could put the last six years of working in the Shoppers Complex behind him. *'Just one more week then I can kick the entire Clique and their manipulative ways in the backside then say adios amigo to this place.'* The thought gave him clarity as he set up the cleaning station. He settled into a groove, making sure he had what he needed then he got down to the routine of the day. The next couple of hours flowed surprisingly seamlessly for him, customers came and went, he smiled whilst making polite small talk as he cleaned table after dirty table for waiting customers. He even saw the off regular who double-checked about when he was leaving so they'd be able to say goodbye in case they missed him. He kept to himself, checked on Sarah to make sure she was ok, everything ticked along without any sort of development. The well-oiled machine of running Café' was running at peak efficiency which was a surprise to Will as Bianca hadn't left the floor at all as they were well into the lunch rush of the day now. *Almost two in the afternoon, only three hours to go. Get me a Corona Extra stat.'* Will was pondering what tonight would bring for him and his friends as he cleared the last of his leftovers into their relevant bins then stepped back out from the cleaning station to see how many more tables he needed to clear. In his general vicinity he found he had no tables awaiting so he remained alert and ready for when someone was about to depart. Then for the third time that day, he saw her enter the Café' again, he was tense like an animal ready to strike out at his prey, Josie was back with another empty crate, this time she was at the front facing fridge for the customers already placing whatever available sandwiches or toasties she could get her hands on. Will had never been more grateful to be far away from her at this given time. Bianca had made her way over to Josie this time rather than just watching her do what she wanted, she had the staff rota under her right arm, she had clasped her hands in front of her, she also got physically closer to Josie who was now turning left to face the Manager, Will watched it all unfold from the relative safety of the furthest cleaning station not knowing of the dialogue that was beginning between the two. Will observed them as he wiped down a table to make himself look busy. The two of them were both calm, they didn't gesture much at all, it all seemed peaceful. Too peaceful in fact. Will knew better than to trust it at all. As their exchange unfolded with little to be suspected as suspicious he saw Josie was still actively putting more than enough stock into her empty crate she had as her gaze never left Bianca who was still talking. Then it all changed the moment Bianca put her left hand on the crate Josie had filled to the brim. What happened next was a split-second reaction that many would have

not even paid any attention too, with the exception of the ever-
observant Will at that given moment. As Bianca had her left hand
on the crate that Josie held, she in turn looked down at her hand
then forcefully removed Bianca's hand from it. No one saw it but
Will, everyone was wrapped up in their own busy agendas, staff
were working, customers were chatting eating and drinking. Yet
Will witnessed it all happening, both Bianca and Josie were now
facing each other head on, both were not backing down. As he was
too far away he couldn't even make out what they were discussing
but he could guess probably most of what was being spoken. *'Go
on Bianca, don't stand for it.'* He internally egged on his Manager
as Josie set her shoulders in an almost unyielding battle stance,
Bianca seemed to be mimicking her. He noticed Bianca gestured
almost delicately in the direction of the crate Josie still held, then
to Will's stunned amazement, Josie put the crate down then near
enough stalked out of the Downstairs' Café. She walked out of his
line of sight in an almost ferocious manner, she was not happy at
all. Will on the other hand was ecstatically proud of Bianca for the
first time since she had begun working in the Café. He watched his
Manager pick up the crate, putting the stock back in the fridge then
she took the now reclaimed empty crate outback, he saw her
disappear with a small smile of satisfaction on her face as well.
'Couldn't be more proud of you if I tried Mrs.' Will smiled as he
got on with some more tables that needed clearing, he ended up

crossing paths with Sarah on the floor. As usual she seemed to be bouncing up and down the spot with giddiness.

"Did you see what went down between Bianca and Josie Will?"

"Did I ever Sarah, I thought it was about to explode into open warfare!"

"And that's just the start of it. That woman does have some nerve coming down here thinking she can take what she likes when she likes…"

"I'm just pleased Bianca finally…"

"*finally what*?"

Bianca's voice came out of nowhere freezing Will and Sarah to their respective spots. They both turned around to face their Manager with sheepish looks in place, Bianca was only smiling back at them with kindness. Will started to grovel.

"Hey there Bianca, look, me and Sarah well we were just saying…"

"We're bloody proud of you what you did there with Josie. Me and Will were both rooting for you no doubt about it…"

"Exactly. Sarah hit the nail on the head!"

Bianca stood there still smiling in her usual way, then she began chuckling as the two looked at her nervously still. Breaking the tension Bianca waved both her hands at them.

"Guys, chillout. I heard what you were saying, and I just wanted to say in return…"

"Yes?" Will and Sarah spoke in unison.

"…I wanted to say, *thank you* to you both. I really appreciate the mroal support. Sarah would you mind giving me and Will a moment to talk? Thanks again as well babes." Sarah seemed to almost run off in the direction as fast as her small legs could carry her which Bianca found even more funny as she sniggered at the retreating co-worker. She looked at Will with an amused look as he laughed to relieve his own tension he held within him. *'Well, at least she knows we had her back.'* He made himself properly relax now as he knew he wasn't in sort of trouble with his Manager, Bianca then got down to what she needed to say to Will.

"Will, thanks again for giving up your Saturday to help us out. I just need a small favour to ask of you…"

'Great, she wants me to stay later, there goes my night out to The Precipice with the lads.'

"…After you've had your break, could you collect some things from the Components Cupboard if you don't mind? We're gonna start running low on a few items that need topping by the end of today's shift, if that's not too much trouble?" Bianca finished by clasping her hands together as she had done to put Josie in her place, this time it wasn't firm it was full of calm, *'she's really found her voice today hasn't she?'* Will appraised his Managers assertiveness.

"Is that all Bianca? Nothing else you need from me at all?"

"Nope, nothing at all. In fact, how long is your break today Will?"

"Only fifteen-minutes, barely enough time to have a decent cup of tea..."

"Well, you've done us a favour today and it's the start of your final week. Take thirty minutes then get me the things I need from the Components Cupboard after alright?" Bianca was now moving off in the opposite direction to Will as she spoke from over her right shoulder, Will was blinking hard, he was sure he had misheard his Manager giving him a longer break than he was properly entitled too, yet he knew he hadn't misunderstood. Bianca was back at the wall separating the Kitchen and shop floor jotting down on a spare piece of paper what he would probably need to get from the Components Cupboard later. *'I guess today isn't all that bad after all then?'* he thought in surprised as he carried on with table-clearing. It was well gone two in the afternoon now; lunch rush was dying down to a more relaxed atmosphere as everyone got on with their duties at hand. Will had guessed correctly that Bianca had indeed been writing a list of goods that she needed him to collect after his break from the Cupboard as she handed it to him before heading out through the Food Department entrance. "Oh Will…" she poked her head back around into the cleaning station "…take your thirty minutes from half past two then get the stuff. Don't worry about anyone taking over just make sure you leave it orderly. I've made sure Sarah will come and collect whatever stuff you leave in here. Carry on." With that Bianca headed back out in Foods once again not giving Will the chance to reply, her mini confrontation with Josie really had caused a change to occur from within her. *'Grabbing life and authority by the balls today Bianca, good for you Mrs.'* He continued to be impressed by his bosses new lease of life as he carried on with whatever leftovers he had to finish. He went over to coffee pod two a few minutes later to find it was fast approaching his two-thirty break time, so he decided to take a slow walk back up to the staffing level for his much-needed R&R. "Sasha babes…" he called out to the mum of two busy in the Kitchen as she looked up at the sound of her name, "…I'm heading up for my break, see you soon!" he waved at her without stopping as he left the Café'. She gave a quick wave out to him on the shop floor before getting back to the food orders she had to complete in the Kitchen as he headed up the escalators, he started to roll his shoulders one after the other to ease any tension he hand been holding in them. *'And now its break time.'* He exhaled as his body began to respond to the respite it was receiving. Before he knew it, he was through the staff entrance on Ladies Wear and heading up the Men's Locker Room where he collected his phone and wallet then made his way to the staff canteen down the long corridor passing the Amin Office and the small interview rooms off their own usual small side corridor. He passed the Components Cupboard as well; he knew he would have to get a key to gain access to the room. He stopped in his tracks to look at the door of the Cupboard again, he did a one-eighty turn then decided to get all the things he needed off the list before he started his break. Getting the key from the Admin Office where it was readily available to all staff if they ever needed it, he marched back to the Cupboard, unlocked the door, switched the light on and then got to work compiling in what he needed. The Cupboard wasn't actually a Cupboard per say, it was just a turn of phrase that had stuck over time so everyone in the Store simply nicknamed it that. It was a converted room, larger than an interview room stockpiled with everything that Departments or both Café's needed to replenish from time to time. It had every wall covered plus a few well place rows of stock that could easily hide someone when they went searching for whatever kitchen towels, napkins, straws, stationary and cleaning products they may be in need of. Whoever did the online ordering always brought in a serious bulk hence why the Component Cupboard never seemed to run dry, it was well stocked constantly for the staff at all times throughout the calendar year.

Right now, someone had once again ordered far too much printer paper than was necessary as it had been piled high neatly in a corner opposite the unlocked door Will he had used, there was at least six to eight boxes of printer paper all piled nicely together, right in front of the kitchen towel he needed to get his hands on currently. *'Seriously, what member of our back of house team does that? Putting heavy printer paper in front of kitchen towel which is needed a hell of a lot more frequently.'* Shaking his heading, he walked over and got to trying to pry out a container that held a bundle of well wrapped kitchen towel, the printer paper was so well pushed together however, you could have sat on it very comfortably like its own throne right there and then. All the while it caused further obstruction to Will as he tried to get the bundle kitchen towel he had a hold of as he found himself leaning over almost a full ninety degrees as he continued to get it out without disturbing the still rather annoyingly heavy printer paper boxes. Just when he thought he had a good grip to successfully hoist it over, it slipped away from him landing with a thud back in its place behind the printer paper. "Ugh fine, fuck you then. You're getting picked last now." He spoke out loud to himself as he decided to get the rest of the items needed on Bianca's list. He got a few sets of crates that were spare, gathered the rest in little to no time at all then he went back to the kitchen towel. After a good five minutes of wrestling around with a bundle, he was able to hoist it over the pile of neat boxes of printer paper that had now become the bane of his existence. He gave the neat pile his middle finger for all its frustration it had caused him. Setting everything up on the crates he had making sure they were secure on the wheels they were on; he inspected all the items he had, double checked his list from Bianca, then he wheeled it out of the Components Cupboard locking the door. He set his pile of items next to the door as he locked it then went back to drop the key off in the Admin Office, he saw a spare sheet of blank paper on a desk where the key was stored normally then came up with an idea. Taking the paper, he wrote a quick message on it then went back to his items still at the locked door. He left the piece of paper on top of his items clearly stating they were going to picked up after his break, so no one was to touch them. Satisfied the message was written in bold capitals which nobody could miss, he set off in the direction of the staff canteen with his phone and wallet plus his stomach now growling in hunger. Entering he got down to making a cup of builders tea before purchasing a sandwich at the counter then surrendering to not doing any work for the full half hour he had. He enjoyed ten blissful minutes of nothing but drinking and eating until he was joined at the table he occupied by none other than his fellow table cleaner of the day Sarah Bailey.

"Blimey, is there anyone left to clear tables down there?"

"Ha-ha Will, of course there is. Today's not that busy for a Saturday."

She opened her own sandwich, tucking into her lunch with hungry excitement, Will finished the last of his sitting back to stretch out in his chair stifling a yawn which made Sarah's eyebrow cock up in surprise.

"Aren't you hitting the town tonight? Not gonna be much fun if your yawning already Will…"

"I'm just yawning Sarah because after today I would have done six full days of working when I didn't ask for this particular day. Then again, I'm too nice so I gave up a day off to help out. Once I'm in that Gay Bar later…

"You'll be any blokes Will? I know your easy an all but then again…"

Sarah stopped as she saw Wills jaw drop in shock at her dig of a joke. She covered her mouth trying to hide the laughter that was slowly erupting from her as she made fun of her co-worker. Still shocked by her sudden joke Will put her in her place.

"*Sarah Bailey*! I never would have expected you to be…"

"To be what Will? So utterly clever with my put downs?"

"No, I was just gonna say what a *cheeky cow* you are!"

They both paused then burst out laughing at the camaraderie they had developed well together, Will was going to miss that about working at Riverside at least. *'I probably won't get the same sort of jokes or banter with others like I have her. Sad but it's true.'* He pondered about what life may be like when he started working at Stratford. Would people like him or hate him, he didn't have the foresight or answers for that question yet, he would simply have to discover it as he went along as was one of life's great mysteries. For now, that was a problem for tomorrow, today, he had to get through this final week.

"Still impressed I came out with that Will?"

Sarah brought him back into the here and now of the his unplanned Saturday as he checked the time on his phone. *'Oy, less than ten minutes left. Half hour breaks are never long enough, I'm lucky I got it though.'* He pocketed his phone away as he turned his attention back to his naughty co-worker.

"I must say Sarah…you've definitely got me prepared for my final week at Riverside in style. So yes…consider me impressed my dear."

He gave her a well-earned high five as he went to get another quick cup of tea before he had to drop his phone and wallet off back in the Locker Room then collect the items he had assembled from the Cupboard. Sitting back down he relaxed as much as he could until his time was up with Sarah. "Gonna miss me when I'm gone then

Mrs?" he asked her as he sipped his tea, Sarah of course gave him a hug-eyed look from above her prescriptions spectacles.

"What a ridiculous question to ask me, of course I am!"

"Ok, ok just checking…" he looked briefly at his phone for the time "…I'd better get on with getting that stuff Bianca asked me. It's not gonna move itself from outside the Cupboard after all."

"What stuff Will?"

"Oh, Bianca gave me that list of items to get from the Components Cupboard, remember? I got them ready before starting my break then left them outside the Cupboard with a note for anyone passing to not touch just leave them there until I collected them after…" He stopped talking as Sarah looked at him with her head at a strange angle, he may as well been talking a foreign language at the moment.

"You do remember seeing Bianca give me the list downstairs right?"

"Yeah I remember that. It's just…" Sarah looked back the staff canteen entrance then back at Will still confused which added to Wills own confusion.

"Just what Sarah?"

"Well, when I walked past the Cupboard, there was nothing waiting outside to be collected. I'm a hundred percent sure as well since I've only been with you for less than ten minutes as of now. But then again, I could have sworn I saw someone coming out of the Components Cupboard before I came to join you in here. I am sure it was…"

"Who was it Sarah?"

Sarah stopped short of replying. She was now looking at Will with an almost fearful look, as if anything she might say now could tip their once playful mood in the polar opposite direction extremely unpleasantly and all too quickly. Will waited patiently for his co-worker to answer despite being suspicious of what had happened to his items he had stored outside the Cupboard with the noticeable sign on top of them.

Taking a deep breathe in then exhaling, Sarah replied at last.

"I could have sworn it was Josie."

Will sat opposite his co-worker in silence, his face neutral, his body language calm. He was breathing just a fraction heavier than he normally would, his mind was alight with an almost intense whirlwind of activity. *'I swear to god, if that person has taken my stuff and discarded my obvious sign, I'm gonna…'*

"Will, don't worry about it ok Mr. Are you…"

Sarah stopped as she was now looking upwards at him. Will had risen sharply from his seat pausing just for a moment to collect himself then he was taking his empty sandwich container and mug over to the staff canteen Dishwasher Area. He then turned around to face Sarah maintaining a neutral look, then he left the canteen without saying goodbye to Sarah. She knew what might happen wasn't about to be a good thing. Will was back in the corridor walking slowly towards the Component Cupboard door. Sure enough, he saw the door was unlocked with a key in it. Next to the door were two pieces of slightly crumpled paper, he picked them up to find his note he had written for no one to touch cleanly ripped right down the middle in two in an almost meticulous fashion. There was only one person who could have done this. And she was still in the Components Cupboard right now. Letting out a frustrated sigh, Will crunched the two pieces of paper together setting off in a march towards the Admin Office, he threw his note into a nearby bin then he asked whatever staff member was in the Office about who was in the Cupboard. Sure enough, he got his answer before he asked the question as he heard footsteps back outside in the long corridor, he half turned his head to look out the window and there she was. Josie Sybille in all her imperious, unforgiving, and utterly unremarkable glory. She didn't pay any attention to him in the Office as she walked past, she went on by without even fully noticing Will. *'That does it.'* Will decided, he left the Office and was back in the long corridor as Josie was about to round the corner clearly heading the direction of the Women's Locker Room, before Will could call out to her she was around the corner, he jogged to make up the distance but stopped short rounding the corner himself as he heard his archnemesis talking in her dulcet tones to what could only be Trudie Harrie who was obviously just heading off as her shift was complete for the day. Will recognised her nasally teacher voice before he would have been seen by them if he had walked round at that moment. Looking back over at his shoulder down the long corridor, he was alone for the time being, so he listened in to their conversation.

"...not a bad day was it Josie, bet your ready to head off soon right girl?"

"Oh yeah, just grabbing some stuff from the Components. I saw a lot of our own stuff waiting outside on wheels about ten minutes ago with a *silly little note* on top saying not to take it can you imagine; it could only be *Will Hardley's* handwriting as well. He always had such scruffy handwriting do you remember Trudie. I ripped that ridiculous note up as well..."

Trudie chuckled loudly with mocking amusement as she hung onto her friends every word. '*Bitch.*' Will thought with added viciousness as he double-checked if he was still alone in the corridor while still listening to the two members of *'the Clique'*.

"…did you get everything you needed in there Josie?" Trudie's awful nasal voice brought Will sharply back to the here and now.

"Oh yes almost. I o*bviously* took his stuff because, why not. I'm just going for a quick wee then I'm going to finish up in there. This place would be nothing without us right Trudie…"

"Ha! You said that Sister. Listen, I'm off, lunch at mine soon? I must show you all what I've done with the eight-bedrooms now I've reworked the house over, see ya later!"

"I'm game for that, we'll get a date in the diaries. Bye Hun."

The corridor went silent, Trudie departed, Josie entered the Women's Locker Room to relieve herself. Will was frozen on the spot. Josie had seen his note, taken the stuff he had put aside for the Downstairs' Café, ripped his note up casually simply because she felt entitled to do so and then bragged about it to one of her best friends without any care to be had. There was pettiness, then there was pure nastiness. This small action may have been trivial, but it fell well into the latter. *'Just seven days to…'* he stopped his train of thought as he realised he was still holding his phone in his hand rather than in his pocket, he was clutching it a little too tightly, then he was staring at it like it was the solution to all his problems in one go. Will looked around towards the Women's Locker Room then back down the way he had come the long corridor from the staff canteen. He was utterly alone.

Will then made another decision.

The consequences could be worried about for another time.

Eleven

The Same Day.

The Women's Locker Room.

3:06 pm.

Three Minutes Later…

Josie Sybille had always been a decisive action taker. She prided herself on it in fact. She always walked with a goal or objective in mind wherever she went, be it in life or work. No diddle-daddling to ever be had for her, she always had things to do. Getting her way was one of these attributes. She came out of the Women's Toilets then checked her complexion in the large landscape mirror that occupied most of one wall of the Locker Room. Her usual

makeup wasn't smeared or out of place, everything was at it should
be. Smoothing down her uniform shirt, she gave her image in the
mirror a curt nod of silent satisfaction then turned in a quickfire
ninety degrees to leave the Locker Room, then she stopped. She
hadn't checked her phone so went back to the her Locker and
fished it out of her handbag. She found messages from her closest
friends she had worked with for many years in the Café on their
dedicated WhatsApp group rather aptly titled *'The OG Café Lot'*.
She skimmed through the messages, Trudie was now suggesting
they all come round to her large eight-bedroomed home in the
coming weeks for a light dinner mixed with what would be a
copious amount of wine or whatever alcohol they all preferred plus
Trudie dropped in the subject matter they would end up discussing
like they normally did. Bitching about work with gleeful
abandonment. Josie finished her reply with a small chuckle, double
checked for spelling mistakes, added the message to the group
chat, locked her phone, placed it back in her handbag then stashed
it securely back in her Locker for safekeeping. She didn't have
long left to go on her Saturday shift as she walked towards the exit.
The rest of the weekdays she came in at six with her girls as it had
always been before the pre-refurbished Café days and after as well,
Coralie on some days came in at the same time yet they just looked
the other way when she tried to order them about or even try to
suggest what they should be doing. The girl may be their
Supervisor in an official capacity, Josie and her girls were simply

Billy Harding © 2021

not to be told what to do, it wasn't their way of doing things. Josie even found it somewhat amusing when Coralie had to try and pull rank on her, she was just about young enough to be her daughter, yet she was trying to Josie, the original Supervisor of Café what to do. It was an absurd notion to even ponder in her mind. So she kept up her normal routine as best she could, she was however a little on edge now that Bianca was starting to assert herself, she was finding her Managerial voice and Josie was none too pleased about this in the slightest, she, Jan, Lucy, Trudie and Sherry, her girls always, would persevere or find a way around the nuisance that was Bianca. They'd done it with Joyce by making her believe she was friends with them, that had been at least half a ruse in the very beginning. Then over time they had allowed Joyce into their inner circle as she proved tirelessly she preferred having them in on the earlies as she wouldn't need to bother telling them how to do their jobs. All the girls over time had persuaded Josie to let her in. In the end she had with good reasons to back it up. When Joyce had resigned rather unexpectedly though, they had all feared what the near future change was about to bring for them. Josie had rallied them up and nipped their concerns in the bud almost immediately the day after Joyce's resignation. It was all about control for Josie every time. Control the situation, then your one in control of all it. Simplistic, cold logic had been her companion for as long as she could remember. And she wasn't parting ways with it anytime soon. Josie stepped out in the corridor to find it devoid of any other fellow Employees or Managers. Looking both ways she breathed in then exhaled a little heavily, normally she would power walk wherever she went whilst in work, today she allowed herself to start strolling leisurely back in the direction of the Components Cupboard where she had first spotted Will's little pile of goodies that she was not going to allow him to take for himself. Truthfully, she didn't need them, yet she saw them, then decided to take the pile of stock just to spite the poor boy. She knew it would annoy him beyond recognition and it gave her immense satisfaction that she could do that to him after all this time. Their run-in last year right before Christmas had been the last line of civility or what was left it between them. She didn't care for him at all after that, and he certainly made it clear he did not like her which was more than fine with Josie. It made it easier to look down at him as the insignificant bug he had made himself to be. She found it internally amusing when he had lodged a formal complaint about in the intervening weeks after their spat, being the former Supervisor that she was though, she knew all the disciplinary procedures off by heart, so she entertained them when the one-on-one interviews began with recounting what had happened. She admitted that she may have spoken out of term when she accused him of being a shit-stirrer contrary to the fact she fully believed in her mind and still did to this day that he was such an odious thing. She knew how to play the game like she always did, she came out of it with a slap on the wrist and the two stayed well way from one another.

Will had wanted her gone from the Store which she found laughable when she told the girls about it over one of the heavy sessions of wine-drinking round hers, all of them found it equally as funny that he had even dared to try and convince the Manager in charge of the complaint to go along with the suggestion. The Manager had found a reasonable excuse to explain away the suggestion to Will and the status quo reasserted itself as it always did. Josie did give him the curtesy of staying out his way for a time after the whole silly debacle came to a close, she even told the girls to play nice if they ever found themselves around him. Being her friends they obliged her as they should. After everything she had done for them over the years of working together, they would do that for her without even needing to think about it. She walked lazily past the Admin Office; the Cupboard was there awaiting her with the key still in the lock where she had left it. She rolled her head from side to side before walking into the room to get the last of the things she needed. The light was still on inside, she nearly walked into the pile of stock she had taken for her own from Will having forgotten she had left a bit too close to the door, she moved it on its wheels to the right side so it wouldn't obstruct the door then she turned left and walked deeper in the Components Cupboard to look for the last of the bits that she needed. Three aisles down she turned into the one she needed, the shelving was quite high in this particular aisle so it partly obscured the light from ceiling, she looked on some of the lower shelves then stood on her tiptoes as far they would allow her then she saw what she needed which was the straws, the very last box of them. Remaining on her toes she reached for the box of straws that was frustratingly further back on the shelf than she liked, her fingers grazed the box then she was able to get a good grasp and got them down at last. She had everything she needed now, so she walked back to the pile of stock she had stolen off Will and placed them in with the rest of the stock she claimed as her own now. After a thorough check she gave her usual singular nod of approval then began to walk to the door to leave the Components Cupboard. As her hand went to the door, Josie paused momentarily. She had taken the key for the Cupboard out of the front door as she had re-entered the room then she had placed it in the lock on the interior side so she knew it would be there when she was about to leave. It was not in the lock anymore and it most certainly had not fallen on the floor as she was checking.

"So where did that go I wonder?"

She spoke out loud to the room as she continued looking at the door with both her hands on her hips still puzzled by the missing key. Then everything changed in the blink of an eye.

"I think you'll be needing this?"

The voice broke the atmosphere like a bolt of lightning.

Josie stood extremely still like a statue; her eyes went wide with shock as she collected herself for a moment. Her normally well-trained bodily functions betrayed her she began breathing a little bit heavier than usual. She hadn't jumped in fright, but she had come very close to doing so. Still breathing heavily, she turned slowly on the spot to face her quarry. And there he was, sitting on a pile of neatly gathered printer paper boxes in a corner of the Components Cupboard. None other than Will Hardley himself. His face was neutral, his shoulders relaxed, his left leg was crossed over his right leg, his right arm resting on the crossed leg and his left arm was propped up with the crossed leg as well. Dangling on his left forefinger under the harsh fluorescent lights of the Components Cupboard was the very key Josie needed right there and then for the door. Will looked Josie dead in the eyes with a calmness she had never witnessed from him until now. The way he continued to look at her made the insides of her stomach flummox as if butterflies were trying to erupt from it. The feeling was not a welcome one for her as she stood still on her spot by the door not even daring to move a muscle.

She hadn't spoken yet either, so Will did for them both.

"I thought it was time that you and I needed to have a little talk Josie Sybille…"

*

The Long Corridor.

Six Minutes Earlier.

3:00 pm.

Will didn't think about anything in terms of specifics. He just did as his body instructed as it propelled him back down the corridor. Before he knew it, he was back in the Components Cupboard. *'What are you even doing Will?'* he asked himself internally as he looked around the room, he was acting on pure instinct. He didn't know why but he just knew it was now or never to do what he needed. He hadn't even thought about it earlier today, it was only after he had eavesdropped on Josie and Trudie's conversation outside of the Women's Locker Room had he made the decision to finally stand up to Josie. It was as if something finally snapped within him, he felt his anger swirling like the storm it was just beneath the surface, it was ready to fly out of him, Will knew when confronting Josie though that he had had to downplay the whole thing more significantly than he liked. *'If in doubt, play her at her own game. Throw the literal shite right back at the bitch.'* He was breathing more evenly now as he saw what he needed to do, he knew she needed something else from here in the Cupboard so he knew exactly where to stand so she wouldn't notice him. He walked over to one of the high shelved aisles that obscured some of the harsh lights, he stood in the shadows just out of sight, he didn't even need to crouch or stand uncomfortably in a certain way. He kept his back to the wall of the high shelving and he simply waited. *'Easy enough I guess, wait here till she comes in, sit down on the printer boxes for comfort then talk to her. Finally get some answers out of her. She can't talk about me like that and get away it. Not anymore, I won't let someone speak about me in a derogatory way even if I am leaving next week. Why on earth am I bricking it though?'* He tried to muster up some courage for what he was about to do. He stopped fidgeting as soon as he heard the door open and close promptly, he heard Josie sighing as she moved down to one of the aisles for what she needed and Will moved in tandem towards the printer boxes silently to take a seat then he stopped midway, he looked at the door and saw the key for the Cupboard hanging there in the lock where Josie had just inserted it, a small smile appeared across Will's face as instinct overtook him once more. *'Play them at the own game.'* The thought gave him focus he took the key out quickly of the lock then he went over tiptoeing to the printer boxes to take his seat, he crossed his left leg over his right then forced himself to relax before Josie came back from her aisle she was still down. He heard her starting to walk back in his direction, he took a measured breathe in then exhaled, a strange calm suddenly came over him like a wave. Josie walked out with her back to him as she looked at the box of straws she had in her hand that she added to the pile of stock he had originally compiled himself until she unceremoniously stole it for herself.

She was now turning to reach out for the doorhandle then she stopped as she saw the key wasn't there. Will readied himself as he raised the key in his left forefinger.

'Here goes nothing. No time like the present as the old saying goes.'

"I think you'll be needing this?"

Josie froze on the spot, he heard her breathing quicken as the shock tried to overtake her senses, she however maintained her posture as if nothing could truly faze her ever, not even an unexpected surprise like Will waiting for her. She turned to face him, she was none too pleased to see him at all, he couldn't blame after the stunt he had just pulled.

"I thought it was time that you and I needed to have a little talk Josie Sybille…"

She looked at him as if he had uttered the most stupidest thing he could ever say, her look made him even more frustrated that she was already not taking this seriously. *'You are going to listen to me Josie. Whether you like it not.'* She hadn't moved from her spot by the door, she had folded her arms, waiting for him to end what she clearly considered as a silly charade that was beneath her.

"Nothing to say then Josie?"

"What would I even say to…*whatever* this is Will? What are you even doing sitting on boxes of printer paper even?"

"Their quite comfortable actually you see."

"I'm sure they are. Can I have the key now please?"

"In a moment absolutely you can Josie. I'm still rather fond of it currently."

Josie's eyes flashed under the harsh lights this time which got Will's full attention. *'Aha, got you now haven't I? Any control that's taken away from you, you don't like it one bit.'* He spotted his entry to get her to open up to him, so he played her at her own game, he simply stayed seated on his throne of printer paper boxes, he added an odd smile to his face then tilted his head to his left side then he slowly uncrossed his legs then crossed them other way. It had the desired outcome he wanted as Josie unfolded her arms her face contorting as more frustration began to slip out from behind her carefully constructed mask she applied whenever in work, her defences slowly being peeled back like the many layers of an onion which may or may not have had a rotten core.

"This isn't funny Will. Just give me the key now."

"I wasn't trying to be even remotely a*musing* as you suggested Josie? I simply want to talk to you, so I am, one co-worker to another. You're a reasonable person after all, you've always prided yourself on your self-control the moment me and you ever met do you remember that Josie? You let me know the *very second* you were *always* in control by simply staring at me, surely you can't forget a moment..."

"*give me the key back NOW!*"

The shout had silenced him, it had gone through him like it was a tonne of bricks also. The ferocity behind it was extremely intimidating as well. Will somehow kept his composure as serene as it could as Josie took one measure step in his direction, her anger fully on display, her mental barriers collapsing before Will's very eyes. Will found the enraged woman before him physically frightening. '*Now there's the real person behind that cool exterior I despise so much.*' The thought flashed through his mind as he pocketed the key Josie needed in his left side, the simple action had the desired effect Will wanted from her as she started to step towards him again.

"*Will Hardley*, I swear to god if you don't give me that key right now, I'm going to..."

"Your gonna what?"

"You *really* don't want to know."

"Sounds to me like your threatening me Josie?"

"Don't try it *little boy*."

She began stepping towards him again, this time however Will was ready for her. He sprung up from his throne of printer boxes as she closed the distance.

"Take one more step Josie then let's see what happens shall we!"

Josie stopped as she saw the look of defiance in Will's eyes. For the first time since the two had ever laid eyes on one another Josie really looked properly at him, she saw the same ferocity she had shown him staring straight back at her and she was unsettled even if only for a moment. Will advanced toward her slowly this time.

"You really are something else aren't you?"

"Excuse me? If this is to frighten me, you're going to have to do a *lot* better than this."

"Who says I'm trying to frighten you Josie? Certainly not me. You're the one who raised their voice at me, not the other way round remember. Then again, you always knew how to play on a Manager's sympathy's didn't you?"

The loaded question landed like an unexploded bomb between the two as Josie recoiled away from Will in surprise, she hadn't been prepared for that at all. *'Got you now deary.'*

"I don't know what your even implying."

"Again? It really is that *easy* for you to act so innocent? After all these years of manipulating this place just so you and your friends can get everything they've ever wanted."

"That is simply not true."

"Oh, but it is. People like me or Daisy Davidson having to take all the shitty late shifts while you and friends do *zero* late shifts ever."

"We've done *our years* of those…"

"Bullshit Josie. You actively m*anipulated* the system and whatever Manager you had assigned at the time to get your selfish way, didn't you?"

Josie wasn't looking Will in the eyes now as she found some stock all of a sudden took her interest, her face however was no longer a picture of calm authority, it was truly unnerved.

Will saw his opportunity opening up before his very eyes.

"*Didn't you Josie!*"

"No. We're done here."

She turned her back to him then stopped as she saw the door of the Components Cupboard which she still needed the key for. She was stuck, nowhere to run, nowhere to hide. It was that or facing Will, so she kept her back to him.

"Open the door the Will."

"Admit it Josie."

"I said…Open. The. Fucking. Door. *You ungrateful little faggot!*"

Josie Sybille had spun around to face him, her face full of uncontrolled fury mixed with shock at the words that had suddenly escaped from her mouth, Will was frozen on the spot, he looked at his former Supervisor and finally saw the rotten core of the onion staring right back at him, it was a truly unpleasant sight to behold such a thing.

'Gotcha.'

"I never thought I would hear that term used in such a way in my life Josie…"

"Will…I erm…I don't know…"

"Admit it. Just tell the bloody truth for once will you." He was looking at her now, there was no harsh tone to his voice, no pleading, his eyes were fixed on her and she looked back at him, her hand had gone to her mouth in complete shock over the choice words she had uttered about him, she took her hand away slowly, then her body language seemed to shift in the blink of an eye. The Josie he had known after all this time was reasserting herself with cold menace. She was revelling in the moment for all its worth.

"I don't understand what it is your trying to prove here Will but let's be honest with one another for the very first time shall we?"

She had moved back to the pile of stock she had taken from him in the beginning, she began looking through it absentmindedly as she kept Will waiting.

"Honest about what Josie?"

"This place was *ours* from the start to do what we like with it you see Will. When I arrived here, that Café was nothing after I got my hands on it you see. Then over time, I worked my way in, ascended up to the Management Team, then I took a voluntary demotion to Supervisor and it was just seemed to click into place when I found out what I could *truly* do. So I did what I needed to do to thrive. Jan, Sherry, Lucy, Trudie. All of my closest allies and friends as well, I positioned them into what worked for them, I wanted something in return though. Do you know what that was Will…"

She trailed off as she half-glanced back at him from her left shoulder, Will simply shook his head which she saw him do then she returned her attention to the stock to continue.

"…I wanted *unconditional loyalty*. Any time things would go south in this place, I wanted those allies of mine to back me up every single time, no questions asked. This place, as I said before, it was a shell of what it could be. That is until me and *my lot* came along."

"And anyone else that may be new that comes along has to suffer under the consequences of who you play *favourites* with Josie? That's not a *fair and equal workplace* and your fully aware of it."

"So what Will?

"So what Josie? Are you serious?"

Will was looking at her shocked once more while she turned to face him again this time her cold exterior fully asserting itself as it always did.

"So you get to be judge, jury and executioner of who can be accepted into your inner circle? I knew you were cold, this though? You're really that *inhumane* aren't you."

"It's served me well after all these years. I'm proud of it in fact."

"And yet, your own Son even *admitted* it to me as well which makes this whole thing even more sadder than I first realised."

Will folded his arms as he observed Josie by the stock, she was frozen again as she held onto it for support.

"What do you mean *my Son* admitted it to you?"

"Oh that? He told me a few weeks ago that you're a handful and he even gave me an *apology* to go with it. Imagine that Josie, your own flesh, and blood having to explain away the person that you are? If that were my Mother, well I certainly can't speak on her behalf but deep down I know she would be not just embarrassed beyond all measure, she would be absolutely mortified beyond belief in fact."

Will looked at Josie with pity yet he didn't feel sorry for her, not after what she had called him a few moments ago. There was no going back from that cliff edge. Josie couldn't look at Will now, she looked at the floor, Will saw it for the first time as well. Shame was plastered all over her face for the world and its Mother to bear witness too.

'I got the answers that I really needed. Now we're finally done here.'

"So you still need that door then Josie?"

"You've got the key Will."

"Yes I do…in fact, here you are".

He fished it out his pocket and he tossed it to her, she caught it without looking at him still. *'Better give her a hand with the door after all.'* He walked over to the door and grabbed the handle, Josie looked at him confused once more as she held the key that was needed to unlock it to permit them both a welcome exit from the Components Cupboard. This time however, the key wasn't needed. Will pulled the door handle down decisively, and the door to the Cupboard opened. Josie looked out at the long corridor of the staff level of the Store then back at Will, the realisation beginning to dawn on her face as her emotions took over again.

"But you...you locked it?"

She half stepped out into the corridor looking around almost widely, her confusion now turning to anxiousness. Will looked at her with a face full of his own feigned confusion.

"I did no such thing? Why on earth would I do that Josie?"

She looked at him, her anger beginning to assert itself in all its ugly glory.

"I saw you Will, you even held the key for the lock out to me!"

"Yes I did Josie..."

Will stepped towards her so they were both mere inches from one another, it was the closest he'd ever been in her personal space before, he didn't like it, but it got him the desired effect that he wanted. Josie was looking at him not angry anymore, she was frightened of him for the first time ever. *'This has got to be the most satisfying moment in all of my years in this place right now. Putting a bully well and truly in their place because they deserve it.'* He smiled innocently at Josie, his eyes though, the determination pouring out of them was everything and more. It was the most powerful Will had ever felt in his entire life so far.

"All I said when I was sitting down there on the printer boxes was *'I think you'll be needing this'*. That's all Josie. I didn't specifically mention that the door was locked. Not once. You remember that don't you?"

He waited for her answer as he stepped away from her back into the Components Cupboard, he continued to hold the door open with his right hand then very delicately he put his left hand on the pile of stock he had originally claimed, then he looked at Josie awaiting her to answer calmly. She stared at him, he mouth partly open, her shocked face gave everything away. She hadn't even checked that the door had been unlocked in the first place. She looked away from him to the key still in her hand, then without uttering anything else, she walked off in the direction of the Admin Office as fast as her feet could carry her, Will heard the door of the Office open then close sharply, then he heard Josie walking further away in what could only be the direction of the Women's Locker Room to give Josie what was clearly needed some breathing room. Closing his eyes for a brief moment, Will let go of the door of the Components Cupboard allowing it close so he could be alone, he opened his eyes as the door snapped shut. Then he went back over to the neat pile of printer paper boxes still in their corner in front of the bundles of kitchen towel. He sat back down calmly; he took his wallet out of his left pocket placing it down next to him, he looked up at the harsh fluorescent lighting then he withdrew his mobile phone from his right pocket.

And there it was, clear as day for anyone to see.

His mobile phone was still recording everything it could hear on the Voice Recorder App in real time.

Will looked at the App as it kept on recording, then he stopped it. He went back to the beginning of the recording and pressed play, listening intently. He heard the beginnings of the fateful conversation with Josie Sybille coming through loud and clear. He stopped the recording then saved the file on his phone to listen to later on when he got home.

'I'll listen to it properly as I get ready for my night out at The Precipice with the lads. God knows I deserve a serious amount of alcohol after that.'

He got back up from his throne of printer paper boxes, he calmly walked over to the stock he had compiled with now added extras, then he cast one last look around the Components Cupboard before switching the light off and wheeling out his stock back into the long corridor. He let the door shut of its own accord as he walked away, deciding to let someone else from the Admin Office to lock the door themselves.

It had been a hell of an unplanned day for all involved.

Twelve

October 21st, 2016.

The Downstairs' Café.

Friday.

12:02 pm.

'I have to be hallucinating. That can't be Judy Howard walking into start her shift? It just can't be.'

It was his penultimate shift working at Riverside. One more day then it would all be over for good. It still didn't feel entirely real to Will. Seeing Judy Howard walk in had made the day all the more surreal as he marched over to Kym on coffee pod two as she stared slack-jawed at the sight of Judy entering the Café.

"Have I finally gone senile Willyboy?"

"My 'Firecracker', I was just about to ask you the very same thing in all honesty."

"What the *actual hell* is Judy even doing here? I thought I'd heard on the grapevine she was getting the sack Will?"

"That's exactly what I've been hearing as well Mrs, clearly she's not for the chopping block yet then.... oh *shit* here she comes!"

Judy Howard wasn't exactly someone you could miss. She walked with a boyish swagger to her stride along with a toothy grin plus greasy blonde hair that was always in a short ponytail, she definitely didn't wash it often. As well having her reputation at work for never really being there that much she let everyone know she fell into the butch category being the proud lesbian that she was, tomboy to boot for added measure and effect.

"Will, Kym! Good to see you two, has this place survived without me ah? Know what I'm talkin about?"

Judy stopped in front of them at the till point of coffee pod two, Will stood on the exit of the pod leading away to tables with a strange look planted on his face, unsure of what kind of words he could form to engage with Judy while Kym stood still at the coffee machine eyeing Judy up and down. She looked back and forth between them with her boyish grin still in place waiting for any one of the two to respond to her, when the silence dragged out even more Judy started to realise the awkwardness developing. *'It's not that I don't want to speak to her, it's the fact that I just don't view her as a member of this workforce anymore. She's been gone too long for anyone to even care if she's back to work properly. And it's entirely her fault for trying to play the system or attempting to at least.'* Will was still looking at Judy with some form of strange fascination as her smile began to falter, she was cottoning on to the way people probably felt about her or was starting too.

"Ok, I get it. I guess I've been well, let's say *awhile* all in all…"

"Stating the obvious aren't ya?" Kym finally spoke from the coffee machine.

"I don't even remember when I last saw you until today truthfully Judy." Will added on from his spot.

Judy looked at them both with a fixed look, it wasn't anger yet it wasn't happiness either. *'Perhaps it will all click into place that she doesn't have any meaningful developed working relationships here in the Café, not after all this time off.'* The thought was Will at his most honest, he felt no shame in thinking it. It was the simple truth of the matter.

"Look guys, we go way back. Remember our days 'The Restaurant' together?"

"Barely, do you recall anything Will?"

"Not off the top of my head 'Firecracker'."

It seemed to be dawning on Judy that the were no bridges that could be built with Will or Kym anymore, shrugging her shoulders she turned around in the direction of the Kitchen where Coralie was watching Judy, she however was looking past her at a busy Nat in the Kitchen. Judy clapped her hands together with vigour, she gave her shoulders a quick roll then swaggered off in Nat's direction, she didn't even say hello to Coralie who watched her blatantly ignoring her as she stepped into the Kitchen to greet the busy Nat.

"Nat! My girl, how are ya my love?"

Nat turned in the direction of Judy who opened her arms as if readying for a hug, Nat kept her face in a deadpan manner then simply offered Judy her hand to shake rather than accepting her hug. Judy's open arms seemed to freeze mid-air as her face contorted into a look of pure shock at Nat's open coldness towards her, she hadn't been prepared for that. As they struck up a polite enough conversation, Coralie turned away rolling her eyes at the way Judy Howard thought she could walk back into the Café after countless months off and think everyone would still treat her the same way they use too when she came in to attempt to do her job like any other normal person. Will and Kym hadn't moved from their respective spots as they had watched Judy try to charm her way back in with the team, it was fascinating for them to see yet they derived no pleasure from it at all. Nat's removed greeting to Judy had them both wincing as she was openly rebuffed.

"Now that one must have hit home for her Willyboy."

"Absolutely 'Firecracker'. I don't know what their waiting for with her. I know tomorrow is my last day and all, I am *not* going to miss that individual over there Mrs."

"I don't blame you either Mr."

They looked at one another with a quick smile of understanding then they got back to their jobs at hand, Will went back to tables and Kym cracked on with her work on the coffee machine. Judy was now attempting to turn her attention to Coralie who was not impressed with her in the slightest. Will gave the whole Judy situation an air of indifference, not when he had just over twenty-four hours left working at Riverside. *'Can't believe there's only one more day of working here. God knows how I'm gonna be tomorrow.'* He picked up a tray of leftovers thanking a customer for their time with his usual service smile in place as they departed through the Foods entrance. He took it back to the cleaning station closest to the Dishwasher Area to start sorting it. Everything he did now, he could feel the sense of finality everywhere he went on his last remaining shifts. Ever since his and Josie's run in on his extra shift, the former Supervisor had steered well clear of him including the rest of the *'the Clique'* which suited Will completely. The more they stayed away, the better he felt. It didn't stop him thinking about all the people he did get on with in work, that was proving to be more emotional for him than he had first realised to detach himself when the time came for it. His resolve was absolute though, tomorrow would be the end of his time in Riverside for good. *'I'm gonna cry tomorrow I know it.'* He wiped down the tray he had finished clearing then stepped back out to the tables scanning as he went. He immediately wished he hadn't walked out when he had. The Couple had entered the Café and the very first person to make a beeline for them was none other than the newly returned Judy Howard. *'Oh god help us all now, those two just had to visit on my second to last day didn't they.'* He watched as she walked up the infamous duo clapping her hands as was her normal routine, they saw her then greeted her warmly in all their sickly amusement. *'I wonder what story she is spinning for them and vice-versa I dread to imagine.'* He observed them all chatting away as he busied himself on tables. It was a quiet afternoon overall, everything ticked along, and people left him to his own devices. Over his final week Will had not only felt the finality of his last working week in Riverside, he felt a shift of some kind amongst the people he had been working with. Each and every employee he

worked with was dealing with the fact that he was leaving as was
Will himself yet there was something else to it. He felt like nearly
everyone, all with the exception of his best friend Kym and maybe
Nat were stepping back from him emotionally. It was by no means
done out of spite or vindictiveness; he still saw it happening with
his own eyes. His soon to be ex-co-workers were going to move on
from him eventually. Will had carved out his own unique identity
whilst working at Riverside after all this time that no one else
could replicate, all good things came to an end before people
naturally moved on. One of the things that was still confusing to
him was there would come a time in the not-so-distant future
where he may well end up visiting Riverside again for shopping
and no one in the In-Store Café would even know who he was. He
would become a thing of the past or the odd story that may crop
up, yet no one could remember or place his name. *'I wonder how
long it will take the majority to forget about me here?'* he asked
himself as he carried on with his table clearing. The answer didn't
come to him as he still saw Judy talking the ears off of The Couple
who seemed to be enraptured by her animated talking. Will
dropped off another tray of leftovers at the cleaning station, as he
was doing so he turned to walk back out to the floor to see if any
more customers needed their tables clearing then he was stopped
dead in his tracks. He may well have been a fair distance away
from Judy and The Couple, there was no denying the noticeable
exchange happen though. The retired Husband with his white afro

hair had gotten his wallet out of his pocket and was thumbing through its contents. Will truly believed he had seen it all in his time at the Store. Arguments, disagreements, shouting, spilt coffee, baby sick, mountains of trolleys in need of dishwashing, favouritism, arrogance, co-workers cracking jokes and all the rest that could occur in a job such as this. Nothing could prepare Will for what he just witnessed happening on the shop floor of his soon to be former Store. The Husband had ceased thumbing through his wallet, he pulled out a series of bank notes, then he placed a handful almost too discreetly into Judy's waiting hand before patting her on her right arm with his Wife standing beside him smiling all the way through the transaction. *'I'm in a parallel universe, that's the only kind of explanation I can offer myself for what I just saw.'* Will found himself blinking hard a few times trying to wrap his head around what Judy had done. She had sweet talked The Couple on the spot, they'd obviously become invested in whatever story she spun them, so they took pity on her and had given her money. All on the floor of the place she was employed at, for however much longer that was for. Will wasn't sure how he ended up at coffee pod two yet there he was. Kym was at the till with no customers to serve so she was topping up the napkin dispenser. She felt his presence then looked up greeting him with her usual cheeky smile, then it changed to a look of a confusion as Will wasn't looking at his best friend, he was looking at Judy Howard who was now running out of the Café in the direction of the escalators with her new wad of cash she had just received. The Couple had headed over to coffee pod one to get their usual order in. Kym was beginning to worry about Will now.

"I know that look Willyboy, what's happened this time?"

"I really thought I'd become used to some of the things I'd seen in this place 'Firecracker'. I really did. But I think this is the moment that's broke me."

"Bloody hell, what is it?"

"It's them my best friend..." Will made Kym look at The Couple then she glanced back at him still confused.

"Them what?"

"Well, they gave Judy..."

"Gave her what? I'm so confused right now."

"They gave her money on the shop floor is what Will is trying to tell you Kym."

The new voice interrupted the best friends. They both turned to look at Coralie who stood with her hands on both her hips, her hair done up in its tight bun like always. Kym and Will's Supervisor was not happy in the slightest either.

"So you saw that happened on the shop floor as well then Will?"

"That I did indeed Coralie, what's gonna happen now?"

"Nothing good for Judy that's for sure, you know she even left the poxy floor without asking either!"

Coralie fished out the work phone from one of her work pockets then began typing the number for Bianca before moving away from coffee pod two, Will could have sworn that she was shaking with anger as she disappeared out to the back of Dishwasher Area for some privacy. Kym and Will looked at each other dumbfounded by what was unfolding.

"I gotta say it Willyboy…"

"I'm probably thinking it 'Firecracker'."

"Judy's done herself no favours whatsoever."

"And the rest to go with it, she's seriously done for now."

News spread of Judy and her actions in the Café' well within the time it took to store the cash The Couple had given her upstairs so that when she walked back into the Downstairs' Café a few minutes later, all eyes from the staff members in on duty were eyeballing her. She noticed them all doing it the second she walked back in through the entrance as she looked at everyone individually.

"What? Is there something on my ass?"

She tried looking at her behind as everyone else looked at her with what could only be described as mutual disdain. Sasha Chase was on coffee pod one with Sarah Bailey, both stood there silently with their arms crossed while on pod two Kym in all her short height, but fiery confidence simply shook her head before turning to the wipe the coffee machine down. Nat was in the Kitchen chopping up some vegetables to go with the side salad for the toasties, each chop of a cucumber became more frequent with her neutral face of indifference she gave Judy while Coralie stood by the wall clipboard in hand, her pen tapping it ferociously as she gave Judy her most reproachful look she could muster. And then there was Will on the tables, he eyed Judy up and down then turned his back to go searching for more tables. Everyone else began to busy themselves with whatever they needed to do, all casting the piss-taker Employee from their minds. Judy stood at the entrance, her face flushed with embarrassment, she did what she could only ever do.

"So guys and gals! Where should I help out? Nat you need me in the Kitchen babes?"

Nat kept on chopping her cucumber without looking up again, Judy moved on.

"Sasha? Sarah? Any one of you wanna swap for something else? Give you a break?"

Both girls on coffee pod one knuckled down to do some cleaning.

Judy walked over to pod two now.

"*Kym*! my woman."

Kym looked at her, Judy instantly ceased her attempt to talk to her. She turned to Coralie, the only person who would talk to her.

"Judy, I believe Bianca needs to speak to you. Right now." Coralie folded her arms, stood her ground then indicated with her head to look back the entrance. Judy stood where she was slowly turning, there was Bianca, her hands typically clasped in front as she always did, there was no friendly smile to be seen this time, there only a face of thunder awaiting Judy. Plus there was a member of the In-Store Security team speaking quietly into their radio standing behind Bianca. There was nowhere to run or hide anymore.

Judy Howard had run out of road.

"Judy…" Bianca took a small step forwards but kept a relative distance from the unreliable Employee.

"…would you come with us please."

She followed in the Manager's wake.

The routine of the Café ticked on, unabated.

*

4:30 pm.

Four Hours Later…

He was on Dishwasher minding his own business.

Kym had gone home only half an hour ago. He had about an hour and half left on his penultimate day to go, work had gotten quiet now so Will was probably wiping the Dishwasher surfaces for what must have been the third or fourth since he been placed on there after his break. It had been a good two hours after Bianca had been seen again, her return was only a brief one, Will had caught the tail end of the conversation she and Coralie had been having by pure happenstance.

"I've just gotta process the paperwork…"

"What about the money…?"

"That's been *handled* through the proper channels this time."

Before he could catch anymore of the conversation they had both departed the Café. Needless to say, a certain employee never came back. Not that anyone else brought the individual up anymore. The consensus Will was getting from everyone who was still on duty was that it was time to forget about the sorry affair which suited him just fine.

'Hell of a penultimate shift to say the least.'

He inspected his handy work, the surfaces of the Dishwasher were gleaming with cleanliness as he went to wash his hands, he'd even wiped down both trolleys from the cleaning station as well. They were waiting in the corner of the Area near the exit for the shop floor for whoever was on tables currently. Will was up to date and didn't know what else he was going to do with the rest of his remaining time. With only one more shift left to do at Riverside, he could feel the minutes counting down till it was over. *'Not long now Will, can't help but feel nervous about what's next for me.'* He wondered as he poked his head out of the Dishwasher Area to find a near empty floor of tables, only a few were occupied with customers on their own or there was the odd duo at best. No families were about today at this hour. *'This is gonna be a long hour.'* Will thought as he brought his head back into Dishwasher. He took the opportunity to lean against the wall and close his eyes for a moment. Since his run in with Josie only six days ago, Will had seen next to nothing of her in work at all which was its own blessing in disguise. After getting home and then taking his time to listen to the Voice Recording of their heated exchange, he had been wondering what was best to do with said recording. As every day counted down to his final shift at Riverside, he was still at a loss as to how to proceed. With only a single day left now, he had to make a decision and stick to it just as he had done when deciding to transfer. Every day since that conversation had taken place he had listened to the recording. Its contents couldn't be explained away even if you tried. It was damning piece of evidence in the proper hands. Will hadn't told anyone about what had happened, surprisingly no one had approached him in work to ask about it either, yet he was sure *'the Clique'* were fully in the knowledge of his and Josie's tete-a-tete. If they did know, they hid it tremendously well. Then again, he had hardly seen any member of them in the week leading up to his last day, he didn't trust it. *'Just get to the end of tomorrow then it will be all change on the Will Hardley Express.'* He opened his eyes looking up at the harsh lights, the silence in the Dishwasher Area was eery to him.

"*Ahem.*"

He was disturbed as he heard the person clearing their throat, looking around he found no one at the end of the Dishwasher who had popped in from the Kitchen, it was from the opposite direction.

"Wrong way Will, over here Mr."

He turned to the exit that lead to the shop floor, there standing just outside in was someone he had not been expecting to see at all. He couldn't believe it.

"*Daisy Davidson*!"

His former Saturday night closer was standing on the spot with a truly happy smile plastered on her face from ear to ear. Will ran to her and they embraced in an affectionate hug.

"What on earth are you even doing here Mrs? I thought you'd be at work today?"

"Ah nope, I've got today off so I thought I'd come say Hi whilst shopping and congratulate you, your transferring Stores!"

"I know Daisy, I can't quite get my head round it at the moment."

The two ex-co-worker's moved out of the Dishwasher Area and took an empty seat near it in case Will needed to jump back on to wash anything soon. Seeing Daisy brought back so many nostalgic feelings of what he had been missing on his Saturday night closes.

"So Will, are your new Store prepared for what your about to unleash upon them?"

"Oh *ha-ha* very funny, their gonna love me Daisy. Well I hope they will at least…"

Daisy grinned at him as they chatted. Will didn't realise how much he needed cheering just by seeing her. *'Absence makes the heart grow fonder indeed.'* He thought as Daisy filled him on her job at the hospital she worked at. The way he and his former Saturday night closer slipped back into an easy conversation was a testament to how relaxed their working relationship had been, she had been his support through some awful Saturday nights while he had been the same for her.

"So, come on Will. How does it feel to *finally* be leaving this place?"

"Honestly, Daisy, I don't know what to think or feel. Six years working in one place does make you become attached to it whether that's in a healthy or obsessive way. You were here for a good five or so years yourself weren't you?"

"That I was…" she was nodding in agreement with him "…I came here and was given the majority of the late shifts all the while having to raise a thirteen-year-old teenager at home whilst *them lot* all swanned off at two in the afternoon. It wasn't easy to begin with."

"How did you cope throughout all of that Daisy? I would have been screaming in frustration with people like *'the Clique'* pulling those kinds of manipulative strings."

Daisy looked him in the eyes after his last comment, he saw what Will could feel as someone who knew his predicament inside out, she placed a comforting hand on his in a motherly way.

"You learn over time Will. I know that's probably not what you want to hear. It's also the truth for every single person who has come to work in this place. We all have our lives to lead outside these four walls when it comes to clocking off time. How we deal with them effectively whilst on the job is proof of how strong every single one of us really are."

She removed her hand smiling in her understanding way, Will found himself in total agreement with her. Daisy got up from the table they were seated at near the Dishwasher Area.

"Well, I was shopping and knew I had to come see you. Bloody proud of you for sticking it out in here for so long Will, one more day to go then that's it!"

"I know, half of me can't believe it yet the other half can. Thanks for popping by Mrs, it's been great to see you."

They embraced in a hug again, then Daisy being as naughty as Will was patted his head, specifically right on his vastly receded hairline. "You cheeky cow!" Will was laughing at her as she departed, she gave him a toothy grin with a quick salute then was off. He was still chuckling as he re-entered the Dishwasher Area to find it still as clean as he had left it. Happily sighing with the last of the laughter Daisy had gotten out of him he turned around lazily to go check tables for any that may need clearing. He found a few that were waiting to be cleared, the Café was in total state of calm, only a couple of tables were occupied, it was very boring so Will kept his busy routine going with an extra spring in his step. Rather than shuttling the leftovers trays to the cleaning station, he took them straight out to the Dishwasher to sort them which saved him some time. With less than an hour to go until his penultimate day was complete the minutes seemed to be taunting him as he put one full tray of dirty plates, dishes, and cutlery into the Dishwasher for a cycle. He walked back out on to the floor to try and find anything else that needed cleaning. He was glad he wasn't closing today yet tomorrow he would be closing on his final shift at Riverside. Of course none of the Management Team had even offered for him to change his shift to a little bit earlier, he wasn't that special in their eyes clearly. He was unsurprised by all of it in fact. It solidified the fact that now was the time to move on from this place for good. *'No more complacency, time to change it up for my own wellbeing. If I don't, I would never leave this place unlike some in here. And that's not a healthy way to live my life.'* He was wiping down tables near the Dishwasher Area as the thought sat in his mind, he inspected his handy work, gave a single nod of satisfaction then moved on to another set of tables in need of wiping. As he got down to it he saw one of his old regulars taking a seat. It was the extra-extra dry cappuccino lady who waved at him as she got comfortable in her booth she had claimed. *'How funny, I've been serving her since 'The Restaurant' days, haven't seen her in a little while and now here she is right before I officially depart. The nostalgia is playing with me today.'* The thought made him snigger just a little as he went over to offer to wipe his regular customers table for her. "Well hello there my dear, how are we today? Is it ok if I give this a quick wipe down for you?" he asked the regular with her dairy issue as he saw she had her frothy coffee to her liking, he still didn't know nor really cared why she didn't just convert to soya milk instead. He would miss serving her all the same.

"Ah yes please, thank you. How are things with you?"

"Oh very good madam, also a bit strange as well."

"How so? I hope you're ok?"

"Hunky-dory actually! It's just that tomorrow is my final day here at Riverside, I'm transferring to Stratford Store. Decided to give myself a fresh challenge you see."

He stopped talking as he wiped down her table for her, she had lifted her coffee up so he could wipe all the sides down so she could see he was properly cleaning. Her face had all of a sudden become rather set in a pointed look once Will had announced to her that he was leaving.

"Your leaving then? Permanently?"

"Yes madam, it's time for a change I believe."

"Oh I say, who will make my coffee as good as you have after all these years?"

"Well I can tell you that there are some good coffee makers in this place that you can trust don't you worry about that."

"Of course I know that it's just…"

"Just what madam?"

"Well it's just, you make this place worth visiting. Why do you think I visit so often? I visit not just for the coffee; I visit as I know the service I receive from you is worth my time. Surely you were aware of that after all these years?"

His regular customer looked up at him earnestly. Everything she had just uttered was the truth, Will could tell as such. He was flattered by the praise she was giving him, yet it also felt like a another moment of finality had hit him firmly square in the face. *'Perhaps I haven't fully grasped the fact of the impression I've made on some people after all this time working here.'* He thought as he decided to respond to his regular customer.

"Truthfully my dear, I hadn't realised I had made that impression on you. For one thing, I am so eternally grateful that I was able to do that for you whenever you visited. It means working here after all this time that it was worth it. But on the flipside it proves to me *why* I still need to leave, and I don't mean that in a negative way at all. Life isn't about staying in once place for an indeterminate amount of time. Life is meant to be lived. Sometimes we have to make those decisions for ourselves when we least expect it, me deciding to transfer is one of those moments. Serving you in all my time here has always been a pleasant one that I will always cherish now after what you have just told me, so I thank you for that. I also don't look at this as an end, I look at it as a door that is about to close while I simply open a brand new one."

He smiled at his regular, it wasn't one of Will's service smiles.

It was a genuine one straight from the heart.

The extra-extra dry cappuccino lady returned her own smile then extended her hand to him which Will took it in a firm handshake of thanks. The was only one thing left to say.

"Thank you for your service young man."

"Your most welcome madam. Enjoy your latest visit with us."

Will finished his penultimate shift more satisfied than he ever was.

Epilogue

October 22nd, 2016.

Riverside Shoppers Complex.

Saturday.

9:15 pm.

'Six Years, One Month, Two Weeks and Five Days.'

Will rounded up to himself as he stared at the Store from one of the benches situated outside. All these years of toiling, smiles, arguments, conversations, disagreements, agreements and so forth had all come to a head today. And now it was time to leave this place for somewhere new. It all felt extremely final yet also felt like it wasn't meant to be happening to Will. *'My last shift here was a close, not that I should be surprised by that fact. As soon as it started then it was over.'* He thought as he continued looking at the Store that had been a secondary home for him after all this time. His last day hadn't been too eventful which he was grateful for in a way. He had come in slightly earlier as Kym had asked him too, so he obliged her. His 'Firecracker' had more than surprised him, she had moved him by buying him a late breakfast before his shift began as well producing a massive farewell card that the majority of the Café team had signed. Of course none of *'the Clique'* had signed their names to his goodbye card, Will didn't entirely blame them either. When your bridges were burnt beyond repair, what was the point even trying to fix it again. Last week with Josie had clearly been the straw the broke the camel's back since this was the least he had ever seen of her. After listening to the Voice Recording almost every day since their confrontation, Will had been wondering what on earth to do with it. Now he here was, his time was officially over at Riverside, he still had this one last issue to make a final decision on, he had partly done something. He had written the necessary email required to send off to Head Office with the recording attached as the appropriate file which he made sure worked when you opened it by listening to it which it did. As he sat on the bench opposite what was now his former workplace he held his phone in both hands, the email was open, he glanced at it then back at the Store. It all came to down to the simple push of a button then it would be out of his hands entirely.

'It always get so simple when it could change absolutely everything in the blink of an eye. All it takes now is me pushing the send button then that's it. Her fate may or may not be sealed. All that power at my very disposal in one email. So simple yet so utterly damaging.'

He thought to himself as he unlocked his mobile as it had self-locked again due to inactivity in the last few moments.

There it was, still waiting for him like a ticking timebomb.

Did he have the courage to do it, press that button then everything could change for one person, then it again, it might not.

It was the unknown that was daunting to Will as the minutes ticked on by for him.

Before he made a decision, he looked back again the Store then at the blue staff entrance doors that were still in dire need of that paint job. They had just opened to permit another member of staff on a late shift as they made their way to their home.

As Will's thumb hovered over the send button for the email, he thought back to a time when he had to say goodbye to the person who had gotten him his job at Riverside in the first place.

His old college friend Ashley Hays…

*

May 13th, 2011.

'The Restaurant'.

Friday.

3:33 pm.

"Do you have to leave?"

He was asking yet it also sounded like he whining in the same instance. Ashley looked at him over her small black spectacles with a goofy grin as she got on with the last of the Dishwashing that was left. It was her last day working in 'The Restaurant'. She was leaving this job with its endless weekends of working for a rather lovely Monday to Friday job where she would have weekend after weekend to do with whatever her heart was content to partake in. Needless to say she was not even remotely sad about leaving Riverside. The rest of team had been wishing her the best of luck in her new venture, all accept a very sullen and moody Will who was now staring at her sheepishly as he stood to the side as Ashely finished loading the last of the plates then brought down the Dishwasher for its cycle. As it got to work she faced Will inspecting him with a once over and feigned seriousness, then she cracked another grin before walking up to slap his left arm.

"What was that for!"

"Your being a silly sod you know Will."

"Oh I'm sorry, one of my close friends is leaving me for a much better job. *Excuse me* for being sad about that!"

He folded his arms then leaned back on the tall shelving where they normally dropped off leftover trays from customers. Ashley tutted at him with a quiet snigger as she also folded her arms partly copying him.

"Will, you're gonna be more than fine you silly sausage."

"Am I? I don't feel like it."

"Well you will, your turning twenty in a few short months, no more *teenage strops* for you when that happens don't you think?"

"Hmm, good point I guess."

"Oh its, an excellent point and you know it! Come on, let's go clear some tables before I finish at four."

Out they went to the shop floor, 'The Restaurant' was quiet today. Lunch rush had been a solid one-hour affair then it had dropped off like a tonne of bricks. Being the middle of May, Summer was fast approaching, the days were longer with a hotter climate as each day ticked down to when British Summer Time formally began on the calendar, less people didn't want to dawdle inside a large Shoppers Complex, they wanted to be on a hill, beach or river walkway soaking up the rays. That meant anyone working in a Hospitality or Retail Unit in Riverside was potentially going to suffer with twiddling their thumbs or doing whatever they needed to do to keep busy. For Will and Ashley, that meant clearing tables. For other members of staff like Sallie and her Chef-lover, that meant flirting some more in the three-quarter enclosed Kitchen away from prying eyes. As they both cleaned up a table of four that recently departed, Ashley was stealing a glance in through the service hatch where hot food normally came out.

"God, I am *not* going to miss seeing that on shift."

"See what exactly Ash?"

"Sallie and her squeeze are essentially *eye-fucking* in the Kitchen right now that's what."

"Ugh, don't tell me that! I've still got to work with them both until seven tonight."

Ashley was now laughing to herself as she loaded the last of the leftovers on to the tray she was using while Will looked at her oddly.

"Ok, those two doing whatever it is their doing right can't be *that* funny surely?

"Ha-ha no it's not that Will…"

"What is it then Ash?"

"It's this place. It just hit me that I'm leaving all of it behind, and do you know what? It's my time. I can feel it. I know that sounds like silly dramatics but I'm sort of serious as well. I've done what I needed to do in this job, proud of it in a way. On the flipside though, it's been nine months of intensely hard work with very little praise to be given to anyone of us. It's a big turntable this place, some people are made for it, others have however long they have then it's their time to leave. This right now, on this rather lovely Sunny day Will, its simply *my time*. And one day my dear Will, it's going to be yours too. But not today Mr."

Ashley picked up the tray with one of her most honest smiles Will had ever seen from her, he felt a little bit like she was making a prediction about him as well. As she started to walk past him, Will caught her arm to stop her, he had a question.

"When do you think it will be my time to leave Ashley?"

Ashley didn't look at him, she cast her eyes around what was about to be her former place of work then she looked at him with assuredness, her spectacles sat smartly on her cute pointy nose.

"Only you can decide that Will. You'll know when it's time, I have a piece of advice for you though. Do not get stuck in this place. This is not the be all to end all for you, not by a long shot, its simply part of your life for now until *you change it*. Don't forget that."

With nothing further to add, Ashely left Will to wipe the table of four down, everything else ticked on by. Will felt like his near future had been mapped out for him by his old college friend. He would take what she said to heart and hold on to it tightly.

'Thank you Ashley. I wonder how long I will call this place work for...'

*

Back To Now.

'We never knew how long it would before I knew it was my time to leave did we Ashley. Guess there's some things we're not meant to know until it just happens, especially when it comes to our working lives, be it long or short.'

His thumb was hovering still over the email that could change everything as he still observed his former place of work. Will had nothing to do but get up from the bench and make his way home. Not before he made a decision. He took one last hard long look at the Store.

'You made your bed Josie Sybille. Now it's time for you and your friends to lie in it.'

Without looking at his phone, he clicked the send button, then the email was sent instantly. There was no going back from it now. Taking a measured breathe, he stood up from the bench, he flung his backpack on his left shoulder and tucked his farewell card under his right arm then he made his way through Riverside. All the shops were closing after their Saturday of trading, even the lights were being dimmed now so the last dregs of customers were making their way to the appropriate exits. As he slow walked through the Shoppers Complex Will took in the sights around him. There was parents with their sleeping children in their prams that should have already been in bed, there were teenagers loitering because they could as they didn't want to go home yet, there were security guards patrolling in their pairs trying to coax people to leave without being forceful about it. There was an announcement over the intercom that any remaining customers should now leave the premises. All had been normal things for Will he would bear witness too whenever he finished his Saturday late night shifts, not anymore from now on.

'I'm gonna miss seeing these familiar sights and sounds.'

The thought was a sad one for him, it was also a reminder that he was leaving for his own benefit and volition. Everyone went through this process in life regardless of what job they had. It was scary yet also exhilarating all wrapped up in one. This just happened to be as Ashley had foretold him all those years ago in 'The Restaurant'. His time. He knew it, he accepted it, it was still sad to go through it as he kept on making his way through the Complex. He passed other shops like Thorntons, Zara, Lipsy,

Lush, along with the independent boutique shops that Riverside allowed to use their Unit Spaces as long as they paid their rent fees every year. All had their own staff finishing up on their shifts, all tired and ready to go to bed or go to whatever plans they had on a Saturday evening. Will observed some of the staff he saw on his final journey through Riverside. All had their own looks of stress, happiness, frustration, sadness, and everything else that came with working in Retail or Hospitality. He knew how they all felt, he'd been put through the wringer enough times as it was after his six long years at the Complex. He'd made it to the House of Fraser end, normally he'd walk through the shop then exit out of their side entrance for the train station. Of course their shutters were down now since it was closing time so he went out of the other side entrance off to the left, finding himself out in the cold again he headed towards the multistorey carpark that had the designated lift that would take him across the interlink connecting to the train station. As always, the lift that was still in need of a complete overhaul maintenance check, he took the six flight of stairs upwards still managing to beat the lift every time. *'Another little tradition I'm never really going to do ever again.'* As he made it on to the interlink walkway he heard the lift arrive at last to deposit whatever customers were getting off as they waited for the doors to open in their slowness. The motorway situated underneath the walkway was abuzz with cars all leaving for their different destinations as was Will, all going about their own routines in their daily lives. He watched them whizzing by as there was partial back log at one of the roundabouts, it worked itself out after a few moments in the end under Will's ever watchful gaze. Each step he took further and further away, the more it felt like it was becoming a part of his past. He felt the change coming for him, he wasn't scared in the slightest. He knew it was now, so he embraced it rather than fighting it. Before he knew it, he was tapping his oyster card on one of the barriers to permit him access to station so he could wait on the platform. He'd time it well as less than two minutes later his train for home rolled up on the singular platform. Boarding with the other waiting passengers, he found a comfortable corner seat that he settled into then he looked out at the window taking in Riverside Shoppers Complex, his past, for one last time.

Like all good things, his time there was over, his future awaited him. With no more tears left to give, he looked away from his past then began looking forwards at whatever lay ahead for him. He had no idea and for Will, this was a new exciting adventure he was embarking on.

He couldn't wait to see what was next.

The trains doors closed, then it began rolling away on its scheduled time like clockwork.

And Riverside Shoppers Complex bid a fond farewell to Will Hardley.

THE END

Character Index

Protagonist:

Will Hardley – Our navigator of all things and events related in The Workplace. Gay and proud of it, he has an opinion on most subjects.

Allies:

Kym 'Firecracker' Harrison – Will's confidant and single Mother of Three best friend. An opinionated force with a heart of gold.

Nat Hardley – Will's original loyal co-worker and former Supervisor from the days of 'The Restaurant'. Level-headed yet caring.

Aaron Connors – The young but mature Teenager with a can-do attitude whilst always a reliable comfort.

Kathy and Sarah Bailey – The Mother and Daughter Duo who always get along with Will.

Sasha Chase – Fellow Café' co-worker and Mother of Two from the pre-refurbishment days who takes no crap from anyone.

Sarah Harker – Will's former lesbian co-worker who moved to Spain for a better life. Never afraid to put Will in his place when needed.

Daisy Davidson – Another former co-worker who resigned for a new job. Was Will's Saturday night closer and great help when he first arrived in the pre-refurbished Café'.

The Management Team:

Coralie Casper – Supervisor of the refurbished Café'. Uptight but her morals are always in the right place.

Emily Arms – the trainee yet naïve Manager from Will's 'Restaurant Days' before she moved up the ranks. Assumes she's doing well until her permanent secondment begins with barely any notice to the Southend Region.

Joyce Cooper – the former Manager who ruled with an iron fist before she resigned. A staunch ally of '*the Clique*' who viewed Will as nothing more than a nuisance.

Bianca Fray – Joyce's replacement Manager from Southend who doesn't do a lot but always wants to be your friend in work.

Enemies:

Josie Sybille – The de facto leader of '*the Clique*' who never likes to be questioned about what she can or can't do. Will's former Supervisor in the pre-refurbished Café' who had unilateral control over whatever she could do.

Trudy Harrie – Loyal ally of Josie and to '*the Clique*'. Infamous for her teacher spectacles plus a known gossip-collector.

Lucy Cricker – another member loyal to Josie and her exclusive only friendship group. Fully believes that doing late-night shifts is beneath her after a certain amount of years.

Jan Betty – Another member of '*the Clique*' who was the friendliest towards Will until she decided enough was enough.

Sherry Michaels – Another loyal member of the '*the Clique*' who would choose them over anyone else any day.

Others:

Jim Hendrickson – Former co-worker/secret crush of Will who eventually transferred out of Riverside to Stratford. Gay and confident, he was alluring yet no to be messed with.

Henry Sybille – Son of Josie Sybille. Surprisingly gets along with Will despite his Mothers predilections.

Niall Rogers – Regional Manager for Riverside who visits every few months.

Judy Howard – The always missing other lesbian co-worker of Will's from their 'The Restaurant' days. She's had more time off than actual working as of late.

The Couple – A retired married duo who are infamously known in the Store and Café for trying to always get free stuff near enough every time they visit.

417

A Message from the Novelist

Well, was that enough of an emotional rollercoaster for you dear reader?

Writing this 2nd Novel in *'The Will Hardley Series'* was another eye-opening experience for me. It took me back to a time when I was a bit younger that I hadn't really given much thought about for a very long while. I always knew in my heart however that this Story is something I have wanted to commit to paper for as long as I can remember.

Why exactly?

It's simple really. There's an old saying, 'write about what you know'. So I did. And here we all are.

419

Now, did I write this particular story for a reason? Of course.

I have always wanted to write a Cautionary Tale about Working Life.

I want people to read this Tale I have written to inform but also warn them that this might be but a few instances of what you can expect or might happen when you work in a people-facing job day in, day out or you may be deciding to try a different career path altogether.

Its hard work facing people as a job sometimes, even facing your fellow colleagues on a daily basis. Yet other times, it can truly be rewarding knowing that you've made someone's day just that little bit better.

I've certainly discovered that for myself from time to time and it still fills my heart with joy that I've been able to do it in the first place.

The point is, I wrote this Novel to get a lot of feelings out that have sat within me for a long time.

Getting the chance to retell them as a fictional Story has done wonders for me to finally express them in a creative literary way.

I hope that you dear reader have found some enjoyment out of this Novel. It sure was a an experience writing it, but the pros far outweigh the cons of it all.

Until next time, stay safe, live your lives happily and I'll see you in the next Story of *'The Will Hardley Series'* whenever that may be.

Wondering when we will see our dear Will next?

Have no fear.

He'll return in the 3rd Will Hardly Novel…

Printed in Great Britain
by Amazon